LEIZAR

Never, ever, ever... Give up

LEIZAR

A struggle
across generations

DAVID GELERNTER

ISBNs:
978-1-3999-1205-1 (soft cover)
978-1-3999-1617-2 (hard cover)
978-1-3999-1616-5 (eBook)

This book is dedicated to my wife Jill with all my love

CONTENTS

Acknowledgements

Although this book is a work of fiction, Leizar, together with some of the other characters really existed, and many of the historical events and scenes really took place. Chaya's journey to Glasgow was typical of how these journeys were made at the time, and the description of cigarette production and the start of automation is faithfully represented. The synagogues mentioned are all real and their descriptions relevant.

I have tried to capture the plight of a family which was typical of many trying to survive during the 100 years or so covered in the book. In WW1 the Zeppelins and in WW2 the unmanned rockets were a very real and ever-present threat, as were Moseley's Blackshirts, outbreaks of violence, such as the Cable Street Riots and the sort of general thuggery described in the Petticoat Lane scenes.

My thanks go to my wife Jill for putting up with me through the long period it took to research and write the book; my grandson, Theo for his production and artistic advice, also my friend Susan Newman for trawling through the drafts, and a great deal of gratitude to Matthew Baylis for his professional help and critique. When I thought it was complete, Matthew's expert suggestions caused me many rewrites, but I believe the book is the better for it.

CHAPTER I

Kingdom of
Galicia
and **Lodomeria**,
and the Grand Duchy of **Cracow**
with the Duchies of **Auschwitz** and **Zator**

Crown land of the Kingdoms and Lands Represented in the Imperial Council
and the Lands of the Crown of St. Stephen

Esther was screaming with the pain of childbirth. There was no-one to hold her hand and her husband, Dawid lay on the bare floor, bleeding from the head. The Russian soldiers had no consideration for pregnant women, especially if they were Jews. Thank God, they felt they had wreaked enough suffering and left. Dawid picked himself up and limped over to his wife just in time to catch his son - born amid the squalor and pain.

For that sublime moment he did not feel the results of the beating he had taken. With a kitchen knife, he cut the cord and wrapped his baby who had also entered the world screaming.

But something was wrong. Esther's screams had subsided and she had gone very quiet. She lay in a mess of blood from the delivery. Dawid's world stood still. The room was spinning. He staggered and almost dropped his new-born child, his mouth open in a silent shriek. He could tell she was not breathing.

Time seemed to stand still, but then he heard the screaming again. This time it was his first-born son, Shmuel – just two years old and terrified by the cruel beating of his father and mother, and then by the scene of his mother crying out in agony, all the blood, and his father's pain.

With the new-born baby in his arms, Dawid staggered to the house of the Benjamin family next door where Esther's mother and two sisters lived. When Anna Benjamin saw the state he was in, she ran with him and the two girls to see the scene of devastation she swung into action. To her sisters she said, 'Moszek, take the baby and the little one next door. Rebecca, let's clean up here' She saw immediately that Esther's body was lifeless: the people of Kawetchka were used to death and destruction at the hands of the cruel Russian oppressors.

And so, Zelman Domansky entered the world.

The Benjamin's house was very similar to the Domansky's. It was built mainly of wood with bare floorboards and sparse, but practical wooden furniture. There was a family room with a large table and a fireplace. It was a bit smaller than Dawid's and there were only two bedrooms, one for Anna and her husband Yossel, and another shared by the two girls Moszek and Rebecca.

Moszek was worried for little Shmuel who had just witnessed scenes that a little boy of two should never see. She needed to settle and comfort him and the baby. At the same time, she was aware that her mother and sister were helping Dawid who was in need of attention to his wounds and support for the dreadful trauma he had been through. And she had a new-born baby in her arms in need of a mother's comfort.

But an amazing calm came over her so, carrying the baby in her arms, she settled little Shmuel at the table with some milk and the sweet little cookies he so loved, and still carrying the baby, she returned to the Domansky house and had Rebecca go and keep an eye on Shmuel.

Her mother was in a dreadful state with blood stains all down her front. She told

Moszek she had cleaned up as best she could, and Rebecca had lit a fire to burn all the bloody mess. Moszek took over, Dawid was still collapsed on the floor, bleeding profusely from the head wound. It did not look serious, so she got some clean cloths and wound them round his head, telling him to hold them tight to the wound. They helped him up and on to the bed and Anna got some warm water and honey to bathe and soothe the wounds.

The next priority was to feed the baby. She went back to the other house and warmed some milk which she mixed with more honey and little Zelman settled quietly in the crook of her arm.

She told Rebecca to run to the Rabbi to tell him what had happened and ask him to inform the authorities about the death, and arrange a funeral.

Anna was now able to inspect the head wound. There was a gash caused by the impact of the Cossack club, and she was surprised that Dawid had remained conscious enough to deal with the birth of his son. After carefully cleaning the wound with the water and honey, she used schnapps to sterilise it. Throughout her life she had seen the suffering of people who had died from sepsis due to untreated wounds. She then took more clean cloths, tearing them into strips to bind up the injury.

The stinging of the alcohol brought Dawid to his senses. His first thought was for his wife 'Esther, where is my Esther?' his voice was cracked and seemed to come from deep in his throat. Anna had to remind him that she had not survived - at which he completely broke down in tears with great racking sobs shaking his body. Moszek thought that the baby might be of some comfort to him, so now he was settled she brought the tiny little package wrapped in a blanket over to him. 'Look Dawid, your new son, one life ends, and another begins.'

This appeared to send Dawid into a higher level of distress. Moszek gave the baby to Anna and put her arms around him. They sat like that for a long time, rocking back and forth and crying together.

The Rabbi was shocked to hear the news, although bad news came often these days. He went straight away to the Russian base and informed the authorities about the death. The administrator made a note of it, but of course showed no interest in the circumstances nor the terrible crime that had been committed. To them, just another Jew had died. Permission was granted for the funeral. The Rabbi then went to Reb Bendle, the carpenter who made the coffins. Together they returned to the Domansky house and the Rabbi enlisted the help of Anna to keep Dawid and the family out of the way while they removed the body.

In accordance with Jewish religious law, the funeral took place the very next day. Dawid had been awake all night and seemed to be in a trance. It was only when the coffin was lowered into the ground that the full force of what was happening seemed to hit him, and he collapsed right there at the graveside. Yossel and the Benjamin women were a great comfort to Dawid. They helped him back to the house and took care of baby Zelman. Rebecca had stayed with little Shmuel and they all gathered round to make sure he was not left on his own. They made sure there was food and tried to coax him to eat.

The Domansky family had endured many tragedies over the years. Since Poland had ceased to exist, and the shtetl where they lived became part of the Russian Empire, atrocities committed by the Cossack rulers against the Jews were commonplace.

In keeping with Jewish custom at the time, Esther's unmarried sister, 16 year old Moszek, was obliged to marry her dead sister's widower. Since observant Jews took God's command to 'Go forth and multiply' at its word, it was assumed there would be further children and the bloodline would be retained. It was also thought to be better for the children as they grew, because they would be more than half siblings. This union was a foregone conclusion between Moszek and Dawid, and the marriage took place just a few weeks later.

Of course, there was no happiness about the wedding, just a simple religious ceremony under a makeshift *chuppah* (canopy). Dawid was expected to continue his work as the younger Rabbi, making time to run the *Cheder* (religious school) and of course, to study Talmud, the bible commentary that the men of the community would peruse in great detail, agonising, discussing and arguing over the nuanced meanings of every word. The community rallied round and although nobody had much to give, there were gifts of food, clothing and houseware.

CHAPTER 2

1850S AND 1860S – POGROMS, BABIES AND MATHS

It was not long after the wedding that Moszek became pregnant and Dawid was proud that she was even more fertile than Esther. She gave birth to another son, Mendel, and then a daughter, Yentl. In a short time, they had become a growing family. Moszek had easy pregnancies and hardly a year went passed when she was not with child.

The births followed of Moshe, Sara, Yossel and Misha. She would not admit it but being so prolifically pregnant took its toll on Moszek. She soon lost her figure and was busy 24 hours a day with all the babies, with no time to herself at all. Yentl did not go to school. Her mother told her she was needed at home to help with the little ones, whilst Mendel and Zelman were able to study, which seemed so unfair to Yentl. 'But Uma, I want to learn too. Why can't I go to school at least sometimes?'

Moszek pretended to spit twice on the open palm of her hand expressing how foolish her daughter was for saying such a thing, but her tone was kindly as she spoke. 'My beautiful Yentl,' she said,' 'It is the work of the men to learn, to study Torah and give thanks to God. The work of the women is even more important, we must run the home, bring up the children and feed the family. Without the women the men could not honour God. Because of us, our families run, we are the rock on which the Jewish home is built. My darling you are learning from your Uma how to be a wonderful home maker, *a balabusta* so that one day you can honour your own husband the same way. Oy, what a lucky man he will be!'

But Yentl was a Domansky, and that meant she had her own mind. She could not just blindly accept what her mother said, even though she knew it had been that way for generations. She would not give in easy, and she resolved that when her father returned, she would convince him that she should also study, even if it meant she had to work twice as hard.

There was no doubt that Zelman was the favourite. As well as officiating as the younger Rabbi, Dawid also ran the Jewish school and Zelman was the star pupil there. He had a very firm grasp of mathematics and by the age of 11 could already speak Polish, Russian and Yiddish, although the Russians had banned the use of the latter language. The Domansky family was highly respected in the little village of Kawetchka. They came from a long line of respected Rabbis. However, that counted for nothing with the Cossacks. In fact it made the family into prime targets.

Zelman hated the arrogant and oppressive Russians and when he was 15, he joined the Jewish resistance movement. The Russians had allowed many of these little villages they called *shtetls* to spring up outside of the Pale of Settlement, a group of about fifty families living in ramshackle houses mostly made of wood with tin roofs. Kawetchka was one of these. In bad weather, rain would pound loudly on the roof, trying to find little gaps in the metal, and the roof would sag in the winter with the weight of the snow. Typically, the Jews were left to their own devices to feed, clothe, educate their families and provide food. The winters were very cold and there was never enough of anything. On top of that they were required to pay local taxes, often settled in bread, milk or hard labour. Some families had a horse and a wagon, others relied only on a horse or donkey, and some had to carry wood and provisions on their back. But everyone helped everyone, and they kept their faith.

Yentl had been stewing on the unfairness of her situation and she was building a head of steam so that when Dawid returned from school with the boys, she unwisely confronted him almost as he walked through the door. 'Upa, I want to go to school and study like my brothers! I have a good mind and I can learn. I can do mathematics like Zelman, and I want to read and write like you and my brothers. So can I start tomorrow, I can go to school with you, and I can make you proud of me!'

All this poured out of Yentl at a hundred miles an hour before her father had even taken off his hat. Zelman and Mendel hurried into their room. They knew what was coming!

Dawid was completely taken aback. His gaze went from his daughter to his wife, who was standing by the kitchen. Moszek was shocked, she'd had no idea Yentl would do this.

'What in the name of God - *Hashem*, have you been teaching her?' He shouted, 'Is this for a man to come home to? Am I such an *alter dumkopf* that I am to be dishonoured in my own house by my own children?'

As was his way, Dawid was winding up as he went, and his voice was getting louder. As he focused on Yentl he started to shake and fixed her with his gimlet eyes. 'Who put you up to this? Who do you think you are to speak to your father this way? What makes you so special? Go to your room, when I have washed up and prepared myself, I will come and talk to you, and you may feel the touch of my belt!'

Dawid wore braces to keep up his trousers, but he also wore a thick leather belt. He had never hit any of his family with it, and never would, but he threatened them and if he was very angry, he would chase them and bang it on the furniture. He was a frightening sight when he was in that mood, the tassels from the white religious under garment he wore flying behind him and his dark beard framing his angry features.

But Yentl had her father's temperament. She ran to her room and slammed the door so hard it nearly fell off.

Wonderful aromas greeted Dawid when he went into the kitchen. Moszek stopped what she was doing and came to him. She let him wash his hands and gave him one of the small fried fish balls she had just made. He sat down heavily in the wooden chair. He sighed, 'What am I going to do with that girl? You have to take her in hand.'

Moszek did not reply, but through the thin wooden wall they could hear Yentl sobbing in her room. It softened Dawid's heart, and he went to her.

As he entered the room, Yentl flinched, expecting another row. But Dawid sat on her bed, 'Yentl, Yentl, Yentl. You are my first born and oldest daughter and Uma relies on you for help with the children and to run the house. You cannot be like a man and go out to shlep and lift. No, you are beautiful, and you have to learn how to be a woman. One day you will make someone a wonderful wife.'

'But Upa…'

Dawid put up his hand and raised his voice slightly, 'I am speaking… Yentl, this is the role of all the daughters in Kawetchka and everywhere. You would not make your mother bring up all these children on her own, would you? And cook and clean the house and look after all of us? If anything happened to her, it would be your fault.' With that he walked out leaving Yentl frustrated and angry.

It was effective emotional blackmail, but Yentl never quite resigned herself to a life of bringing up babies and cooking and cleaning, and she always yearned to be treated like her brothers.

It was Friday 25 September 1860. The family were preparing for the new year festival of Rosh Hashanah. There had been a pogrom at the place where Zelman's elder brother Shmuel worked, making prayer shawls and religious items. Shmuel had been attacked by Cossacks wielding swords and clubs. In terrible pain and dragging his left leg, he had staggered home to his wife Chava Devora. Chava ran to the Domansky home, crying and distraught.

'Moszek, Moszek help me. It's Shmuel – the Cossacks - he is covered in blood and his leg – I think it's broken.'

Moszek saw the bloodstains on Chava's dress, and interrupted, 'Go back to him straight away! I will bring the doctor.'

She ran to the house of Joseph Galitzer, who had been studying to be a doctor before the Russians forbade Jews to follow a profession.

'Kim shoyn!' Come quick, she screamed as soon as he opened the door. 'It's Shmuel, there's been an attack.'

Dawid had returned from work to hear what had happened. He and Zelman ran to the home of Shmuel and Chava and were shocked with the scene that awaited them. Shmuel lay in the dust outside the door with his leg turned so that his foot faced backwards, and his knee joint twisted at a horrible angle. He was covered in blood and barely conscious.

Dawid, Zelman and Joseph lifted Shmuel as gently as they could and took him into the little house.

They placed him on the table and Joseph found wood for splints. He and cleaned and dressed his wounds as best he could and reset the leg into its natural position while Shmuel screamed in pain. Chava brought schnapps and Dawid made him drink as much as he could, but Joseph was shaking his head. Shmuel would never walk properly again.

When Shmuel seemed a little more settled, they placed him on the bed, where Chava could tend to him, while Dawid and Zelman went to the workshop where the attack had taken place. The smell that hit them was almost physical. There was horse excrement all over the floor, mixed up with prayer shawls and religious artefacts. The place was a disaster.

Although Zelman had often witnessed violent behaviour from the Russian aggressors, the pogroms up to now had largely been demonstrations, aimed at disrupting the homes and lives of the Jews, as an example to those who did not pay their taxes. At the age of 17, he was profoundly shocked at this atrocity resulting in the injury to his brother. Shmuel was a kind person and had spent much time with Zelman as he grew up – setting him mathematical problems which Zelman enjoyed solving. It was Shmuel who'd inspired Zelman to become a teacher at the Jewish school.

The news of the tragedy spread like wildfire among the inhabitants of the shtetl and such was the community spirit that the Domanskys were quickly inundated with offers of help. People brought food and fuel, blankets, and clothing. Most importantly, the men brought wood to repair the workshop, ensuring that Shmuel could return there when he was able.

Between them, it did not take long to repair the damage to the workshop, but the damage to Shmuel was profound. His leg had been set by Joseph, but without the proper instruments it could not be straightened. Joseph fashioned a crutch and taught Shmuel how to use it to take pressure off the leg, visiting him twice a week to ensure he was rehabilitated as best as was possible. The psychological damage was something else. Shmuel did not sleep at night and often woke with nightmares, writhing in pain. This went on for a long time, during which Chava Devora was of course, a great comfort to him.

So, it was with some trepidation that Zelman received a message from Dmitri, the Russian army captain in charge of the local garrison. He apologised for the recent pogroms and asked if Zelman would meet him alone at the big oak tree in the centre of the village at noon next day. Zelman was really worried. Why had he been singled out by this important soldier? What could he possibly want? Would it lead to yet more hardship and suffering for his family?

He spoke to his father that night and showed him the message. Dawid nearly choked when he read it. Nothing good could come of this, but Dawid saw right away that the option to ignore the 'summons' and not turn up was not open to them either. That would lead to even worse retribution. He suggested that he, Dawid, should go with Zelman, but after much discussion and stroking of beards, they agreed that this could also be perceived as a snub, since the message had specifically said that Zelman should go alone. Yeshiva and Talmudic studies taught Jewish men to carefully examine every detail and possibility, and in the end, they agreed that Zelman had to go to the meeting on his own.

When Zelman arrived, Dmitri was already there waiting with his horse tethered to the tree. The captain was in his fine uniform made of stout woollen cloth, jodhpur style trousers tucked into his beautifully polished leather boots, while his gleaming cap badge denoted his rank.

It made Zelman conscious of the way he looked. Old trousers and a long shirt with holes. A shirt that had been worn by older members of the Domansky family and handed down to him. He did not have proper shoes and his feet were protected by two pieces of worn leather bound together with strips of cowhide. He walked boldly, but with inward trepidation, fearful that some further atrocity might be visited on himself or worse – upon his family.

However, Dmitri thanked him for coming and offered him his hip flask. This was strange and Zelman warily refused at first, but Dmitiri laughingly took a drink from the flask first to show it was not poisoned. Zelman followed suit.

It was a beautiful clear day, if a little cold and they sat on the ground under the tree.

'I want to ask a favour,' said the Russian. 'I know you are a teacher at the Jewish school, and they tell me you specialise in mathematics. My son needs some special tuition. Would you be prepared to help him? I would make it worth your while.'

This took Zelman completely by surprise, he had not considered for a moment that he might be in a position to help the Russian. His first reaction was to tell the Dmitri to go find some other poor Jew to help. He felt it would be a betrayal to work for the Russian. How would his family feel about him helping the people who had just caused such pain and suffering?

Quietly he said, 'You ask me this when your men attack our homes and our workplaces and smash up our possessions?'

Dmitri expected this, 'Look, you have to understand. We know your families for many years, and we know you are good people, but we are instructed to carry out these atrocities upon the very people we know. You must understand I am only following orders; it is not personal.'

Zelman knew he was in a difficult position, but he could not let it go. 'Tell that to my brother Shmuel and his family. He will never walk properly again.'

Dmitiri actually had the grace to look embarrassed. 'Yes, I heard about that. It seems a couple of my men got over-enthusiastic. I have dealt with them. If you can help my boy and he passes his exam, I will make sure this sort of thing never happens again to your family… and I will pay you.'

Zelman was, on the one hand, afraid to refuse. What wrath might the captain visit on him and his family, if he said no? On the other hand, wasn't it possible that he could protect his family from more of this terrible persecution.

'I must speak to my father,' he said.

'Very well,' replied the Russian, 'but don't take too long – I will meet you back here in two days at the same time. Tell your father I *strongly advise* him to agree.'

Zelman had no wish to stay and chat. He was fearful of this thinly veiled threat and could not wait to get away. He excused himself and left, leaving the captain leaning against the tree smoking a cigarette and smiling. Zelman worried about the conversation all day, but he began to think more and more about how this could work to the family's advantage.

When his father returned home that evening, Zelman wanted to tell him about his conversation with the Russian. But he knew it would be difficult. His father understandably harboured a lifelong hatred for the Russian military.

It was Friday evening, Shabbas, the start of the Sabbath, a meal that was very significant for Jewish families. It was a time for them to come together. Moszek and the girls had been working all day to provide the meal. The butcher had provided two kosher chickens which had to be killed, plucked and cooked. Every part of the chickens was used – nothing went to waste. They made soup from the bones, chopped liver which they mixed with onion and boiled egg, *magela* (stuffed neck) even the *pippick* (belly button) was cooked until it was soft and succulent. From the baker they bought their weekly plaited loaf of *cholla* bread and from their own land there was cabbage, onions and potatoes. They also had a little kosher wine. The rest of the week could take care of itself, but the Shabbas meal was special.

Round the table were Moszek, Dawid and Zelman, Mendel, who was 16, 12 year-old Yentl, Moshe, nine, Sara, six, Yossel, four, and the baby of the family, Misha, who was just three. Everyone stood at their place around the table and Dawid *kvelled* with pride at the head of his family.

The boys wore *kippot*, the little skull caps and everyone stood while Moszek made the *brocha* prayer of blessing over the candles to welcome the Shabbas. Dawid did the ceremonial washing of hands and recited the *brocha* over the bread and the wine. There was a moment's silence after the *Omayn* at the end. And then the quiet was split by loud chatter, everyone wanting to tell about their day, their week, who they had met, what did they say, what were the rumours, who was marrying whom… So much gossip while everyone helped themselves to the food, being careful not to take too much and be greedy, even though they were all hungry and the food smelled and tasted delicious. The older girls helped the little ones lest they be left out.

Zelman was quiet, waiting his time.

Gradually the younger children left the table to be put to bed, until in the end there was only Dawid and Zellman – and the schnapps Dawid had had taken as payment for the beautiful Hebrew prayer book he had printed for the Old Rabbi. Moszek could sense that there was a sensitive conversation to be had, so she made herself scarce in the kitchen. Dawid seemed very relaxed.

'Upa,' started Zelman, 'today I spoke with Dmitri Belakov the Russian captain.'

'That *momzer* bastard, may he rot in hell!' Dawid made as if to spit on the ground. 'We should break his legs like his men did to your brother Shmuel'

'He was very sorry about that, Papa. He said his men should not have done that, and he has dealt with them for it.'

At this, Dawid's face darkened and he started to get agitated. Zelman realised he had said the wrong thing. His father stood and knocked over his chair, banging the table as he spoke. 'Sorry? Sorry?' He shouted, '*A viste pgire oyf dein!*' (*He* should die a dismal death like an animal.)

This was not going well. Zelman lowered his voice in the hope it would calm his father.

'Upa, please don't lose your temper, listen to what I have to say. Dmitri says he is only obeying orders. He says he does only the minimum of pogroms he can get away with to stop his superiors from taking over and throwing him in the salt mines. He says that would be far worse for us.'

'Why are you telling me this? Why are you even talking to this *farshtinkener chazer*?' (stinking pig)

'Because he wants me to teach his son mathematics, and he says if I do, then there will be no more pogroms against our family, and he even offered to pay me. Upa, just think, if the family was protected from further violence…'

'Are you crazy!' Dawid was shouting now at the top of his voice, his face red with anger. He stood up again and again knocked the chair over which this time fell with a clatter. He kicked it away. 'You are telling me you would do this? Make a deal with the devil!'

'Underneath it all, he is not all bad, Upa – he is a man in a bad position.'

Dawid's eyes were rolling – he was shouting and banging the table as Moszek came running in.

'*A chazer bleibt a chazer*!' Dawid was shouting. A pig is always a pig. He turned to Moszek: 'You want to know the idea of your lovely son? He makes a deal with that *momzer* Dmitri. Are you crazy?'

Moszek said, 'Calm down Dawid, you'll make yourself ill. Zelman, go to bed and let's hear no more of this nonsense.'

Zelman knew that his father would think about the idea even though he had reacted badly to it. That was the way he dealt with things, reacted first and considered afterwards. So, he went instead to see his brother Shmuel who was slowly recovering. He sat down on the bed with his brother, and they were joined by Chava Devora, Shmuel's lovely wife who, Zelman always thought, was wise beyond her years. If anyone, Shmuel and Chava had the most reason to hate the Cossacks, but Zelman knew his brother was a thoughtful man and discussion between the three of them would be objective in spite of all that had happened.

Zelman went through the whole meeting from the time he got the message and took pains to make it clear that Dmitri had not put him under any pressure, except for the veiled threat at the end.

'And,' said Chava thoughtfully, 'if you were to refuse, what do you think would happen?'

'Of course, you are right' Zelman replied, 'I am sure he would find ways to make us regret it.'

'I understand Upa's reaction,' Shmuel spoke up. 'After what happened here, and I bear the scars of it, no-one hates these *momzers* more than me and the thought of helping them in any way is abhorrent. I wish them nothing but bad luck.'

'Yes,' said Chava, slowly, 'but maybe this is an opportunity for us all. It's very rare for them ever to need something that we have – other than taxes, and we can be in control this time. Also, Zelman, maybe you can get to know this *momzer's* family and exert some influence. And I must say immunity from future pogroms – if he keeps his word – that would be a good thing for the whole family, no?'

Shmuel knew there was sense in Chava's comments, yet the pain in his leg reminded him of the suffering the Cossacks could inflict. He was torn. On the one hand he could see the possible benefit, on the other he truly hated the Russians. '*Az men shloft mit hint, shteyt men oyf mit fley,*' he said. (If you sleep with dogs, you get up with fleas). But Chava brought some tea in tall glasses with lemon, and they tried to look at every possibility. It was quite possible that, even if Zelman was successful with the boy, Dmitri would not keep to his word, and there would be no benefit. It was also possible that the boy would not learn no matter what Zelman did, and then what would happen? And even if he was successful, how could the Russian be trusted?

But they had to consider what would happen if Zelman refused. Surely there would be retribution against the family, and he would have brought it down on them. So, it seemed there was no real choice.

After much discussion, they agreed he had to say yes, and that despite the odds, it could just turn out to be an opportunity for Zelman and the family. Shmuel's advice was to let Dawid calm down and try to speak to him again tomorrow. They both knew that after he had let off steam, their father would think carefully on it.

When Zelman returned, he could hear his father and Moszek arguing. Well, it was not really an argument. That requires at least two people. Dawid was the sort of man you could put in an empty room, and he would have an argument! Moszek was not saying much, but whenever she did say something – especially if it was an opinion – she would get another mouthful as Dawid descended into a further diatribe. The Domanskys all had that in their character. They could be compassionate and understanding with incredible insight, but if they thought they were right (which was most of the time), they could be very stubborn and vocal.

'That young *boychick*,' he was saying as Zelman walked in – 'who does he think he is? To make a deal with the devil! He is not *gepipchged* yet!' (He still has his umbilical cord). 'I should have gone with him and told that Russian *momzer* what we really think. Just wait until I get hold of him.'

Zelman went straight to bed, and heard nothing until the morning when Dawid, as expected, was calmer and able to consider the options.

As a result, two days later Zelman met Dmitri as agreed. 'Okay, I will try with your son if you promise no more pogroms for the Domansky family. Let me meet him first and see if I believe I can make progress with him. I will not take your money if I don't think I can do the job. But if I am successful, then I will spend two hours three times per week and for this I want 10 zloty per visit. I also want your word that the Domansky family will be protected from any further pogroms.'

'Are you mad?' Dmitri exclaimed. 'Look, think about what happens if you *don't* help me. It will be the worse for you and your family. I will pay you 10 zloty per week, not per visit. Take it and be thankful. If you improve his grades so that he passes his exams, I will pay a 30-zloty bonus, and you have my word on the other thing.'

Truly, Zelman was delighted with the result. It would mean the family could maybe have chicken more than once per week, and maybe he could even buy himself a real pair of boots.

He had not forgotten the risk of what might happen if he was not successful with the boy, nor whether he could trust Dmitri's word. So, he knew he would have to be careful.

In spite of his misgivings, Zelman was smiling to himself as he walked home. When his father returned, of course he wanted to know how it had gone. Truly it was a relief to Dawid that his son had returned unharmed, he had been worried that there may have been some sort of ambush.

They settled down in front of the fire and Zelman explained to his father that he had done a deal. He had managed to get a promise of safety and also some good payment from the Russian. Thankfully, as Shmuel said, Dawid had calmed down and listened carefully. The money was certainly tempting. 'But you can't trust these momzers,' said Dawid. 'He says he will keep us safe, and he will pay you money, but it may not last, or the promise of protection may be broken. He may not pay you anything and what would you do?'

'It's very risky,' said Moszek who had come in from the kitchen 'And what happens if the son has no brains, he's just a *schlemiel,* and you can't teach him?'

'Yes, it is risky,' replied Zelman, 'But I think I have a good chance and I want to do this.'

'Alright, try it', said Dawid after a lot of beard-pulling. 'But my lovely Zelman, keep your eyes and ears open. Remember you can't trust these pigs. At any time, the Cossack *momzers* can come and take what little we have.'

Zelman thought it was better not to bring this up again, so it was not discussed. A few days later he went to Captain Dimitri's home to meet the son and decide if he could work with him. Dmitri lived in Stoiczov, about two hours walk from Kawetchka. It was where most of the Cossacks lived. The only Jews living there were servants. It was a small village, but the homes were built with bricks and the roads had grass verges. It was altogether a much more pleasant place. Dmitri's house had carpets on the floor and curtains at the windows. His son Alexei was 11 years old, and he even had his own room with a desk.

The boy looked up as his father entered his room, 'Alex, this is Zelman. He has come to help you with your maths. You are to listen carefully to what he says and with Zelman's help I expect you to pass your school exams so that you can go to university when you are older. You can't do that without maths.'

The boy looked up at his father as if he was telling him to fly to the moon. Then he looked Zelman up and down, taking in his old shabby clothing and his makeshift shoes. Zelman could see he was not impressed. Winning the boy over would not be easy.

Dmitri left the room and Zelman first asked to see Alex's schoolbooks to assess his understanding of the subject. He was quite shocked to find pages covered with food stains and spidery work that made no sense at all. 'Ok Alex, perhaps you can tell me what you find difficult about this subject?'

'It's rubbish and the teacher is rubbish and when my father talks about it – that's rubbish, and I think probably you are also rubbish!'

'Ok, then let's see what we can do together. I will only suggest a way of thinking about it to you, and if you don't like it that way, we will do it another. What do you think of that?'

That peaked Alex's curiosity. No-one had ever taken account of how he would like to be taught. 'What do you mean? he asked.

'Well, there are many ways of learning things. When we were all babies we had to learn to walk and then to talk. We did not have boring lessons on how to do it, did we? How do you think it happened?'

'Well, I suppose we just picked it up as we went along,' said Alex

'Yes, and isn't it strange that everyone learns those lessons, and no-one ever fails to learn them?'

This achieved its purpose and got Alex thinking about a different way of learning. So, for the first lesson they did not do any maths exercises at all, but just discussed all the different ways of learning things. Alex liked the fact that Zelman was treating him as an equal and not a lowly student who couldn't understand anything.

At the end of the lesson, as Zelman was about to leave, Dmitri wanted to know how the boy had got on with the subject. He was not pleased to hear that they had not done any maths at all. 'How do you expect him to learn if you don't do exercises?' he asked. 'He has to be made to do it. He doesn't like it. That doesn't matter. Force him if necessary!'

All this was said in front of Alex, who ran back into his room. 'You said you would let me know if you could teach him, if he doesn't listen, I will beat him until he does.'

Zelman didn't comment, he just said that he needed a little time, and he would be back in two days.

Zelman had a lot to think about on his way home.

On the second occasion Zelman spent two hours with Alex, going through his schoolbooks and trying to explain where he was going wrong. To be fair the boy was trying very hard to understand, but Zelman's heavily accented Russian did not help, and at the end, Zelman felt he had not really made any progress. As they discussed his schoolwork it was becoming clear that the boy really did not like the subject and found it boring. Again, Zelman left after a ticking-off from Dmitri.

That night, Zelman decided to discuss the problem with Dawid. His father was, after all, a teacher and had taught children of all ages in many subjects. Zelman explained that the boy was frightened of his father and had not greeted Zelman well. But he had won him over and he felt there was now a rapport between them.

'Hmm,' mused Dawid thoughtfully. 'So why don't you try to impart the joy of mathematics in everyday life, rather than doing exercises and calculations? Do you remember some of the ways I taught you when you were small?'

'Yes!' Zelman exclaimed. 'Of course. Try to get him interested in the application of maths in his life. I know how to do that! I think it may work!' Zelman thanked his father and could not wait for the next lesson. He was already planning how it would go.

On the following Wednesday, Zelman arrived at the Russian house. Only Alex was at home and answered the door himself. They went into Alex's room and Zelman saw he had already got the books out and arranged them for the lesson.

To Alex's surprise Zelman put away all the books and sat down.

'Look Alex, maths is everywhere around you. In life the way we calculate time, make food, money, puzzles and games, all sorts of things and we don't realise it all has a basis in maths.'

Alex was looking at Zelman with a strange look on his face.

'My father said we have to do lessons and if I don't do what you say, he will beat me.'

Zelman frowned, 'Alright, but I want to talk to you about life and see what you think, take a simple thing like probability.'

'What is probability?'

Zelman gave Alex a coin and asked him to toss it to see if it came down with the head or the back side showing. He did it three times and it came down twice on the head and once on the back. Zelman explained that, as there were only two sides it could come down on, the probability of it landing on one side or the other was 0.50 or one divided by two, and it was always 0.50, no matter how many times you tossed it.

Zelman had brought a bag of marbles and he took out five; four blue and one red,

'Look, when you pick out one of these five, there is also a probability.'

He picked one marble out of the closed bag. It was blue. He put it back and asked

Alex to pick one, it was also blue. Then he picked another and this time it was red.

'Ah!' said Zelman, 'But if we do the same thing again, the red could come out first, last or in between. But if we keep doing it then the average, if we do enough, will be consistent. That is the probability, and we can calculate it.'

Alex was interested, so Zelman wrote on a piece of paper. 'The probability of picking the red without looking is 4 divided by 5, or 0.80, but in this case it was different. Once you'd taken out one blue, there were now only three blues and one red left, so the probability was reduced to 0.60 – there is now a higher chance of picking the red. And that would continue until you had only one blue and one red, and then the probability would be the same as the coin, 0.50. An even chance.'

He was pleased that this approach seemed to interest Alex, who started looking at more examples and working them out for himself.

When Dmitri arrived, he told Zelman he had been disappointed so far, and he wanted to see what Alex had done in this lesson. Zelman explained his different approach and that for this lesson they had focused on probability. Dmitri looked puzzled until he saw the work that his son had done, and he started to smile. He was understandably impressed.

Zelman said, 'Alex and I have been discussing how maths can be applied to almost everything we do, and I think he sees how interesting this can be.'

He turned to Alex, 'Alex, would you like me to continue to teach you, so we can explore more exciting ways of applying what we learn to life?'

Alex was smiling and with enthusiasm, he told his father he would very much like Zelman to continue. And he turned back to Zelman, 'Please! And I want to do some work on this, so I will have more examples to discuss when I see you next time.'

'Then on that basis, I would be happy to continue with the arrangements as we agreed.' Zelman said to Dmitri.

'Good! Then we continue with that agreement. Alex has exams at his school in the summer next year, said Dmitri. 'If he gets good grades, I will keep my extra promise.'

So, Zelman continued to work with Alex and sparked his interest in mathematics by using practical examples and relating them to the curriculum that Alex was following at school. Dmitri was pleased that his son was not only making progress, but was actually looking forward to Zelman's visits, and on one occasion when Moszek was giving birth yet again, and Zelman could not attend due to having to look after the family, Alex was really upset.

Dawid was grateful for the extra money that Zelman was bringing in, and Dmitri, true to his word, stopped the pogroms for the family. Moszek gave birth yet again, another daughter, Aryeh, so they had already grown to quite a large family. Moszek and Dawid now had seven mutual children, in addition to Zelman and Shmuel who were, of course, from Dawid's marriage to Esther. It was a lot of mouths to feed, but it made them a very important family in the shtetl.

CHAPTER 3

1871 SHIDDACH TIME

Dawid and Moszek felt that at twenty one it was time for Zelman to take a bride and to strike out on his own. Zelman's older brother Shmuel had already married Chava Devora and ran his own home, and Dawid and Moszek were torn. On the one hand they felt it was time to seek a wife for Zelman. On the other, they knew they would miss the money he brought in. 'Go and have a little chat with Chana,' said Dawid.

True to tradition, Moszek as the mama was the prime mover in arranging the lives of her family. Zelman was 21, a fine age to be married, and she had her eye on a girl from the Blass family. So, she went to see the Chana Bubitke, the *shiddach macher* (matchmaker). But before she left, Dawid took care to remind her that, as the papa, he would always have the final word.

'Oy, have I got a girl for your Zelman!' was the greeting before Moszek had even got through the door. 'I was talking to Misha Rabinski. She is looking for a shiddach for her daughter Faygel.'

'But Faygel is 30 years old, and she was married before.'

'Yes, but poor Aba passed away and she is a good girl, a *balabuste*, a homemaker.'

'No, no she is too old for my Zelman. I want to talk about Ryfke Blass.'

Chana knew the Blass family very well – it was her job to know all the families, and especially those with sons and daughters of marriageable age. Moszek was giving her a problem because Ryfke was a beauty and at seventeen, it was going to be easy to find a shiddach for her, whereas with Faygel it was not so easy. It was Chana's job to find shiddachs for all the offspring of the local families and she was kept busy because the families were all so large.

'Ryfke's father is a poor man. He works as a cleaner for the Russians. Ryfke will have no dowry.'

This was indeed difficult for Moszek, because Dawid had already pointed out that they would lose Zelman's income; if the bride came with no dowry, too, then that would be a problem. But she was up to Chana's little tricks, and she knew what she wanted for Zelman. At Rosh Hashanah last year, she had noticed the two of them looking at each other in that certain way young people do. Above all, she wanted her son to be happy.

Chana offered lemon tea which they drank the traditional way, through a sugar lump held in the mouth, and they talked.

'Moszek darling, please think about Faygel. She is a lovely girl and I know she would make your Zelman a lovely bride. She is not too old to have children, she is a hard worker and a good cook, and you should taste her lokshen pudding! Oy, he will grow fat on it. And her father is the tailor. He has a wonderful business, even the Russians go to him with their uniforms. She would come with a very fine dowry.'

Moszek would not be deterred. The more Chana tried to schmooze her into accepting Faygel, the more determined she became that she would not allow it. This went on for some time until finally Chana could see she was getting nowhere.

So finally, Chana promised to speak to Ryfke's parents, and Moszek said she would speak to Dawid.

Moszek went home and fed the children. She asked Zelman to go into the other room with them because she wanted to speak to his father, and she prepared a special supper for Dawid. Chicken soup with noodles and *kreplach* matzo balls followed by roast chicken and then lokshen pudding with fruit. She made the lokshen herself and the meal was very filling. It was a favourite of Dawid and when she gave him a little of the schnapps she had left over, he knew something was up, and that it had to do with the shiddach macher.

When she thought he was in a good frame of mind, she broached the subject. She started talking quickly to prevent him interrupting.

'So, I went to see Chana Bubitke today, to talk about Zelman. She was very excited that we thought the time might have arrived for him to seek a shiddach, and in fact she said she had been thinking about him herself. She suggested Faygel Rabinski, the tailor's daughter, but she is thirty years old, and she was married before. I said that was not right for our Zelman. So, she tried to *gib mir avek* with other ugly *meiskeits*. (Fob me off with unfortunates) Always she tries with what she calls her bargains - *matzeers*. But I know how she works, she got nowhere with me. I said Ryfke Blass would make a perfect shiddach. And I know they like each other.'

'What about the dowry?' said Dawid, straight away. 'Ryfke's father is a *mak kliner* (muck cleaner) the Russians pay him *chai kak*. (fancy shit) She will come with nothing, *goornisht*.'

Moszek knew this would be the problem.

'But Dawid, I know in my heart she is right for Zelman. She is a lovely girl, and I can teach her how to be a *balabusta*. I would love to have her as my daughter-in-law. Dawid, this will make me happy and above all, it will make your son Zelman happy.'

Dawid was worried that he had four daughters to marry off and that, without a dowry, he could end up looking after Zelman's family as well as his own.

But for all that he was such a stubborn man, he had a soft centre, so after the schnapps and some *schmoozing* from Moszek, he relented.

'All right – for you I do this, and for my son. I hope she makes you both happy.'

Moszek was beside herself. But she had to wait to hear from Chana to see if the *shiddach* was possible. But she went to bed with a smile on her face.

The next day after breakfast of corn bread with eggs and quark cheese that she made for the whole family, she hurried round to Chana Bubitke.

'Well? Well? What did they say?'

Chana was smiling. 'I spoke with Ryfke's parents, and of course, they wanted to know that this *shiddach* would have my blessing. Pah! Pah!' she said spitting on the palm of her own hand in the customary way to show that she was telling the truth about a very serious matter.

She puffed out her ample breast. 'They would not do anything without the approval of the qualified matchmaker, so we sat down, and we talked. We discussed forwards and backwards and then backwards and forwards over a nice glass tea.'

'So, tell me already!' Moszek exclaimed.

Chana was clearly enjoying the suspense. 'Well, I explained that this was a very serious decision for their daughter, and you know, Ryfke is very beautiful. They have the pick of the young men. I had to use all my powers of persuasion.'

'So *nu?*' Moszek was impatient to hear, and Chana was dragging it out.

'Well… This was not an easy conversation you know, and it needed all my skill…'

'Yes, yes… we know you are the best, but tell me already!' Moszek was really wound up.

'In the end they said yes! They would be proud to have Zelman for a son-in-law.'

Moszek had a habit of squeaking when she was very excited, and now she couldn't stop. It was very disconcerting for Chana, who gave her lemon tea and water to calm her down.

'Lena Blass is speaking to Ryfke right now, and you had better go and speak to your Zelman, then we can start to make wedding arrangements.

Moszek tripped over twice on the way back home – she was so excited. She couldn't wait until Zelman came home, and as soon as he arrived, she took him aside. She could not help squeaking as she told him. He was delighted to hear the news. The truth was he had been noticing Ryfke quite a lot and knew she had been looking at him. He readily agreed to meet with Ryfke if she was in agreement.

The way these things were arranged was that first, the parents had to agree, and then the young couple met each other on a 'date.' They would go for a walk with a chaperone and maybe sit and talk somewhere – keeping a respectable distance, of course. If this went well, they were effectively engaged, and they could start making wedding plans with their parents. During the engagement they were allowed to meet only under the same circumstances.

Ryfke and Zelman hit it off straight away. Zelman thought Ryfke was the most beautiful woman he had ever seen, and Ryfke found herself very attracted to Zelman. Apart from physical attraction, their conversation was wide reaching and intelligent, even though each of them held somewhat differing views and they were not afraid to challenge each other. To his delight, Zelman found that whilst Ryfke was not a maths aficionado, she had an extremely bright and enquiring mind, her grasp of Yiddish, Russian and Polish was excellent, and she could even write and translate

Cyrillic. On top of that she was a beauty. She was perfect.

In due course, both sets of parents went to the Old Rabbi and agreed a date for the wedding. Dawid would not be allowed to officiate at the wedding of his own son. Everyone in the village of Kawetchka was excited at the prospect of the wedding. Ryfke and Zelman were allowed to see each other in the meantime, but never in private.

CHAPTER 4

THE WEDDING

Gradually the days passed, and the wedding drew nearer. As was incumbent on Jewish girls in preparation for their wedding, Ryfke attended the Mikvah – a ritual bath – every month after her period and the wedding date had been calculated so that she would be purified before her wedding night. An observant Jewish man was forbidden to go near his wife before this ceremony had taken place. The women of the community had been busy making a *sheitel* wig for her. Married women were required to keep their hair covered, so the custom was to wear a wig. Ryfke spent a lot of time with Moszek and her mother and they showed her special recipes for meals she should make and they talked a lot about how to make your man happy.

But there was no talk between the parents and the betrothed couple about sex, or what to expect. Such talk was considered unclean and not to be uttered. So, the couple would have to find out by trial and error on their own. It's fair to say that Zelman had heard stories from the boys at the Yeshiva school, and Ryfke had heard her sisters and cousins say things that were frankly terrifying for a young girl. But she knew that all married couples did it, and that it was the way children were conceived. They both wanted as large a family as possible.

As the great day drew nearer and the friends in the village knew there was no dowry, the villagers, who had very little themselves, began to deliver presents for the new home. The butcher gave them two live chickens so they could always have eggs. Menachim, one of the best-off villagers gave them a cow, that they could have milk and cheese, and there were many gifts of household articles, linen and bedding. But the best gift of all was from Zelman's brother Shmuel and Chava Devora. They had a barn on their property which they gifted to the young couple and Zelman, Shmuel, Dawid and his other sons worked every spare moment they had to convert it into a home. By the week of the wedding, it was almost complete. They had a kitchen, admittedly only a stone structure with a metal cover to cook and heat food. They would have to light a fire underneath. They had a shower arrangement, too, but no hot water unless they heated it on the fire. But it was a start, and Zelman and Ryfke knew the family would be very forthcoming and welcome them into their own home any time.

Lena Blass and Moszek worked together on a wedding dress for Ryfke, complete with a veil. They managed to buy some white taffeta fabric and a little bit of silk ribbon and by the time the wedding came round, they had created a dress that took Ryfke's breath away when she saw it.

The wedding took place in the open air outside the Domansky household. Zelman stood anxiously under the *chuppah*, the open canopy which signified the hospitality of Abraham. He didn't feel hospitable – he wished everyone would go away. He was getting a headache from having to smile and look composed in front of the people standing with him under the chuppah: his father, the Old Rabbi and his future mother-in-law.

But his anxiety vanished when he saw his bride. Tenderly, trembling only a little, he performed the *bedeken*, placing a veil over her face as a pledge to protect and honour her his whole life. The Old Rabbi asked him to repeat the Hebrew vows and as he did, he smiled at Ryfke, sure she was smiling back under the veil. Then it was her turn to repeat the vows, after which Dawid's rich, powerful baritone sung the seven blessings, and he kept looking for signs that she was smiling, as she circled him seven times.

The significance of the number was to acknowledge that in the bible God created the world in seven days. Two cups of wine were sipped by the couple and the families. Zelman then took the ring that was also a gift and said, in Hebrew, 'Behold you are betrothed to me with this ring according to the law of Moses and of Israel' before placing the ring on Ryfke's forefinger. The bride was not required to say anything, and at that moment the couple were married.

A glass was placed on the floor and Zelman shattered it with his foot to represent the destruction of the temple in Jerusalem. Everyone shouted 'mazeltov' (good luck) and the clapping and happy dancing started. The men danced only with the men and the women with the women.

Families and friends had contributed food and wine and the long table was groaning with good things. After much dancing which became more and more energetic and frantic, the bride and the groom were each lifted on a chair while the dancing continued.

Eventually the rabbi recited the grace before meals and the blessings over the food and everyone could eat. It was a great celebration.

The only two without happy faces were Misha Rabinsky and her daughter Faygel, who thought it should have been her!

Against the background of the hardship in their lives, the people partied with great enthusiasm and gusto for a long time, and when the time came it was with some trepidation that the couple made their way to their new bedroom. Everyone knew they would now consummate their union. Both were of course, virgins and had only a sketchy knowledge of what was required.

Moszek had thoughtfully placed what was left of the schnapps in the room, and they gratefully finished it off as soon as they entered. Of course, not only did neither of them have any experience or knowledge of how to proceed, but they really hardly knew each other. The schnapps did not really give them much in the way of Dutch courage and neither knew how to start. Zelman felt that as the man, he needed to lead. 'Let's just sit on the bed and talk for a bit. Let me know when you are ready.'

Ryfke nodded nervously. She had an overwhelming desire to please her new husband, but the nerves were making her shiver.

So they talked about the wedding, the beautiful ceremony, the food and the dancing. After a while Ryfke knew Zelman would never force her, and she took comfort in that, so she would have to initiate things.

A large bedsheet had been strung up and Ryfke went behind it to undress. She took as long as she could to stave off the moment and when Zelman called her, she wrapped another sheet around her and ventured back into the room. Zelman had stripped down to has underpants. He was trying to project some machismo, but he was very conscious that this was very frightening for Ryfke. He took her in his arms, and she felt his manhood against her straight away.

'Ryfke, I have never done this before and I know it is scary, but we must learn to love each other in every way, just as our parents have done before us. And Ryfke you can see the effect you have on me. I think you are the most beautiful girl I know, and I am proud to be your husband.'

If Zelman thought that this little speech would provide some comfort for her, he was mistaken. Ryfke started to cry, and the tears streamed down her face. He could feel her trembling against his body. It took considerable effort, but Zelman knew he could not rush her. They both sat on the bed again.

'We can take this slowly, my love. Let us get to know each other first.'

He started to kiss her on the lips, and then the neck. Gradually the tears stopped, and he took the sheet from her shoulders so that just her breasts were visible. Although small, she had beautiful breasts with erect nipples. Zelman nearly fainted at the sight of them. He had an ache in his loins and he wanted her more than ever. Ryfke started to kiss him back, but when he made an attempt to remove the sheet altogether, she jumped up and walked away.

'I am sorry, Zelman,' she said. 'I am a bad wife, but I know what you have to do to me, and I don't think I can face it. I do want to do it with you, but I am so scared. Will it hurt?'

'I don't think so,' replied Zelman. 'In fact we are both supposed to enjoy it. Please take off the sheet and let me see your beauty. Trust me, I would never hurt you.'

He was speaking in a soft voice which gave Ryfke a little more confidence, and the truth was that she did have desire for him. Gradually she removed the sheet, and he was able to see the soft, white skin beneath. He took in the swell of her hips; the curves of her body and for the first time he saw her mound of Venus with its soft covering of hair leading to the crease that was the beginning of her vulva. When he saw this, Zelman could not contain himself. He removed his own underpants, leaving his erect penis standing proud.

'Ryfke, Ryfke, you are the most perfect and beautiful thing I have ever seen.'

But Ryfke could not take her eyes of the wild snake that confronted her and shuddered at the realisation that he intended to put it inside her.

Zelman walked toward her and put his arms to embrace her again and she felt the hardness of him against her. Zelman felt he must take control and he gradually eased her toward the bed. He noticed that she was moist, and he could feel her sexual juice against his thigh. He knew he should take it slowly, but an urgent and wanton desire had taken hold of him. He climbed on to her and pushed himself into her, but he found resistance. By now he was overcome with need. He pushed harder, and this time he gained complete entry, but Ryfke screamed with pain.

Alarmed, he withdrew, and the door burst open. Moszek and Lena had been listening outside and rushed in when they heard Ryfke's scream.

The young couple immediately jumped up and tried to cover themselves. 'What the…?' shouted Zelman and then he saw blood on the sheet. He was terrified he had done something bad to Ryfke.

The two women urged the young couple to sit down. 'It's alright,' said Lena. 'This only happens the first time. You must feel a little pain at first so you can understand the pleasure in the future.'

'Yes, yes,' said Moszek. 'Don't be afraid. Every married couple go through this and you will get over it. I will bring a glass tea and some *kichels*, cakes, and you just relax, go to bed and get to know each other. Tomorrow is another day, and it is the first day of your life together. You will make lovely babies.'

Zelman and Ryfke were completely stunned that their mothers had been listening outside the room, and shocked that they should burst in. But they were grateful for the tea and *kichels* and above all for the reassurance. Moszek explained that it was not unusual for mothers to listen outside on the first night so they could help where they could. Ryfke cleaned herself up and they both went to bed comforted by the warm touch of each other's bodies.

The next morning was much more successful and both succeeded in a stuttering but fulfilling lovemaking. The mothers came again to the house and this time they were both proud that things seemed to be back on course. They both went back to report to the respective fathers that all was under control. There would be babies.

Chapter 5

Ada Ochter

Zelman continued to work hard, and he and Ryfke were as happy as they could be. They had fallen in love. Ryfke was taking in washing and mending for Dmitri's family and as much as she and Zelman were enjoying each other, there were no babies yet.

Chana Bubitke had found a *shiddach* for Zelman's brother Mendel: Ada, the daughter of Menachim Ochter, whose wife had just passed away. Truly Mendel was not keen, she was not a beauty like Ryfke, but she was a good girl, and she made the best chicken and lokshen soup in the village.

When Moszek told Dawid that the marriage had been agreed, he wanted to be happy for his son. On the one hand he was pleased that she would come with a dowry from Menachim and it was understood that the young couple would move in with him, so they would have a home immediately. On the other hand, he knew Menachim's motivation was that Ada could continue to look after him, Menachim would provide for the home and Mendel would work, and Ada would look after them both. That was why he was so keen.

'Can't you find anyone else for Mendel?' he asked Moszek after they had finished their meal and the children had retired. 'After all a man cannot live by chicken soup alone.'

But Moszek was set on it, and in the end Dawid gave in, they could start planning another wedding.

It was a dark night with no moon, in November. Snow was already on the ground, and Ada had been in the field gathering vegetables for dinner which she carried in a basket. She became aware of a presence behind her. She looked round and could not quite make out what she was seeing. There was a dark shape entirely black against the white of the ground and the trees. The shape seemed to be moving behind her.

She started to run, but the shape got closer, so she threw the basket with the vegetables behind her, gathered her skirts and ran for all she was worth. But it was dark, and she did not see the pothole. Her foot went into it, she felt a snap and then terrible pain shot up her leg. Before she could move a large man in a black cloak and hood stood over her with a knife which he pressed to her throat. Of course, she was terrified. He held the knife so firmly to her skin that she thought if she as much as coughed, it would go in.

'Move or shout and I will kill you now,' rasped the voice between closed teeth.

Consumed with terror and pain, she went numb as he put bindings he had already prepared over her wrists and pulled them tight. He had a filthy cloth that he stuffed in her mouth and another he bound round her head to hold the gag in place. He dragged her out of the pothole to flatter ground and pulled down his trousers. She saw he was already aroused, and he put it into her bound hands and told her to stroke it. Then he pulled up her skirts and put his fingers inside her.

Between the pain and the discomfort, mercifully she passed out. When she came to, he was inside her and she felt his seed on her leg. She thought that maybe it would be better to die so she found her voice and screamed for her father. It was futile. No one would hear her out here in the field, and the momzer pushed the knife so it cut into her throat. Then he used it to cut away her clothing and she lay naked and shivering on the snowy ground. 'Do that again and you will never live to see your family.'

He smoked a cigarette while she lay there and then he raped her a second and a third time. Then he cut her throat.

When she did not return, Menachim started getting angry. She was a friendly girl and always stopping to talk to friends or people she met. As the time passed, his anger turned to anxiety, and he began to trace the steps she would have taken out into the field.

It was the worst sight imaginable. Menachim was holding a flaming torch to light the way. As he approached, he could make out the site of a disturbance and as he neared it, he became aware of a bundle on the ground. He arrived at the site with his heart in his mouth and saw the carnage that had been wrought. Blood and clothing were flung around as if by some maniacal bloodthirsty giant. And then he saw the worst. It was his daughter Ada. She lay naked, her body white and twisted against the grass. The bright red blood making a grisly contrast against her body and the snow. Her mouth was open in a rictus scream and her head was half severed from her body.

Menachim fell to his knees and then prostrated himself on the ground 'No, no, no…' he kept crying into the night. 'Not my little *shapsele*.'

He started to bang his head with the branch of the torch, and it was only when he burned himself in the flame that he stopped. He repeatedly walked away from the scene and returned as if hoping that it was a dream.

He stumbled around with unseeing eyes and tears streaming down his face. He had lost his wife and now his only beloved daughter had been viciously murdered. The hours passed and the first rays of morning were approaching. Menachim did not know what to do.

An early Cossack horse patrol was approaching, and the leader surveyed the scene. 'What happened here?' was the uncaring comment.

Menachim could not speak, but the scene spoke for itself. One of the men in the patrol knew the family and explained that this was father and daughter. The Russians put the body on a horse together with the father and took them back to the shtetl.

The village was just waking up and Mendel was starting his morning round. He was a *Yeshiva Bocher*, a young man whose days were spent studying Torah and Talmud with the religious scholars of the village. This was considered to be a *mitzvah*, a blessing, and among religious Jews, it was the most important occupation. But he also made a few zlotys by helping deliver milk in the mornings. Mendel was the first to see the patrol enter the village with its grisly luggage.

He first saw Menachim on the horse and thought it very strange that he should be led by the Cossack patrol. As he got nearer, he saw that what he thought was a blanket was actually a woman and even when he was beside the horse his brain would not register that he was looking at his wife to be, Ada. And she was dead.

He turned away and felt a blackness come over him. The world was spinning, and he passed out. A woman from the house where he had just delivered came out. She knew Mendel and Ada. She cried out when she saw Mendel on the ground, but nearly fainted herself when she realised the grisly package on the horse was actually a woman covered in blood.

The Cossack let the body slip off and fall indecently to the ground. It was then she saw it was Ada and made the connection to Mendel. She stood frozen to the spot until the Cossack told her to get water and tend to the living. She ran inside and returned with water and a cool cloth with which she bathed Mendel until he came round. A crowd was beginning to gather, and people were standing in varying states of shock.

At first, Mendel thought he'd had a bad nightmare, until he looked up. The Russians had helped Menachim off the horse and they were carrying the body with Menachim following.

He seemed to be in a dumb trance, staring blankly.

Suddenly he stumbled, prostrated himself on the ground and started to wail. This was heard by others and pretty soon more people had gathered. Zelman and Dawid came running but everyone pulled back when they caught sight of the body. To gaze on a dead body was considered to be a sin – and this was someone they knew.

The body was taken into Menachim's house and laid out as decently as possible. It was covered in a sheet that served as a shroud. Dawid took Menachim back to his house where Moszek tried to comfort him as best she could, offering the famous chicken soup. But Menachim was inconsolable. He kept banging his head repeatedly against the wall and wishing himself dead. He had vomited several times.

Meanwhile Zelman was trying to console his brother at the scene. Mendel was a hothead and a fighter. Often, he would come home with bruises from a fight he had got into over nothing. His face had a black look and he wanted to kill somebody. Zelman spoke to the Cossack leader who was still mounted on his stallion. 'Who will investigate this vile murder of a sweet young girl?'

'Well, I will report it,' replied the Russian doubtfully. 'But since she was a Jewess, maybe we will never know.' This was intended as a hurtful slight to ensure the Jews knew their place, and it hit its mark.

According to Jewish law, bodies had to be buried as soon as possible. The Russians knew this, so the leader advised Zelman to get it buried right away. 'But don't you want a doctor to look at it and do some investigation?' Zelman asked, shocked at the offhand attitude.

'No, we know what happened, she was raped and murdered. We will try to find out who did it, but there is a lot going on. We have to run the country you know, and there is much to do. I will report it and you will hear when we know something.'

Menachim was completely distraught, oscillating between violent anger and desperate misery. Zelman took him home and insisted he stayed with the Domanskys. Ryfke was wonderfully sympathetic, wrapping her arms round Menachim, whom she hardly knew, and Mendel who was numb with shock. Zelman and Dawid went from door to door to see if anyone could throw any light on how this could have happened, but incredibly for such a small community, they could not find out anything relating to the atrocity. There were no witnesses, it seemed that the attacker was not known to Ada and no similar crime had ever been committed that they knew of. Of course, the Russians were no help at all. Clearly, they were not interested in solving the disgusting crime. After two days, they had no choice but to arrange a funeral.

This left a terrible scar on the memory of all in the shtetl.

Chapter 6

Birth of Leizar

Zelman had gradually developed a cautious friendship with Dmitri. He had kept his word and the family were free of the pogroms which were visited from time to time on other folk in the village.

On a beautiful clear day in the Spring, Ryfke had wonderful news. She was pregnant. The family were ecstatic and Moszek and Lena bustled around her giving lots of advice. 'You must be very careful; this is your first.'

Zelman's sister Yentl was now 20 and she was charged with taking over the heavy work – washing, ironing, cleaning of the floors and the house and much of the cooking. Although she was ably assisted by their sister Sara who was now 15, Yentl didn't like these household chores one bit, and protested loudly all the way.

For years she had never given up hope that one day she would be the Torah student instead of the skivvy around the house. But as always, Zelman overruled her.

'Listen to Uma. This baby is precious', he said. 'Your job is to look after Ryfke and make sure the baby and the mother is healthy and happy.'

This annoyed Yentl all the more. She bit her tongue and stormed out into the kitchen. 'One day', she thought, I will take a husband, and HE will be the one to look after the home while I study and learn!'

Time passed slowly for Ryfke. It is a Jewish tradition not to do much preparation for the arrival of a baby especially the first, so as to avoid a *nahora*. Not to tempt fate.

But it annoyed her that the mothers interfered so much in their lives.

However, Zelman quite liked it, especially when they used the old-fashioned way to tell the gender of the baby. At first, because Ryfke was quite slim, her bump stood out more than usual at the front, so they were sure it would be a boy. 'If the front is more, it's a boy for sure. With a girl you carry differently,' said Moszek.

'Yes, with more all round, a girl will be found,' agreed Chava.

But as the pregnancy progressed, Ryfke began to put on more pounds towards her rear, so the mothers tried a different system. A *magen dovid* - Star of David pendant that Moszek wore round her neck - was warmed by the fire. They had Ryfke lie down and suspended it above her stomach. 'If it starts to spin round, then it is a boy,' said Chava. 'And if a girl, then it swings from side to side.'

After a few moments, behold! The star began to spin. 'What did I tell you?' said Moszek, to Zelman's delight. 'You are having a boy!

Ryfke carried her child all through the summer and as the weather got colder and winter approached, they knew the time was near. It was in the early hours when Ryfke got up to use the bathroom, as she returned to bed, she felt a rushing sensation. She looked down to see water on the floor. 'Zelman, Zelman, get my mother right away. I think the baby is coming.'

Zelman had never woken up so fast. He jumped out of bed and ran to his parents and then to the Blass house. '*Kim gishvint*, the baby is here!'

Because of his alarm and the way he said the baby had arrived, both mothers were very concerned. Had something gone wrong? How could the baby come so quickly? They both ran to the house, still in their nightclothes.

But when they arrived, they saw that Ryfke was only at the early stages of labour and contractions had just started. 'Calm down, *tatele*,' said Moszek. 'You have a long wait for your baby. He's just started the journey.' They banished the men from the house and started to prepare with hot water, sheets, and towels. As the labour progressed, the contractions came more often and were more severe and when Zelman first heard Ryfke scream with pain, he burst back into the room. The sight did not give him comfort. Ryfke was on all fours on the floor with the two mothers at her rear. She was hot and sweaty.

'What have you done to her?' shouted Zelman.

'Just get out,' said Moszek – this is normal. 'Go speak to your father.'

Zelman had been around when his brothers and sisters were born, of course, but his memory was more focused on the recent ones, Moszek's sixth and seventh deliveries, which as such had been much easier, and he certainly never saw her on the floor.

Yentl had been commandeered to fetch lots of hot water and clean towels. She was horrified when she was in the room to see the indignity, pain and suffering of her sister-in-law and vowed that this was another thing she was never going to do!

Zelman was pushed out of the door and went to find his father, who reassured him that the women knew what they were doing. So, it was around midday when he heard the wonderful sound of the first cry of his new-born son. Yes, the women's tests had proved correct. The baby was a boy.

The women allowed Zelman and Dawid into the room. Ryfke was sitting up in bed with the broadest grin on her face and holding in her arms a tiny, little baby boy. Zelman did not know what to do. He was beside himself with joy. His beautiful wife had produced his first-born son. And they were both perfect. 'Come and meet your son,' said Ryfke, with not a little pride.

Zelman approached the bed and sat on the edge. Ryfke placed the little bundle in his arms. Zelman felt that his heart would explode, until he felt wetness down his front. His wonderful first-born son had just pee'd on his father. But he didn't care.

Dawid, a smiling *zeider* took over, then handed the baby to Reuben Blass, the other *zeider* and one by one the other children came to meet their brother or nephew. Zelman noticed that one person was missing. His brother Mendel who was still grieving the death of poor Ada.

Zelman went to get him. 'Come, Mendel. I want to share this with you. One life closes, another begins.' Mendel followed him into the room, and Zelman put the baby in his arms. The little one was cooing and Mendel, for the first time in a while, was smiling. Dawid looked on, nodding. And even Yentl thought the outcome was not too bad.

Eventually the mothers shooed everyone out, saying that mother and baby needed some time and some rest. It was a big job entering this world. They proceeded to help Ryfke to breastfeed which was another challenge. It was painful for her at first, but eventually with encouragement and patience, mother and baby both got the hang of it and afterwards they fell asleep – both were exhausted.

Outside, celebrations were starting. Wine and schnapps were made available and Yentl and Sara had made *latkes,* the fried potato pancakes, fish balls and *rugelach,* the small, sweet pastries. Dawid, Reuben and Zelman were in a corner deep in conversation with the Old Rabbi. They had to plan for the *Bris Milah* circumcision. Jews must have their new-born sons circumcised on the eighth day of his birth. Since this was the first-born son, there would also be a *Pidyon Ha Ben,* the traditional ritual by which the father symbolically offers the boy to a Cohen, a member of the priestly caste, and 'buys him' back again. This would take place on the thirtieth day. Both of these rituals were considered a *mitzvah,* a divinely-imposed duty that resulted in blessings, and each would be the subject of celebration.

The *mohel* who performed the circumcision was the subject of many jokes because he also happened to be the butcher, Aaron Gabinsky. 'I hope he remembers which job he is doing today!' 'It's the best cut he's had all week!' 'He does very well with his tips!' But it was Aaron everyone called on when the job had to be done.

As the days passed, there was much discussion in the Domansky family about names for the child. Everyone had a different idea, but in the end, it was Zelman who put his foot down. 'He is my son, and he will be named Leizar. A fine strong name after my great grandfather.' Grudgingly Ryfke and her family agreed. Little Leizar grew stronger every day, so on the eighth day, as prescribed in the Torah, everything was ready for the *bris.*

Aaron said he would be delighted to assist. 'Of course, I have to ask, as you know, in the Torah, God commands that the father shall circumcise his own son. Do you wish to delegate that *mitzvah* to me as the *mohel?* It is not a job for the faint hearted.'

Zelman was very happy to confirm that the mohel should perform the procedure. He told Aaron that the *sandek* who holds the baby during the ceremony would be his father Dawid, and the *kvaters* who bring the baby to the *sandak,* would be his brothers Shmuel and Mendel.

These duties were considered to be a *mitzvah,* but a dubious one, because the baby will cry and quickly need to be comforted. Women did not take part, but of course it was their job to comfort the little fellow afterwards.

It all went smoothly, and after the appropriate *brocha* blessing, the baby was named and all the merriment started with much eating, drinking and dancing.

There was similar celebrating and feasting on the thirtieth day when the *Pidyon Ha Ben* ceremony took place. This time only the Rabbi was required to bless the child and the parents and instruct them how to figuratively hand the baby to him and then buy him back for a silver zloty.

CHAPTER 7

BIRTHS AND MISCARRIAGES.

Time passed slowly in Kawetchka. Zelman continued with his work, Dmitri was very pleased that Alex was now progressing well at his studies and although the pogroms continued in the shtetl, true to Dmitri's word, the Domansky family were spared.

Ryfke became pregnant again. This time it was less dramatic, and she gave birth to another little boy, whom they named Mendel Yaacov. Little Leizar was into everything. He was an early walker, and his first word was uttered when he was only 13 months old. It was *Bubba* - Grandma. Of course, Moszek beamed with pride. 'You see, the first word is *Bubba*.' She picked him up, 'You love your *Bubba* don't you?'

'Not so fast!' Anna Benjamin had walked in. 'How do you know he means you? Am I not also his *Bubba*?'

'Of course, of course, He means both of us.' And she handed him to Anna.

------◆------

Ryfke was keen to see all the family round her dinner table, so one evening in the autumn when the nights were cold, but before the snows came, she put the little ones to bed early and with the help of Moszek and her sister, Anna and Yentl who did not stop grumbling, they lit a big fire and made a lovely dinner for everyone.

Dawid loved being at the head of the family and it was wonderful to see everyone round the table. When the meal was finished, Dawid decided this might be a good time for them to learn a little bit about the world they lived in. He sat in front of the fire in the big wooden chair with pillows at his back and a glass of schnapps at his side. He gathered the whole family around him, some in chairs, but mostly on the floor.

'Well, my beautiful family. First, we must thank the women for making us such a lovely dinner, and it's wonderful to have you all here. We are so proud! So now I've got you, I want to tell you a little bit about where we live and where the Domansky family come from.'

He placed a large piece of rough, brown paper on the floor, on which he had drawn a map of Galicia.

'Now gather round,' and he pointed with a stick. 'We call this country Poland because that's what it used to be before the Russians and the Austrians got their hands on it. Now, our little town of Kawetchka is in the Western Region of the Russian Empire under the rule of the dictator Mikhail Vilensky, they call him the Hangman of Vilnius. The area is called The Pale of Settlement and we Jews, as you know, have the privilege of being blamed for everything that goes wrong.'

At this, there was a little wave of ironic laughter. Everyone seemed willing to listen.

'But you see, we are a very old family in these parts, and we can trace our roots back hundreds of years. My *liebchens*, we should all be proud of our heritage.'

He knew he had their attention.

'In 1495 this land was part of the three kingdoms of Hungary, Croatia and Bohemia ruled by King Matthias Corvinius. Among his subjects were a very large number of Jews and this king understood that he needed a Jewish advisor who the Jews would respect as a leader.

Of course, there were many Rabbis who were the leaders of their own communities, but the wise king wanted harmony with the Jews and a voice to speak on behalf of *all* the Jews in the land. Rabbi Zacherie Mendel, our ancestor, was honoured with the title Supremus Judaeorum, he was given the name Domansky and was effectively the Chief Rabbi of all the three kingdoms.'

Zelman's youngest sister, Aryeh had been listening intently, 'But *Zeider*, why was he given a new name? He already had a name, didn't he like it?'

'Very good question!' said Dawid. 'In those days, people didn't really have proper surnames. As you know from your Hebrew name Aryeh bus Duvid, it simply means Aryeh the daughter of Dawid, so people used their fathers' names, or the towns they came from, you could be Aryeh Kawechka or maybe their work like Reb Schneider, the tailor, and in a lot of cases, they used the sign over their house. Mendel means almond. Only very important people had real surnames and the king bestowed the name Domansky on our ancestor to show his importance. It comes from the language of the Romans, Latin, and it means Belonging to the Lord. So he was a servant of the King and also of God - and only the King and God could overrule him. He was the royal personal advisor'.

Dawid continued to explain how they were all descendants of this Rabbi and through the ages there had been many very famous Rabbis who were also descendants. Eventually the younger ones started to yawn. Moszek, sitting next to Dawid, gave him a not very subtle kick to let him know it was time to finish and let the families go home.

———————✳———————

Zelman and Ryfke were delighted when, a year after Mendel Yaacov was born, Ryfke fell pregnant again, but all the *mazeltovs* they received were to be short-lived. She was unable to carry successfully and suffered a miscarriage at three months.

So, six months later, when Ryfke eventually announced she was again pregnant, it was greeted with delight, but tinged with trepidation. She was once again waited on hand and foot by the mothers and the family, and she put on quite a bit of weight, being fed with all her favourite food all the time. She lost count of how many times she was told 'You're eating for two.'

At around eight months, she started having pain and some bleeding, but the pains turned out to be false alarms and although she was uncomfortable, the mothers were very reassuring. 'Don't worry *tutele,* this baby is going to arrive healthy, we know about these things.'

But there were whispers between them that it looked like this was going to be a difficult delivery for her.

'She's been lucky,' said Moszek, 'she delivered the first two as if they had just fallen from heaven.'

A week before the due date, Ryfke's waters broke, and labour started. The labour pains were much more marked than before, and progress seemed very slow. After several hours, Ryfke was getting weaker, and the mothers called Joseph Galitzer. When he examined her his brow was furrowed.

'The baby is in breech position,' he said. He tried to turn the baby in the womb without success and just succeeded in hurting Ryfke much more. It was all Zelman could do to restrain himself from throwing the doctor out.

Dawid and Zelman were very frightened. To Dawid, the memory of how Zelman had been born was only too stark, and they were scared they would lose Ryfke. To make matters worse Joseph explained that the cord was caught around the baby's neck, and he had to deliver the little chap as quickly as possible. But Ryfke was growing weaker all the time and could not push as hard as required and then have the strength to refrain from pushing when necessary.

Eventually, amid much blood and screaming, the baby was born. Moszek took the new born while Joseph attended to Ryfke who was in great distress. The baby was quite blue, but they wrapped him up and kept him warm while rubbing his little chest and back and he perked up. Dawid was outside praying. Zelman was beside himself with worry. Eventually, to everyone's relief, there was a faint cry from the baby. He was breathing. Ryfke heard it, and it was a tonic that raised her spirits. Everyone was relieved.

When Joseph felt it was alright to leave Ryfke, he went to examine the little one. Everyone watched for any clues that might appear on his face, but there were only deep furrows. 'Look, this baby has been through a lot,' he said, mainly to Zelman. 'Don't tell Ryfke, but the heartbeat is weak. He will need a lot of nurturing and care. Also, his breathing is irregular.'

In the ensuing days, the families and friends arranged twenty-four hour attendance for the little one, whom Ryfke and Zelman decided to call Aaron. He could not latch on to his mother for feeding, which actually worked in his favour because it meant any of the family could warm milk for him. Ryfke and Zelman did not sleep much and thankfully Moszek and Lena were available to look after Leizar and Mendel. But they were fighting a losing battle. On his fortieth day on this earth, poor little

Aaron drew his last breath and closed his eyes forever.

This left a massive scar on the family. Ryfke went into depression, feeling it must have been her fault and that she had let Zelman down. Zelman tried to reassure her, but it was often through tears. In his mind he resolved to avoid any future pregnancy because it was too dangerous.

It is difficult to overestimate the love between Ryfke and Zelman. To her, Zelman was her hero for whom she would make any sacrifice. To him, Ryfke was the sun, the moon and the stars all shining together. They had grown to respect each other's intellect, and the physical love had grown in care and intensity. Since all marriages were arranged between the *shiddach* maker and the mothers, love really did not enter into it. The couple were usually told they would learn to love each other, and to be fair, most of the time, most couples relaxed over the years to a compromise that was at least comfortable. But a love such as Zelman and Ryfke shared was precious and rare. When Moszek thought back to how she'd stood up to Dawid and Chana and brought these two together, she felt that she had really done something good.

In the case of Ryfke and Zelman, they really had found their soulmates, which made them wonderful parents for Leizar and Mendel Yakov, but the loss of two babies - the second in such a dramatic and dangerous way - tested their relationship. An air of depression seemed to settle over their house. This was exacerbated when, according to Jewish law, they had to arrange a funeral for their son and, instead of celebrations this time, a tiny coffin had to be made. On a cold rainy day, the families stood round a grave and Zelman had to recite the *kaddish* prayer for the dead.

He looked up and gasped with surprise to see Dmitri's son Alexei, standing behind at a respectful distance. His nose had gone red with the cold, and he was shivering in a donkey jacket with a simple cap on his head. Zelman walked over. 'You were one person I didn't expect to see today.'

'I am so sorry to hear what happened, Mr Zelman, and I hoped you wouldn't mind if I paid my respects.'

Zelman was impressed that the boy had come specifically for that purpose, and he felt he could not leave him in the cold. 'Come into the house, I will just say you are a student of mine, and you can stay for the *shiva*.'

Alex looked at him quizzically.

'It's Jewish custom to mourn the death of an immediate family member for a period of seven days following the funeral. During this period the house becomes a house of mourning and parents, siblings or children of the deceased are expected to discuss their loss and accept the comfort of others. Prayers for the departed are recited every evening, but there is food, drink and warmth. Come, you look freezing cold.'

Zelman and Ryfke sat on low boxes wearing clothing they had torn at the funeral. Leizar and Mendel were too young to sit shiva. But friends and family were with them all the time and when the prayer service was held, Zelman had the opportunity to say *kaddish* for his lost son, after which he stood and walked over to Alex. 'It was very good of you to come Alex, and I want you to know how much I appreciate it. Does your father know?'

'No, this was my choice, Mr Zelman.'

He gave the boy a hug, 'Well, go back to your home now. You look a lot better than before, and I will see you at your next lesson.'

During this time, Zelman found himself arguing with his father and his brother a lot. And because they were all serious, strong personalities, the arguments became very heated. The death of the baby also tested his religious beliefs and feeling bitter, Zelman picked a fight with his father the Rabbi, who was trying to explain that God decides who should live and who should die, and indeed who should not be born at all. Zelman, he said, should accept the deaths as God's will.

This struck at the heart of how Zelman saw things at that time. 'What sort of God is it that makes my Ryfke suffer like that only to deliver a baby with no chance to live?' With tears in his eyes, he went on, 'Ryfke never did any harm to anyone. Why did God decide she should suffer like that? And what did my third son do that he did not deserve to live?'

'God works in mysterious ways, Zelman. It is not for us to question the ways of God. He put us on this earth and only He can decide when we should leave it. You must be thankful for what you have. A beautiful and bright wife – as the bible says, *'A woman of true worth.'* And two beautiful sons. You also have both your parents and your family. Give thanks to God.'

But Zelman was not prepared to be told to be thankful for what had happened. 'He is a vengeful God, your God!' he said. 'He curses us with the Cossacks, and he kills my son.'

Dawid slapped him round the face quite hard. 'I forgive you because of all you have been through,' he said. 'I love you and God loves you, never let me hear you say anything like that again.'

The family were shocked. Dawid had never done anything like that before and the little ones started crying. Zelman walked away with his father's finger marks on his face.

Gradually these deep scars healed, and the Old Rabbi was right, their children and family were a great comfort to them both.

The two boys, Leizar and Mendel Yaacov were lavished with love from their parents and the family, who overcompensated for the loss of baby Aaron. The boys were never short of attention. Leizar was proving to have an exceptional mind. He remembered everything and already at the age of five, he could read Hebrew and solve rudimentary maths problems. Of course, he spoke Russian and Yiddish, although, under the new regulations the family were not allowed to speak Yiddish in public. He was a serious child with a strong and healthy thirst for knowledge.

Mendel had also been an early walker and what his parents called a *'Yachner'* - someone who talks a lot! He didn't stop and at only three years old whatever was in his mind was on his tongue. In contrast to Leizar, he was always laughing.

CHAPTER 8

DUVID AT LAST

·

As the years passed following the death of baby Aaron, Moszek and Dawid started to say how nice it would be if the boys had a sister. They knew this was a very sensitive subject with Zelman and Ryfke, but it gradually crept into the conversations. At first Zelman was vehemently against any talk of another child. 'I would never put Ryfke through that again. It could kill her, and that would kill me. We are content with our lovely boys. I don't want to hear any of this talk again.'

But after a couple of years had passed, Ryfke began to get a little broody. She would not say anything to Zelman, but she could not help but think how lovely it would be to have a little girl, soft and lovely, whom she could nurture and bring up in her own image. She shared this with Moszek and Lena and they resolved together to work on Zelman. Lena spoke to Ryfke's father Reuben but got little sympathy. The men were always focused on bringing more boys into the family, so that they could become *tzadiks* (religious leaders). Traditionally the *tzadik* in the community leads and promotes spirituality through revealing divinity in new Torah interpretations, and through awakening his generation to return to God. Of course, this was not an ambition of Zelman's in any case.

The older Jews also believed they had a duty to do as God had said to Noah in the Torah, 'Go forth and multiply.' Every child was a blessing, and it was their duty to procreate, so families were large. Ironically this added to their poverty and suffering, but they saw it as upholding Jewish Law and the will of God.

So after much persuading, eventually Zelman began to relent; they started trying again for another baby, and in the spring of 1878, Ryfke became pregnant again. This time Joseph Galitzer kept an eye on her. He visited the home every few weeks to check on how the pregnancy was going, although somewhat uncharitably, Dawid thought he really saw it as a way to get a regular helping of Ryfke's chicken soup with lokshen and kneidlach. Dawid maintained that this chicken soup – the recipe for which had been handed down through generations – was the reason the Jews were so resilient.

Ryfke carried well this time. She remained fit and hardly ever took to her bed despite Zelman's imploring her to take it easy, and as she got larger, the boys loved to touch her stomach to feel the baby moving.

'But how did the baby get in there?' said Mendel, four years old. 'Uba put it in there,' replied Leizar who already knew a bit too much about how babies were made and wanted to share it with his little brother.

'But if it is in Uma's' tummy, then all her food must fall down on its head.'

They were both fascinated, but Mendel could not work it out at all, and there was no one in the family who was ready to explain. There were many things that were not spoken about in front of children, and the making of babies was certainly one of them.

As she got bigger, it seemed to Ryfke that the days and weeks got longer. She developed a sort of waddle when she walked that Mendel found very funny and tried to copy. What Mendel did, his younger brother was sure to follow and even Zelman had to laugh when he saw both the boys waddling along behind Ryfke like little ducklings.

Ryfke knew the day was very near and she could feel familiar movement in her body readying itself for the birth. On this occasion, the waters broke exactly on the day appointed. Ryfke had a short labour and delivered after only two hours.

In fact, Joseph Galitzer arrived at the same time as the baby, but the mothers and Ryfke were now an experienced team, and the baby was just fine. Pink and warm. Joseph cut the cord, and the baby started to cry. Dawid, Zelman and Reuben who had been waiting and worrying burst into the room. Joseph checked the baby over and handed him to his proud father.

Yes, Ryfke had delivered another boy. Zelman was delighted. It was Leizar who pointed out that the probability of a girl was always 0.50, no matter how many times she delivered boys. Zelman smiled, making a mental note to explain that human biology did not always conform to the principles of mathematics.

All three men were delighted and of course so were the women, even though the delight of Ryfke and the two grandmothers was tinged with the longing for a little girl.

They decided to name this baby Duvid, the more modern equivalent of the Polish Dawid. In Jewish communities, it unusual to name a child after a living ancestor, but the Old Rabbi pointed out that there was nothing in the Torah preventing it, and they wanted to honour Zelman's father, who was of course, filled with pride.

With the approach of *Chanuka* that year, the family got to hear of the terrible unrest in Warsaw. A gypsy vendor passing through told tales indicating that anti-Semitism seemed to be on the increase, and he said that a mass panic had broken out on Christmas Day 1881. There had been a fire in the Holy Cross church and a lot of people had been killed in the stampede to get out. Someone said the Jews had started it and he had seen a mob forming and starting to loot Jewish stores and residencies in the streets near the church. He had left the next day, but the rioting was still going on, and the police were arresting people, it seemed to him, for just being there.

In the evenings after dinner, especially on Friday nights, the men would gather round to drink some schnapps and talk about what was going on in the country and the world in general. Leizar loved to hide under the stairs and listen. On the Friday after the Warsaw pogrom, he heard his father saying that the life of a Jew in Russian Poland was becoming too dangerous.

But Dawid and Reuben said there had been times when it was much worse. Reuben said that Jews were made to suffer. This had been the case all through history, starting with the Pesach story when Jews were slaves to Pharaoh in Egypt and God allowed them to escape by sending miracles. But the people had become so glad to be free that they started partying with debauchery and turned away from God. For this reason, God had made them wander for 40 days and nights in the wilderness.

'We must keep our faith,' he shouted. 'Never turn away from God. We are His Chosen People and if we suffer, it is part of his plan. Always remember,' said Reuben, '*S'iz shver tsu zayn a Yid.*' (It hurts to be a Jew)

They went on talking long into the night, and Leizar listened intently until he was afraid he would fall asleep right there, so he went to bed. But he lay awake wondering why Jews had to suffer and whether there was a better life to be had somehow, some way, somewhere.

CHAPTER 9

LEIZAR'S BAR MITZVAH

Leizar had been going to *cheder* for three years and he had an extremely good grasp of ancient Hebrew which he could read and translate, but now he was eleven years old, Zelman said it was time for him to start to learn and prepare for his Bar Mitzvah.

His father and his grandfather sat him down at Dawid's house and Zelman started, 'My dear Leizar you've been doing well at Hebrew school, but Bar Mitzvah is a very important matter. When you are thirteen, you will no longer be a boy and you will be able to take a full adult part in the community and in religious services. As you know, *Bar* means son and *Mitzvah* in this context means commandment, because after your Bar Mitzvah, you can perform all the *mitzvahs*, the Commandments of the Torah and all the duties and commitments that come with it. You will be a man, and you will make the whole family proud of you.'

Dawid continued, 'You are now ready to start your deeper studies into Torah and Judaism. You will attend special teachings to learn the Hebrew chants and prayers. Every week in the synagogue a new portion of the Torah is chanted aloud, each portion is read on a specified day, and you would find the same portion read in every synagogue all over the world. The Hebrew from the scroll must be chanted accurately in every detail. You must learn how to do this perfectly because you will be required to lead the community on that day. You must also learn how to put on *tefillin* that the men wear on their forehead and arm during morning prayers. If you can do all this perfectly on the day, we will have a big party to celebrate, and you will be the star!'

So, the special teachings started two years before the great day. As it turned out, due to the date of his birth, Leizar's portion was one of the largest, so there was much to learn. But Leizar was a very bright student. He had an extremely retentive memory which enabled him to perform his studies quicker than most. But being Leizar, he began to question why it was necessary for every boy to do this, and he got the usual religious answer. 'This is a commandment of God; all of your ancestors have done it for thousands of years. Who do you think you are to question it?'

He would never go against his father and his grandfather, but this did not satisfy Leizar, nor did his attitude go unnoticed. Questioning the rituals and the learning of the religion was not done. The religious men of the Yeshiva together with the rabbis were shocked to hear this and considered it something in Leizar's character that had to be eliminated. He found very little sympathy for his questions – and to be fair, very few answers.

Leizar could not keep his mouth shut, 'But Upa, why does this ceremony make me a man? And maybe I don't want to study Torah.'

'Never talk like that!' exclaimed Zelman, 'Every Jewish boy has undergone Bar Mitzvah for thousands of years. You must study and work hard so you can take your place as a man and so your mother and I can be proud of you.'

But doing something simply because people had been doing it the same way for thousands of years seemed to Leizar a reason to challenge and change it, rather than keep on doing it forever.

As his studies continued, Leizar found it boring, especially since he was able to learn quicker than the rabbi was teaching. His father would fly into a rage if he dared to mention how he felt; the only person to whom he could express some of his feelings was his mother. She was more sympathetic, although she also could not contemplate any Jewish boy, let alone her own son, not having a Bar Mitzvah. And in fairness, Leizar could not contemplate that either, not out of respect for tradition, but because at that tender age he could not bear to do anything to cause pain and disappointment to his father and his grandfather, let alone the rest of the family.

So Leizar continued and prepared for the big day. On the first Saturday after his thirteenth birthday, the rabbis and officials together with Leizar and his father were in the synagogue involved in preparatory prayers at 8.30am. Leizar was short for his age and he could not see the scroll on top of the reading desk, so they had to get a box for him to stand on. Until the day of Bar Mitzvah, boys do not wear the *tallis* prayer shawl, so for the occasion his Uncle Shmuel had purchased some fine white woollen material and sewn the traditional tassels on the ends. He had trimmed it with black and blue Stars of David and presented it to his nephew as a bar mitzvah gift together with a matching woven *kippah* skullcap.

The Rabbis, including his grandfather were gathered on the raised wooden *bimah* platform in front of the 'Ark', a sort of wooden cupboard with lovingly carved emblems and an 'eternal light' above. The sacred handwritten scrolls were stored in the Ark, 'dressed' in beautifully embroidered coverings. On the *bimah* was a raised reading table where the precious scrolls would be placed. The doors of the *Ark* were open, and a curtain was drawn across. All the rabbis were dressed in their white coveralls with their *tallisim* around them and all wore tall black satin *yarmulkas*. Their fringed *tzitzis* peeked out of their clothing. They were all totally engrossed in chanting their prayers.

Gradually more and more people arrived, filling up the wooden benches, men at the front and women at the back, until at 9.30 the Sabbath morning service began. By then the synagogue was packed.

The morning service commenced with more ritual and prayers, this time the congregation were invited to join in and various verses were sung by all. Leizar and his family were seated at the front waiting for the reading of the *Sefer Torah*, at which point Leizar would be 'called up' to read and chant his portion directly from the scroll. The *Sefer Torah* or book of Torah scroll had been written by hand, in Hebrew on parchment made from the skin of a kosher animal.

As the time approached a quiet, but audible buzz grew in the congregation. The *Sefer Torah* was removed from the Ark and carried round the synagogue for all to see, and many men lifted the corner of their *tallis* to touch the scroll and kiss it. On returning to the bimah, the scroll was placed on the reading table and opened at the appropriate place for this particular Sabbath service.

There was a strict order of *aliyahs*, the men who received the honour of being called to the reading of the Torah. Firstly, a descendant of the tribe of Cohen, then descendants of the tribe of Levi, and then descendants of the tribe of Israel. They did not actually read from the scroll themselves, but they would assist the *oleh* (reader) by pointing at the words. For this they would receive a blessing from the rabbi. Being a Levite, Zelman was the second person to receive the *aliyah* and Dawid the third. After that the uncles took their turn.

Eventually, the Rabbi's voice boomed out, 'Leizar ben Dovid ha Levi - bar mitzvah!'

Leizar, resplendent in his new *tallis* ascended the *bimah*. He recited a blessing and commenced to read and chant his *maftir* portion of the Torah reading for the day. It had to be chanted perfectly. Not a syllable nor an intonation could be incorrect. If he made the slightest error, it would be immediately spotted by the rabbis, and he would be corrected. That would not be welcomed.

But there were no corrections; although it was very long, Leizar knew his portion and could have done it entirely from memory. After he had read it perfectly, the *Sefer Torah* was held up for everyone to see, and then rolled up and dressed in its covering. The second scroll was taken and placed on the reading table and Leizar proceeded to read the *haftorah* from the book of Prophets. When he had finished and recited the blessings, he returned to his seat and the service was concluded with normal Shabbas prayers and songs.

At the end of the service, the Old Rabbi addressed the congregation. He talked of the talents Leizar was clearly developing and what an asset he was to be for the community. He linked it to religious passages in today's reading and was full of praise, saying how his father and grandfather were excellent role models and he should grow up to always remember God's Commandments to honour his father and mother, and lead a pious and fulfilling life. His family were all beaming with pride.

After the ceremony, there was a *kiddush* – wine and small sweetmeats were brought into the synagogue and after the rabbi had recited the various blessings, everyone was invited to honour the bar mitzvah boy and his family.

Of course, Jews being renowned for their ability to eat, drink and make merry, the party continued outside with much dancing and music. There was again a table loaded with food and drink, but of course, according to Jewish custom, the men and the women remained separated.

Chapter 10

Marcia and Moshe, Karl Marx and tragedy

The family continued to grow, and they did not have long to wait before Ryfke was pregnant again. And this time it was the little girl the women had been yearning for. She was beautiful and healthy, and everyone was smitten with her. She was to be called Marcia. And the following year another little boy arrived, Moshe.

At fifteen, Leizar was multi-talented. He had taught himself to play the Devil's fiddle, a stringed instrument like a violin. He also played the zither and a sort of recorder that he made himself out of carved wood. For that reason, he was very popular at celebrations, and also in the synagogue especially at Rosh Hashanah, when, as part of the service a ram's horn or *shofar* is blown. This is very difficult to do, the blower had to have very strong lungs, so few people could do it. The blowing of the shofar was meant to signify the start of the New Year, and during the service it would be blown 30 times with up to 100 blasts.

But for all his talents, Leizar questioned everything – which caused consternation among his elders. Due to their suffering over all the years, the Jewish way was to rely on God's will and accept their way of life. But Leizar saw it differently.

'Why, when there are so many of us in the shtetl, do we allow a few Cossacks to control us? Why do we accept that our country is divided, and we have to pay taxes to the Tzar? Why do we not speak Polish or Yiddish in public anymore? Why are there a few very rich people and so many very poor people? We are told God created every man in his image – surely we should all be equal?'

These questions drove everyone crazy. Leizar was prepared to take on anyone who had a view on these and many other things. And he would turn the argument every way. But at the heart of it was a growing feeling that a few could not control the many, if the many bound together without fear.

Zelman's friendship with Dmitri had continued, and it transpired that some members of the Russian military were also very unhappy with the way things were going. Dmitri told of the palaces in Russia with unbelievable treasures of gold, diamonds, precious artwork and even one palace where the very walls were painted with gold. And yet, he said that the people of Russia had to pay taxes too, and there was often not enough food to go round. He told Zelman that under Alexander II it had seemed that there was recognition that things needed to change and there had even been whispers in private of representative government, but that all changed on his death in 1881. The Tsar was succeeded by his second son Alexander III, who reinforced the autocracy and bore down on the proletariat and especially the Jews.

Knowing Leizar was interested, Dmitri gave Zelman a book for him. He said there was a groundswell of feeling among poor people in Russia, that with enough support it might be possible one day, to change the political system. He said the book's author had written about the type of equality that Leizar was often talking about. This book was banned in Poland, so he told Zelman to be very careful with it. The book was called The Communist Manifesto by Karl Marx and Friedrich Engels.

Leizar devoured the book, which spoke of public ownership of assets, services for the good of all the people and distribution of wealth in an equal manner. The book stated that the working class or proletariat would inevitably triumph over the capital-owning class, the bourgeoisie, and win control over the means of production, forever erasing all class distinctions and privileges. The phrase that stuck in Leizar's mind from the book was, 'From each according to his ability, to each according to his needs.'

The winter of 1887 had been very cold, and it had been hard for the families to keep warm. Wood for burning was becoming more difficult to find. Zelman and Ryfke were worried about their parents. Dawid was always cold and shivering, even when there was a fire to warm them. His mind was also not as sharp as it had been, and he would often wear several layers of clothes. Ryfke did not like to say it, but she had noticed that he was starting to smell.

Bad eyesight ran in the family and Dawid's had worsened. This had affected his confidence when walking and he did not always see what was in front of him. One cold morning Moszek came over to Ryfke's house for a glass of tea. She was wrapped up in a thick sheepskin sheath for warmth. There was just a hole where her head popped out on which she wore a sheepskin hat. She was wearing all that over her woollen jumper and trousers, and Ryfke had to smile. She looked like a large fat ram standing on its hind legs. 'Meh!' Moszek said, when she saw Ryfke's expression. 'It keeps me warm, why should I worry what I look like?'

Ryfke had a fire going and she brought some hot tea. They sat down. 'What is wrong with Upa? Between you and me, he is getting a bit smelly, and I tried to speak to him yesterday and he had to walk up really close to see who I was.'

Moszek had become very close to her daughter-in-law, treating her almost like a friend. 'Yes, yes – he is becoming very difficult, and I know he is getting worse. I spoke with Joseph Galitzer a few days ago.

He said, 'I'm afraid it's old age, keep him warm and make sure he eats properly.'

'But I have to tell you Ryfke, the truth is it is hard to get him to eat at all. He just wants to *daven* - pray - most of the day. I don't know what to do with him. He said he wanted to come over to see the children when they come home for lunch. I left him davening and he said he would make his own way.'

Just then they heard a cry from outside '*Oy* a *broch*!'

They ran out to find Dawid collapsed on the icy ground where he had slipped in the treacherous weather. It was starting to snow again, and the freezing fine powder was swirling around. The women could not lift him, and Ryfke was only clad in her nightclothes and dressing gown. Moszek hurried to the school, taking care not to slip. When she arrived Leizar was in the middle of a story for the smaller children about a factory run by alligators to produce ducks which they would fatten up and eat, when Moszek burst in together with an icy blast of air.

'*Mach gishvint*- quick! It's your *zeider* he is on the ground.'

Leizar remained calm. 'Ok, you go and tell Uba. He is teaching the older kids in his room, my uncle Yossel is also here, tell him to come and look after the children here. I'm coming right now.'

He put on his thick coat, worn at the elbows and threadbare from the years of wear, together with his woollen hat and boots. When he opened the outer door, the icy wind whipped into him and threatened to pin the door back on its hinges so that he had to struggle to close it. He trudged the short distance to his home, his boots crunching the snow, full of trepidation at what he might find,

As he approached, he saw Ryfke crouched over Dawid. She was shivering and wiping Dawid's brow with a flannel that she had warmed in a pot on the fire.

He arrived at the same time as Moszek with Joseph. They could see that Dawid was conscious, but very disorientated and the side of his head was already discoloured with bruising. Joseph sat him up and between them, they managed to half-carry and half-walk him into the house. They laid him on the bed, gently removed his great-coat and Ryfke got water. Joseph examined him with a worried look while Leizar, Moszek, Zelman and Ryfke anxiously waited for news.

Moszek had tears in her eyes, and they could already tell the news was not good. Dawid was not talking, which was very unusual for him, a man who in the normal way, was never short of something to say, and usually quite loudly too. Indeed, a characteristic of the whole family, was the quantity of noise they generated when they all got together.

Eventually Joseph came over to speak to them. 'He has a broken ankle, and his spine is twisted, but he has also suffered a major blow to the head when he fell. I am more worried about that.

Ryfke said he lost consciousness for quite a while. He is very confused. I have tried to straighten out his spine by manipulation, and I have bandaged up his ankle. The best thing is to leave him here tonight and I will call tomorrow to see how he is.'

Zelman and Leizar returned to Dawid's home to collect what he would need for the night, leaving Ryfke to explain to the children. She was quite frank with Mendel Yaacov, who was old enough to understand, but the younger ones were just told that *Zeider* had fallen over in the snow and would be staying there tonight. The older girls were told to look after the little ones and of course it meant changing beds and sharing, but that was not unusual.

They also went to the uncles and aunts to let them know and Zelman's brothers, Mendel and Moshe, trudged back with Zelman.

They arrived to find Moszek in tears. She was crouched over her husband with tears streaming down her face, and speaking to him, but he was not responding.

'Dawid, Dawid, *liebe fun meyn lebn*, what has happened to you? Let me take the pain.'

She said this over and over, all the time crying and alternating between wringing her hands and digging her nails into her own palms as if the pain she felt would take it away from Dawid.

Ryfke was standing over Moszek and gently rubbing her back to try to comfort her, but there was no response from Dawid. The men stood over the bed with grave expressions, they could see this was not good, and Zelman's brother, Mendel started praying in an undertone. This brought a worse response from Moszek, who broke out into sobs. Zelman quietly led Mendel away from her.

There was no change and after a long time with no response Ryfke tried to feed Dawid with a little warm chicken soup to no avail, and gradually, the family managed to coax Moszek away.

Zelman and Ryfke had four children: Leizar was seventeen, Mendel sixteen, Duvid ten and Marcia four. Ryfke had a *chulent* that she had cooked yesterday. It was a kind of stew which when simmered overnight, could be kept for days and was always ready to heat up if anyone was hungry. She took *challah* that she had been saving for the Ssabbath, and she brought out a big steaming pot of it. They all sat at the table, from where they could keep an eye on the patient. No one felt like eating and Moszek kept returning to the bed to try to elicit some sort of response, and to rub his temples.

Ryfke made sure that at least the children ate, and then she put them to bed. She made a sandwich for herself and Zelman, but could not persuade her mother-in-law to eat anything. They agreed that Moszek would sleep next to Dawid to keep an eye on him, Mendel and Duvid shared a bed anyway, and Ryfke went in with Marcia. Zelman made do with some straw and a sheet on the floor.

They were awakened in the night by screams and they ran into the bedroom to find

Moszek screaming and shivering. Dawid was on the bed, but he was now shaking violently, his body arching backwards as if something was pushing his spine upwards at a crazy angle. The scene was horrific.

Suddenly he collapsed back onto the bed and lay still.

Moszek then started to lean over Dawid and shake him. 'What has he done to himself, wake up, for God's sake, wake up. You hear me?'

Ryfke and Zelman gently, but firmly persuaded her to come away, but she kept returning, crying, wailing and completely distraught. It was clear that Dawid had passed away.

They took her into the family room and sat her down. Ryfke gave her a glass tea, and Zelman went to wake up Joseph Galitzer. They had all been traumatised by the awful sight of Dawid in a some kind of seizure and however dreadful that had been for Zelman and Ryfke, it had affected Moszek most profoundly. Suddenly she seemed old and bent over. From time to time, she would shake, her breathing seemed laboured, and she did not seem to respond when spoken to.

Joseph arrived with Zelman, followed by Shmuel and Mendel, Zelman's brothers. Joseph examined the body and spoke softly to Moszek, explaining that Dawid had indeed, passed away. The finality of his pronouncement was too much for Moszek and she collapsed on to the floor. They gently picked her up and took her into the other bedroom so she would not have to gaze at the body.

Joseph asked if they had any schnapps and he put a few drops into a small glass. 'Make sure she drinks this,' he said. 'It will make her relax and sleep.'

In his opinion, given the circumstances, Dawid had suffered a brain haemorrhage when he had fallen and hit his head. This meant there was internal bleeding that Joseph could not have diagnosed, and the subsequent pressure on the brain had led to the seizures and eventually his death.

As dawn broke, the men started to think about a funeral and the formalities according to Jewish law and tradition. This would have seemed premature in some faiths, but Judaism required, as a mark of respect to the deceased and the family, that the burial took place as soon as practicable. The first person to contact was the Old Rabbi, who would inform the authorities so that the death would be recorded. Assuming there was no objection, they agreed the burial could take place the next day, and the body could be taken to the synagogue and kept overnight in the ante room.

The Judaic rules are that a body must not be left on its own, so it was agreed that Zelman would perform the unwelcome task of the *shomer*, the watchman, and stay with his father until the burial. His brothers would make the simple white shroud and help prepare the body. This entailed thorough washing and obtaining a simple box or coffin for the burial. Reb Bendle, the carpenter always had coffins ready.

The Rabbi completed the formalities, and the funeral was arranged for one in the afternoon on Friday; the timing was important because as soon as dusk settled the Sabbath was said to have begun, and during that twenty-five-hour period, no work could be carried out, not even ae burial.

Moszek did not take this period well. She continued with the keening; she would not eat or drink. She would not even wash or change her clothes. She just sat rocking back and forth, her long, grey hair hanging down like rats' tails. The family tried to rally round her, but if she heard or saw them at all, she did not show it.

As the time approached for the funeral, the immediate family – the designated mourners – gathered. This was Moszek, and all nine of her children – all adults now - including Zelman who had 'handed' the body over to Reb Bendle, plus Shmuel, both of whom were actually the sons of Dawid and Esther. Grandchildren were not included among the official mourners, no matter how much they might be grieving. The Rabbi performed the ceremony of *kriah,* the tearing of the clothes of the mourners, and the whole family proceeded to the graveyard.

A grave had already been prepared and the coffin was waiting, draped in a simple black cloth. The weather was dreadful, with high wind and driving snow, but despite this, quite a crowd of villagers had come to pay their respects.

The Rabbi commenced the service which of course, was entirely in Hebrew, with the traditional prayer. 'O Lord what is man that Thou regardest him? Man is like a breath; his days are like a passing shadow. You sweep men away.'

At this point, Moszek, who had been supported between Zelman and Mendel, let out another piecing scream and with tears streaming down her face, she threw herself on to the coffin. The young men gently helped her up and supported her again. It is Jewish custom not to try to offer words of comfort and support while the deceased lies unburied, and the ceremony must be completed out of respect for the dead.

The Rabbi cleared his throat and finished the prayer. 'The dust returneth to the earth as it was, but the spirit returns to God who gave it.' There followed a memorial prayer which ended, 'May the Lord of Mercy bring him under the cover of his wings forever, and may his soul be bound up in the bond of eternal life. May the Lord be his possession and may he rest in peace. Amen.'

At this point, the men manoeuvred the coffin with ropes and gently lowered it into the grave. It is an important part of the ritual that first the mourners and then others in attendance, begin to shovel earth on the coffin until it is completely buried. Shmuel went first. He took up a shovel and loaded it with a large lump of the frozen clay that was piled by the side of the grave and with a grunt he heaved it into the grave, where it landed with a loud thump on the lid of Dawid's coffin.

Moszek screamed 'No, no – my Dawid – you will not go without me!' And she wriggled free of her two sons and threw herself into the grave, landing with a loud scream on to the flimsy wooden casket, which split with her weight, revealing the body beneath.

The shock that permeated the gathering was almost palpable. One or two of the women screamed to match Moszek and, as if they were all pushed by some invisible force, the whole crowd moved backwards. Mendel's face turned white with shock, and he stood for a moment before starting to babble.

Zelman, however, swung into action right away and carefully lowered himself into the grave. It was clear that Moszek was badly injured, and she was bleeding profusely. Between the men, it was eventually possible to manoeuvre her back up.

The snow was driving in the biting wind now, it was bitter cold. and the scene was like some bleak, dismal painting.

Joseph came to the front and Reb Bendle suggested they use a spare coffin lid to carry Moszek back to her house. Once there, Joseph staunched the blood which was coming from an open wound on her hip.

She was conscious, but incoherent and after a long examination Joseph was grim faced. 'She has a fractured tibia and fibula and a dislocated shoulder. I think she has also cracked a couple of ribs. I can reset the shoulder, but she is in a great deal of pain. I have a little morphia which I will give her, but she is in a bad way.'

He returned to Moszek, and after another half hour or so returned. 'I have done all I can for her. She should sleep now, but you must keep an eye on her.'

It fell to Zelman to take charge of the situation; although Shmuel was the oldest son, it was normally Zelman who would take the lead. Moszek's sisters had arrived, and they remained with Moszek while Zelman returned to the graveyard to ensure Dawid's grave was properly covered. Ryfke returned to let her family know that their Bubba was very ill. Everyone else returned home.

Anna and Rebecca, Moszek's sisters, stayed by Moszek's side for several hours. She was in a deep, drugged sleep. Anna thought they should try to rouse her to see if they could persuade her to eat or drink something, but Rebecca said to let her sleep.

Eventually Anna got a shock. She placed her hand on Moszek's forehead, and it was cold. Then she noticed that Moszek was not breathing. Immediately, Rebecca ran to get Joseph, but by the time he arrived there was nothing he could do except to pronounce her dead. This was a tragedy of tragedies for the families and the whole shtetl. One day Dawid and Moszek had been at the heart of the community and the next they were both dead. A cloud of grief descended on everyone.

The next day being *shabbas,* nothing could be done at all, and it was Sunday before the Rabbi could go through the same procedure again. Moszek was buried alongside her husband. Again, there was a big crowd and many tears, the prayers were completed, and the devastated family returned home.

The mourners this time were not only the Domansky family, but also the two Benjamin sisters – a total of twelve mourners to sit *shiva*, which lasted for the whole week. The mourners sat on low chairs while family, friends and well-wishers came to pay their respects, to bring food and drink and wish them 'long life.' Every evening at dusk, the Rabbi came to conduct prayers and give the opportunity for the male mourners to recite the *kaddish* prayer. It was very hard for the families and the children to come to terms with. In an instant they had lost both parents and their grandparents and sister.

CHAPTER 11

Life never really returned to the way it was after the dramatic deaths of Dawid and Moszek. Leizar was becoming more vocal in his leftist views. He found, to his surprise, that there were Russians who had read the works of Marx and Engels, and he became aware of an organisation called the Polish Democratic Society, the TDP.

The brave people of this organisation had been agitating for change for many years in Poland. Needless to say, the Society and its views were not welcomed by the Russian hierarchy, nor by many of the traditionally poor families in the shtetls. They had been so beaten down over generations that they believed it was dangerous to plot against the regime and that it could only come to no good.

The TDP published a newspaper *Demokrata Polski* with the slogan 'Everything by the People and for the People.' When they became aware of this publication, the Russians came down hard on the whole organisation and it was disbanded, but the movement continued to exist covertly, and Leizar joined it. He attended clandestine shtetl meetings and encouraged his brothers, Mendel and Duvid to join as well. They called their movement *'Lud Polski'* – the Polish Peoples' Movement.

This put Leizar and his father on a collision course. Zelman, now a leader in the community, could sympathise with the philosophy, but he thought that the young people involved had no idea what they were messing with, and that it would all end in tears and bloodshed. Most of all, he worried that the pogroms and violent demonstrations from which his family had mostly been protected, would start up again, with the sort of terrible consequences they had witnessed in years gone by.

For this reason, the movement, its philosophy and aims were not discussed openly in the family home. Whenever Zelman became aware of them whispering in a corner, he would fly into a rage. 'Will you stop with this stupid nonsense? Do you want to get us all killed?'

And when Zelman was in a rage, everyone knew it. He would thump the table and shout at the top of his voice. The younger children would run and hide, and poor Ryfke would end up with the job of trying to pacify him while Zelman sat with his head in his hands.

Leizar quickly became a leading thinker in this group and began writing its aims. First was to abolish all political and social privileges. Influenced by his study of Karl Marx, he envisaged an egalitarian society based on public ownership of all factories, farms and sources of consumer supply. 'Levelling Social Status' was their slogan. But the group found it very difficult to make any progress. They heard there were other groups in other parts of Poland, and indeed in Russia itself, with similar views and aims, but communication with them was almost impossible and this left Leizar very frustrated.

The Domansky men were considered to be learned, probably because the thoughts of most men were entirely taken up with making enough to put some food on the table and pay the taxes. But the Domanskys were definitely thinkers as well, and their interests went further than that. They were not tall in stature, and they had serious faces which did not smile easily. All of them had poor eyesight which, it was said, came from spending so much time with their noses in a book.

Unlike Zelman, Leizar did not have a beard. He took the trouble to shave every day, which was not the way of the traditional, observant men in the shtetl. He always wore a cap and changed his clothes regularly, he took a pride in his appearance, so far as it was possible with very few clothes. But like his father, he had a terrible temper which was never exhibited physically, though he could be vicious with his tongue. For all that, he was a kind man, understanding of the plight of others.

As a result of his father's acumen and insight, Leizar had developed an enquiring mind which was never going to accept the lot of the poor in Poland, especially when he found out how the aristocracy lived in Russia. They had gown fat upon untold and obscene riches, acquired mainly from the heavy taxes forced on the poor.

Very few people ever visited the shtetl from outside. It was really a tiny village where everyone knew everyone and as a result, most people married within the community. Why would anyone visit anyway? There was not much there to see. That was why the *shiddach macher* could be so successful: the lack of choice. But by 1891, even in Kawetchka, there was a bit more mobility, and socialism had a few covert champions.

One morning in spring there was a knock on the door of the Domansky home. This was unusual in itself. No-one ever knocked. If they had a visitor, they just walked straight in – which could sometimes be a bit embarrassing both for the family and the visitor. Zelman had already gone to the school and Ryfke answered the door, worried that a knock on the door might not be a good thing. Her foreboding was intensified when she opened it. She was confronted by very large man dressed entirely in black, with a long coat and upon his head a *shtrimmel* type of hat worn by religious Jews. He had a long shaggy black beard and the coiled sidelocks called *payot*.

'Oy veh!' Ryfke exclaimed, 'Who died?'

The somewhat serious face of the visitor split into a wide smile. 'Oh, no, no, there is nothing to be concerned about. My name is Moshe Vasilinsky from Warsaw. I am looking for a young man called Leizar Domansky. Have I arrived at the right house?'

Nonetheless Ryfke was very suspicious and quite agitated. 'Who are you? I don't know you. You are a stranger in the shtetl. What are you doing here and what do you want with my Leizar?'

Hearing his name, Leizar came to the door. 'I am Leizar Domansky, what do you want of me?'

'Reb Leizar, I am here with my friend, Edvard Abramovski. Perhaps you have heard of him?'

Now it was Leizar's turn to be suspicious 'No, I know of no such man, and if you are from Warsaw, how do you know my name and what do you want with me?'

'Please, there is no need to be concerned. Can I come in and explain? Edvard waits in our carriage.'

By this time the neighbours were wondering what was going on. In Kawetchka conversations never took place on the doorstep and the houses were close. One by one, the other doors opened and although there were no raised voices, people looked out to see what was going on. Two men in a carriage and one knocking on the door of the Domansky household. But the big man was smiling and speaking in a soft tone and somehow, Leizar felt he was not a threat. He invited him in.

He sat down at the table where his bulk was almost too large for the chair, which creaked in complaint. He beckoned Leizar to come close. 'Reb Leizar, we must speak carefully and what I say must not fall on Russian ears. Who is in the house, apart from your lovely Mama?'

Leizar's apprehension was heightened, but his curiosity got the better of him. 'Only her.'

'Good, then I would like you to meet my friend Edvard. We have heard that you are interested in the Socialist movement. Edvard is a philosopher and a psychologist from Warsaw, and he is the founder of the Co-operative Movement. Perhaps you have heard of it?'

Leizar was wary. It was not unknown for the Russians to send someone pretending to be a Socialist to trick people, but there was something about this man who seemed very calm.

He went to speak to Ryfke, to explain that he would like to invite this man into the house and hear what he had to say. Ryfke's views on Socialism were not as extremely opposed as her husband, but she worried that if Zelman knew about this meeting, he would react very badly. Although she loved all her children and she would never admit it, Leizar was a favourite, and she knew he had a vision.

'Leizar, my *liebchen* – how do you know who this man is? He could be a thief or a villain. He may want to steal everything we have. And you know if your father hears about this, he will go crazy.'

'I don't think he will harm us, Uma. I think he is genuine, and he says he heard about me. I would like at least to hear what he has to say. He is waiting, Uma, let me invite him in. I promise I will ensure it is a very short visit.'

So, Leizar told Moshe that he would be happy to meet Edvard, but he regretted that he had to leave in half an hour, so he had not much time. Moshe's face reflected disappointment. They had travelled all the way from Warsaw, and it seemed they were receiving short shrift. However, he brightened up and said he would go to fetch

Edvard and return with him shortly. Leizar had to hide a smile when Moshe stood up with the chair still connected to his rear end. It was such a tight fit that Leizar had to pull it off him. With that done, the big man departed.

Ryfke was very concerned. 'Leiza *Liebchen*, be careful. I hope you know what you are doing. Everything he says may be a *bubba meister*. Who is this person he is bringing to our house?'

'Uma, Uma, don't worry so much. I'm not stupid, and we will see very quickly who he is and what he is. But I have heard there is an important socialist group starting up in Warsaw, part of a growing Marxist movement, and you know how I feel about that, Uma! No matter what Upa says, we can't continue to be downtrodden forever. Sooner or later people have to do something about it.'

It was only a few minutes later that Moshe returned. Again, he knocked on the door and on opening it, Leizar was confronted by two formidable looking men. Moshe seemed even larger than when he left, as if that was possible, and next to him stood a tall man dressed entirely in black, with a black astrakhan hat, great-coat and boots. But his most striking feature was his bushy beard, starkly white against all the black. He had a weather-beaten face and bushy eyebrows which strangely were not white, but black.

Moshe's face split into a smile. 'May I introduce Edvard Josef Abramowski? Edvard. This is Leizar Domansky.'

Leizar stood aside and made a sweeping gesture with his arm to indicate that the men should come in. 'Please take a seat at the table and may I offer you a glass tea? You've travelled far.'

Moshe noticed that, to avoid the same embarrassment as before, Leizar had placed a different chair with no arms and a larger seat, at the table. He gratefully took it and both men were seated. Ryfke entered the room and Leizar introduced his Uma. He excused himself while he went to the kitchen with Ryfke to help with the refreshments.

The visitors took the opportunity to look around. They took in the ramshackle house with bare floorboards, the utilitarian furniture – wooden chairs, a large family table, and a fireplace with logs which were not lit. Around the walls were pictures drawn or painted by the children with their names and ages appended. They understood that a large, and growing family lived here, one whose artistic efforts improved with age. They noticed, as well, that there were no pictures by Leizar.

Meanwhile, Leizar and his mother used the time in the kitchen to exchange first impressions. 'His appearance is very striking,' said Ryfke, 'and I have to say he is quite tall and handsome, but to me he looks Russian. Look out. *Hytn zikh.*'

Leizar smiled at his mother's caution, 'Let's give them a chance, Uma.'

They returned with three glasses of tea, slices of lemon, sugar lumps and some of Ryfke's special *kichels* - a delicious cross between a biscuit and a cake. The men all sipped the tea in the Russian way, sugar lump in the mouth and sucking the tea through it.

The visitors were clearly grateful for the refreshments. Edvard spoke first. 'Thank you for this, and I have to say Madame Domansky, the *kichels* are delicious. And the pictures from the family are very impressive. But we noticed there are none drawn by you, Leizar?'

Ryfke was quick to respond, 'Yes, I always keep plenty of *noshes* around. With a family like ours they don't last long. Leizar has never been very interested in visual art. He has always been a writer and I have kept a lot of his work since he was a little boy. He is very talented, and we are very proud of him.'

'I'm sure you are,' said Edvard, and there followed a slightly awkward silence. Ryfke took that as her cue to excuse herself and leave the men to talk. She retired to the kitchen where she stood by the door, out of sight, but so she could hear everything that was going on.

After a few moments, during which there was much slurping of tea Leizar said, 'Well, gentlemen, I am flattered that you have come here to our little shtetl to see me. What can I do for you?'

Edvard finished his *kichel* and took a sip of tea. 'Let me explain a bit about myself. I was born in the Kiev Governorate and I moved to Warsaw in 1879 after the death of my darling mother. Life in Kiev was very hard, and my father knew it was wrong that the aristocracy and bourgeoisie were living in opulence while we were starving to pay their taxes.

He moved us to Warsaw where I could be taught by a brilliant teacher, Maria Konopnicka. She first introduced me to the members of the First Proletariat. This is a powerful movement growing very fast, and we want to enlist the help of people across Poland. Our ambition is that this momentum will spread throughout the Russian-controlled countries and maybe even beyond. We believe in what the bible says, all men are created equal, and equality is therefore a God-given right. Our cause is just, and we work to distribute wealth and ensure a fair society.'

Leizar was impressed by this speech and flattered that they should have come to speak to him about it. 'I am familiar with the works of Karl Marx and I passionately agree that people should no longer live under the boot of the like this while they eat caviar and drink champagne. I even heard there is a palace in St Petersburg where the walls are painted with real gold.'

Edvard nodded. 'But we must be very careful because as you know, if the Russians get wind of how this is growing, we will be severely punished. We are prepared to fight, but we are no match for the Russian army. We believe in the co-operative organisation of the workforce, leading one day to the overthrow of the bourgeoisie.'

'Leizar, although I very much wanted to speak to you, that was not the only reason for my journey. Some Russian army officers are also very unhappy with the way things are in Poland. Do you know of a Cossack Captain Dmitri Belokov?'

'Yes, my father teaches his children, and he is the reason my family has been spared the pogroms.'

'Dmitri has been sympathetic to our cause. He has done little things to help. I am sure you can see how useful it can be to cultivate a relationship with a Cossack officer. I had a covert meeting with him, and the truth is he is a corrupt individual. Although he will help, he wants paying. He has agreed to help our movement if we pay. That means we could have some undercover influence in Kawetchka. We have seen some of your writings, and we believe you have strong feelings that are largely in line with our movement. We believe we can change things. Would you like to join us?'

Leizar was inwardly very excited at the prospect of joining up with a real movement whose aims were similar to his own, but he was torn; not so much because he knew this would be at great personal risk to himself, but more that he could be putting his parents and family in danger. 'What would you want me to do?'

'At first not much. Mainly we are trying to recruit as many people as possible to the movement. I believe you are a very good writer. We are hoping to publish a magazine. It would not be openly subversive, but it would carry articles to attract socialist-leaning minds. It would be a magazine for the poor and for the workers. And it would be free. We would get it printed in Warsaw, but it could be distributed everywhere. Perhaps you would like to be the founder and the first editor?'

Leizar could hardly contain his excitement. A magazine! And he could be the first editor and in charge of the content. He could write articles that others would actually read, and he might be able to influence people. This was beyond his wildest dreams.

He remained thoughtful for a minute, letting it all sink in, before he said, 'Look, I worry about my family. My father does not agree with any of this, and I would never forgive myself if I brought risk to the family.'

'Understandable of course, and I can't say you would not need to worry. You must make a decision for yourself. But if you are clever and careful, you can minimise the risk. We have many young men in the movement who are in exactly the same position. Think about it.

Moshe will return in one week. Let him know your decision. But in your deliberation, balance the risk against the possibility that you may become very influential in the rise of the workers' co-operative, the overthrow of the system, and a permanent change to the life chances of all of us and everyone who may follow us.

'But I need your word that whatever you decide, you will treat this meeting as if it never happened.'

Leizar gave his word and they all stood up. Ryfke had been listening to every word, and she came into the room. Edvard and Moshe bowed and thanked her for her hospitality. The men all shook hands, and they left. Leizar sat back down with Ryfke. It had all happened so quickly and unexpectedly. His heart was thumping. 'Uma, this is a chance for me to make a real difference. I could really help to change things forever.'

Ryfke's face was lined with worry. 'And you could get yourself killed or worse and bring trouble on the family.'

Of course, Leizar knew that would be her reaction and he carried on as if he didn't hear it. 'Someone has to do this, or nothing will ever change. It is a risk, but change does not occur without taking chances. Just think what a risk Columbus took, when everyone believed the world was flat and if you went too far you would fall over the edge. Think about Charles Darwin when he challenged every religion's idea about how we got here! Think of the risk Moses took to take the Children of Israel out of the slavery in Egypt – although I will accept, *he* had a little help from God.'

Leizar realised he was getting carried away and his mother was just standing open mouthed. 'The children will be home from school soon and your father will follow. They will all be hungry; I have to prepare for them. Do not mention this to your father and we will talk some more tomorrow.'

But that night Leizar could not sleep. His head was full of the possibility for real change. And not only, he realised, in their little shtetl of Kawetchka, but also in the play a part in that, small, but still a part. By morning he had convinced himself that he was going to accept and work with the movement in Warsaw whatever his father said. He awoke early and with great energy. By the time his siblings had dressed and readied themselves for the day, Leizar could not wait to get going. He would speak to his father that evening and join the movement tomorrow.

So it was that when Zelman returned from the school next day, Ryfke had prepared a nice dinner of *chulent* with a little meat and dumplings and an *apfel strudel* she had made with sweet raisins and honey. When the children had retired, Leizar was still seated at the table, and Zelman could see he was itching to speak. 'Well, my lovely first-born son, what have you got to tell me?'

Leizar hardly knew where to start. He told his father that he had an unexpected visit the day before from two gentlemen from Warsaw, Moshe and Edvard.

'Well Upa, it all started with a knock on the door.'

Zelman interrupted right away and in his usual bombastic way, 'What? You mean you let strangers into our house? And you didn't tell me?'

He turned to Ryfke, 'You were in on this?'

Ryfke had of course, seen this coming, and she had learned over the years that the best thing when Zelman was angry was to let him rave on. To attempt to argue only wound him up more. So, she said nothing.

But Leizar was not afraid of his father, 'Upa, these are good men with a fine reputation, Edvard Abramovski is the founder of the Polish Co-operative movement in Warsaw. He is well known and very influential.'

Zelman was not so easily placated, 'So what did they want, these big shot *groisse knuckers* from Warsaw?' And Leizar went on to explain the offer they had made to him.

Zelman was not entirely unaware of the left-leaning movements that were beginning to appear under cover in Poland, although the possibility of any of them reaching a member of his family had never occurred to him. And of course, his past family experiences had instilled a healthy fear of the brutal way in which the Russians would deal with dissent. Zelman saw his role in life to protect his family above all, to teach in the school and study Torah and Talmud. The Domansky family had a stubborn streak which kept them completely focused on their aims, which was very effective in achieving goals, but it could make them somewhat blinkered to other possibilities.

Leizar was somewhat surprised that Zelman's reaction was not as extreme as he had expected. His voice had dropped a few decibels, though. 'You know this is dangerous, don't you? If the Russians find out, we will all suffer. Why do you want to put yourself and your family in this position?'

'Upa, I want to do something with my life. I can see that this existence for poor people is not right, and I want to help. I believe the Austrian side of Poland is beginning to recognise this, and Socialism is beginning to rise in other parts of the world. In America and in England they have democracy, and people vote to decide who should rule them. People have a say in the laws that govern them. They have courts of law with independent judges and ordinary people can go to them to put their case. I want to bring that here.'

Zelman was still very angry, but now this was becoming more directed at Ryfke for keeping this meeting from him. But she knew how to get round him, so it did not bother her. To Leizar he said, 'All right. If this is something you must do, then be sure to keep it very quiet. Just between us. And if you have any problems, make sure you come to me with them, you understand, *vershtay?*'

Leizar could not get this meeting out of his mind. He discussed it with his brothers, who thought it was a great opportunity. So, when Moshe returned to the house to find out Leizar's decision, he was delighted to find him so enthusiastic. 'That's good to hear, Leizar. There is nothing much to do now, but we will contact you shortly and from time to time you will get a visit from somebody.'

At first Leizar was disappointed that nothing much happened. He thought that, having agreed, things would start moving right away. But after a month, and just as he was beginning to think it had all been hot air, he was contacted again, and the planning started for the magazine. Leizar's brother Mendel Yaacov was equally excited, and together they started planning articles.

The next visit was again from Moshe. He brought a copy of a book written by Edvard. It was called *Socialism and the State*. Moshe told him it was a very important work and contained his political philosophy. The two young men read it avidly.

CHAPTER 12

MOSHE, WARSAW AND COMMUNISM

The main thrust of Abramowski's political philosophy was to find the best strategy for the transition to Communism, which he called Stateless Socialism. He envisaged the gradual establishment of educational initiatives, workers' unions, agricultural and consumer co-operatives, starting with individual sympathisers and gradually merging into larger groups. The brothers stayed up many nights discussing these concepts, along with the works of Marx. On the one hand Communism seemed to be an antidote to the feudal system and the excesses of the hereditary, oppressive rule of the Tsars. On the other, they were gazing enviously at the democratic type of government exemplified in the United States, which seemed to offer equality of opportunity and reward for talent and hard work.

The brothers worked subversively for the movement. It was not easy to spread the word in a community as small as Kawetchka whilst avoiding the attention of the authorities. Also, they were frustrated because the articles they wrote for the magazine had to be sent to Warsaw, where they were edited and altered before printing. So, they never saw the finished article, and although Leizar was supposed to be the editor, he was unable to exert any real control over the content of each edition until after it was printed and circulated. Also, the brothers wanted the magazine to reflect their twin ideas: freedom from oppression via the route of Communism, and via democracy on the other.

Leizar was growing more and more unhappy with his life in the shtetl. He wanted to influence major thinkers inside and outside the movement, but it seemed impossible from where they were situated, so isolated from the outside world. Unlike his father, he was not prepared to accept their meagre living as a way of life, he knew he had to get out or he would die there. He discussed this with Moshe on one of his visits.

'Yes, yes,' Moshe nodded wisely, his black beard and enormous head with the black *shtrimmel* hat nodding up and down slowly. He took a sip of his tea and a little of it dribbled down his beard and on to his waistcoat. 'I thought you would come round to this way of thinking.' He paused and stroked his beard, 'Well, why don't you come and live in Warsaw?'

Oddly, although he realised the limits of living in the shtetl, Leizar had never thought that he might be able to escape, especially to Warsaw, a big city with lots of possibilities.

'But how would that be possible?' he asked. 'I have no money or transport. How would I get there? Where would I live? And more importantly how would I live, feed myself and so on?'

Suddenly, now that he had admitted the idea, although his head was full of questions, he was thrilled at the very thought of being a real magazine editor in Warsaw and close to Abramowski, one of the deepest thinkers and influences among the proletariat in Poland.

'Don't think that this possibility has not been spoken about,' Moshe took another sip of tea. 'I wouldn't say it is easy, but we have some good contacts in the Russian army who are sympathetic to our cause, and we have a lot of friends and colleagues in Warsaw. I know Edvard was very impressed with you and I think we may be able to pull a few strings. But we would need the help of your friend Dmitri Belakov from this end.'

'But where would I live and what would I do for money?' Leizar asked.

'I am not promising anything, but we have a colleague who owns a cigarette factory. In the past he has helped us by providing a job in his factory in similar circumstances. Leizar, if this man would agree, and I have to warn you it is hard work, long shifts and not much pay, but if he would employ you, it would be enough to rent a small room and provide food. You would have to edit the magazine and attend meetings in your own time.'

'What about my brother?'

Moshe shook his head, 'I am sorry, but this would only be for you. Perhaps if things work out well eventually, you could send for your brother.'

Leizar's heart skipped a beat. This had gone from a pipe dream to a real possibility, but then his heart sank. What about his father? Could he convince Zelman to allow him to go? And he would be leaving his mother and the rest of the family for a very long time. He had never been parted from them. He felt a churning in his stomach when he thought about it.

Moshe read the look on his face. 'Think on it,' he said. 'I will be back in a few days. In the meantime, I will tell Edvard of our conversation, thank your Uma for the tea.'

He stood up, and once again Leizar was surprised at the sheer bulk of him. He seemed to be even bigger than Leizar remembered him.

Leizar was not surprised to find that Ryfke and Mendel had been in the kitchen with their ears pressed to the door. They had heard most of what was said.

'Leizar, my *shapsele,* you can't be serious about this.' Ryfke was wringing her hands. 'Tell me you would not think of leaving us all and going to the big city to live on your own in a little *shtibl,* and more importantly – going into the unknown. Surely, surely you would never do that?'

'And they would only take you,' said Mendel 'That's not fair. I write articles too, and you said some of mine are better than yours. I could go with you; we could share a room and I would work hard. What do they think, I can't make cigarettes?'

Leizar's head was spinning. 'Uma, I love you, and the family so much and I never thought there could ever be an opportunity like this for me. My head is *farmisht* and I can't think straight. Give me some time. Please, please, don't mention it to Upa until tomorrow when I have had a chance to think? Can you not say anything to him, I know he will not like it, but I need to get things clear in my own head first.'

'Oh, Leizar, don't put me in that position again. He was very cross with me last time.'

There were tears in Ryfke's eyes. She knew her son well, and she also knew that if he had no intention of taking up this offer, he would have said so straight away, and now she was torn between loyalty to her husband and her son.

Leizar's voice softened when he saw his mother was upset, 'Uma please don't worry, you heard what Moshe said. He can't promise anything anyway, and we would need the help of Dmitri. So, nothing may come of this anyhow, and I have to think about how to tell Upa. Please do this one thing for me.'

Leizar went on his knees with his hands together to implore his mother.

'All right, all right *hak mir nisht kayn tshaynik*. Again you make me choose between my son and my husband.'

'*But Uma, you know how to shmooze round Upa. It will be alright.*'

'*Let me get on with the dinner before the children get home.*' And with that, she disappeared into the kitchen.

Mendel looked thoughtful, 'Let's go somewhere we can talk, I would like to discuss this with you.' So, they went outside and sat on the fallen tree.

'Leizar, I have been thinking a lot about this. I know you are excited to think you could be an influence to draw people towards communism, but let's think for a moment of the other alternative. Democracy. It's only a thought, but if you were working and living in Warsaw, and perhaps there is a possibility that after a while I could come and join you, maybe there could be a way we could leave Poland and go to America?

'Not just you and me of course,' he added quickly. 'I am talking about the whole family, and maybe even others from the shtetl too. Think of it, the land of the free, where it is possible to follow the American dream. Where everyone has an equal opportunity, even Jews.'

'Slow down, Mendel,' was Leizar's response. 'I haven't even been offered this chance yet, and we have to convince Upa, and enlist the help of Dmitri. Nothing at all may come of this. But I have to say, I had not thought of that possibility. I have heard that quite a few Jews have found a way to arrange passage on a ship to the United States. But would that be better than life the way Marx and Abramowski envisage it, with equality for everyone?'

Thoughtfully he continued, 'I don't rule out your view, but we are talking of opposite ends of the spectrum. On the one hand, free market capitalism under the democratic system, allegedly this creates equal opportunities to reward enterprise and hard work. But there are bound to be casualties too. Clearly not everyone is going to be a winner. On the other hand, Marx speaks of equal distribution of wealth and assets to everyone. What is for certain is that we have to shake off this yoke the Russians have placed on us.'

There had been many revolts against the Russian occupation. The land had been granted by the Congress of Vienna – the Poles had very little say in it, and recently another large revolt in Warsaw had been put down. But Warsaw was the place from which some Poles had been able to escape; it was possible, if you knew the right people and you had the money.

They went inside to help Uma prepare for the evening meal and get the children ready. Mendel became very quiet and thoughtful, 'What about if we could get our whole family out of Poland altogether? Wouldn't it be wonderful if we could find a way to get to America? I hear there are people who have done it.'

It was a thought, although they had no idea how this could be achieved – simply another pipe dream.

The whole Domansky family was a very close unit. Although everyone had great respect for Zelman as the father, they were all independent thinkers. Mendel was a thinker and he had inherited some of his mother's softness along with the Domansky single mindedness. The whole family shared the short, stocky build, but Mendel was the tallest. He was also a talented writer.

Later Zelman returned from the school, and found the table prepared as if it was a Shabbas meal, but it was only Thursday. There was kosher wine and chulent, fresh vegetables and cholla bread. As soon as he entered, he realised something was up.

'Aha! So, what's going on? What are you up to? What do you want from me this time?'

He went to have a wash to prepare for dinner and have a private word with Ryfke. 'Well, I can see something is going on, what have you all cooked up for me? I am getting used to this now.'

Ryfke gave him a knowing smile and poured a little of the wine, 'You'll have to wait until the children are out of the way. Come, let's sit and enjoy the special dinner I made for you.'

There was as usual, much noise at the dinner table, but punctuated with little knowing looks that passed between Ryfke, Leizar and Mendel some of which were picked up by Zelman. When the dishes were cleared and the children were allowed to leave the table, Zelman spoke. 'Well, I have waited patiently, what *bubba meister* have you got for me this time? It had better be good.'

It fell to Leizar to start the ball rolling. At first, he could not look Zelman in the eye, knowing he was about to get angry when he heard what Leizar had to say. 'Upa, you know it is my burning ambition to be an effective influence in the Socialist movement?'

'Yes, yes,' shouted Zelman as if he knew what was coming. 'And you two are helping with that *farkukte* magazine.'

'Yes, but it is very difficult to really be an influence here in Kawetchka, and the articles we write get edited and printed in Warsaw, so we don't get to see them before they are published.'

Now Zelman's attitude had changed to one of caution mixed with anger. 'So, what do you suggest, my two fine boys?'

Leizar went on to explain about the conversation with Moshe and the possibility of transport and accommodation in Warsaw combined with work in the cigarette factory.

'You mean you would leave all your family and live in Warsaw?' Zelman was shouting louder. 'Why would you want to do that? This home is not good enough for you? This shtetl is too small? You want to be a big shot? A *Moishe Groisse*?'

There was irony in his voice now. 'Who the hell do you think you are? I want my family here. What you are talking about is dangerous and who knows what can happen. We don't even really know who these people are who say they may help you.'

Zelman was standing and shouting, and they knew there was no point in trying to reason with him until he had calmed down. 'I don't want to hear another word about this *mishigasse*.'

With that Zelman went into the bedroom and slammed the door so hard, it seemed to shake the whole house.

Ryfke was not surprised. 'Let me talk to him,' she said, and she followed him into the bedroom.

The next day Zelman went to see his uncle Shmuel. Although he had the Domansky stature, Shmuel's nature was softer, he was a thinker and Leizar respected his advice. He bore the scars of the Russian cruelty and even with his stick, walking was difficult. Like the rest of the family, he was short and stocky and even in the coldest winter, he always wore a white shirt with short sleeves and a waistcoat. He sported a generous beard and always wore a *kippah*. Everyone liked Shmuel.

Leizar told him the whole story, including how Zelman had reacted. Shmuel was a good listener and sympathetic to the socialist ideals. 'Ok, I will speak to my brother. He will come round I am sure, but he is right, what you are about to do is dangerous and it may not work out. There are pogroms in Warsaw too, you know.'

Leizar was grateful for his uncle's support, he was altogether more controlled than his brother, but they were very close, and he knew his father would at least hear him out.

The next day, Shmuel visited Zelman at the school, and they sat to eat their lunch together. Zelman was calmer than when he first heard about it of course, and they discussed it for quite a while. Zelman's brow was furrowed with concentration and he kept pulling on his beard. Shmuel was not telling him anything he didn't know. 'Your Leizar is very headstrong, and if you forbid him to do this thing, it may have the opposite effect and make him more determined to do it.'

'So, said Shmuel. 'It may come down to…. Do you want him to do it with your permission… or without it?'

That evening Leizar was surprised that the subject was actually brought up by his father. His uncle and his mother must have done a good job for him.

'So, tell me Mr Big Shot, when do you expect to hear from your contacts?'

'Moshe said he would be back in a few days.'

'Oh, Moshe said! And what about us? Have you thought what this might do to your mother? You want to give her all this *tsorris* on top of everything else she has to worry about? So go! Go! Go! Don't worry about us! Go change the world while you still know everything!'

This was not going well. 'Upa, I will be able to come and visit, and if things don't go well, I can come home. I don't know what will happen, but I know I have to try.'

'What did we do that you don't care about us? You know nothing about that world. The Russian *momzers* are everywhere, and you want to go and poke the bear! Why won't you listen to me? And why? Because some stranger comes with a story about starting a revolution – let him start the *farkukte* revolution! You stay here with us.'

Leizar's mind was made up and he knew if he showed any sign to his father that he could be persuaded, then he would never get away. 'Upa, I love you all. You know that, but the time has come for me to make a decision for myself.'

Zelman stood up suddenly knocking over the chair. He looked at Moszek and banging the table with his fist, he shouted 'What have we done? Why won't my children listen to me?' And with that, he walked out.

Mendel had not mentioned any of his own thoughts, well knowing that it was going to be hard for his father to accept Leizar's intentions, if they came about, without adding to it. He knew the move to Warsaw was against Zelman's wishes, and it was certainly not the time to introduce the possibility of emigration for the family in the future.

The generations of Domanskys were so ingrained in the life of the Kawetchka community, and they had learned to live with, and overcome so much adversity, that it had made them very tight knit and to some extent co-dependent. It would be very difficult, if not impossible for Zelman to contemplate leaving his family home and going anywhere, let alone another country.

Moshe did not return the following day, and the next day was shabbas. The family had been to the synagogue and returned for lunch and the atmosphere was so thick you could cut it with a knife. But Zelman had calmed down. 'If this Moshe of yours shows up, I want to talk to him.' Moszek looked up in surprise. It seemed that perhaps the feud was over.

Seeing her reaction, he said, 'Nothing I say will make any difference to your bull-headed son. So, if this *shmegegge* idiot comes, I want to talk to him.'

So, on the Sunday, Leizar waited impatiently. He was excited when he heard Moshe's horse drawn carriage arrive around lunchtime and he ran out and welcomed him to come inside. Mendel ran to get Zelman from the school. 'I hope you have some good news for me.' said Leizar.

'Yes, yes, don't worry.' Moshe was heaving his bulk down from the carriage.

'Good, I hope you don't mind, but my father wants to meet you.'

Ryfke had prepared a light lunch and Moshe went to wash up from his journey. Zelman arrived and they all sat at the table. Ryfke was gratified to see that Moshe had a ravenous appetite and seemed to relish everything on the table.

To everyone's surprise, Zelman and Moshe hit it off really well. They were both Levites and shared the same birthday. As a result, they had the same portion of the

Torah at their bar mitzvah, which had included a notoriously difficult stanza that had taken them both time to learn. And of course, they were both pleased to share it by singing after lunch.

Eventually Zelman's face took on a serious look and he leaned across the table to Moshe. He wanted to know the plans of how it would all work, and Moshe tried to answer honestly, but although he could assure him that the factory owner was trustworthy and he would have accommodation, their motivation was to help to effect real change in Poland and that was a major task.

He could not say exactly how it would go. 'But we do believe that your Leizar has an exceptional mind. He will be a great asset to us, and he will make you proud.'

And so, it was agreed that Leizar would go to Warsaw. 'Look after my boy, he's very precious,' implored Zelman. 'Don't worry, he's in good company and to be honest, we all think he will be a great success. '

'*Frum dein moil tsu Gott's erin* (From your mouth to God's ears)'

They arranged that Leizar would finish up at the school and Moshe would collect him. 'How long do you need?' He asked.

Leizar had a think, 'Today is Sunday. I can be ready by Thursday.' There were lots of hugs and shaking of hands as if Moshe had suddenly become a friend of the family, and with that he left.

An excited babble broke out. Everybody wanted to speak at once. The children were home from school, and it was explained that Leizar would be going on an adventure to the big city, and they might not see him for a long time. Even little Moshe who was only three, got involved and started crying at the noise.

Zelman banged on the table for attention. 'Now everybody listen, you should all be proud of your brother Leizar. He has been selected to go to Warsaw to become a cigarette maker and work with some very important people. Maybe one day he will be famous – who knows? So everybody settle down and Uma will make dinner. Leizar has a lot to do in the next few days.'

Mendel and Leizar again went outside to talk. 'I have an idea about how we can communicate while I am in Warsaw,' said Leizar. 'Tomorrow I will have a word with Dmitri. Moshe says it is safe to talk to him, and he sends and receives messages from Warsaw and from Russia. If we pay him, I think he will help.'

Mendel looked sceptical. 'But surely it is dangerous for him, and where do we get the money to pay him?'

'I will be working and earning some money. I don't think we have to pay him much. Don't forget, he has already been helping the movement. All it takes is for someone to let his superiors know and he is finished. He knows that.'

A change seemed to be coming over Leizar. He seemed sure-footed and confident. He even spoke a little differently, as if he was in control, and it got under Mendel's skin. He was irritated by his brother's assumption that he was the chosen one.

'You may be a little older than me, but I can write every bit as good as you, and sometimes even better. And we are a team you and I, why should it be only you who goes to Warsaw?'

Leizar did not handle this well. He smiled rather condescendingly, 'Yes, little brother,' he began, but he was interrupted when Mendel threw down the book he was holding, his lip curled, and he took a step toward his brother.

'Don't you *little brother* me. When Moshe returns, I will tell him that I write as much of the articles as you. If he won't take me to Warsaw, then I will tell Upa we should both stay here. You were always Upa's favourite, and you got away with a lot, while I took the blame. Well, not this time!'

Leizar's temper started to show. 'You will do no such thing!' They both knew it wouldn't take much for Zelman to stop Leizar going to Warsaw, and Mendel could easily be the catalyst.

'I am the older brother, and it was me they approached. If you do this, Mendel, I will never forgive you!'

Mendel turned on his heel. '*Geh shlogn zich kop in vant!*' he shouted and stormed back into the house.

CHAPTER 13

THE ACCUSATION AND ARREST

The next day, Leizar went to speak to Dmitri, but he was in for a shock.

He waited outside the command hut as usual, until Dmitri was alone. As soon as he entered, Dmitri rose from his desk and, walking towards him, made a statement that felt like a physical blow. 'Leizar, we need to talk, we have a big problem, I have to arrest your brother Mendel Yaacov, where is he?'

Leizar was a man who normally spoke in a measured way, but he had inherited the Domansky way of shouting when he was shocked, the volume rising as he went on. 'What? What are you talking about? Mendel has done nothing, why would you want to arrest him? For what?'

'He stole a side of beef from the Russian army store. He was seen by a woman who worked there, and he hit her with an iron bar he used to lever his way in. She is in a coma and the doctor says they will fight to save her life, but she may die. Another officer saw the whole thing and identified Mendel.'

Leizar was astounded at Dmitri's tone as well as the accusation. 'Are you mad? My brother Mendel would never do such a thing, when is this supposed to have taken place?'

'Last night at around midnight. Do you know where your brother was at that time?'

'Yes of course, he was in bed asleep.'

'How do you know? Did you see him around midnight?' Dmitri knew enough about the Domansky family to know that Leizar shared a bedroom with his little brother, Moishe. Mendel shared with Duvid. 'I was with him all evening until we both went to bed. This is ridiculous! Of course, he was in bed asleep. How can you think Mendel would do such a thing? You are a friend of the family. My father taught your son Alexei, and I know you help with the Movement.'

Even as he was speaking, Leizar felt his stomach tightening. Again, his voice got louder. 'What's going on, Dimi?'

Dmitri was already halfway out the door, and he was calling to another officer to accompany him. Talking as he walked, he said 'Leizar, this is very serious. The penalty for this type of crime could be death.'

This was like a physical blow in the face to Leizar. Why was Dmitri acting like this? Over the years he had kept his promise and shielded the Domansky family. He visited the home and took tea and schnapps with the family. 'Look Dimi, you know Mendel. I don't know what this woman saw, but it wasn't Mendel. She is clearly mistaken; you can put a stop to this nonsense.'

There was no further talking as Leizar followed the two Cossacks at a half-run towards his home.

On arrival, the Russians burst into the house and found Ryfke in the kitchen mixing ingredients for chulent with Marcia and Mendel helping to clean and wash vegetables. 'What is this? What do you want in my house?' Ryfke screamed.

'Mendel Yaacov Domansky, come with me at once!'

Dmitri and the other officer went straight over to Mendel, who was completely shocked. One grabbed each arm, and they frog marched him out the door. Leizar could see that the first priority was to comfort his mother.

'Uma, they think Mendel has committed a crime, but it is a mistake, we will deal with it, and I can assure you all will be well. Marcia, go and get Upa from the school.'

When Zelman arrived, Marcia had already told him what had happened, that they had *shlepped* him away and Leizar said they thought he had committed a crime, but it was a mistake, and everything would be alright. But Zelman knew there would be more to it. He walked so fast that Marcia could not keep up with him.

As he walked through the door, he saw Leizar. 'You spoke to the Russian?'

'Yes Upa, I went to his office to talk about going to Warsaw and I walked straight in when he was about to come to arrest Mendel. He had some rubbish story from a Russian officer who said she saw the whole thing. It was around midnight and he identified Mendel and said he hit a woman with an iron bar.'

'Has he gone mad?' Zelman hit his head with the palm of his hand. 'You told him he was here with us all night? And what has come over him?'

Leizar went closer to his father and spoke quietly. He did not want to alarm his mother. 'Upa, this was not the Dmitri we know. He was aggressive and not listening to me. Something has happened and he has changed.'

Although they had no doubt that this was mistaken identity, there were many cases where good innocent people had been accused of crimes and sentenced to severe punishment or even death. Indeed, it was largely thought that the Russians had a policy of meting out severe and public punishment to endorse their authority, and they did not care too much whether they had the guilty party or not, or perhaps whether the crime had even been committed. So, the family were justifiably worried, especially when Leizar told them that Dmitri had mentioned the death penalty.

'I must speak with Dmitri,' said Zelman. 'He owes me something for all the years I worked with his son Alexei, so he will speak to me, I'm sure. But first I must speak with Duvid. He will be the witness that Mendel was asleep all night. I will return to the school to find him.'

When Zelman asked Duvid, he could only say that he went to bed before Mendel and then he was asleep all night. It was not a good alibi, and Zelman would not ask him to lie and say he saw his brother asleep around midnight because not only would he not put his young son in such a position, but it would be unlikely that he would be able to maintain the story in the face of questioning, and to be caught in the lie could actually make it worse for Mendel as well as landing Duvid in trouble.

He went to the command hut. The Russians had already put Mendel in irons, and he was in a cell. In those surroundings he looked like a guilty prisoner. When Dmitri asked Zelman, he had to admit that although Duvid had been in the same room and he was sure Mendel had been there all night, he had himself been asleep and could not say with certainty what time Mendel had come to bed.

Dmitri closed his office door and dropped his voice, 'Zelman you are my friend here, and you know I would do what I can. I am in a lot of trouble. The Russian High

Command have been here, and I am under investigation. They have heard about the Communist movement growing in Kawetchka. I am accused of being too soft and allowing dissent to build. They are watching everything I do. And there is more I can't even tell you. My own life is at stake.'

'But you can't take this out on my innocent boy!'

'First, I am not sure he is so innocent. We have an eyewitness officer who saw the whole thing and identified Mendel. I am afraid he will have to go through the procedure, but he will have a chance to say his side of things. That will be before three officers of which I will be only one. I have spoken to him and of course, he denies it. He says he was at home in bed.'

'Let me speak with him. He is my boy, and he is as honest as the day is long. I can assure you he would not and did not do this thing.'

Zelman was allowed into the cell and went straight to hug his son. Mendel was very distressed. His movement was restricted by the chains and there were tears in his eyes. Zelman persuaded Dmitri to release the chains and he even brought them two glasses of tea. Zelman sat down and looked into his son's eyes. 'I need to hear you tell me about this accusation,' he said. 'Whatever you tell me I will believe you.'

Mendel looked at his father. The tears were rolling down his face now. 'Upa, I swear I have no idea what they are talking about. I already told them, last night I went to bed as usual. By midnight I was fast asleep. Why don't they believe me?' he sobbed.

Mendel also knew that sometimes people were wrongly accused of committing crimes on trumped up charges, and he had seen them punished. Mendel grabbed his father's hands, 'Upa, I am scared.'

Zelman held his son close, 'Don't worry *tateleh,* we will get this straightened out, I promise. Dmitri knows me and he knows the family. I will get to the bottom of it. You just sit tight here until I can come and get you.'

He stepped outside the cell and went to see Dmitri. 'Listen my friend. You know my boy could not have done this thing. He was asleep at home and if he stole the beef, where is it? You have known him all his life. He has never put a foot wrong, why would he do this thing now? He is a gentle boy; can you honestly imagine him hitting a woman over the head with an iron bar?'

'Look Zelman, I would like to help, but you have to see I have a problem here.

We have an officer who identified Mendel by name. He has since been here and confirmed his identification, and there is no evidence to the contrary except Mendel says he didn't do it. It will have to go before the tribunal in three days. If he didn't do it, bring me some evidence, or find the other person who will admit it was him.'

Zelman went back to the family, and they all sat round trying to figure out what had happened. They all went to bed that night with heavy hearts. Two days passed, and they got nowhere. Zelman spoke to everyone he could think of that might be able to help, but the Cossack officer was adamant he saw Mendel.

Zelman even went to the Old Rabbi. 'Rabbi, Zelman didn't do this thing, but he can't prove himself innocent. What can we do?' The Rabbi pulled his beard in his usual thoughtful manner.

'Well, first of all was the crime committed at all, or are they making it all up?'

In answer to his own question he went on, 'If it was committed, then obviously someone else stole the beef and hit the woman with the iron bar. Can it have been someone else from our community? After all, the beef was not kosher, it could not be eaten by any of us, so it would have to be a non-observant Jew, or a Gentile. But at least that is something we can say in his defence. What would Mendel want with the non-kosher, *traif* beef, that the family would not touch?'

Zelman and Ryfke went to see Mendel. Being a good Jewish mother, Ryfke took food. *Gefilte fish*, potato *latkes* and *bubeles* (sweet fried patties). They were freshly made, and the smell brought the Russians gathering round. Of course, she had made enough for everyone in Dmitri's unit. She left the food and ran to her son. They embraced as best they could despite the chains. She cried when she saw the state of him.

Zelman explained to Dmitri about the non-kosher beef. The way Zelman put it, Mendel could not be the perpetrator for that reason and there must be a mistake, apart from which the family knew he went to bed before midnight.

Dmitri smiled. 'And can anyone swear that they were not in bed until well after midnight, so that they can say they saw Mendel go to bed before 12pm and that he did not come out of his room. They would need to swear he was definitely in bed at that time, and could not have crept out.'

He went on, 'Yes you make a good point about the non-kosher beef. I know the family would not touch it, but Mendel could easily have sold it for quite a lot of money. I am sorry my friend, but that will not do.'

On the second day, Zelman returned to the Rabbi, and they went to see the butcher, Aaron Gabinsky. He swore he had not heard of anyone trying to sell beef and, in any event, if he were to allow the *traif* anywhere near his meat, it would render all the rest of his meat also *traif*.

Zelman asked all the students at school if any of the families had some nice beef for dinner, but the older students laughed, they had not seen beef for a long time. Leizar went from door to door in the shtetl to explain what had happened and to ask if anyone had any idea what the real circumstances were. Nobody had seen nor heard anything. The Rabbi spoke to all the men who attended the religious services, with a similar lack of success. By the morning of the third day, they were getting desperate.

Chapter 14

The trial

The tribunal hearing was arranged for the next day, Wednesday at noon.

It took place in Dimitri's office. He was to conduct the proceedings himself. He sat between two very large Cossacks in full military uniform. They both looked very stern and very much like each other. They could have been brothers, both had neatly trimmed beards and large black moustaches. On their heads they wore large astrakhan hats. They were very tall, and with Dmitri in between they looked very intimidating.

Mendel was brought into the room by two more soldiers. They were not dressed in such splendid outfits as the officers, just simple grey shirts done up to the neck and a bit crumpled, and grey trousers tucked into their boots. They were no taller than Mendel, but they looked very tough, and they handled him roughly, shoving him to the middle of the room where he was forced to stand in the chains. He did not look good. Three days of beard growth and dirty clothing with what looked like blood stains. Ryfke drew in her breath when she saw him.

The family were allowed to sit on wooden chairs at the back of the room. Leizar began to fear that the tribunal had already made up its mind.

Dmitri sounded his gavel and spoke loudly, 'Mendel Yaacov Domansky, you are accused of stealing a side of beef from the Russian store and striking a woman with an iron bar causing loss of consciousness. I have to inform you that the tribunal has heard this morning that the lady has sadly died. So, the charges are theft and murder.

How do you plead?'

The whole room seemed to gasp when they heard the word 'murder'. They knew now that the penalty if he was found guilty would be death.

Mendel was stunned at first and did not answer. Dmitri spoke even louder 'How do you plead?

'Not guilty.' Mendel's voice was weak. He looked over at his parents and his brother as if pleading for help. Zelman's face was very stern, and he nodded to his son and mouthed 'don't worry.' But inside his guts were wrenching.

'This is a very serious matter, which could result in the death penalty, do you have anyone to speak for you?' Zelman stood up, 'Yes, I will speak. Can you tell me who will make the decision in this case?'

Dmitri looked a little irritated, 'After hearing the evidence, the guilt will be decided by myself and my two colleagues sitting here.'

Zelman scoffed, 'But you are presenting the case for his guilt, are you not? How can you then judge the case impartially?'

Dmitri was really cross at what he saw as a smart-ass observation. He raised his voice again, 'I am the officer in charge here. You will do as I say, and at the end I and my colleagues will decide. Do not think you are among equals here, Mr Domansky. You are not!'

'How can this be justice?' Zelman had raised his voice too, and he was starting to shake with rage. 'I want to speak to your superior!'

Ryfke and Leizar were both worried that if Zelman lost his temper, he could make matters worse.

This time Dmitri dropped his voice for effect. 'Mr Domansky, *I* am the authority here. I represent the Russian authorities who have vested in me the responsibility of trying the accused and deciding the outcome.'

Then he shouted at Zelman 'If you do not respect this court and behave in the appropriate manner, I shall have you thrown out!'

Ryfke was pulling at Zelman's arm. 'Liebchen, sit down please, you are making it worse.'

The trial proceeded and Dmitri went through the procedure as he saw it, of presenting the facts.

The big surprise came when he presented the eye witness who had seen the whole thing take place. The Cossack on his left stood up – it turned out that *he* was the eyewitness. So, the guilt or innocence of the defendant would be judged by a tribunal who not only had a vested interest in the outcome because it was their beef that had been stolen from the army store, but also the tribunal contained the officer in charge who presented the prosecution case *and also* the officer who was the eyewitness for the prosecution.

When the witness stood, Leizar could not control himself, 'This is outrageous!' he shouted at the top of his voice. 'How can my brother get a fair hearing here?'

One of the guards stepped towards Leizar with his *shashkra* sword drawn. Dmitri stood and took a couple of steps towards him. 'You will hold your tongue, or you will be thrown out!'

Zelman could not believe what was happening. He asked Dmitri for a word in private, which was forcibly denied. Dmitri had turned from a friend for whom he had worked for years, into a bullying ogre intent on bringing tragedy to the family.

Needless to say, the trial was a sham. Dmitri presented the 'facts' and the witness said that he had seen Mendel take the beef that night at midnight. He saw him walking out with the beef over his shoulder when he was approached by the Russian woman shouting 'thief.' He had a heavy iron bar in his other hand, and he hit her a mighty blow on the head, and she collapsed, bleeding heavily. The woman had been taken to the Russian doctor's surgery and remained unconscious until that very morning when they heard that she had died from her injury.

Zelman was invited to speak on behalf of Mendel who had been allowed to sit otherwise he would have collapsed. His head was lowered, and he seemed a shadow of the young man he was only a few days before.

'I would like to ask the witness officer how he could be sure it was Mendel when I myself, know he was at home at that time as he always was, and fast asleep.'

'I am quite sure it was the man sitting opposite me,' he replied indicating Mendel, who sobbed loudly.

'Wasn't it dark in the store at that time? And how close were you to the perpetrator.'

'I was quite close, and as an officer in the glorious Russian Army, I am trained to recognise people when the light is not so good. I am quite sure it was the defendant.'

Zelman turned to face the tribunal, 'The beef was not kosher, it would be of no use to Mendel or his family, or indeed any other Jewish person, so why would they try to steal it?'

'He probably sold it for a lot of money, beef is very expensive.'

Zelman was becoming more anxious and frustrated. He was making no headway. He felt his chest tightening as he tried to suppress his anger. 'This is madness.' His voice got louder, 'I tell you my boy was at home asleep, the beef is no good to him and it was dark. You say he was somewhere else stealing meat.' His hands were clenched in front of him.

Dmitri interrupted. 'Do you doubt the word of an officer of the Russian Army?'

'But this is not justice! There are three of you to decide, and one is the prosecutor and another is the main witness.' He was shouting now, and Leizar grabbed him by the arm and made him sit down. And a good job too, because Dmitri had stood and indicated to the guards to grab him. When he sat down, they stopped.

'Another outburst and you will be in the cell with your son!'

It was clear that they had made up their minds before anyone stepped into the room. They said a crime had been committed and they had the culprit. They wanted to hang Mendel!

Ryfke was in floods of tears and Mendel had shrunk back into his chair with his head down in despair. Leizar was in shock; the realisation suddenly hit him like a train: his younger brother actually die for something he did not do.

Zelman approached the tribunal. Tears were now streaming down his face too. 'Please, please, I beg you. We are good people. We have never done anything wrong. We work hard and we pay our taxes.'

He moved closer to Dmitri and the guard with the *shashkra* moved toward him in case of an attack. 'You know me for all these years, I taught your son. I have been to your house, and you have been to mine, you know all my family. How could you do this? Don't take my boy.'

Dmitri stood and shouted at the top of his voice 'Enough! The tribunal will retire and make a decision.' And with that all three of them filed out.

As soon as they had gone, the family all rushed towards Mendel, but the guards kept them away. He was reaching out as best he could, to his mother. He was sobbing,

'Uma, Upa don't let this happen. I will do anything they want. Tell them they have the wrong person.'

Only a few minutes passed before the three officers returned and with exaggerated formality, resumed their seats. Dmitri's face was like thunder. He looked at Mendel.' The tribunal has found you guilty of theft and murder. You will be hung by the neck until you are dead. This will take place tomorrow at dawn.'

They rose and filed out again, and the guards roughly took hold of Mendel by each arm, and he was dragged back to his cell.

A guard was posted at the door leading to the cell and the family were told that they would be allowed to see Mendel only one at a time. They should come back in two hours as he had to be 'prepared'.

Zelman was horrified to hear those words, but he could get no more information from the guard who just repeated that those were his orders.

Ryfke had to be supported as she could hardly walk, and the family trudged slowly back home. .hocked when he stood at the door and saw the pitiful group approaching.

'Leizar, you explain to Duvid, I am going to see the Rabbi. Maybe he has an idea of what we can do.'

Ryfke offered food, but no one was hungry. Marcia was six and little Moshe only four, and Leizar just told them enough to stop them asking more questions. Ryfke was sobbing and every now and then it would build to a wailing cry. The evening was drawing on and it was getting dark.

When Zelman told the Rabbi, he was stunned. 'How long do we have?' he asked.

'Not even 24 hours, it is set for tomorrow at dawn.'

The Rabbi questioned Zelman quite closely about the events at the trial. There was much stroking of beards. 'Rabbi there must be something we can do?' Zelman broke down again. 'They are going to kill my son!' he said, between great racking sobs. 'And I swear to you he has done nothing.'

'It is impossible to go over the head of Dmitri. He is in charge here and even if we could, whose version do you think they would listen to? No. I must go and talk to the Russian. Maybe I can bring some sense to this. To be honest this is not the first time I have heard of these terrible murders by these *momzers*. It has happened in other shtetls. I am going to go talk to him.'

Zelman staggered to his feet as if the weight of the world was on his shoulders. 'I must return to my family, and then we have to go to Mendel. Rabbi you must do something.'

'Pray that I can make a difference,' said the Rabbi.

Zelman staggered back home. Ryfke had not taken off her coat since she had arrived from the trial and Leizar sat with his head in his hands. Duvid and the children were in the other room.

'Come,' said Zelman, 'let us go to our son.'

They went out the door, a pitiful trio with heads bent against the wind. On arrival at the command hut, they found Dmitri with the other two officers seated in front of a roaring fire drinking schnapps. The rabbi was standing to one side with his hands clasped in front of him.

'Only one at a time!' Dmitri said in his loud authoritarian voice as soon as they entered. 'The others can wait outside.'

Ryfke was the first to enter the cell. She had brought soup and bread. Mendel rushed to hold her. 'Uma, Uma I am so scared. I don't want to die. Please, please Uma, make them stop this.'

Ryfke held him as if he was a child, cooing and speaking softly. 'The rabbi is speaking to Dmitri. I am sure he will make him listen to sense. Your father and the rabbi have known Dmitri for so many years.

Zelman was allowed to join the Rabbi speaking to the officers while Leizar waited outside. The rabbi had been pleading with the Russians to no avail. Zelman decided to try a more desperate approach. 'Dimi, we have known each other for more than thirty years, I know your family and you know mine; you have never had any trouble with us.'

Zelman was a little surprised that the Russians were allowing him to speak freely without interruption. It gave him a little more confidence. 'My Mendel is a good boy, and he has never put a foot wrong. I don't have much, but I swear if you spare him, you can have everything I've got. My house, my milk cow, even my clothes. I will work for you for nothing. My wife Ryfke will wash and clean for you. We will do anything, please, you have it in your power. Spare him.'

Dmitri leaned back in his chair and put his shiny boots on the stool in front of him.

'Zelman, you don't understand, do you? There is nothing I can do even if I wanted to. There is strong evidence against your son and nothing to disprove it. This was a terrible crime, and he has to pay the price. There has been a trial, and Mendel has been found guilty. He must face the ultimate penalty.'

He looked at each of his colleagues and then back to Zelman, 'And I have instructions from my superiors to ensure the law is upheld in this shtetl as in all the others. I have no choice.'

Ryfke came out from the cell after about an hour, and Zelman went in. He did everything he could to comfort Mendel and give him some hope, but he could see the situation was becoming hopeless. After Mendel, Leizar was allowed to see his brother while his parents waited. Mendel would not be alone that night.

While Leizar had been waiting, his emotions had been running riot. For a few minutes he sat on the step, closed his eyes and imagined this was not happening. It had all been a terrible nightmare. But reality kicked in with a brutal force when he thought about this dreadful miscarriage of justice that could be perpetrated by the Russians simply because of the rotten system, his anger boiled up inside him. By the time he was able to see his brother, he was torn between sympathy and anger. Weighing heavily on his mind was Mendel's anger last time they spoke the night before. It had ended in a row which was not resolved.

When he entered the cell, Leizar was shocked at his brother's appearance. He seemed to have physically shrunk in size, his face was white, his clothes stained and dirty, but worst of all were his eyes, which seemed fixed in a wild terrified stare.

Leizar tried to distract his brother with the plans they had before all this happened. But Mendel couldn't concentrate. And he seemed fixated on their last row which he said, had been playing on his mind all night. He was still bitter about it. 'So, it looks like you win again,' he said, with pain in his voice. 'You get to go to Warsaw, and I get to die!'

This hit its mark. Tears came to Leizar's eyes. He did not want to carry the guilt of this, Mendel had not been aggressive in this way before and the small rows they had in the past were soon resolved, but this was different. 'Mendel, you are my brother, my flesh and blood. If I could stand in your place now, I would. I am so sorry about last night. It was my fault and whatever I said, I didn't mean it.'

Mendel was shaking now, 'Well, you did a good job. Look what has happened to me!' And he broke down in tears.

Leizar left the cell with his mind in a rage that this could be allowed to happen and there was nothing they could do about it. He staggered out of the cell with the heaviest of hearts.

The family stayed with Mendel all night, and each spent time in the cell. Leizar went home to ensure the children were fed and put to bed and returned two hours later. He asked to see his brother again. This time he found a strange calm had come over Mendel as if he had accepted the inevitable and was consciously coming to terms with it.

The wild eyes were gone and instead he sat with his head in his hands. Leizar went straight over and hugged him, and Mendel didn't resist – he hugged him back. Between sobs he said, 'Leizar, I do not let you off the hook for what you said and did, but I want you to promise me that you will find the way to change this. If my death is to mean anything at all, then let it be in the name of change from this disgusting and vile regime.'

Leizar could hardly speak, he was hugging and nodding. Mendel continued, 'And I want you to give me your word that you will try to get our family out of this place to a country that treats their people fairly, like human beings.' Again, Leizar was nodding. 'Give me your word,' sobbed Mendel.'

'I give you my word, my brother.'

Leizar stayed for hours, with their parents interspersing, sensing this time was precious for them all, but especially for the brothers, and it took all Leizar's will power to remain calm when he was boiling over internally with the injustice of it all and the guilt he felt at what had occurred between them. They knew time was short, but Mendel had become resigned to the inevitable, and Zelman told Leizar to try to keep him calm.

Mendel wanted Leizar to understand how things would be if they ever got to America. Although Leizar was not ignorant of the democratic way, Mendel had studied it, 'In the United States and in many European countries under one person one vote, the people have a real say in how they are governed and who should do it.

'Elections take place on a specified day, and if the people don't like the way the country is being governed, they can vote and change the governing party. There is a true freedom of speech. You can write almost anything in the newspaper, even criticising the government, and above all the Judges are independent and impartial. Atrocities like this would never be allowed.'

Leizar said he still felt that Communism was the panacea where everyone was equal and all worked for the common good, but he found it hard to concentrate with this dreadful situation fogging his mind. Mendel seemed to appreciate that the idealistic discussion was taking his mind off things. They talked and talked, batting it back and forth until Ryfke knocked on the door.

Chapter 15

The Outcome

Leizar exited the cell to allow his mother time with her son. His father was standing and banging his head on the wall. Leizar was struggling hard to contain his anger and frustration and several times Zelman had to physically prevent his older son from storming into the living quarters of the Russians.

As the time approached, Leizar's aggression grew. 'Why should they be able to commit this heinous injustice with their lies and deceit? And the only reason we cannot appeal to a higher authority is that the whole lot of them are corrupt.'

The more they spoke in this way, the more emotional Leizar became. He was forced to accept that they were powerless to prevent the dreadful thing that was about to happen, which filled him with anger, but at the same time, strengthened his resolve enormously to effect change to prevent further atrocities of this sort.

Just before dawn, a Russian came in with a meal for Mendel which he refused, and Leizar kicked it out of the hands of the Russian in anger. 'Tell your masters we don't want any of their *traif!*'

Ryfke, Zelman and Leizar were allowed in the cell together, and the rabbi came to pray for Mendel. Ryfke could hardly stand, and her body was racked with heart rending and sobbing grief. Tears were running down Zelman's face and into his beard. He avoided direct eye contact with Mendel because he could not bear to face the reality of what was to happen while Leizar paced back and forth on the small room.

The rabbi was chanting in Hebrew.

Too soon, three Russian guards entered and grabbed Mendel. The rabbi intoned a prayer in Yiddish.

'We acknowledge before You, Adonai, God and God of our ancestors, that the healing and death of Mendel Yaacov Domansky is in Your hands. May it be Your will to grant him a complete healing. If it be Your will that he is to die, let his death bring him peace forever more at your right hand.'

Ryfke ripped her shirt top and fell, first to her knees and then prostrate on the ground, body shaking. Zelman staggered against the rabbi, who held him and gently stroked his head.

Leizar stormed out of the cell and through the outer room. His face was red, and his rage was incandescent. He started to kick and punch the wall making his skin bleed. When his fists were too painful, he too started to bang his head on the wall until one of the guards came out to stop him.

The execution was primitive.

Behind the command hut was a large oak tree. It had a sturdy branch about ten feet from the ground. The family stood some distance away. Zelman and Leizar did not want Ryfke to witness the horror that was about to take place. 'Uma, please – let Duvid take you home, there is nothing to do here now.'

Ryfke was shaking and a low-pitched keening was coming from her, she did not speak, but they could not move her.

Several Cossacks were gathered round the tree. They had strung a rope over the branch with a roughly fashioned noose at the end. The rope was secured around the tree branch so it would not move. A box was placed under the rope.

Zelman and Ryfke were leaning into each other and holding on as if one would let go the other would fall. Ryfke couldn't help herself. As Mendel was led out, she shrieked 'Ney, ney. Not my baby! Here take me!'

And she let go of Zelman and ran to the guards. They all stood in front so she could not pass, and she fell to the ground, screaming and sobbing. Leizar and Duvid gently picked her up and led her back to their father.

Mendel was compliant. He was led quietly with his hands tied behind his back and helped up on to the box and the noose placed around his neck. The three officers had gathered at the site and they stood like that, a macabre gathering waiting for a signal from Dmitri.

The sound of a horseman was heard. As it got nearer, a Cossack appeared riding a beautiful Palomino. He dismounted in front of the officers and saluted. He had a small pouch in his hand, and he approached Dmitri.

He saluted again, and handed over the pouch, which the Captain opened and removed paper from it. He opened out a letter. The family held their breath. Leizar gasped, 'This is it.' He whispered to his parents. 'It must be the reprieve, he will live!' And as the realisation dawned on him, his voice became louder, and others looked round.

'*Frum dein moil tsu Gott's erin*'. Is it possible?' Zelman's eyes were closed as if in prayer, and Ryfke's tears were in full flood. She was digging her nails into her hand, the female family trait.

'It must be, why would they send a horseman at the last minute? They know they have the wrong man.'

The captain slowly read the letter. He showed it to the uniformed Cossck standing next to him, who read it and gave a confirmatory nod and returned it to the Captain, who folded it carefully and returned it to the pouch.

He nodded at the horseman, who turned on his heel, remounted, and rode away in the direction he had come from. The family held their breath for what seemed like ages, while a gentle breeze picked up some of the leaves and the tree rustled.

Dmitri put the letter back in the pouch and handed it to one of the officers.

He raised his gloved hand high above his head and brought it down sharply.

The box was kicked away,

Mendel's body dropped and was abruptly halted by the noose which immediately tightened and snapped his neck.

Leizar put his hand over his mother's eyes, but she fell to the floor. He was glad they had chosen to stand some distance away, but they couldn't help but see the awful, hideous scene unfolding before them.

As they saw and heard Mendel's neck snap, Zelman's body gave a sudden jolt as if it had happened to him.

After the audible crack of his neck snapping, his legs and torso went into a wild spasm for what seemed like quite a while but was probably only 30 seconds and then the body began to swing.

This seemed to be a signal for Leizar's rage to subside and he realised his parents needed support. He averted his mother's eyes and put his arm round his father and his brother and quietly led them away, holding Ryfke with his arm around her waist.

Together they staggered back home.

Chapter 16

The move to Warsaw

Nobody slept that night. Ryfke sat shaking. Every now and then she would start a gentle mewing and rock back and forth. It had fallen to Zelman and Leizar to explain to the children that God had decided to take their brother Mendel away. Aunt Yentl brought food, but only the children could be persuaded to eat anything. The Old Rabbi stayed for some time, until his platitudes about this all being the will of God really started to get on everyone's nerves. He was politely asked to leave. The shock of what they had witnessed seemed to have struck everyone dumb and the house became deathly quiet.

Leizar laid on his bed thinking. Tomorrow was the day Moshe was due to come and take him to Warsaw. He kept turning things over in his mind, he was supposed to enlist the help of the traitor Dmitri, how would the Movement react when they found he had betrayed them?

Of course, there was no way he could leave his parents and his family at this time? He was sure Moshe and Edvard would understand when they heard what had happened.

On the other hand, his determination to effect changes and start to fight back was burning in him, especially after the vow he had made to his brother, but he knew his first duty was to his parents and his family.

Late in the evening, Uncle Shmuel came round and, after spending some time trying to placate his brother Zelman, and of course, Ryfke, he came in to Leizar's room where he found him lying on one bed with Duvid on the other. Leizar was pleased to see Uncle Shmuel. When he was in trouble Shmuel was a good sounding board, often helping Leizar to figure a way through his most difficult problems.

'Uncle Shmuel, I'm so glad you are here,' said Leizar, with tears in his eyes. 'I need to talk to you.'

The two men hugged tight for a long time before Shmuel let go. He went over to Duvid and did the same. Even at his young age, Duvid had picked up Leizar's anger, and he had been around both his brothers enough to have an idea of what might be on Leizar's mind. 'Can I stay while you talk?' he asked.

So, the three sat on the edge of the bed and Leizar started to explain. 'You know that I had this unbelievable offer to go to Warsaw and work with some very important people in the Movement, but that was of course, before all this happened. I need to tell you everything.'

He told Shmuel about his long-held views about the way in which poor people were subjugated and used by the Russian oppressors, while the Tzar and the bourgeoisie lived in luxury.

He explained briefly about his study of Karl Marx and communism and his passion to influence change in this oppressive system. It's fair to say that Shmuel was not that surprised. People were beginning to mutter this sort of thing more and more, away from Russian ears. What did surprise him was that this was on his mind today of all days.

'You see, Mendel and I have been working for some time undercover, writing articles for a socialist magazine that they publish in Warsaw. That's how I got the offer to go.'

'Yes, Zelman told me'

'But while I have been studying Marxist principles of equality, Mendel also looked at the Western democracies. Change has to come, Uncle Shmuel, but Mendel thought one person, one vote creates equality of opportunity within the freedom.'

'And you?'

'Karl Marx believes all men are equal, and should be treated equally, wealth should be distributed as evenly as possible. Under Marx there would be no Tzar, and no Russian oppressors I am all in favour of that..'

'Interesting!' Shmuel nodded.

'But Mendel felt democracy was a better alternative because all men had an equal opportunity to succeed. And the one man one vote system enabled ordinary people to decide who should govern them.'

Shmuel was surprised at the conversation. With his brother lying dead, how could Leizar be talking about this now? Nevertheless, he thought it was good to let him talk.

'I don't know much about how the system works in the USA and UK, but I do know they are powerful nations, perhaps more so than Russia.' Duvid was listening quietly.

Shmuel started to question Leizar about the idealism of each system and Leizar explained as best he could. Apart from his interest, Shmuel also thought this was a good way to distract the boys, but after a while this was testing Leizar's patience.

'Look Uncle Shmuel, I haven't got to the matter I wanted your advice on.'

His voice started to rise again. 'My brother Mendel is dead, cruelly killed for no reason today by the disgusting oppressors under which we live. The night before he was arrested, Mendel and I had a big row. He thought it was wrong that I was the one to go to Warsaw, and he was not given the chance. A lot of things came out that he had never said about me being the favourite over him and he was really angry.'

As close as he was to the family, Shmuel had never seen the boys have anything other than a Domansky disagreement. He was surprised.

Leizar continued, 'Uncle Shmuel, I didn't handle it well, and we ended up with a really big blow up and Mendel walked out on me. The very worst of it all was I didn't see him again until he was in the Russian cell.'

'Oh my God, and your father has told me of the dreadful, heart-breaking ordeal he went through. Was the row forgotten?'

'No, that's the whole point. Not only did he not forgive me, but he made me make a vow before he died.'

'What sort of vow?'

'As I explained, I believe that Communism or Socialism is the change that is needed in Poland and Russia, and if I went to Warsaw, I would work hard to try to influence that for the whole country, but such change can take decades and much heartache and sacrifice along the way.

'Mendel's idea was to get the family out of Poland altogether and emigrate to the USA. He made me vow to do all I could to make that happen.'

Shmuel's eyes opened very wide, 'Are you crazy? How would you do that?'

'I would go and work in Warsaw. I would have some money coming in – not a fortune, but I could save some. Many Poles have managed to emigrate to the USA from there, I'm sure I could find the way and, maybe not all at once, but gradually and in time we could do it. Listen I have no illusions, this might take several years, but I have a young brother and sisters and I don't think my parents have finished their family yet.

'In the meantime, I would work very hard for the TDP cause where I believe I can make a real difference. Otherwise, I would not have received this generous offer. Mendel knew all about that.'

Shmuel's eyes opened wide. There was such enthusiasm in his nephew's voice.

'Uncle Shmuel, this is an unbelievable opportunity and as you know, I already discussed it with Uma and Upa and you helped me a lot with that. After they met Moshe and understood what it was all about, they agreed I should go.'

'Wait a moment, slow down. This is going a bit fast for me,' said Shmuel. 'So, they agreed, but that was before…' his voice trailed off as if he could not speak of what happened today.

Leizar was getting very agitated now, he was about to speak when Shmuel stood.

'I see. Well, my advice is to sleep on it for a few days. Let the family try to come to terms with what has happened. It will take time and it will never heal, but now it is raw and impossible to think straight. You may have convinced your parents then, but now is completely different. I'll talk to them in a week or two.'

Leizar jumped up. 'No, you don't understand!' he shouted. 'Tomorrow is the day Moshe returns to pick me up and take me to Warsaw. I must decide tonight. If I refuse and he has to return to Warsaw empty handed there is a good chance someone else will be offered the opportunity, and it will be lost to me.'

Leizar told him about the TDP with whom he and Mendel had been working and the approach from Edvard Abramovski via Moshe to allow Leizar to go and live in Warsaw where they would provide a job and accommodation.

'So, you see my *hartzshklupinsht*? My brother lies dead, and we must go through the worst of all grieving for him. I must support my parents through it, and yet I have made him a vow that I can only realistically have a chance to deliver on if I go to Warsaw tomorrow.'

Silence reigned for a while until it was broken by Duvid who had been listening intently and saying nothing. 'I think you should go. There's nothing you can do here.'

This broke the tension and Leizar smiled 'Thank you little brother, but I have to think about Uma and Upa. There will be a funeral and a shiva for our brother. How will it be if I am not there?'

Shmuel sat silently for a long while and nobody spoke. Eventually he stood up again. 'I think you should go too, we can speak to your parents tonight and explain to everyone else that you have a marvellous opportunity to work in Warsaw and if you don't accept right away, it will be offered to someone else. That is most of the truth anyway – beyond that nobody needs to know.'

But it wasn't as easy as they thought. When they returned, Ryfke was in the bedroom still sobbing, and Zelman was sitting at the table with his head in his hands. The pain of suffering seemed to fill the room. Spontaneously, Leizar went to his mother while Shmuel put his arms round his brother. This was a night for comfort, not serious discussion.

After a while Shmuel went home to collect his wife Zelda, and they both returned with food. Zelda laid the table with comfort foods she thought might be tempting, and they managed to persuade Zelman and Ryfke to sit and eat. The truth was they were actually starving and despite their grief, the whole family ate and were grateful. They felt better for it.

Shmuel and Zelda went home with a promise to return in the morning. This left Leizar quite anxious. Moshe was coming tomorrow, and until he was able to speak to his parents, he was unable to make this massive decision. So, for another night all the adults lay awake with their sorrow and in Leizar's case, also anxiety.

Dawn broke the next day, and everyone except the children, were up and about already. Ryfke's face looked as though it was cast in white stone, and Zelman as if he had aged during the night. But at least the crying had stopped. Ryfke made breakfast and got the children up, breakfasted and off to school. After that, Shmuel arrived and although the pain was still very raw, he and Leizar asked Zelman and Ryfke to sit down with some tea because they wanted to speak.

Leizar went first. He had been thinking all night how to approach this, but there was no easy way. 'I have been talking to Uncle Shmuel. Do you remember that this is the day Moshe is coming to take me to Warsaw?'

Both of his parents had been sitting with their heads down, staring at the table as if almost in a trance. But at this, they both looked up with a jolt. Zelman's eyes opened wide 'Of course, I had forgotten that. Well, he'll understand, things have changed. Today we have to make all the arrangements.'

He could not bring himself to talk directly about the hard fact that he had to bury his son and then sit shiva for him, but Zelman was a perceptive father, and he knew his Leizar well. He would not be talking about it now, with Shmuel as well, if he was simply going to send Moshe away. He looked across at Ryfke who had started crying again.

Shmuel spoke softly, 'I didn't know about this until last night,' he said, 'And Leizar has been in agony about it. On the one hand, of course, he loves his family and wants to be by your side. On the other, this is a chance of a lifetime, and he fears that if he lets it go, it may be gone for ever.'

Zelman stood up, 'Don't tell me you are thinking to leave us here on this day?'

Ryfke spoke between sobs, 'So it's not bad enough we have lost one beautiful son, now we have to lose another? How can you think like that? Have I been such a bad mother to you, that you want to hurt me some more?'

Zelman interjected loudly, 'And you have to sit shiva for your brother! That is the Jewish Law.'

Leizar felt the adrenalin rising, 'Upa, there are things you don't know. Mendel and I were in this together.'

He went on to explain how they both did work for the TPL in furthering the cause, but it had been limited because the movement was based in Warsaw. Their perception was that Leizar was the wordsmith and contributed more than Mendel, and that was why it was he who received the offer. He told how Mendel's focus was to find a way to get the family out of Poland and emigrate to USA.

He didn't mention the row, but he did tell them about the vow he had made to Mendel. He said they had agreed that Leizar should take the opportunity and work for the movement and at the same time assess the possibility of emigration and work towards it.

Zelman shook his head and interjected, he sighed, 'You were always a dreamer, Leizar. Listen, life may not be great here, but at least we are all together.'

His voice raised and he stood up, 'Nobody leaves here unless we all leave …. And I will *never* leave. Kawetchka is not much… but it's my home. Yes, yes, we have spoken of leaving for years, but how? This is what we can't come up with. We are poor people, we have no money for bribes, so every time we speak – every time the answer is the same. There is no answer!'

'Upa look, I gave my word to my dying brother. I will not renege on that. Yes, I admit my way may lead to a revolution and it may take years, and maybe Mendel's way could be a solution. I owe it to my brother to do everything I can to find this way out, if it is in any way possible. But one thing is for sure… if I don't go with Moshe today, I probably won't achieve much in either direction.'

He looked at his father and then across at his mother, 'Uma what do you think? You didn't say anything.'

Ryfke started sobbing again and they waited until she patted her eyes and was able to speak 'My darling Leizar. You are my first-born son and the light of my eyes. I will never, ever get over the loss of my *liebchen* Mendel and I don't want to lose you. But…' and she looked at her husband, 'I do know that you are the clever one. I believe if you put your mind to it, you can change the world. No wonder Moshe chose you, and you say he will give you a job and a home in Warsaw. You will pay him back a thousand-fold. He knows a *matzeer* when he sees it. Zelman, I say we must let him go, or he will regret the lost opportunity and come to resent us for stopping him.'

'*A mama hot glezerne oygen*,' said Zelman. What next?' He turned to Duvid sitting quietly, but listening intently, 'Where do you want to go? China? And Marcia and Moshe, it must be time to send them off somewhere.'

But Zelman's voice was softening. 'Just remember, this is where you live, and we are your family. Find a way to get messages back to us. There must be travellers who, for a few zloty, will bring us a message. We will worry about you, you know. I want to know how you are getting on. Oh! And don't worry,' he said with a note of sarcasm in his voice.

' I'll find an excuse to make people understand why Mendel's brother is not here to attend his funeral and sit shiva. And that's another thing, you make sure wherever you are and whatever you do, you sit shiva for your brother for seven days - even if you are on your own. And be sure you say *kaddish* for him. I won't know, but your brother will know and above all….' He pointed to the heavens… *HE* will know.'

Leizar knew it was unimaginably hard for his parents to accept what he had told them in their hour of grief, and as much as he loved them, he looked at them in a new light, realising they had come to terms with it because of their love for him. It was his turn to shed tears.

Zelman hugged his son close. 'Now, you'd better start to prepare. Do you know when Moshe will arrive?'

Over Leizar's shoulder he caught the eye of his brother Shmuel. They looked at each other, and Shmuel smiled. That was all the confirmation Zelman needed that his brother thought they were doing the right thing.

Leizar hugged both his parents, and Ryfke held him too long, as if she didn't want to ever let him go. 'We will be proud of you Leizar,' she whispered in his ear. 'Go with God.'

Leizar found himself charged with a strange energy and conflicted feelings. He was very excited about the move, and the promise he had made to Mendel and subsequently to himself to pursue Mendel's plan. On the other hand, he felt badly that he was leaving his grieving family and not even staying for the funeral. He spent the morning packing his things and going round all his uncles, aunts and cousins to say goodbye, and to attempt to explain why he was going without giving too much away.

The truth was that most of the villagers thought he was being selfish and disrespectful, especially his aunts and uncles. He couldn't tell them about the TPL of course, but he did the right thing and went to see them all before he left.

Moshe arrived that afternoon and Leizar was waiting for him. In order to avoid too many questions, he asked to leave straight away, he said he had a lot to tell him on the way.

Moshe was a bit disappointed. He had been looking forward to tea and *kichels*, but Ryfke had given food and drink sufficient for both of them – and being a Jewish mother – enough to feed a few more people. For Moshe she added in a few more *kichels*. The family were there to see him off. He hugged and kissed them all, and of course, there were tears among the good wishes. Zelman and Ryfke watched the carriage slowly disappear from sight and both stood silently even when they could not see it anymore. Life was certainly going to be different from now on without the two sons.

On the way Leizar explained the whole story, starting with the shock arrest of Mendel, through the sham trial and the execution including of course the complete *volte face* of Dmitri Belakov. Moshe was so shocked that at one point he stopped the carriage and turned to Leizar. 'Wait a minute! This was Dmitri Belakov, the one we have been working with?'

'The very same. He should rot in hell for a thousand years.'

'But we have been paying him.'

'Well, it looks as though someone else was paying him more.'

Moshe sat thinking for a while, and then said, 'And you mean this happened over the last few days, and yet you still come with me to Warsaw?'

Leizar went through the whole story with Moshe, explaining his thinking. He told about his vow to his late brother and his passion to be involved in the movement. Of course, he didn't disclose that part of the vow was to find a way to get out of Poland. Moshe shook his head in disbelief and drove on.

CHAPTER 17

ARRIVAL IN WARSAW

It was dusk when they arrived in the outskirts of the city. On the way, Moshe had explained that there are many Jews living in Warsaw, and the Russians held a strong grip, but due to the very large Jewish population, life was completely different to the shtetl and Jews had a lot more say over how they lived.

As he drove Moshe explained, 'About thirty percent of the population of Warsaw is Jewish and there are over 300 synagogues, including of course, the Warsaw Great Synagogue which can hold 2000 people.'

Leizar was surprised, he had no idea this was the case, 'And there are still pogroms?' he asked.

'Well, there are not many pogroms now, but there is plenty of anti-Jewish feeling. People blame us for everything. A headline in the newspaper yesterday suggested that Jews had planned the assassination of the Tzar.'

As they approached the centre, Leizar was shocked at the bustle of people and carriages, all in a hurry to go somewhere, and he was somewhat overawed at the grand buildings. There was a cacophony of noise the like of which he had never experienced, coming as he did, from the quiet of the shtetl.

As they rounded a corner, Leizar was shocked to see a sign daubed on a wall that read 'A home for Jews in Israel.' Under which someone had added 'Go, we don't want you here.'

He asked Moshe about it, 'Yes, they're Zionists. They believe the only hope the Jews have left is to return to the homeland.'

'So, they're religious?'

'Some of them, like the Mizrahi, believe they will be fulfilling God's plan, but some of them want to build socialism over there. We believe in building it here, where we live, not where we used to live centuries ago. We've got more in common with the Maskilim than the Zionists.'

'The Enlightenment? The ones who want to become non-Jews, *goyim*?'

Moshe smiled. 'Maybe it seems like that in Kawetchka. They believe our future is here, where we've lived for a long time, alongside the Poles and the Russians.'

'So, we try to become like them, in the hope that they will stop hating us?'

'Perhaps… For me, the hope is not 'for the Jews', it's for all of mankind. The sooner we recognise our common humanity, the sooner we can make a world that's fair and just.'

'All these posters suggest people like to focus on their differences.'

Moshe chuckled. 'I didn't say it was going to be easy'

They approached the Vistula river that runs through the city and arrived at the Town Square. For a young man from the shtetl, the city was overwhelming. Moshe explained that Leizar's lodgings were on the other side of the Castle Square, and they would drive down Jerusalem Avenue to arrive there. Leizar was impressed by the crowds of Hasidic Jews milling about in their long, black *kapotes* coats, and when they came upon the Royal Castle with its grand monuments, he was completely stunned.

Eventually they entered a dark, narrow street with high four-storey ramshackle buildings either side. On the ground floor were little shops with no frontage. Some had fruit and vegetables on display. Others simply offered wood for burning or cloth to use for coverings. There was a blacksmith and an artist sitting and painting. They stopped outside one of the shops which was empty. They had arrived.

Moshe showed Leizar the way to the back stone stairs which they had to climb to the third floor. There at the top was a small room with bare walls, a bed and a stove for cooking. In the corner was a sink with running water. It smelled a bit damp, and it did not look very welcoming.

Moshe explained that they had some bedding for him, and the stove would warm the room up. He suggested Leizar brought his things up and settled himself in. He told him he was invited to the home of Edvard Abromovski for dinner where he would meet some other members of the movement. Moshe would return in an hour.

Leizar sat on the hard bed after *shlepping* his few belongings up the stairs. There was some kindling wood next to the stove, so he started a fire in the grate which slowly began to warm the room, and he lit a candle which cast weird shadows on the walls. The ceiling was quite high, but the walls were bare stone and plaster, and the floor was bare boards. This was not what he had expected. His home in the shtetl had been fairly sparse, but there were always nice smells of Uma's cooking. Above all, there were always people around him and the thing that hit him hardest and very quickly was. loneliness. For the first time in his life, he was totally on his own. And it drove home the realisation that success or failure would be entirely down to his own efforts.

It was not long before Moshe returned. By the time he got to the top of the stairs with his large bulk, he was sweating profusely, breathing very heavily and mopping his brow with a handkerchief. He said he had left everything in the corridor on the ground floor and was worried it would get stolen, but Leizar feared if he let Moshe go back down, and then up again, he would have a heart attack. So, he told him to sit on the bed and he would fetch it.

Although he was delighted to find a thin mattress and sheets, and some rudimentary breakfast food; bread, jam and some apples, he had to make two journeys to shlep them up on his own. Nevertheless, he was grateful and thanked Moshe who by now had recovered. Together they went back down the stairs; it was quite dark and Leizar led the way, fearful of the treacherous staircase. He did not want Moshe's bulk to fall on him should he lose his footing. He was glad when they made it to the bottom.

They walked to Edvard's home in Leszno Street, which while it was not the smart part of town, was certainly better than where Leizar was living. They stopped at number 32 and Moshe rapped on the door, which was opened by a very tall and quite intimidating looking lady. She had grey hair tied up in tight pleat and a lined 'lived in' face. She was dressed entirely in black. She did not smile or greet them in any way. The door opened on to a tiny lobby and then directly onto the stairs. There was not room for two people to pass, so she simply turned and started up the stairs, indicating for Leizar to shut the door behind him.

At the top of the stairs, another small landing opened out on to a well-lit and welcoming room. Edvard stood, also dressed all in black. In his own environment, his white beard and black eyebrows seemed even more stark than when Leizar had first met him. He was smiling and held his arms out wide to greet both men with a hug, but in Leizar's case the hug enveloped him and lingered.

'Welcome, welcome to my home. It is lovely to meet you again, Leizar. I am so pleased you are here. Moshe told me what happened to your brother, we wish you long life, and we are very impressed that despite that, you decided to make the journey and join us today as arranged. We have assembled a few people for you to meet, but tonight is really to eat, drink and relax. You have had a long journey.'

Seated at the table were Moshe, a rather well-dressed man, and two other women, one wearing orthodox clothes and a young lady of around Leizar's age dressed in modern clothing. Leizar did a double take, he had never seen a woman dressed that way before.

'Thank you so much,' replied Leizar, 'But I am a little embarrassed. As you know I am sitting shiva for my brother, so would you mind if I could ask the men to be kind enough to join me in prayers before we start?'

Amongst orthodox Jews, women did not take part in prayers, and a proper ceremony could not take place because it required 10 men over the age of 13 called a *minyan*.

Edvard smiled, 'Of course, let me first introduce you. You have already met my wife, Zelda and you know Moshe of course, and this is his wife, Gitte.'

Strangely, considering Moshe's bulk, his wife was quite a small woman with long black hair which Leizar assumed was a *sheitel* wig, and she wore a shapeless long grey shift dress. But she had a pretty smile and a certain impish expression.

Edvard continued 'And this is Herschel Eisenbaum. He is a very good and trusted friend of myself and of the movement. Without Herel we would not be able to make the progress we have, and he owns the cigarette factory.'

Herschel was a serious looking man dressed in a tweed jacket, flannel trousers and an open necked shirt. Of all the men, he looked the most modern. He was tall and slim with black hair, greying at the temples and a trimmed moustache with no beard. His greying hair was receding, and he wore wire rimmed glasses. Leizar thought his gaze was intense as if he could see into his mind, but he smiled easily and Leizar liked him.

He had the air of a man who was very comfortable in his skin. His handshake was firm, 'Good to meet you at last, Leizar, I've heard a lot about you, and I know Edvard thinks highly of your work for the movement. Let me introduce my daughter, asked Chaya.'

She remained sitting and gave Leizar a demure smile, which made him feel a little awkward. She was quite lovely with long auburn hair which she wore swept back at the sides and in ringlets at the back. She wore a dress of violet colour with a tight bodice and bolero top. Leizar felt his face redden, and not knowing what else to do, he simply smiled back.

Herschel continued,' My wife passed away a year ago, and Edvard kindly invited Chaya tonight in her place.'

There was a small room off the dining room which Edvard clearly used as an office and Edvard suggested they conduct the prayers in there. Since they did not have the numbers for the full service, it did not take long. Leizar was able to say the memorial prayer for the departed, but not the traditional *kaddish*. He then sat on a low chair and the women joined the men in wishing him the customary long life.

When they returned to the table and sat down, Edvard said the brief Grace Before Meals and blessing over the wine. He then tore apart the *challah* bread and distributed a small piece to each which they ate together with a glass of wine, and Zelda uncovered the food. While they helped themselves to herring, egg and onion and gefilte fish, Edvard asked Leizar to go through the story of what had happened with his brother.

Leizar was embarrassed to go into detail with people he had just met, and if the truth were told, he was especially intimidated by the presence of Chaya. But he took a deep breath. 'Following your suggestion, I was on my way to speak to Dmitri Belakov, the Russian captain to seek his assistance. My family has known him a long time, he has been many times to our house and my father tutored his son. Imagine my shock when his first words were that he was going to arrest my brother. He locked him up, conducted a sham trial and sentenced him to death.'

Edvard stroked his beard thoughtfully. 'But what happened to him? We have worked with him before, I would never say he was completely trustworthy, but the arrangement seemed to work for both sides. As long as we paid him, he would assist and keep his mouth shut.'

Leizar explained what Dmitri had confided, that he was under investigation from the Russian High Command, who had heard that there was subversive work going on in Kawetchka, and they were watching closely. 'I think he needed a dramatic example to demonstrate his local power.'

'Do you think they were on to you and your brother, and maybe that is why he picked on your family?' Asked Chaya, who had been listening closely.

'I wouldn't be surprised,' replied Leizar.

'And then what you and your family went through,' said Chaya again.

Leizar went on to describe the fear and dread that his brother and the family had experienced and their efforts to prove his innocence with an alibi. 'It would have made no difference anyway, because justice was completely absent. They said the crime took place at midnight when we were all asleep. It is entirely possible that the crime never even took place.'

Herschel had not said much up to this point, 'I would like to hear about the trial, if it is not too much to bear,' he said.

Leizar went through it and there was much gasping and drawing of breath when he explained the wanton bias, trumped-up evidence and foregone conclusion. At the point when he described the passing of the 'verdict' and the sentence, Leizar was overcome and struggled hard not to break down in front them. So, they did not push him to go any further and the execution was left to their imagination.

They were all taken aback by the extraordinary injustice and brutality of the story. 'And this only happened yesterday?' said Chaya.

Leizar nodded trying to control his emotions. 'And yet you made the journey?'

Of course, he did not disclose the vow he had made to his brother, 'To be honest this was one of the hardest decisions of my life. I knew Moshe was returning to collect me today, and I had no way to contact him, and I was excited to have the opportunity to come to Warsaw and work for the Movement. Please understand there is nothing else that would have torn me away from my parents and family… at… this …time.'

His voice was broken, and a massive heart-rending sob broke forth from his chest.

'Leizar, Leizar,' this was Edvard, 'there is no need. You don't have to justify anything. You are here, and we are grateful.'

Leizar regained control, but with tears streaming down his face, and embarrassed in front of strangers, he managed slowly, 'I... loved... my brother... with all my heart.'

Gradually regaining some control, 'And I would never, *never* leave my family at this time... But your offer was... so generous, and I worried that if I did not come the opportunity may pass.'

Edvard, sitting next to Leizar, gripped his shoulder. 'Leizar, we understand what a wrench this was for you, and please understand, we really appreciate your sacrifice.'

He said that he had heard this sort of thing was going on throughout the country. The Russians felt threatened by the socialist movements that were springing up, and this was a show of strength to strike fear into the hearts of the proletariat, and especially the Jews.

Herschel was nodding along as the story unfolded 'Yes, things have not improved in Warsaw since the great pogrom in 1881', he said, 'and I am not surprised to hear that in the shtetls it has got worse. Workers in my factory tell of being spat at in the street and sometimes prevented from buying food in the shops. The poorest are treated the worst. And with your family you have suffered like this and yet you are still here tonight!'

Moshe's wife, Gitte however, was absolutely shocked, 'That poor man, and what of the family, your parents how they must be suffering. And you lost your younger brother...'

Her voice trailed off and what was left unsaid was 'How can you be here when your family suffered this terrible and tragic loss?'

Edvard intervened, 'Leizar has worked for the movement for some time, and he is an accomplished writer. It was pre-arranged that Moshe went to collect him today, and of course we knew nothing about this until Moshe arrived, it is indeed impressive that he still wanted to come. He will become a rising star in the movement.'

Leizar had composed himself, he regretted his show of emotion and felt the need to respond. 'Yes, you are right, the whole family is devastated, and my parents are racked with grief. It was a very hard decision to leave, but I have to tell you I am passionate about the need to effect change for Polish people. I hope through the Movement, I can have some small influence on it. I also made a promise to my brother before his.....'

His voice trailed off and he cleared his throat, 'He made me promise I would not miss this opportunity and he was as passionate about the Movement as I am.'

Herschel continued, 'There are many groups and movements growing up in Poland now. Have you heard of the Jewish Enlightenment, Haskalah? They are another group who are pushing for integration and assimilation of Jews. Also, the Musar movement who are concerned with the very future of Judaism. Then there are Poale Zion and Polish Mizrachi, both socialist Zionist groups. Edvard here is seen as a leading light and recognised by all these groups. I am proud to know him.'

The women cleared the plates, and Gitte returned with a pot of stew with potatoes and invited everyone to help themselves again. It was delicious and Leizar was starving – he took two helpings. His head was spinning. The journey, the little room of his own, two glasses of wine and this food. But he could not take his eyes off Chaya. She ate in a very feminine way, taking a little portion and eating slowly. She didn't say anything, but he thought he'd caught her stealing a glance or two at him.

Moshe, on the other hand, was taking very large portions and finishing them off as if it was the last meal ever. When the pot was empty, Moshe wiped his mouth and used his napkin to wipe a few dribbles of gravy from his beard and his waistcoat. He sighed as though he had just eaten the best meal of his life, then he turned to Leizar. 'My boy, it is due to this man (indicating Herschel) that we are able to support the work of the Movement and offer this position to you.' He turned back to Herschel. 'Since he will be working for you, perhaps you could tell our young prodigy a little of your background?'

Herschel had clearly noticed these little glances and he knew his daughter well. He also saw that her mannerisms had not escaped Leizar to whom he leaned closer and fixed him with his intense gaze. 'My family arrived in Warsaw from Amsterdam at the turn of the last century. My grandfather was a diamond trader, and the story is that he came for a visit, met my grandmother and stayed. It was my father who started us off in the tobacco business. Although smoking was very popular, he saw that the supply was patchy. He had a few people hand rolling cigarettes in the building we now occupy.

'Then came the partition and we ended up under Russian rule, but by then my father was supplying cigarettes and cigars to the Tsar. When I was old enough, he took me to the factory, and we started the business we have now. We have been protected from the pogroms ever since. I met and married Chaya's mother in 1865 and she was the softest-natured, most beautiful creature you could ever imagine, and she gave me the most treasured gift of my beautiful daughter. One day I will tell you how she met her death, but for now she is gone and my purpose in life is to assist in destroying the injustice and oppression of the *momzer* Russian rule.'

When Herschel spoke of his wife and daughter, he leaned even closer, and his eyes seemed to take on a needle-like focus which made Leizar feel very uncomfortable. He felt the need to comment, 'I am sorry to hear of the loss of your dear wife,' he said, 'and I am unimaginably grateful to you for giving me this opportunity. I promise I will not let you down.'

Herschel leaned back and although his face remined impassive, Leizar thought he had said the right thing. 'You will be employed at the cigarette factory where you will learn to be a cigarette maker. You need only work three days a week, so you will have plenty of time for writing and to look after the magazine.'

Leizar was nodding.

Herschel continued, 'You will be paid 90 zloty per week less your rent which is 40 zloty, so you should have sufficient for what you need. You will not receive any favours and you will need to work hard and master the work quickly. You start tomorrow. Moshe will show you tonight where the factory is. We start at 8.00am. Report to me and don't be late.'

Again, the plates were cleared, and Gitte returned with a large round plate on which was an enormous yellowish slab of cake. Gitte explained it was her home-made cheesecake fresh out of the oven. She gave Leizar a large slice which was still steaming, and it tasted like nothing he had ever had before. Made with three different types of cheese it contained dried fruit and it melted on his tongue. It was neither sweet nor savoury and he finished the lot.

After dinner they remained at the table and the conversation led by Edvard and Herschel surrounded serious aspects of the future of Judaism and the lot of Jews in Poland.

Leizar felt very tired after a long day and a more substantial meal than he was used to, but his ears pricked up when Edvard mentioned that Jews were finding ways to leave Poland, mostly bound for the US. He was too tired to probe that but tucked it away in his mind for a conversation at another time. Leizar also noticed that although Chaya did not say much, what contributions she made were shrewd and insightful.

He didn't wish to be rude to his hosts, but he really wanted to go to bed, so he was delighted when Moshe suggested they leave so that he could show Leizar where the factory was, and then drop him home. Whilst thanking everyone, he noticed that Gitte had not smiled all the evening and still had a stern face now. He wondered if he had upset her somehow and made a mental note to speak to Edvard about it when he could.

Fortunately, the factory was only a ten-minute walk away and then another thirty minutes to return to his room. Leizar was relieved when he arrived. He hauled himself up the stairs and felt he had never been so tired. After lighting a candle, he gratefully collapsed onto the bed. However, although he only wanted to sleep, he could not help revisiting the events of the day. And what a day it had been!

It seemed an age ago, that he left his parents and his family mourning the dreadful loss of his brother. That thought came flooding back to him and brought tears to his eyes once again. How he wished he could speak to his father and mother and share the pain. Instead, he had to wonder how they were coping with it, and he suddenly felt very lonely, realising that this pain he felt in his heart would have to be borne by himself alone. But it reinforced his determination to fulfil the promise he had made to Mendel and work hard on everything they had agreed upon.

He turned over the experiences of the day. There was the long journey with Moshe, and upon his arrival in Warsaw so many new experiences in such a short time. He had never been in a big city, and he felt overawed by the scale of it. The grand buildings and the crowds of people. Mostly in his life, Leizar had been surrounded by Jewish people a lot like him, or a few Russian soldiers. In the shtetl, he knew almost everyone, and the place was full of gossip, but he was immediately struck by the different atmosphere in the city, with its more cosmopolitan population. He realised the great irony of a city like this was that you could be very alone in its crowds, more alone than anywhere else, and the thought made him shiver. This was how he was going to have to live.

As he looked around his room, he became aware how unwelcoming it really was, and he resolved to personalise it as soon as he had some money. He had to get used to the idea that he could not just walk out and chat to his family or friends. He also needed some writing materials and a desk.

Then there was the whole evening at the Abromovski home. They had certainly made him very welcome. He thought about how they lived. Their flat above the shop was not large, but adequate for two people. The ceiling was high, and the walls were bare. There was a rug on the floor and the furniture was simple wood. It was the home of someone who was not poor in the sense that his family was poor, but certainly not the home of someone well off. The people he had met were interesting.

Edvard was clearly an observant Jew and an intellectual. Leizar was sure he would learn a lot from him, but he was curious about his wife, Gitte who seemed so stern, but such a good cook. Moshe and his wife seemed like very nice, warm people. Leizar was just surprised that such a large man should have such a small wife. It seemed a mismatch.

Herschel was going to be his boss and although he had an aura of authority, Leizar had warmed to him. He seemed the least observant Jew and the most modern man in the room, and clearly as a business owner he was better off than the others.

But his daughter Chaya... Well, Leizar could not get her out of his mind, and he was anxious to meet her again. Despite the implied warning contained in Herschel's words, he thought he would really like to talk to her one to one. She seemed a rare combination of beauty and intelligence. He wondered if he would see her again at the factory.

Eventually, thinking of this, he did finally drift off to sleep.

Chapter 18

Starting work in Warsaw

Leizar was used to rising early and he awoke at 6.00am. He lay there for a while surprised to have slept so well considering the events of yesterday. He felt a pain in the pit of his stomach when he thought about the death of his brother, and he did not want to let go of the thought for fear he was being disloyal and dismissing it too quickly. However, he forced himself to think about the possibilities today might bring, and he jumped out of bed and splashed some water on his face.

He ate some of the bread and jam that Moshe had left and was surprised to find a bottle of water alongside. Leizar had been used to drawing water from the well, but this bottle appeared to be from a factory. Anyway, he was grateful, and he drank it, making a mental note that one of his first purchases would be facilities to make tea.

Feeling a lot better, he got dressed and started to walk to the factory. The streets were quite wide, allowing the watery sun to cast shadows without containing much warmth. But he felt optimistic about the day ahead of him. There were already quite a lot of people and carriages about. Warsaw woke up early. He had plenty of time, and he paused to look in at the shops and stalls on the way. He added to his shopping list as he went. Fresh fruit, cooking utensils, some pictures for the walls, crockery, and above all, some new clothes. He only had the one pair of trousers and a couple of long shirts. Fortunately, he had brought changes of undergarments.

He arrived at 7.45am and found the factory doors open and the place already operating. The factory was huge with bare cracked walls and a very high ceiling. There were workbenches in rows, 20 to a row and five rows, so a hundred benches. On the far side were large wire containers full of tobacco, the smell of which pervaded everything. Herschel was in a blue overall walking down the rows of benches. He would stop and pull a tray of paper from one, tidy up and wipe the surface of another. Only a few of the benches were occupied. He spotted Leizar.

'Good morning, come over here,' he shouted.

As Leizar was walking toward him, he indicated toward an old man who was sitting and working away. 'This is Avram. He has worked here in the factory for many years, and he is the fastest and most experienced cigarette maker you could find.'

Avram looked up at Leizar and just nodded. Leizar was struck by his dark yellowy brown face which was deeply wrinkled and an almost bald head except for a small patch of longish grey hair growing right out of the top of his head. His hands were yellowy brown and wizened, but his fingers were working away very fast. Leizar thought the long piece of hair and the speed of his fingers made him look like a silver-grey squirrel. A completed cigarette appeared perfect in his hands as if by magic.

'Avram will show you how it's done. You spend a couple of hours watching him and then we will give you a bench of your own,' and with that, Herschel walked away to greet people who were beginning to arrive. The newcomers went quickly over to a bench, took off their coats and started work.

Leizar turned his attention back to Avram. 'Please will you do one slowly so I can see it?' he asked.

Avram just nodded. The paper was on a roll beside him, he had a wooden stick which he used to measure how much paper he needed. The roller had a blade against which he cut the paper cleanly.

He placed the paper on the bench and took some tobacco from the bin beside him which he spread on the paper. He then worked what Leizar thought was magic, kneading the tobacco inside the paper and gradually rolling the paper up as he did so. When he had done the cigarette looked perfect. He licked the edge of the paper and stuck it down and then used a clipper to nip the tobacco strands at each end and then handed it to Leizar who was astonished. The cigarette was firm, tightly packed, with no loose ends and Avram showed that you could stand it on its end, and it would not fall over. The operation had taken only a minute or so and Avram had been working very slowly to show how it was done.

Avram's face split into a wide grin at the look of astonishment on Leizar's face. 'You have a try,' he said.

And he stood to let Leizar sit down. He went through the simple procedure, but of course, he ended up with an object that looked like something a child would do. Fat, misshapen and lumpy with the tobacco falling out. Leizar could see the skill was in the kneading of the tobacco at the same time as rolling.

Avram smiled again and took it from him. 'Ok to start, you use this,' and he brought out a small hand-rolling machine. 'You put in the paper like this, then the tobacco,' which he again kneaded and spread evenly, 'then you roll like this almost to the end. Lick the paper and finish.' He took out another perfect cigarette, snipped the ends and it was as good as the first, although to be fair, not quite as quick.

Herschel came over. 'You sit at this bench and practise. Show each one you make to Avram until you get the hang of it. I need you to make 50 cigarettes per hour. You work from 8am to 12.30pm and then you have a break half an hour for lunch. You get sandwiches and a few other things from the canteen through that door, Avram will show you. Then you work from 1pm until 6pm. You can get as much tea as you like and drink it on the bench.'

It didn't take Leizar long to work out that he was required to make 475 per day, and the other workers were quicker. All of the benches were full now. So, if a hundred workers were making 475 cigarettes per person, per day, that was at least 40,000 per day allowing for wastage. Leizar could see why Herschel was quite well off. He continued to practise, handing each one to Avram, and by the end of the day, he was making cigarettes which, whilst not as perfect as Avram's, would certainly pass for sale. With the making of them more or less mastered, the next challenge was to start making them more quickly.

At six in the evening, everything stopped. Work was finished for the day, and this particular day was Shabbas. Leizar was hungry and started to wonder how he was going to eat. He had no money. Herschel was standing by the door saying goodnight and *Git Shabbas* to each of his workers as they filed past him. He pulled Leizar to one side. 'Not a bad day, Leizar,' he said, 'Avram tells me you catch on quickly and you can make reasonable cigarettes after one day. Good. So, tomorrow is *Shabbas* and the factory is closed. I am not religious, but we must have respect for the religion and those who are. I would like you to attend the *Shabbas* service at the shul with me tonight. I can introduce you to a lot of people. Afterwards, I would like to invite you to a *Shabbas* evening meal at my house. So, wait here until everyone has left, and we will go together. Leizar was both grateful and relieved. He knew he would get a meal, and he also had an excited feeling in his stomach at the thought of meeting Chaya again.

The synagogue was only a short walk from the factory. It was a very impressive building and large enough inside to hold around 1,000 people. Although Leizar was wearing his cap, so his head was covered as required, the head coverings among the men were either *shtrimmels*, the round fur trimmed hat worn by the *hasids*, or the *cuppel, kippah or yarmalka* skullcap. Herschel took two *kippahs* from a box. The shul was already packed, men were on the ground floor and women were separated upstairs, and Herschel had reserved seats at the front. As they walked down the central aisle, many people wished him *git shabbas,* he was obviously well known. Leizar was familiar, of course, with the service, which was conducted entirely in Hebrew, but he was overwhelmed by the size of the place and the numbers of people. Also, by the *bimah,* the raised platform on which stood several rabbis, dressed entirely in white standing in front of the Ark containing the Torah scrolls.

The service lasted about two hours, and by the end, Leizar was starving. But Herschel wanted to introduce him to some of the men. He met owners of local shops and businesses, and importantly, Yitshok Peretz a name Leizar had heard of. He was a famous Jewish writer and had written some important works. Herschel explained that Yitshok was the driver of the publications the Movement put out, and he would be Leizar's mentor in Warsaw. Yitzkok suggested Leizar came to the office tomorrow and they could have a chat about how they could work together. Leizar was very impressed.

A short while later they arrived at Herschel's house. It was on the other side of the river and overlooked it. Leizar expected something quite grand, and he was a bit disappointed really. The house was in a better part of Warsaw, but it was nothing special. Just a terraced building with three storeys alongside many properties that looked more or less the same. In fact, the outside was in need of some repair and painting.

However, once through the front door there was a small hallway with a crystal chandelier. The only place Leizar had ever seen a chandelier before was the synagogue he'd just visited. Another doorway opened into a lounge with settees and an easy chair in front of a fire. The room was bright and warm and quite unlike the general atmosphere of Warsaw, which was rather grey. And best of all, seated beside the fire was Chaya. She looked even more lovely with her long hair completely down over her shoulders and just a simple band on top. She wore a long gown cinched at her tiny waist. She rose and smiled as they walked in.

She held her hand out to Leizar, 'Lovely to meet you again,' she said, and then rather took Leizar aback by adding, 'I don't know if you are religious, if so, I will not be offended if you don't wish to shake hands.' Leizar felt very awkward, not knowing what to say, so he simply took her hand in his and smiled.

He followed Herschel into the kitchen where they both washed their hands at the butler sink in the corner. There were two women working there and the air was full of the most delicious smells which almost made Leizar faint. 'Come and have a drink before we start,' said Herschel.

They returned to the lounge and Herschel poured two glasses of schnapps explaining that Chaya did not drink, before handing her a bottle of water. This prompted Leizar to ask about the water. It was the same as the one Moshe had left for him.

Herschel indicated for them to sit down, and he spread his legs out and leaned back comfortably. 'Warsaw has always had a problem to find sufficient drinking water. A few years ago, in 1886, a man called William Lindley devised a system to filter the water. It was brilliant, involving a group of slow sand filters, clean water tank, pump depot and a water tower. This system could filter as much drinking water as we want. It is bottled and distributed to all who need it, and it is funded by a local businessman.'

Leizar must have shown his surprise because Chaya said, 'Leizar, there will be many things in the city that will surprise you coming as you do, from a small shtetl. Perhaps when you have settled down, you may be able to spare a little time for me to show you around.'

This knocked Leizar back. She seemed awfully forward and the idea of being shown around the city by this beautiful woman was to his mind extraordinary. Of course, there would be a chaperone.

They went through yet another door to the dining room where the table was laid out with hors d'oeuvres. 'Leizar,' said Herschel, 'Let me be very blunt. Chaya and I are not very religious, and so we light the candles on Friday nights, and we have a *shabbas* meal, but unless we are with others who are observant, we don't really do the rest of the ritual. Would you be offended if that was the case tonight?'

'Of course not!' Leizar could hardly get the words out quickly enough. He was so hungry, and the sight of the food was making it worse. The last thing he wanted was to wait while prayers were recited.

Herschel indicated that they should help themselves, and Leizar feared he had taken too much, especially when the cook brought in the soup. It was tomato soup with rice, and it was delicious, but quite filling. That was followed by roast chicken with potatoes, and shredded vegetables, and then a dessert called Napoleonka, a sort of cream pastry with more cream on top. They also had a very good red wine.

Halfway through Herschel put down his fork saying that he was full and could not finish. Leizar was grateful. By now, he felt if he ate any more, he would explode, especially as he noticed that Chaya only had small portions of everything and took only tiny mouthfuls at a time.

They retired back into the lounge. Herschel sat in the easy chair, and Leizar and Chaya sat at either end of the settee. Leizar felt wonderful. His belly was full, he was warm and in lovely surroundings with welcoming people. The cook brought in a bottle of something called Krupnik with some glasses. She poured a small glass for each of them. It tasted like nectar. Sweet and yet with a slight warming sensation as he swallowed. Leizar looked at the bottle and Herschel explained that it was a traditional sweet alcoholic drink similar to a liqueur. It was based on vodka and honey.

'So, let us talk a little bit of business,' he continued. 'You will report to Yitshok Perez on Sunday at the office and discuss how you will work together. On Monday, Tuesday and Wednesday, you report to the factory where you will work at improving your rolling speeds under the supervision of Avram. Remember I need 50 per hour from you. Thursday and Friday, you work with Yitshok and I expect you will be doing some writing in the evenings as well. Edvard will also supervise your work.

So, you are going to be busy. I know that you have no money, and you need things, so here is 50 zloty. It is the equivalent of your weekly wage less your rent. It is not a gift, and you will always owe me this money, but you will only be required to pay it back if you leave.'

Leizar did not wish to overstay his welcome, so he said he thought he could find his own way back to his room. Herschel said that was fine and he would ask Moshe to come and show him to Yitshok's office on Sunday morning at nine. He was offered and he took again, the soft hand of Chaya and shook hands firmly with Herschel. He thanked him profusely for all the help and for the wonderful *shabbas* dinner. 'Don't mention it,' said Herschel, 'I am getting something out of it too, and I have a feeling you are going to do a lot of good here.'

For the second night, Leizar walked back to his room with a warm full comfortable feeling.

The next day, Saturday was *shabbas*, so Leizar rose a little later than usual. Although religious Jews did not do anything other than pray on Shabbas, Leizar used the day to buy food and provisions he needed. He made lunch and spent the afternoon trying to make his room into some sort of home. By the end of the day, he was tired, and after a little reading, he went to bed and slept soundly.

CHAPTER 19

WRITING WITH YITSHOK

Moshe arrived at 8.30am, a little earlier than Leizar expected, but he was up and ready to go. Moshe suggested they stop and get some tea on the way. Moshe knew a tea shop where they also had good pastries. Leizar felt bolder with some cash in his pocket and readily agreed.

When they were sitting down, Moshe leaned a little closer to Leizar. 'A few things you should know,' he said quietly. 'Herschel is a very important man in the community, but he does not want the gentiles or the Russians to know it. That's why his house looks so modest from the outside. He is a philanthropist, and he uses his income from the factory to fund projects. He pays for the office where you are going, and he told you about the water purification? He pays for the research and the upkeep.

He is a Zionist, but not a religious Jew, even though he donates to the synagogue. His wife was very ill, and he nursed her for a long time. She finally passed away a year ago. She was a beautiful and wonderful woman, and he misses her a lot. You see Chaya? It is like looking at a younger version of Breindel. Chaya is his most precious possession, and he dotes on her. Be very careful! I saw the way you were looking at each other, and so did everyone else.'

Leizar was taken aback, he didn't realise it was so transparent.

'Herschel will be a very good friend, but he would be a terrible enemy. He seems to like you but take this advice seriously.'

Leizar was certainly listening carefully, he was grateful to find out more about the people he had only recently met, but who it seemed, would be influential in his life. 'What about Edvard?' He asked.

'Well, everything he told you when you first met him is true. He is well known here in Warsaw, and with various socialist movements throughout Poland and Russia. He is a philosopher and a psychologist with a brilliant mind. He has written important books which you would do well to read. Apart from his political philosophy, he is prolific in the field of experimental psychology, especially the subconscious mind. He is brilliant, Leizar.'

'Why is his wife so stern?' said Leizar, 'She made us very welcome, and we had a wonderful dinner, but I don't think she ever smiled.'

'Edvard and Gitte have no children and as Edvard says, that is not their fault, it is God's fault. They tried for a long time. Gitte was pregnant on two occasions and miscarried at a late stage. A few years ago, she delivered a beautiful baby boy. They were ecstatic, and she nursed the child for more than one month. They woke up one morning and the child was dead. Since then, she has not smiled much. However, don't be misled, she is a good soul, a *gutte neshuma.*

'And what about Yitshok? '

'Ahh! You are so lucky. He is a wonderful man. Not only a writer, a lawyer too, but they took away his licence to practice law because of his socialist views. He has a Jewish school named after him here. The office is on Jerozolimskie Street, across the river from here. He calls it a literary hub, and he has inspired some great writers like Sholem Asch, Pinkhas Kaganovitch and Dovid Pinski. Maybe you will be the next one.'

They finished their tea, and with great anticipation, Leizar followed Moshe again, walking to meet with Yitshok.

They arrived at a narrow street between buildings either side that consisted mainly of three storeys of apartments. Due to the height of the buildings, the street was overshadowed. Moshe knocked on one of the doors, and they waited for a while with no reply. He knocked again and after a while it was opened by man in his late forties with almost white hair, a round face with a moustache that turned up at the ends. He wore a rather wrinkled, grey three-piece suit with a wing-collared shirt and a tie. His eyes were wide, and he did not smile. 'Shalom Moshe, and you must be Leizar. I've heard a lot about you.'

They entered a rather dingy room with two desks and a window looking out on the street. It smelled of stale ink. 'Come sit and we will talk,' he said.

But Moshe remained where he stood, 'Yitshok, I will not stay, I have to return to work, and I don't think you need me anyway. So, I will leave now.' Yitshok nodded and Leizar thanked Moshe and said he could find his own way back.

Yitshok leaned back in his chair, 'Well young man, this is a bit different from the shtetl, no?' When Leizar nodded, he continued. 'Here we do a lot of writing and publishing. Next door we have typesetting, printing and binding. I know you are here to work on Edvard's magazine, but I will explain a little more. It's not just politics. I am concerned with moral dilemmas, psychological and social conflicts. Jew against gentile, Western versus Jewish views of beauty. I am writing a book now called the Mad Talmudist about a man who is torn between physical, spiritual and intellectual urges; a critique of a husband who becomes a public benefactor at the expense of his wife. What do you think of that?'

Leizar felt the urge to call him sir, but Yitshok immediately disabused him of it. 'Well, where I come from such radical thinking would not be permitted. In fact, because of the Russian yoke that the poor have borne for so long, most have become completely submissive. It is as though they have their foot on our throats all the time.'

And he proceeded to tell Yitshok what had happened to his brother. Yitshok listened intently. His face a picture of concentration although without any expression. When Leizar had completed the story, Yitshok continued to gaze at him with the same expression, saying nothing for a while.

'I am very sorry for you and your family,' he said at last, 'And I wish you long life. But there is so much we must change about the world.'

'Yes,' said Leizar, 'I have never aired my thoughts, but I have often felt that it is time someone addressed the plight of Jewish women. They are allowed no ambitions, and are required to be subservient, almost second class to men.'

'Yes, yes!' exclaimed Yitshok. 'I can see you have a mind, and you can think. I want to broaden it and we can do some good work together. We must push the boundaries.'

The two got on very well and Leizar was excited by Yitshok's keen, challenging mind. He could not wait to work with this man. Yitshók showed him the printing room and introduced the two people who ran it. They had some tea, exchanged further views and talked for a long time. Eventually, Yitshok leaned back in his chair again, 'Well, my boy I think we will get along. I understand I will not see you again until Thursday next week because you have to earn your keep at the cigarette factory. Think about what we have said here today. I want to do much more with you than just a magazine about socialism. We must lead and enlighten those with closed minds. Now you go home, have a sleep and work out how you can make cigarettes so fast that we can get more time together.'

On the way back, Leizar passed a little book shop, selling second-hand books. Back in the shtetl, the only books he came by were those given to him occasionally, or passed round from one person to another. But he was an avid reader and could not resist going in to have a look. He was surprised to find at the bottom of a pile, a rather worn book entitled *Sipurim be-shir ve-shirim shonim* (Stories in Verse and Selected Poems) by Yitshok L Peretz. Needless to say, he purchased it and hurried back, anxious to start reading.

CHAPTER 20

CHAYA

When he arrived at his room, Leizar cooked up some of the rice and vegetables he had bought and sat down at his desk. He spent two hours reading Yitshok's book and turning things over in his mind. Life seemed to be moving so quickly in Warsaw, and he reminded himself that his primary aim was to fulfil the promise he had made to his brother to find a way to a better life for his family. That reminded him that it was only a few days since his death and the funeral would have taken place. He lit another candle and said some memorial prayers. That in turn, made him homesick for the first time, and he started to think about his parents and his family and how he missed them. He resolved that he would ask Moshe when it would be reasonable to return for a visit, and if Moshe would take him?

He was not worried about the work in the factory, he knew he would easily meet Herschel's expectations, and although he was really not interested in the formality of the religion, he could see that the synagogue would be a good place to meet people and maybe find out more about emigration.

Then his thoughts turned to Chaya. He couldn't wait to meet her again and spend some time with her. She had suggested she could show him around Warsaw. Did she mean it? Would her father allow it? He had a glass of schnapps, went to bed and drifted off to sleep.

Her lips were soft and moist against his own. He could feel her breasts heaving as their bodies interlaced, her nipples hard against him. She reached for his sex, and he held her down and prepared to plunge into her. But his seed exploded too soon, and he felt his own wetness. He looked up; she had no face, just blank skin where her face should be. He had to get away, get away from her, what was she doing to him? But now she held him down and she was immensely strong, he could not move. She put her nothing face close to his. 'Where is your brother? Did you kill him? Now you are mine.'

Leizar awoke to find he had truly exploded. This was the first time this had happened to him, and although he knew what the wetness was, he had never seen it before. He jumped out of bed and lit the candle. His penis was red and throbbing and still quite hard. He was shaking and frightened from the dream.

His member still ached somewhat, and a quick look confirmed what had actually happened. He thought about it. Clearly this was to do with his sexual attraction to Chaya. He felt guilty that he must have been subconsciously thinking about her in that way. He must exercise self-control. The Rabbis taught that lust outside of marriage is an emotion that must be controlled. It cannot lead to procreation. But she was beautiful and intelligent and unlike any woman he had ever met. The words of Moshe returned to him: 'She is Herschel's most treasured possession. Be very careful, she has broken many hearts. Take this advice seriously!'

His work at the factory went well, and very quickly Avrom did not need to supervise him, and he was exceeding 500 per day. There was an incentivisation system, Avrom explained. If any operative hit 550 per day, they would receive a cash bonus of 5 zloty for each day. If they hit 600, there would be a further five zloty, and on the rare occasion that anyone hit 650, there would be a bonus of ten zloty. Nobody had ever exceeded 650. But it was not long before Leizar was making an extra fifteen zloty per week for regularly hitting 550 per day.

He started going to shul on Friday nights and Saturday mornings, where he became quite friendly with the Rabbi and the shul officers. Because of his retentive memory, he was quite good at reading ancient Hebrew and he started to read up on the Torah portion to be performed for the next Shabbas. He let the Rabbi know that if they needed, he could lead the congregation, chanting the *leining* from the Torah.

This is considered quite a feat and to be asked to do it is considered a *mitzvah* blessing. It has to be done very accurately and any mistake must be corrected immediately. Very few men in any community are able to do it, and the Rabbi was delighted. After he had tested Leizar's competence, he invited him to be *baal korei* (expert Torah reader), and he was able to do that on many Saturday mornings when there was no bar mitzvah. On those days of course, the bar mitzvah boy himself was taught how to do his particular portion. There were another two *baal korei* in the community, but they were old men, and they were delighted to have a young man do it.

The dream kept coming back to Leizar. He found himself thinking about it from time to time, and when he did, it often caused an embarrassing, unwanted erection. He desperately wanted to see Chaya again, but was there something wrong with him? Why was this happening? After a few days of worry, the dream had not recurred, and he felt more in control.

So eventually, he asked Moshe about Chaya. 'She offered to show me around Warsaw,' he said. 'Do you think that would be permissible, and how should I go about it? I don't want to offend Herschel.'

Moshe smiled, 'Well, first of all I know she has been speaking about you, and enquiring as to how you are getting on, and Herschel knows this. Not much gets past him. So, it will not be a surprise if you follow that up. Chaya is a very emancipated young woman, and Herschel is much more open minded about his daughter than most Jewish men. So why don't you just call round there and make arrangements?'

Although this was of course, music to Leizar's ears, he was nevertheless filled with apprehension. Did Moshe really mean he should meet with Chaya without a chaperone? And not even with an introduction from a *shiddach macher*? This was unheard of throughout the whole of Leizar's life.

He resolved to speak to Herschel first to make sure he would not be out of line, and he did not want to bring up such a personal matter at the factory, so he waited until *shabbas* at the synagogue. At the end of the service, he was able to draw Herschel aside and ask his permission to approach Chaya. 'Of course, my boy! But just let me tell you that Chaya is not short of admirers, and if she is not interested, she will let you know.'

So, on Sunday after working at the office, he stopped by at their home. Chaya opened the door and smiled broadly when she saw him. He was invited in for tea, and Herschel, knowing why Leizar was there, made himself scarce. Leizar did not know how to go about this, and he was mightily embarrassed. Chaya brought in tea, and they sat again at either end of the sofa. Leizar stood up as if he was about to make a speech. His palms were sweaty, and he started to stutter, something he had never done before. 'I, I, I w-w-was just w-w-wondering, Chaya, if y-you would, would c-consider.'

Chaya, who may have been tipped off by her father, interjected, 'Oh for goodness' sake, Leizar, do you want to take me up on my offer to show you round Warsaw?'

'Yes! Yes!' he exclaimed with relief and sat down heavily.

Chaya suggested they meet next Saturday. As it would be *shabbas*, they could walk with no worry about being home by a certain time.

Of course, Leizar couldn't wait for Saturday, and on that morning, he spent much time shaving and putting on his new breeches, tweed jacket and cap. He wanted to look his absolute best. Walking out with this beautiful woman, he felt nothing could be better in the world, even though they got a few tuts when passing older Jewish women who, seeing Chaya with a young man, and without a *sheitel* wig, realised they were not married.

They walked and talked and even when they had nothing to say, the silence was shared and comfortable. First, she showed him King Sigismund's column with the Royal Castle opposite. They passed many statues and monuments and Chaya seemed to know them all. They explored the narrow-cobbled streets, visiting the Stone Steps which rose so high you felt on top of the world, the Palace on the Isle built by the last king of Poland, and in the evening, they stopped at the Old Town Market Square with the famous mermaid in the middle. They sat on a stone wall, and Chaya told Leizar about the legend.

'A long time ago, when Warsaw was a fishing village, the sea and the river were inhabited by golden-haired mermaids. One day, one of them set off from the Baltic to the south. She swam along the Vistula, and when she got tired, she decided to rest on the sandy bank of the river at the foot of today's Old Town.'

Leizar was captivated. He had to keep reminding himself to listen to her story, and not make it too obvious.

'There the mermaid would sing a beautiful song about the Vistula. The animals listened to her singing: the beavers raised their snouts from their burrows, and the cormorants sat on drifting logs. Leizar, whatever is the matter? You seem miles away. This is a great legend of Warsaw, would you prefer not to hear it?' Her voice contained a genuine note of irritation.

'Oh no! I am so sorry, Chaya. It was the sound of your voice and just sitting here with you.' His voice had become a little breathless. 'I am listening I promise, please continue.'

Chaya frowned and looked away, and he cursed himself for getting distracted. She pursed her lips, paused and turned to him. 'Alright, but if someone's bothering to tell you something, then do them the honour of paying attention,' she said, quite sharply.

'One day, a greedy merchant decided to get rich on her beautiful voice by putting her on display at fairs. He tricked her, kidnapped and imprisoned her in a wooden chest. The mermaid's crying was heard by the young son of a fisherman who with his friends, released her and punished the evil merchant severely. The joyous mermaid, thankful for being free again, pledged to the fishermen that she would always guard them and their village.'

Leizar clapped, 'What a lovely story! Thank you.'

But Chaya looked away again. They continued walking, but the atmosphere between them seemed to have changed.

Eventually, when they got hungry, she took him to a street where there were two kosher restaurants. She explained that you had to know they were Jewish and kosher, because they were targets for attacks from anti-Semites, so they did not advertise it. It was warm inside, and the owner, a very large lady with long curly hair and a massive smile clearly knew Chaya quite well. 'Chaya, *shalom aleichem*, lovely to see you, how is your father?' And then, with barely a pause, but a meaningful inflexion in her voice, she added: 'And *who* is this lovely young man?'

'Hello Batya, aleichem shalom, it's lovely to see you too. My father is well, thank you and this is my new friend, Leizar.'

'Oy, you are a *friend* of Chaya?' The emphasis was obvious. 'You are a lucky man. And you, Chaya, are also lucky to have this young man for your *friend*.' She winked at Leizar. 'Come, I have a wonderful wine for you, drink and enjoy.'

As she walked away, Leizar and Chaya looked at each other, and both burst out laughing at Batya's enthusiastic welcome. Whatever ice had formed between them, it was well and truly broken now.

They sat and Batya brought bread, herring, soup and then a main course of stewed lamb. It all came without asking and Chaya explained, 'There is no menu here. In this place everyone has the same meal, and it's different every day.'

Leizar looked embarrassed, 'I'm sorry Chaya, you'll think me foolish, but I come from the shtetl. I don't know... what is a menu?'

'Oh, you lovely boy! Of course, I keep forgetting. Just eat and enjoy, Batya's cooking is always delicious.'

While they sat, they talked, and Leizar found that Chaya was not only beautiful, but she had a quick and bright mind, with strong opinions. They found they had a lot in common and there was one area where their views were very close. They were both convinced that the rule of iron exerted by Tzar Nicholas II could not continue and that if the people could bind together, there would come a day when change was possible. After dinner, they walked back to the Eisenbaum house, where Leizar once again became tongue tied and unsure.

Stuttering, he thanked Chaya for a lovely day. He was again taken aback when he became the lucky recipient of a little kiss on the cheek. 'Thank you, Leizar. I have had a wonderful time and enjoyed your company. I would like to see you again soon.' And with that she turned and entered the house.

Leizar stood at the doorway for a few minutes, really quite stunned, before he slowly turned and made his way home. He was besotted with Chaya, and it seemed she quite liked him. How could he be that lucky? The words of Moshe were again ringing in his ears. 'Be very careful. Take this advice seriously!'

Chapter 21

Visit home

Leizar had been making very good progress at work. His factory speeds were nearly on a par with Avram and with the bonuses, he had been able to save some money. Yitshok had given him projects for the magazine, which he had enjoyed. The system they adopted is that one or other of them would make a controversial statement and they would argue about it. When the argument ran out, Leizar's job was to present that argument in written form, reflecting either a consensus view – if they could reach one, and if not, then both sides of the argument.

The first such subject was 'A home for Jews where everyone is equal...'

'Since the diaspora, Jews have continued to be distributed over many parts of the world. And there is no shortage of prominent Jews who believe it is time for a Jewish country, and that the land of Israel is the obvious place, a return of the Jews to the Holy Land. Theodore Herzl in his book Der Judenstaat argues this very eloquently, and perhaps his connections with the Ottoman court may bear some fruit.

Zionists believe the land of Israel should be delineated again as the Jewish state, but could that happen? – what is the incentive for the Ottomans? - and could it be recognised by the world?

Israel is placed in the heart of the warring Muslim nations, so surely this is not the ideal location for such a state, and bearing in mind that throughout history, Jews have been persecuted wherever they go, maybe it is not such a good idea to have them all together in one target place for the persecutors to ravage?

But we want to address another aspect of such an event, should it happen.

In the new Jewish state, should there be a system of government to ensure the terrible inequalities of Eastern Europe could never arise? And should all Jews be required to live there? . . . .'

The article continued presenting arguments for and against the creation of such a state, whether it was possible, and how it should be run, reflecting the differing views of Leizar and Yitshok. It provoked a great deal of interest and response from readers, and Leizar enjoyed his role in it.

Despite all the work, Leizar was terribly homesick, so when Herschel suggested that he could arrange for a carriage to take him back to Kawetchka and pick him up again the next day, it took him by surprise. Why would Herschel do such a thing? Did Chaya have a hand in it, he wondered? He accepted gratefully, and the prospect certainly lifted his spirits.

'After all,' said Herschel, 'the timing and manner of your departure must have left you all wondering what has happened, so take a couple of days off. The carriage will collect you tomorrow morning.'

Leizar was so excited at the prospect of seeing his family that he didn't sleep well that night, in addition to which, the dream re-occurred several times, interrupting his sleep whenever he had dropped off, so he was a little bleary-eyed when they departed early next morning.

Ryfke started to cry immediately he walked through the door. She was as usual, busy in the kitchen, but she could see the front door. She dropped what she was doing and Leizar had to go to her quickly lest she should fall. 'Oy, my *tuttele* Leizar, what a wonderful surprise.'

And they hugged each other tight while tears of joy rolled down Ryfke's face. 'Uma, I have missed you so much, sit down a while, I will make a glass tea. I am here until tomorrow, so we have time. I have so much to tell you.'

'Yes, yes, my darling boy,' she said, and she sitting down quite heavily. 'I must go to the school and tell your father.'

'Don't worry Uma, you sit a while and drink some tea. I will go to the school and see Upa and the children.' He put the tea on the table and gave her another hug, 'I will return very soon.'

When Leizar appeared at the door of his classroom, Zelman's face was a picture. He went through all the emotions, from surprise and shock to overwhelming delight. He broke off his lesson and hugged his son so close Leizar could hardly breathe. But eventually he said, 'I am in the middle of a lesson here, go back home and I will gather up Duvid, Marcia and little Moshe and be home early. Have you returned to us forever?' he asked, hopefully.

Leizar explained that this was a short overnight visit and Zelman's face dropped, but Leizar said he couldn't wait to tell Zelman all his news.

He didn't have long to wait at home before they all arrived. The children ran in first and there was lots of hugging and kissing and Ryfke had something delicious cooking in the kitchen. Eventually Zelman told Marcia to take her little brother and run to tell all the uncles and aunts and the cousin, that Leizar was visiting, and they could come after dinner this evening. Ryfke said she would make some little *noshes* to eat.

So, they all sat with tea and kichels and Leizar commented on how grown-up his brother Duvid was. He seemed to have got taller in the six weeks since he'd last seen him. 'Yes, said Zelman, 'He is nearly 13. We are planning his bar mitzvah in December. You must note the date.'

They were all bursting to hear about Leizar's adventures in the city. So, he ran through the whole story: the factory work, his one-room flat and how he had deco-rated it, Herschel, Yitshok, Edvard, the work he was doing for the movement and how he had been welcomed by almost everybody. 'But how do you live, who cooks your food?' said Ryfke.

'Uma, I get paid, and because I am so fast, I get bonuses too. I buy my food and I cook it myself.'

Ryfke was astonished, 'Oy! You cook your own food? It has come to that?'

Leizar continued, 'You have to understand life is different in the city. Look at my clothes. I buy them in a shop that only sells clothes for men. I buy food from special shops that sell different things. One sells fruit, one sells meat and so on.

'Is it kosher, or at least *khochick?*' Ryfke asked.

'Yes, Uma,' Leizar smiled, 'There are many Jews and many shops that sell kosher. I go to the synagogue every *shabbas* and I am meeting a lot of people. The Russians still weigh heavily on the Jews, but there they have others to worry about also. Catholics, Muslims and even the Poles themselves. So, every now and then, we hear of someone who got arrested and tortured. Someone who got their property trashed, or worse, confiscated and, yes, the authorities are still brutal.

'But you know it has made me see that things do move forward... everywhere except here. In Kawetchka time stands still. It's made me more determined to help things to change. Anyway, how are things here? Tell me.'

This last remark about his home got under Zelman's skin. 'Let me tell you my boy, you are in the big city, and I am proud life is going the right way for you, but Kawetchka is our home, and it is your home too. Things move forward here also, but slowly, and sometimes slowly is better. Remember when you were little, I told you about the tortoise and the hare?'

Despite his words, Zelman thought his son had become much more mature in the weeks he had been in Warsaw. Independence sat well with him, and he was truly making his own way. With an effort, the old man determined he would hold his tongue.

He cleared his throat, 'The *levaya,* the funeral was awful, and to tell the truth it is still too painful to talk about. The whole shtetl turned out and the *momzer* Russian Cossacks were on horses carrying long clubs. Every now and then they would hit one of us and that person would go down. They were doing nothing, Leizar, you know how those *momzers* are. There was a eulogy by the Rabbi who, among quotes from the *sedra* of the Torah, told of our lovely Mendel, he should rest in peace, *olav ha sholom,* and how he was put to death for something he didn't do, and at the mention of that heinous act, the whole congregation murmured and some shouted *Shame.'*

'Did that provoke the Russians?'

'Yes, the *momzers* hit out at that, and there were some broken limbs. The shiva went on all week and of course, I can't hide it Leizar, people wanted to know where you were. You had best take care while you are here, because we could not convince them that you had a good reason to miss your brother's funeral and shiva.'

Leizar nodded along, he had expected this, but it brought tears to his mother's eyes again.

'And what else?' said Leizar, beginning to well up himself.

Zelman grimaced, 'Hmm... life doesn't get any easier here. They put up the taxes again, and I have to say, without your help here, it's hard to pay.'

Leizar was waiting for this, and he interjected, 'That's one thing I wanted to tell you. I've been earning some very nice bonuses at the factory, and I've been saving them for you. Here.'

He opened the little leather bag he had been carrying and on to the table he tipped money, mostly notes. 'I've been making around 50 zloty per week in bonuses. I don't need it, my wages cover everything I need, so here is nearly 200 zloty. It should be a big help and it more than replaces what I was able to give when I was here.

'And,' he said, quite loudly, 'You don't have to feed me!' He looked at his mother, who was sitting open mouthed, 'But I miss your wonderful *chulent,* Uma.'

'But you need this money to live, Leizar, you have to buy food and clothes. This is your money.' Ryfke pushed the money across towards her son, as she was looking at her husband.

'Upa and Uma, I have all the money I need from my wages at the factory. I am going to save all my bonuses and I will come to see you as often as I can – maybe every two or three months. It's not easy because it is a long journey, and I have to ask a favour of Herschel for the transport and the time off. So, I can't ask too often. But you can count on this money, and it should make life easier.'

Now it was Zelman's eyes that began to water. The truth was, he was finding it very difficult to put sufficient food on the table. He had lost the income of Leizar and Mendel, and with the higher taxes, life was very difficult. This money from his son was a blessing from heaven. It would not only supplement the family income, but provide for other things they could not afford before.

Leizar could see his father was struggling to hide his emotion, so he quickly changed the subject. 'But I have not told you the biggest news of all,' he said. All three heads suddenly went up, 'I have met a girl. She is the most wonderful creature you could imagine. Beautiful, smart and from a very good family. She is the daughter of Herschel, and I think she likes me.'

'Who made the *shiddach*?' asked Ryfke, right away.

'Uma, in Warsaw things are not quite the same. Sometimes people meet and marry because they fall in love!'

'Pisht, what a lot of nonsense,' she replied. 'What do you know about this girl? Is she a *balbattishe* homemaker? Does she cook? What about mending and sewing? Does she help her mother, and does the mother show her how?'

Zelman interjected, 'Does she come with a dowry? How will you make a home?'

'Wait a minute!' Leizar exclaimed. 'You are all getting too excited. I just said I had met her, and we were getting along well. Yes, we are seeing each other, and we enjoy each other's company. That's all for now. I have no idea of the answers to your questions. Uma, in the city things are a bit different. You can meet someone and be attracted to each other, without a *shiddach macher*, and it may develop into a marriage, and it may not. It all depends.'

'All depends on what?' Ryfke retorted. 'With no *shiddach macher*, how do you know you are suited to each other? How do you know the families will get along?' Leizar smiled, 'Uma, it all depends on love. If you fall in love, then everything else can be worked out. Maybe, if we are still seeing each other, then next time I will bring her to meet you. And I am sure you will love her too.'

Zelman was clearly not impressed, but he could see that his son didn't want to carry on this particular, so he just snorted in a disapproving way, and said nothing.

The ensuing silence was broken by Duvi., 'I want to go back with Leizar,' he said.

Zelman looked at him with angry eyes, and responded loudly, 'Oh! Yes, let's all go and live in Warsaw, the whole *mishpocha*. We can all live in Leizar's room.'

Leizar smiled and put his arm round his brother, 'One day, little man. First you must concentrate on your bar mitzvah, and study hard to get a good job. Then – who knows?' He just let it hang in the air, and Duvid's face showed his disappointment.

Ryfke had made a *chulent* for dinner, knowing it was a favourite of Leizar, and Marcia helped her to lay the table and bring out the *chulent*, together with some herring and bread.

After dinner, the uncles, aunts and cousins started to arrive and pretty soon the place was full of people, chattering away, all keen to see their intrepid family member. There was a lot of cheek pinching, which was customary for adults to do to the children as a show of affection (although the children hated it), and it was all very noisy.

Leizar spied Aunt Clara, the wife of Yossel, Zelman's brother and he made a bee line over to see her. He'd always liked Aunt Clara, and when he was little, he often would go to their house. She kept a jar of sweets which were a very rare treat in the shtetl, and he knew where she kept it. She always had time for him, and they would play Klobyosh, a card game requiring a good memory. Leizar occasionally let her win and she knew it, but it was all part of the fun. They played the game for sweets, so Leizar always went home with some in his pocket. She was a large lady with an ample bosom and a kind face that laughed easily. She would always give Leizar a big hug and he loved the softness of her.

But on this occasion, as he approached, she turned to speak to Marcia. She was aware he was standing beside her, and yet there was, he knew, something wrong. He tried a direct approach. 'Hello Auntie, I am so glad to see you!'

She turned toward him and as he stretched out his arms and moved forward as if to hug her, Aunt Clara reached out to shake his hand. 'Hello Leizar, nice to have you back with us.' And then she turned back to Marcia.

This was very strange. It was clear that something had changed. He determined to find out what was going on.

Leizar also noticed that the only person missing was his Aunt Aryeh, which was a bit strange as he had always got on well with her and he would have liked to see her.

Eventually, one by one, all the guests left and quiet reigned again. It was quite late and Leizar was very tired and looking forward to relaxing in his old bedroom. He kissed and hugged his parents, lay down on the bed and went to sleep immediately. It had been a long day.

The next day at breakfast, he asked Ryfke why Aunt Aryeh had not been there last night. Ryfke made as if to spit on the palm of her hand three times, a custom thought to ward off evil. 'Psht!' she said. 'We don't mention her name in this house.'

'Why ever not?' asked Leizar. 'What has she done?'

Ryfke was talking as she cleared the table and walked back into the kitchen. 'She married out,' she said quietly, as if people were listening.

Leizar knew that she meant his aunt had married a *goy*, a non-Jew. In those days it was rare. 'So, who did she marry?'

'You remember Dmitri, the *momzer* Russian, may he rot in hell? Well, he had another son, Igor, and Aryeh had been seeing him without anyone knowing. One day she walked out of the house, and they went to Warsaw and got married in the Russian way, no *chuppah*, nothing. When your father and his siblings heard about it, straight away they said kaddish for her.'

In those times 'marrying out' was considered a sin, and of course, kaddish was the prayer for the dead. So that was how family were treating her. Henceforth they would have nothing to do with her.

She continued, 'Not bad enough she marries out, but it has to be the son of that *momzer*,' and she again spat on her hand three times. 'He should be cursed,' she said. '*A meesa meshineh oyf im.*'

Leizar was shocked at first. He had no experience in his life of anyone 'marrying out', and it was unbelievable that it should be the son of a Russian, let alone the son of the very Russian who had facilitated the state murder of her nephew.

But he liked Aunt Aryeh and he had, himself, come to understand that you cannot necessarily chose whom you fall in love with. When he thought about it, was this really a reason never to speak to her again?

'Uma,' he said. 'Why would you do this? She is still the same person, and I remember that Igor was also very intelligent. He is the only Russian I know who ever bothered to learn Yiddish. What would be so terrible to invite them over occasionally? She is our flesh and blood.' As soon as the words were out of his mouth, Leizar knew he'd made a mistake.

'You don't know what you are talking about!' Ryfke had actually raised her voice in anger, something that happened rarely. 'First of all, they are not like us. She will go without her *sheitel*, and he does not cover his head. There will be no more *Chanuka*, or other festivals for her, and she will celebrate with the *goyim*. But the worst is to think about their children. They won't know who they are.'

This was a heartfelt reaction from his mother.

'By the *Din,* the children are Jewish because it is the mother's line that prevails, but their children will not be given the chance to grow up as Jews. And they will be half-bloods of that monster's family. This is a terrible thing.'

Zelman had entered the room and overheard the conversation. 'You see?' he said, 'This is what happens when you stray away from your roots, *ale tsorris vos ikh hob oyf mayn hartsn, zoln oysgeyn tsu zayn kop.* Promise me you will stay true to your heritage, Leizar. Remember who you are and where you come from. We think about you every day.'

Leizar wanted to do a quick tour of the shtetl, to see his family and friends, and the first house he visited was Aunt Clara and Uncle Yossel. He had not visited their home for a very long time, and he had not had a chance to speak with his favourite Aunt the night before. He was greeted at the door by his Aunt and two small cousins. But it was not the welcome he'd expected. Aunt Clara's face was stern, and she did not smile. At first, she did not even invite him in, just stood at the doorway, said a brief hello. She said that Uncle Yossel was away working in the fields and she had work to do in the house.

Leizar stopped her. 'Wait Auntie, what's wrong, what have I done?'

She did an exaggerated sigh and opened the door further indicating he should follow her. They sat at the table. 'You are not so popular around here, you know? What? You couldn't wait to go and find your fortune with all the big shots in Warsaw? You couldn't even attend your brother's funeral and sit *shiva* for him out of respect. What's the matter with you?'

Leizar was taken aback. He was fond of Auntie Clara and her words stung him. He tried to explain that this was a once-in-a-lifetime opportunity, and he had promised Mendel he would pursue it. But he did not feel he could tell her what the driving force behind it was, and it was as if she had not heard him.

'Yes, yes,' she retorted, 'we heard all that from your parents. Do you know how upset they were? They just had a beautiful son taken from them, and the next day they lose another one. And why? He says he has a great opportunity. Listen sonny, you may want to be a big shot in Warsaw, but to me you are still a little boy, and you should stay here now. As the Torah says: 'Honour thy father and thy mother.'

Try as he might, Leizar could not talk her round, in fact as they were talking, she was getting angry, so finally he said he was sorry, and he said he would come to see her again on his next visit.

With that he returned home. Ryfke was not surprised to hear the reaction. 'Yes, Leizar, you can't expect them to understand. They don't know the whole story, and even if they did, they see the shtetl as their home, and nobody ever leaves it except to go to the big shtetl in the sky.'

The carriage arrived to take him back and Ryfke gave him a sack full of food to take. He was embarrassed because he knew they were finding it tough to provide sufficient food for the family, while he was able to feed himself and still put away some money. 'Uma, please, this is not necessary, and I don't need it.'

She had packed the sack with *chulent* in a covered dish, a piece of chicken from *shabbas* dinner, some lokshen and kreplach soup and homemade jams and vegetables they had from the field. 'You must eat and keep your strength up, and what sort of a mother would I be to let you leave empty handed?'

Leizar sighed. He could see that it was no good arguing, and that his mother needed to feel she had done something for him. So, he finally accepted it and left. She waved him off and when the carriage was out of sight, she fell to the floor weeping.

CHAPTER 22

CHAYA AND HERSCHEL

Time was passing very quickly, Leizar was earning good money with bonuses, his daily production was now very close to Avram's, and his pay had exceeded all of the other workers. He'd become aware of mutterings and looks from some of them that seemed less than friendly.

Herschel was delighted with his progress, but Leizar felt the need to speak to him about the other workers. 'Yes,' Herschel replied, 'I have noticed it too, and it is not surprising that there is some jealousy. Why don't you speak to one or two of them, maybe over a sandwich or tea? They don't know you and here you are in five minutes earning more than them.'

Leizar took his advice and that lunch time, he sat next to the man working opposite who was often giving him dark looks. 'I apologise, I have not introduced myself before, I am Leizar Domansky from Kawetchka, and he offered his hand.'

The man was clean-shaven with dirt marks on his face. He wore a tweed cap and a dishevelled, old-looking tweed jacket. He stopped mid-bite and stared at Leizar. A few seconds passed and he did not offer his hand in return. 'I am Arbar Veshinsky, and I have no wish to shake hands with you.' Another man came over and sat opposite them. 'You have a problem with this one, Arbar?'

'Nothing I can't handle,' he replied. He turned to Leizar. 'Who do you think you are? You come here and the boss helps you, and straight away you make more money than us. I have been working here for five years.'

Leizar could see he had made a mistake not being more friendly, and he had not seen this coming. 'I'm sorry, Arbar,' he said, 'I am here to do other things and the job in the factory is just to pay my rent.'

'Oh, *other things*. Well, look out for yourself shtetl boy, or you may have an accident.'

The two got up and walked away. Leizar knew the conversation had not gone how he intended. He resolved to speak to them again and see if he could do a better job next time. He got on with his work and he was pleased that tomorrow was Thursday and he could turn his thoughts to the magazine.

He enjoyed working with Yitshok, with whom he had deep, challenging conversations. They spent much time arguing the pros and cons of Communism, Zionism, Democracy and Judaism. And as a result, he was writing some very thoughtful articles. Edvard had commented that his editing of other features was creative and added to the appeal of the publication.

Chapter 23

Arbar and pain

He decided to have a proper meal, so he found his way to the kosher restaurant he had visited with Chaya. Batya recognised him straight away. 'Welcome, *shalom aleichem,* you were here with Chaya, weren't you? Come, sit down I will bring challa and cream cheese, and you can eat.'

Batya was a typical Jewish mama. Plump and friendly, she wore a long dress which had once been a shade of green and a loose, faded, pink head-covering. The dress went all the way to the floor and over it she wore a light beige pinafore. Leizar felt warm and homely.

She brought the *challa*, cheese and a small glass of kosher wine and while she busied herself in the kitchen, Leizar thought about how things were going.

He had met some prominent Jews at the synagogue and in a short time he was beginning to be quite well known in Warsaw.

Most importantly though, he had seen Chaya again, and each time he saw her, he could not wait to see her again.

The Movement was gaining much support throughout the Jewish community, which at that time accounted for around a third of the population of Warsaw and was connecting with Haskalah and other movements throughout the country. Edvard, Yitshok and now Leizar were well known among activist groups. This was not without danger, because the more these movements grew, the harder the Russian overlords tried to curtail their traction, and the pogroms and atrocities persisted.

However, poverty and pogroms kept the Jewish community largely subjugated and most families survived by providing labour at very low wages and inh very poor conditions. Alongside this, the Mayor of Warsaw was encouraging industrialisation. Plans for the first sewer and water system were being drawn up, even telephone lines were being spoken about.

Batya brought chicken soup with lokshen and then a boiled chicken leg with stuffed neck, broad beans and onions, and then a large piece of apfel strudel. By the end, Leizar was stuffed. He paid for the meal, thanked Batya and left.

It had grown dark outside, but Leizar knew the way back. He got to the end of the street and turned into the small alleyway that led through to Pokoma street where he lived.

'Now!' It was the only word he heard before something hard hit him on the head and at the same time strong arms gripped him from the back so he couldn't move. It was pitch black in the alleyway and he could not see a thing. Another blow to the head and the arms let him fall to the ground. He lay for several seconds mistakenly thinking the attack was over, until he was kicked so hard in the stomach that he retched and brought up the meal he had just eaten. There were two attackers, he realised, by counting the blows, and he was being kicked repeatedly in the guts and the back. The pain was unbearable, and he passed out.

He didn't know how long he had laid there, but he became aware of people standing over him and was half-afraid the kicking would start again. His head was throbbing, and he felt pain everywhere. When his vision gradually cleared, he saw two large women looking down at him. They were speaking Russian.

'What is your name?' It was all Leizar could do to moan. He couldn't seem to make his mouth work. '*What is your name?*' The woman repeated, much louder this time. With great effort, he managed to mumble 'Laaay… sheeer.'

'A Jew?' the woman asked.

Leizar didn't answer. 'Thought so. Come Matilda,' and with that they walked off and left him lying there.

He managed to sit by propping himself up against the wall. The pain was unimaginable, and he sat for a long time. He was only a short walk from where he lived, but it might as well have been the other side of town. He knew he could not stay where he was, so he tried to haul himself up by gripping a drainpipe, but when he did the pain came over him in waves and he passed out again.

Voices woke him this time. He opened his eyes and when his vision started to clear he thought he was hallucinating. It was Batya from the restaurant and a man. She didn't seem to recognise him straight away. When she did, she screamed aloud. 'It's the young *boychik* who was in the restaurant, what happened to you?'

Leizar couldn't answer, but he tried to smile. His clothes reeked of sick, and the smell made him retch again. Batya took a step backwards. 'Where do you live?'

He tried to communicate that he lived nearby, but as he tried to mouth the words everything turned black, and he slumped to the cobble stones.

'Manny, I think he is coming round.' The pain came flooding back, and he nearly passed out again. He was laying on a table in the restaurant with his shirt open and Batya was bathing his wounds.

'We need to get you home, darling.' She said, 'Where can we take you?' This time Leizar found he could manage a few words, and he gave the address of Herschel, thinking that he would never get up the stairs to his room.

With Manny supporting him on one side and Batya on the other, he managed to limp out to the horse and cart they used to carry supplies. Between them they managed to get him onto the cart where he could lay flat and endure the painful journey.

They went slowly and by the time they arrived at the address Leizar had given, the first rays of morning were beginning to coat everything with a hazy outline. To Leizar, everything seemed unreal. After several knocks, the door was opened by the cook wearing a hairnet and wrapped in a blanket.

She recognised Leizar and motioned them inside. Herschel appeared at the top of the stairs in a red velvet dressing gown. 'What is all the noise?'

As he descended the stairs, he stumbled at the sight before him. Leizar, clothes dirty and torn and still quite bloody and bruised, was being supported by Batya and her husband, whom he knew from the restaurant. He helped them take him into the spare room on the ground floor and they managed to lay him on the bed.

Batya explained how they had found him, and Herschel sent his maid to fetch the doctor. After he had managed a little of the schnapps that cook had given him and he had drunk a whole bottle of water, Leizar began to feel a little better.

The doctor diagnosed two broken ribs and head injuries which, although they had bled quite dramatically, he did not consider serious. He was badly bruised around the mouth and chin which was hampering his speech, but he was now able to communicate verbally, albeit painfully. The doctor cleaned the wounds with a mixture of alcohol and carbolic acid which proved to be as painful as the injuries themselves and then used honey as a salve. He then bound his head and chest so that by the time he'd finished Leizer was hardly recognisable, but the patient felt a lot better, especially after the doctor gave him a dose of laudanum the and cook had fed him some chicken soup.

Herschel had gone to inform Chaya and now she burst into the room. She gasped, 'Oh my God, what has happened to you?'

Leizar was a little ashamed that Chaya should see him in this state, but he was feeling a lot better, and decided he would try to explain. His speech was laboured, 'Tank...you....' he said to Batya and Manny. 'I... would... have... die.'

Slowly and painfully, and with as few words as possible, he gave them to understand that he had been attacked and he didn't know who the attackers were. He was becoming very drowsy from the laudanum and Chaya thanked Batya and Manny for bringing him. She suggested that, since there was nothing more they could do, they should return home.

The next morning, Herschel went to the factory and Leizar slept until midday, when he was able to eat some more soup with lokshen and shredded chicken.

The doctor returned later and administered more laudanum which again made him drowsy. His speech had improved, but he could speak only slowly, 'I don't want to be a burden,' he said to Chaya. 'If... someone will... assist me I can... return to my...' and by the last word, he had dropped off to sleep again.

Chaya left him to sleep. That evening, after they had eaten, Herschel was frowning. 'I am not happy that he is here, Chaya. He does not know much about us, and it is better to keep it that way for now.'

'But you can't throw him out, father. Look at the state of him.'

'As soon as he can walk, we must get him back to his room. I will ask Moshe and Cook to look in on him. I don't want him here.'

Leizar woke the next morning and although he felt in pain everywhere, it did not seem as acute. Cook have him a glass of tea with some soft *challa* bread and honey and he drank two full bottles of water. The doctor called again and suggested he try to stand lest he should become too stiff; with a lot of effort and help from the doctor, he managed to stand on his own. But he was in great pain.

He collapsed back on the bed and tears came to his eyes. 'What am I going to do?' he asked. 'I have to go to work; I cannot let Herschel down and I have writing to do at the magazine.'

'This will help.' The doctor gave him two small phials, one labelled coca and the other laudanum. 'You can take five drops of coca twice a day, to help with the pain. Take the laudanum with tea or milk at night to help you sleep.'

During the day, despite the pain in his chest, Leizar tried to walk and caught sight of himself in the mirror. His head was swathed in bandages, and it was all he could do to stagger back to the bed. Chaya came to see him and made sure he ate some of the food cook had prepared; he drifted in and out of sleep until the evening.

When Herschel returned again, the first thing he did was to look in on Leizar. 'I hear you have been up, and the doctor has given you something for the pain.' Leizar nodded, Herschel seemed very business-like and different from the way he had spoken before.

'We must make arrangements for you to go back to your apartment. You will go tomorrow with Moshe.' And with that, he walked out the door.

This was a side of Herschel that Leizar had not seen before. He didn't want to overstay his welcome and in fact, he was embarrassed to be in the house. He was glad that he could return to his room, but depressed at the thought of being stuck there. Chaya had not been to see him since midday, and he hoped he had not somehow offended them.

There was a knock on the door and Cook propped it open. She said she had a tray of food that she would bring for him. With the bedroom door open, Leizar heard a loud knock on the front door, and he saw the maid escort a young man up the stairs. Cook entered carrying a large tray with more soup, soft boiled gefilte fish, mashed potatoes and soft challa. There was even a small glass of wine.

'I see there is a visitor,' he said.

'Yes, it is one of Chaya's admirers.'

This landed on Leizar's ears like a bombshell. He was so taken aback that although he opened his mouth to ask a further question, nothing came out, and he was left with his mouth open as Cook walked out.

He nibbled at the food while he tried to come to grips with what he had just heard. 'How could I have been so stupid to think I was the only one? She is a beautiful young woman, and she has not spent her life waiting for me.' He turned it over and over in his mind and as he did, he cringed at his naivete. He remembered the wet dream and how he had been unable to get her out of his mind. The pain in his chest was overtaken by the pain in his heart, as he thought of the way he had spoken about her to his parents. Tears welled up and ran down his face. He had to get out of there and he hoped Moshe would come early in the morning. He took some of the laudanum and just before he drifted off, he remembered Cook saying, 'He is *one of her admirers.*' And so, of course, he concluded: Chaya has many.

To add to his embarrassment, Chaya entered his room just before Moshe arrived. Leizar had managed to dress himself and when she brought breakfast, Cook had helped him remove some of the bandages. Chaya looked stunning in a long-skirted dress with a bolero top and an embroidered hat perched on her head, slightly to one side. Leizar could not look her in the eye. 'How are you feeling today? I hear you are returning to your apartment.'

This was a conversation he did not want to prolong. 'Much better, thank you,' he mumbled, and he was grateful that, just then, Moshe entered the room. He turned away from her, 'I am ready to go,' he said to Moshe, and Chaya turned and left.

It was with much pain and enormous effort that with Moshe's help, he managed to climb into the waiting carriage, and it took them a very long time to get him up the stairs into his room where he collapsed onto the bed. Moshe was sweating from the effort and breathing heavily. He, too, gratefully slumped on to the bed, which creaked and groaned in protest.

When he had recovered, Moshe made them both a glass of tea, 'Well, my boy, they certainly made a mess of you. Herschel has arranged for Cook to send food, so you will not starve.'

Leizar decided to open up to him, 'Can I confide in you, Moshe?'

'Of course, nothing you say will go any further.' Moshe had become quite attached to this young man who, in his view, still had a lot to learn about life.

'I feel so embarrassed and depressed. I thought everything was going so well, the work at the factory, the writing at the magazine and above all….' He looked down unsure if he should admit this, even to Moshe, 'the relationship I thought was developing with Chaya.' And he explained the events of last night includingCcook's comment.

'Look, the world is a tough place. Don't take anything for granted. You've been doing well at work, but Chaya is a beautiful and independent young lady. It's true she has many admirers, and I did tell you that Herschel allows her to make her own decisions at the same time as being very protective of her. Leizar, this is Warsaw, and believe me, the city is full of lovely young women. You must not get fixated on Chaya. She will break your heart.'

Leizar nodded thoughtfully. He knew these were wise words, but they did not help the way he felt. 'I have to tell you something else.' He explained about the animosity he had experienced with Arbar from the factory, and that it had been shortly afterwards that he was attacked.

'It was my fault because I didn't trouble to make friends with the other workers, and they saw that Herschel treated me differently, and I was making more money than them. I have a strong suspicion this was what led to the attack. And now I am letting everyone down.'

The words were coming quickly as Leizar felt the need to unload his feelings, 'Herschel, Yitshok, Edvard, all the people who put their trust in me, I have brought this all on myself.'

Tears welled up in his eyes. 'Look, the doctor has given me medicine for the pain, and I feel better already…'

This was not true, he still had excruciating pain in his chest whenever he moved, and the headache was with him all the time. 'I want to go to work tomorrow, I need to talk to Herschel. I will work at the factory and continue at the Magazine on Thursday. Can you help me to get there?'

Moshe looked sceptical. 'You don't look ready to me, but if you are sure that is what you want, I will collect you with the carriage tomorrow morning. Be careful what you say to Herschel. He is not as easy going as you may think.'

When Moshe left, Leizar took some of the coca the doctor had given him, and he was surprised that within minutes he started to feel less pain and much better about himself. He started to think he had exaggerated all these problems in his own mind. He laid back on the bed and closed his eyes.

The pain in his chest woke him an hour later. It seemed even worse. Cook had sent the maid with some food for lunch, but he had no appetite. He looked around his dark room with no daylight and dark shadows from the constant candle burning and he felt so alone and miserable. After a while he took another dose of the coca which worked its euphoric magic again, and he got off the bed, and managed to do some writing at his desk. But after a short time, the pain and depression returned. More food was delivered, and the maid took the previous, untouched, tray away.

As he lay on his bed, the dark cloud seemed to be growing around him. He had never felt so low. Eventually he took another dose of the laudanum and went to sleep.

Moshe arrived early next morning and helped Leizar down the stairs into the carriage and within minutes they were at the factory. Leizar had removed almost all the bandage from his head, leaving only abrasions and bruises visible. He did his best to walk upright, but he could not help holding his chest at the site of the pain. The place was not yet full, but those who were there all looked up as saw him stumble in. Herschel stopped him on his way to his workbench. 'Come to my office,' he said, and then turned on his heel.

Laizer slumped into a chair. 'You can't work like this, and you should not have come in. I want you to take a few days off. I have spoken to Yitshok and he knows what has happened. He said maybe you can do some writing from home, and Moshe can take it in to him.'

Leizar welled up again. 'I've let you all down. I'm so sorry. Maybe I am not the right person for this wonderful opportunity you have given me.'

'Why do you blame yourself? It's not your fault. Many Jews are attacked, but from what you've said, it sounds like they were waiting for you. Why do you think that might have been?'

Laizer explained about the conversation with Arbar, which might be connected, and how he thought that it was his fault for not making friends whilst being singled out for special treatment and training and for making more money than them.

Herschel was thoughtful. He said nothing for quite a while. 'Go home. You have given me a lot to think about. Do not return until you can walk properly, and you feel better.' And with that he walked out into the factory, leaving Leizar to wonder how he was going to get home, until Moshe came to the rescue again.

With great effort, and help from Moshe, he had managed to get back up to his room and again Moshe dropped his considerable bulk on to the bed which protested even more with a loud creak and a groan. Seeing that Leizar was at a low ebb, he made tea, and put in some honey and lemon. He helped himself to the little box of *kichels* that Cook had sent over, and then he said simply, 'Talk to me.'

It was as if a dam had been breached. It all poured out of Leizar. The episode with Arbar, his suspicion that it had led to the attack, the pain he was in, his loneliness and, above all, the pain from his arrogance in thinking he had a chance with Chaya.

'So, what do you want to do?'

'This is not what I thought, Moshe. Warsaw is a frightening place. Too much happens too quickly, and I miss my parents and my family so much. And now I have enemies here also.'

He was holding his ribs as his chest was heaving. He could not fill his lungs with air without pain and tears coming to his eyes.

'Well, you sound to me like a young man who is really feeling sorry for himself.'

Leizar interrupted, 'I want to go home, Moshe. My father was never in favour of me coming here and I think he was right. I am a shtetl boy and I have had enough of this big life and these great ambitions. I want my life back.'

'Look, you have a think about it overnight. I don't think there will be more food from Cook, so I will go out now and bring you something to eat. Have a good rest and I will call back tomorrow. See how you feel.'

When he had left, Leizar took another dose of the coca, and as before, it had a profound effect. He quickly felt much better, and the pain subsided, he wondered if he had said too much. Moshe returned with bread, cold meat and cheese. He was pleased to see Leizar standing up and making more tea.

'Eat and sleep tonight. I will be here in the morning,' he said, and swiftly left.

But as before, the euphoria he felt after taking the medicine was soon exceeded by the dark cloud of depression and he felt even more miserable and alone. The darkness and shadows made the walls appear to move as if they were closing in on him. He took another small swig of the coca straight from the bottle and marvelled at how quickly it made him feel better. He became suddenly, ravenously hungry and ate all the food Moshe had brought and washed it down with some wine he had from before.

It sustained him for a while, but again the black dog of depression returned. He laid on the bed and the shadows seemed to take human form and move toward him. He saw Chaya's face, but it was twisted, and pock marked, and she came to him with arms outstretched, her fingernails long and black reaching to scratch him. He could hear an undercurrent of voices as if many people were struggling to be heard, but he could not make out any words. The voices got louder, and Chaya had turned into a snorting boar-like animal with large tusks that seemed to want to climb onto him. He tried to push it away and felt its disgusting hot hairy hide. He started to itch and saw insects on his arms. He screamed and screamed, but of course, no-one heard.

Suddenly it all went black, and it took a few minutes before he realised his eyes were closed. When he opened them, the visions and the noises were gone and he was aware that what had happened was not real, even though it had seemed so at the time. He was extremely frightened that such a thing could happen, and he knew it must have been induced by the medicine. The candle had gone out and he lay for a while in the darkness. He longed for the warmth and comfort of his shtetl home. The words of his father came to him: 'I will *never* leave. Kawetchka, it's not much… but it's my home.' His father was right, who did he think he was to change everything?

'Well, have you decided what you want?'

Leizar awoke to find Moshe standing at the end of his bed. He had laid awake for a long time, turning things over in his mind and had finally taken a dose of the Laudanum and overslept. He quickly came to, got out of bed and went to make tea. With some trepidation he invited Moshe to sit. The only place was the bed and he thought it might finally give in. But with another loud creak and what Leizar thought was a crack, the bed held up and they both sat.

He was aware that the tone of the conversation, first with Herschel and now with Moshe had subtly changed. 'Moshe,' he said, 'I don't want anyone to think I am ungrateful for the wonderful opportunity you all gave me and the kindness and help since I arrived. But I have learned that I am not cut out for this. I am just a shtetl boy and that is where I should be. With my parents and my family and helping to teach the children, and maybe writing a few articles. I made a big mistake, Moshe, and I want to go home.'

Moshe was nodding along as Leizar was speaking, 'Yes, I thought so. I have already spoken to Herschel, and when I left you, Edvard, Yitshok and Herschel had a meeting at the magazine office. They all agreed that if this is what you want, then there is no point in trying to persuade you otherwise. So, you don't have to do anything. Pack up your things and I will take you back to Kawetchka.'

Chapter 24

Home Again

Leizar's misery was compounded all the way. There were awkward silences, and he felt the pain over and over of how badly he had let everyone down.

'It's Leizar, Leizar.' Ryfke had heard the carriage pull up, she had run from the kitchen where she was baking, and she was at the doorway with flour all over her hands and spilling down her pinafore and hopping from one foot to the other with excitement. 'What a lovely surprise... Oy! What has happened to you?'

She covered her mouth with her hands and gasped for breath when she saw Moshe helping her son down from the carriage. She ran to Leizar, and he had to fend her off, lest she should try to hug him.

'It's alright Uma, let me get inside and I'll explain.'

The wooden house was exactly the same as when he had left, with the same delicious smells and comfortable warmth. He went through the whole story of what had happened since his last visit, how ashamed he felt at making the wrong decision and having ideas above his station. She listened carefully and interjected with a lot of *Oys!, Oy vehs!* and even the occasional, *Oy veh iz mir.*

When he reached the part about Chaya, she couldn't help herself. 'You see, no good can come of it without a *shiddach macher*!'

As she sat with him, he stroked her hair and felt he was really home at last. 'Uma, this is where I belong,' and he laid his head on her shoulder.

Zelman, Duvid and the children all returned together, and the house was a babble of excitement with everyone talking at once. Leizar was grateful that Ryfke took charge right away. Not wanting to go into detail in front of the children, she winked at Zelman and Duvid and said quite loudly, 'Our lovely Leizar had an accident in Warsaw, he fell off a horse and he has come home to be with us while he recovers.'

This only half-worked because then the children were full of questions about the horse and how it had happened, but Zelman picked up the thread and told them all to wash and get ready for Friday night dinner, during which he guided attention on to the excitement of living in the big city. Eventually Marcia and Moishe were packed off to bed, and Leizar shamefully, his voice catching from a sudden thickness in his throat, repeated what he had told his mother.

Zelman was uncharacteristically quiet and listened intently. When Duvid tried to interject, he 'shushed' him to be quiet. He had tuned in straight away to his older son's anguish. It was only when Leizar came to the part about the attack and his suspicion about it being connected to the animosity at the factory, that they both became animated, Zelman thumping the table, his eyes growing wider as the detail unfolded. 'Those *momzers*, they are worse than the Russians'.

And Duvid, whose fists were clenching, added, 'I wish I was there, I said you should take me to Warsaw with you.'

Finally, Ryfke calmed them down. 'Well, Thank God, you are home now with the people who love you. You need to get better, and you can settle down to your proper life.' Her voice dropped, and she said conspiratorially, 'Don't worry, *tutele*, I will find a nice *shiddach* for you!'

Leizar began to relax into the bosom of his family home. Duvid was happy to share his old bedroom again, and for the first time in a while, he went to sleep peacefully, without the help of any drug.

Joseph Galitzer, the pseudo doctor came to see him the next day and dressed his wounds, after giving Leizar a thorough examination, 'Well, after what you have told me about the attack, I would say you have had a lucky escape.' Leizar didn't feel very lucky. 'You have two cracked ribs, but they will heal, and your face and head wounds are superficial. No bone injuries. You will have bruises for a while, but it will all heal up. Now you say the doctor gave you medicine, can I see it?'

He sniffed the first bottle. 'Laudanum to help you sleep. My advice is to use this only if you have to.' When he sniffed the second phial, he wrinkled his nose, and without a word, he went straight to the kitchen and emptied all the liquid out.

'This is dangerous stuff,' he said, 'I suppose he gave it for the pain, but it can have very bad effects and you can become addicted to it.' Leizar thought about how the coca had made him feel invincible, and then how depressed he became. He said he thought he could manage without it now.

He relaxed at home for a couple of days and his mother fussed and spoilt him with special food, but as his health improved, he became restless. He started helping out at the school and his mind turned again to the quest for equality in the world. He thought about Mendel and how his brother would have reacted to the recent events.

As he always had in the past, he went to see Uncle Shmuel. 'Well, I think you took on too much and you've learned an important lesson. You need to rebuild your life again, here in Kawetchka. Take on a job where you have to go to work every day – maybe that is at the school, maybe something else, and if you feel the need, you could start writing again like you did before you met all the big shots. That way you would still have some influence on your socialist ideals.'

Leizar nodded along, he knew Shmuel was right, 'Yes, I know things are not so easy here and I must find a way to help my father put food on the table.'

'You are lucky Leizar, you have good parents and a family who all love you. You have a clever mind and I believe you can be whatever you want. So, make up your mind, and settle down. Remember to honour your father and mother and one day you will have lovely children and they will honour you. You will be proud of them and that is what I call *nachas*, the real blessings of life.'

And he left determined to follow this advice, returning home with a renewed attitude. 'Uma, I want you to talk to Chana Bubitka, the *shiddach macher*. I am going to speak to Upa and see if I can get a permanent job at the school and I want to start to settle down.'

Needless to say, Ryfke welled up and hugged her eldest son close. 'Tomorrow I will speak with her, don't worry, now eat!'

Leizar felt sure that part of his mother's plan was to fatten him up. She was a typical Jewish mother, she always thought slim people looked ill. So he ate the tea and *kichels*, while his mother hummed happily.

Zelman was equally happy with his son's new resolve. 'At last, my boy has seen some sense, my prayers have been answered.' It was only Duvid who had any doubt.

'Are you sure this is what you want, Leizar? I always thought you were going to change the world.'

'Look, little brother.' Duvid hated it when Leizar called him that, but he said nothing, 'We need to know our purpose in life. I didn't know until now. This has made me realise you should count your blessings and not look at what others do. I will build a strong family here in Kawetchka, with children that will live after me. That's the real *nachas*,' he said, echoing the words of Uncle Shmuel.

The next day Ryfke could not contain her excitement. The children were already back from school, and she couldn't wait for the men to return. As soon as they walked through the door she was beaming, 'Gittel Farshinsky!' she almost shouted with excitement.

All the men were startled so she said it again, 'Gittel Farshinsky!' Even louder this time as if they hadn't heard.

'Who?' said Leizar.

'What?' said Zelman at the same time.

Ryfke had started hopping from one foot to the other again as she did when she was really excited. 'Gittel,' she said, 'I went to see Chana and she told me about Chaim Farshinsky's daughter, Gittel. I have seen her in *shul*, she is a wonderful catch! We went straight away to talk to Chaim, and he knows about Leizar. And what do you think?'

With a gleam in her eye and her voice rising, she almost squealed. 'He agreed on the spot! So Leizar will marry Gittel.'

'Not so fast Uma.' Leizar was stunned. 'I don't even know her, who is she?'

A smile had come over Zelman's face. 'You know Chaim, don't you? He owns the farm up on the hill with the milk cows and the chickens. He makes a good living supplying all the chickens to the butcher and all the milk to the milkman. She would come with a very good dowry, and you and your family would want for nothing your whole life. She is his only daughter and his wife passed away last year, so one day that farm would all be yours. She is what my father would have called a *matzo pudding*, full of good things.'

This was all happening too fast for Leizar. His head was spinning, and he was glad that they all went to wash up and have dinner. When the children had gone to bed, he wanted to know all about Gittel. What did she look like? Was she intelligent? What were her political views? Ryfke said, 'Don't worry, she is a good match. We'll arrange a meeting. You'll like her, *tuttele*.'

So, a meeting was arranged at the Farshinsky house. It was a long walk up the hill which exhausted Leizar and he had to rest twice along the way. Leizar and Ryfke approached the large farmhouse which was encircled by a spiked wooden fence, with fields beyond. They heard the sound of cows mooing and chickens clucking, and every now and then the urgent cry of a rooster. It was built of far more substantial wood than the other dwellings, and it had a gabled metal roof. They entered through a gate and walked up a winding path to the front door which was raised on four steps with a metal portico above.

Leizar raised his hand to knock on the door, but before he could knock, the door was opened by a short, fat lady with enormous breasts that threatened to escape from her dress, which was of a faded blue and white stripe material, with a white apron at the front. She had a ruddy, beaming face and a smile that became even wider when she saw them. '*Kim, kim*, welcome, we are expecting you.'

The house was warm and smelled of burning wood and chicken soup, 'I am Chaim's sister, Izabella, I come most days to help Gittel in the house and Chaim asked me to act as chaperone today.' As she was talking, they entered a small lobby, and she opened a door to a very large living room. The floor was wooden, but with woollen rugs which were soft to walk on. 'And this is our lovely Gittel'

Seated in a chair by the fire was a wholesome-looking young lady with striking red hair. She stood to greet them but in a demure way, she would not look directly at Leizar. She wore wire rimmed glasses and a blue loose-fitting dress with a white floral design. It was tied at the waist. Also quite amply busted, she was about the same height as Leizar, and when she took off her glasses, he had to admit, she was very pretty, with rather a lovely smile.

Izabella brought tea and a big round cheesecake which she cut into portions, taking care to let them know that Gittel had baked it specially, and then she and Ryfke went to sit towards the back of the room, leaving Gittel and Leizar to rather awkwardly, talk to each other. It was a difficult, stilted conversation and it was clear to Leizar, that Gittel was trying very hard to say the right things.

Leizar was surprised to learn that she knew of his writings for the magazine. She kept looking down when he spoke to her, but she came alive when he coaxed her to reveal her own views about equality and a home for the Jews, and they had some lively exchanges.

But Leizar felt uncomfortable, and he knew Gitte did too, the whole thing was so contrived. Eventually he apologised and said they must leave, but he had enjoyed talking to her, and would like to continue their chat another day. She smiled and looked him in the eye for the first time, and he could not help but think that she really was quite beautiful.

Ryfke came forward with Izabella. 'Thank you for the tea.'

To Gittel and Leizar she said, 'I hope you two young love birds got on well with each other.' Again, to Izabella she said, 'I will go speak to Chana in the morning.' And they left.

Before they had even got to the garden gate, Ryfke said 'So nu? What did you think? She is pretty, no?'

Leizar said nothing for a few moments, and then thoughtfully he said, 'Uma. I don't know what to say. She is beautiful, and I think she is intelligent, and she has good well thought-out opinions, which we can discuss.'

'So this is good, no? She is pretty and strong, and she will make lovely babies with you. Did you see her beautiful hair? In the house she doesn't have to wear the sheitel... Leizar, I think she liked you.'

Ryfke was starting to gabble, 'And she is a *balabusta,* she can cook and look after the house. And look at the size of that house. There is room for a large family. You will be happy, Leizar trust me. I know what is best for you. Listen to me this time.'

Ryfke kept this up all the way home, as if, the more she said it, the more convincing it became. But with Leizar, it had the opposite effect. Laying on his bed at home, he couldn't help but think about Chaya. He knew she was out of his reach, and his mother was right, Gittel would make a good wife who would look after him, cook his meals and give him babies, and on top of that, one day he would own a large house and a farm. And actually, he liked her. It was a good solution for all the family, but still he had another stone in his shoe.

Everyone he spoke to said he would be crazy to turn down this opportunity. His father was making arrangements to meet with Chaim to discuss the wedding and the dowry, and it all seemed to be moving along with its own momentum.

He agreed to meet Gittel again, and arrangements were made for Ryfke and Izabella to chaperone, so that the young couple could 'walk out' together and then have dinner at the Domansky house. The arrangements were made for the following week. Meanwhile the word had spread quickly around the shtetl that there was a *shiddach* between Leizar and Gittel and over the next few days, Leizar became a little irritated when people started wishing him *mazeltov*.

The second meeting with Gittel also went well. She had been a good student at school and had a quick mind, while her views on socialism and equality were different to Leizar's. She believed that state ownership was the best way, with a minimum wage for everyone, and distribution of wealth by the state. Leizar enjoyed discussing it with her. Although she tried hard to hide it, Leizar saw he had offended her when he suggested that she could not really evaluate these concepts because, in the relative terms of life in the shtetl, she was one of the privileged.

She pursed her lips and to his surprise, said she would like to discuss it further on another occasion. Leizar's heart opened, knowing that she would not argue with him, but she had her own views.

They were not allowed to touch, but Leizar really started to feel some attraction toward her. He went home that night very confused. Gittel had everything, and he was growing very fond of her. But she was not Chaya, over whom he had dreams and fantasies. But on the other hand, Chaya was out of reach. So, should he settle for what was possible?

The weeks went past, and Leizar was returning home from teaching at the school. He had worked a little late to mark the work his students had done during the lesson and the daylight was fading.

'Leizar! Leizar!' He could see a man and a woman at the foot of the hill. The woman was waving and shouting his name. As he got nearer, he was surprised to see it was his Aunt Aryeh and although he had never met him, the man with her had to be her husband, Igor, the son of Dmitri the Russian captain.

'I heard you had gone to live in Warsaw,' he said. 'What are you doing here?' Leizar felt a little uncomfortable. He knew Aryeh was an outcast from the family, although he didn't agree with it, he was not sure that he wanted to be seen talking to them.

When she introduced Igor, Leizar interrupted quite gruffly, 'I know who you are!'

Igor was unfazed by this and continued to smile. Aryeh continued, 'Yes, we are visiting. Igor wanted to see his father and his brother. You remember his brother, Alex? How are the family, Leizar? They are never far from my mind. How is Uma and Upa, Duvid and the children? I miss them so much. But I heard you had gone to Warsaw, and you were very successful. Is this a visit for you too?'

Leizar had no wish to go into detail, especially in front of the Russian, so he just replied that the family were all well, and yes, he was here on a visit.

When he said that, Igor looked up sharply and gave Leizar a quizzical look, as if he knew he was hiding something. He took Leizar by the arm. 'Excuse me Aryeh, I just want a word with Leizar.'

This was very strange behaviour, and Leizar's pulse quickened. His first reaction was to shake off Igor's grip on his arm and stand his ground. Igor leaned in so that he could speak quietly into Leizar's ear. 'Please, I just want to say something to you in private.'

There was no threat in his voice, so with some trepidation he walked a few paces away from Aryeh who was also looking quizzically and wondering what was going on.

'My father has been talking about you…' Leizar put up his hand and went to walk away. He didn't want to hear that any Russian, let alone Dmitri, had even mentioned his name.

Leizar's whole body had tensed, and he was clenching and unclenching his fists, 'Look, leave me out of it. We all just want to be left alone.'

But Igor held on to his arm again. 'He heard you had returned to Kawetchka, and he knew we were here. He said if we ran into you, he would like to have a word. I am sure there is no harm in it, Leizar. He was struck down with a strange illness.'

Leizar couldn't help the thought that maybe this was the result of all the curses from his father. 'He is not the man you remember,' Igor continued. 'He is frail and weak, and I fear he has not much longer to live.'

Leizar knew if his father had heard those words, he would have looked up to the heavens and said *Gott zei danken* Thank God. 'Igor, you know my father would be furious if he knew I was talking to you. My family has said *kaddish* for Aryeh already because she is with you.'

Igor winced as if a pain had struck when he heard that. 'Yes, my Aryeh suffers every day, but I know it does not compare to the pain and suffering of your family for things that happened in the past. Please, don't ignore this opportunity. Meet with my father for a few minutes and you may find that some of the pain is blunted by what he tells you.'

Igor seemed to be sincere, and now Leizar was intrigued by his last comment. He was still very unsure, though. 'I will think about it overnight. But if we meet, it has to be somewhere in the open, and he has to come alone. Can you bring your father to the big oak tree in the centre of the village? It is the place where he first met with my father, he knows it well. Tell him to be there at noon tomorrow. If I am not there after fifteen minutes, then I am not coming.'

Igor didn't seem overjoyed with these arrangements which were not only completely one-sided, but involved finding a way to transport his sick father, and he was not at all sure that Dmitri would agree. But he nodded. 'I will tell him,' was the only answer he could offer.

Aryeh had become impatient, and she came forward to Leizar. After some hesitation, they hugged each other, with Leizar hoping all the time that nobody saw them.

He said nothing to anyone when he returned home, and that night, as he lay in bed, he turned it over and over in his mind. Was he about to walk into the mouth of the lion? Was Dmitri really so sick and frail? What was it that he wanted to tell Leizar that might 'blunt the pain of the past'?

It was this last thought that was uppermost in his mind the next morning when he woke. He decided he would risk it. He had chosen the venue wisely. No-one could hide and yet it was quite secluded. They could sit under the tree and talk.

So it was that history was repeated. Leizar arrived deliberately ten minutes later than the appointed time. It had been a long walk, and although the pains in his chest had dulled, they did not let him forget what he had been through. As he approached, he saw a small, covered wagon and a single horse that had been let out and was grazing. As he got closer, he recognised Igor, but no sign of his father. He began to worry that this might be a trap. He stopped and looked around. It was a fine day; the sky was blue and clear, and the only sound was the chirping of the birds. The terrain was flat with little vegetation and no-one else in sight, which was the reason he'd chosen to meet here. The thought flashed across his mind that although they were unlikely to be seen, it was also a perfect place for an ambush.

He shouted to Igor, 'Where is your father?'

'Oh! So, you arrive. Come. come, we cannot shout to each other!'

Nervously, Leizar ventured forward. Igor remained still, watching him and the only movement was from the horse who looked up and whinnied as he approached.

As he neared, Igor suddenly moved towards the wagon, and Leizar was about to turn and run until he heard him say, '*Batya*, Papa, he is here.'

Igor climbed into the wagon and with much effort, half carried his father to the clump under the tree and gently sat him down. Leizar peered into the wagon to make sure no one else was in there.

Dmitri was a pale shadow of the man Leizar remembered. He was very thin with sunken cheeks, and he seemed shorter and smaller. He had only whisps of hair which were white. He was dressed in grey loose jacket and trousers, and Igor had placed a blanket round him.

When he spoke, his voice was croaky. 'Leizar, my boy… '

At this incongruous greeting from the cruel enemy he remembered, Leizar snapped, 'I am *not* your boy, and you are *nothing* to me. You killed my brother. Did you think I could ever forgive you? I came only because Igor said you have something to tell me that may blunt the pain you have inflicted on my family. If you have something to say… Then say it and I will be gone.'

'Leizar, Leizar, you can see I am very ill, and I shall not see many more sunrises.'

'Good,' said Leizar. 'Then the world will be well rid of you.'

'Just sit and let me talk.' He beckoned for Igor to give him some water.

'Before Mendel was arrested, I was helping the Movement and my superiors got to hear of it. They knew you and your brother were writing pieces and to be honest, the Movement was gaining ground.' He was struggling for breath, and he had to pause.

'They came to my house in the night with many Cossacks. They gave me and my wife a terrible beating in front of my boys… They took my wife away screaming. It was a shock to see General Gromysikov, one of the highest generals in the Russian Army, enter my house.' Here there was a long pause and Dmitri seemed far away, as if pondering whether to say the next sentence. He took a deep noisy breath.

'He told me what I must do to save my wife.'

He continued, panting in between words.

'The whole thing was planned… from start to finish to serve as a warning to your family and the whole community. He told me if it did not do exactly as he said, I would never see my wife again. And he… said this in front of my two sons.'

Another long pause. There were tears in his eyes.

'They took my wife and said I would not see her until it was over. I am so sorry Leizar… For me it came to the choice between your brother… and my wife, the mother of my children, and if I refused, then it would probably be all of us.'

Despite his long-standing hatred, Leizar saw a frail, dying man crumpled on the ground struggling for breath. He helped Dmitri to drink a little water, and neither spoke. Dmitri stared with pleading eyes as if looking for forgiveness. Leizar turned away and walked a few steps. There was a picture burned in his memory of his brother Mendel with the rope round his neck as the box was kicked away, as his body snapped, and life was taken from him.

His own body tensed at the thought. Why should he feel any compassion for this man? He turned and in a louder voice, 'Is that what you called me here for? To seek my forgiveness. I lost a beautiful young brother in the most brutal way, and my parents will never get over it. You carried on with your life. What happened to your wife?'

'I said I wanted them to put in writing that if I committed this outrage for them, they would spare my wife. The Cossack who arrived that day brought the written confirmation before I gave the order.'

Leizar remembered it. The man on horseback. The letter. It had given them a moment of hope. 'And then?'

'They killed her anyway.'

This took Leizar aback. Dmitri took some more water and a deep breath.

'How did you know I was here?'

'This you ought to know. There is someone inside the community in Warsaw… He is close to Yitshok and Edvard and he also knows what goes on in the factory and the Eisenbaum family, amongst other things. I asked him to keep an eye on you. He told me everything that happened to you in Warsaw… and why you have returned to Kawetchka.'

Leizar gasped. He took a step back. What Dmitri was saying was outrageous. Was it possible that they were watching everything that was going on in the movement and the community in Warsaw?

'Leizar, listen carefully, come closer… you must return to Warsaw. Life does not always go how you want, and sometimes you have to fight for what is good. '

'What do you know about this? Why are you telling me?'

' Believe me… I know everything. The factory, the attack, even about the girl… You can and you *must* return and fight for what you want.'

'Why would you care? What's this all about?' Leizar could not believe what he was hearing.

Dmitri coughed loudly and a little blood and spittle came from his mouth. But it seemed to clear his breathing.

'I hate this Tsar. I hate them all as much as you. Look what they have done to me. You were doing very good work in Warsaw and the truth is they need you. They need you in the factory and they need you at the magazine.

He paused for breath and took a rest before he continued.

'What I did to your family was a vicious and evil deed. I have not much longer to live, so what can they do to me now? I know you will not be happy living here in the shtetl and you will always wonder what might have been.'

He propped himself up on one elbow. His eyes were wide as he tried to get nearer.

'Leizar, you have a brilliant mind. Return to Warsaw and put it to good use against these *momzers*.'

The use of the Yiddish word by the Russian seemed incongruous. Dmitri went into a coughing fit and Igor came running. He tended his father and lifted him up as easily as if he were a child. 'I don't think he can speak any more, he needs to rest. I will take him back now.'

As he drove away, Leizar was left standing, lonely and confused. This was not what he had expected. He sat down under the tree and replayed the conversation in his mind. How could he have known all this? Was it a trap? Surely, he could not trust the word of this man.

He knew what his father would say.

But then his father had not seen him. He was a dying man, what motivation would he have to lie now?

And he had to ask himself if he given up too easily in Warsaw. Was Dmitri right? Maybe if he stayed in the shtetl, he would always wonder about what might have been.

This was the first time in his life that he had been faced with a real obstacle, a challenge to what he wanted to achieve. And what had he done? He had given up.

As he started to walk, he realised that although life was not easy in the shtetl, whatever goals he had set for himself, or that others had set for him, success came easy to him. Even when he started in Warsaw, he easily reached and exceeded his target production, and his work for the magazine was well received right from the beginning.

He had been targeted and beaten up, perhaps due to his own foolishness, and he had found that Chaya was not hopelessly in love with him to the exclusion of everyone else. He had failed. And so, he had run away.

The more he thought about it, the angrier and more ashamed he became with himself. Was this something to be proud of? To tell his children in the future? Is this the sort of man he is?

And then above all, was there any chance he could win Chaya back?

As he neared home, his mind was beginning to race through the possibilities of how his life may turn out if he gave it one more try.

Then suddenly he was struck with the most obvious reason he had to return. How stupid he was only to think about himself. This was far more important.

He must let his friends in Warsaw know that they had at least one spy amongst them, who was watching everything they did. They had to be warned before there was some terrible consequence. If the Russians harmed any of the people who had shown him such kindness, and he knew about it and didn't warn them, how could he live with himself?

By the time he arrived home, his mind was made up. He was convinced that he had taken the easy way out from Warsaw, and that he must return and warn his friends of the traitor in their ranks. He would fight for what he wanted, and he may get beaten, but he would *never, ever, give up!*

He had not told anybody at home about his meeting with Dmitri, and he felt it would be better if he kept it that way.

That evening he confidently told his family had been giving it a lot of thought and he was returning to Warsaw. He did not divulge anything about his meeting with Igor, Aryeh or Dmitri. The family didn't expect it and they were shocked. They tried to get to the bottom of his *volte face*, asking what had led him to this decision, and doing their best to make him realise this was the wrong choice. He was part of Kawetchka again. Why would he put himself through all that *tsuris* in Warsaw?

Ryfke sat with her hands up to her mouth. 'What about Gittel and the shiddach? Everyone thinks you are going to settle down and marry her. Your father has spoken to Reb Farshinsky. They are making plans for the wedding.'

'Uma, I said I wasn't sure, that I would need to think about it. I'm sorry, but I have to do this.'

Leizar decided to be stubborn and immovable, simply saying he had thought it through, and he had to go back and continue what he had started. He had been doing important work and he was not prepared to let this setback end his ambitions. He had made a promise to his brother, and he was determined to do all he could to deliver on it.

No matter how his parents tried to dissuade him, he was implacable. They tried reasoning, anger and emotional blackmail, but Leizar was having none of it. At the end he said he was going to ask Reb Bendle if he could borrow his horse and cart to travel to Warsaw. It would be a long journey, and he would have someone return it the next day. If Bendle agreed, he would leave tomorrow.

Ignoring their protestations, he went to see Reb Bendle after dinner, and after he explained why he wanted to return, Bendle didn't seem surprised. 'I'm proud that you want to fight and honour your promise to your brother. Look, I don't have much work tomorrow, I'll take you there. The horse and I can rest overnight, and I'll return in the morning.

The family could see there was no point in trying to change his mind, so after breakfast next morning, he kissed and hugged them all. Again, tears were shed and again Ryfke gave them plenty food to eat on the way.

'Uma, don't worry, I will visit again when things are settled,' and quietly to Zelman he said, 'And I will start to send money again.'

As he prepared to climb up on the cart next to Reb Bendle, his father gave him a kiss, which was the first time he had ever done that and wished him, *mazel und brocha* - luck and blessing.

The farewell from his family buoyed his determination to overcome the issues in Warsaw and succeed.

Chapter 25

Warsaw and back

After a long and very uncomfortable journey, they arrived at the outskirts of the city. The cart drew attention as it clattered over the cobblestones. Leizar directed Reb Bendle to the house of Moshe Vasilinsky who was delighted to see Leizar. Gitte came to the door and told them both to come in. She had just made some fresh soup and she had been frying fish, which was evident as they could smell the delicious aroma from the front door.

Leizar explained to Moshe, 'I have had time to think. I should not have run away like that. I just needed a little time to heal and think. If Edvard, Yitshok and Herschel will allow it, I want to pick up where I left off.'

Moshe was listening carefully and smiling, which encouraged Leizar.

'I have to tell you, this has made me more determined than ever to influence the magazine and I have some great ideas for Herschel's business too.'

They sat down to a delicious dinner, but of course Leizar could not discuss anything further in front of Reb Bendle.

'Across the road there is a hostelry, it is owned by a friend of mine. I'll have a word with him, and I'm sure they will be able to put up Reb Bendle and look after his horse. Leizar, I suggest you stay with us tonight, and tomorrow we can go and speak to Herschel and the others.'

Reb Bendle was delighted. He thought he was going to sleep in the cart. And

Leizar was pleased, because there would be nothing in his little apartment, even if it was still available.

When Moshe returned from settling Bendle in the hostelry, Leizar couldn't wait to speak to him. He told him the whole thing about the meeting with Dmitiri and what he had said. Moshe listened carefully, stroking his beard in concentration. 'Hmmm, this is serious. We must waste no time in discussing this with the others.'

When he went to bed, Leizar didn't know why he felt uncomfortable with Moshe's reaction. He would have expected more animation. What he had told him, Leizar considered, was a bombshell. Moshe had taken it seriously, but somehow not with the anxiety and shock he had expected.

As usual, he turned it over and over in his mind until he came to the conclusion that it was just Moshe's way. He had a pretty relaxed attitude to everything, and he didn't make decisions. He would leave that to others.

The next morning they saw Reb Bendle off after breakfast, and went first to the factory to see Herschel. He was also delighted to see Leizar, and listened carefully to what he had to say. He asked several questions about the Domansky family. How did they feel about Leizar's return to Warsaw and his new determination? Also, about the attack, how would Leizar feel if it happened again? Indeed, his questions seemed directed towards Leizar's state of mind and how he would deal with any future problems.

Eventually, Herschel suggested they all go over to the offices of the magazine and meet with Yitshok and Edvard to see how they felt about things. On the way there, Leizar again had an uneasy feeling that this was not quite unfolding the way he had expected.

When they arrived, Yitshok sent a message to Edvard, and when he arrived, they all sat down to tea and *kichels*. Leizar again went through the story about Dmitri, explaining that he was very ill and frail, and he didn't expect to live much longer. And then he dropped his bombshell.

'He told me that they have a spy here who is so close to all of you, that he knows everything you are doing. He knows about the factory, about the magazine and he even knew about the attack on me.'

The three men nodded along, but they did not react with the shock that Leizar expected. What was going on?

'So, of course, if nothing else, I had to return right away to warn you all before something terrible happened.' Again, there was just nodding. No questions. No shock.

In fact, glances were exchanged between them, and Herschel started to smile at Leizar's quizzical expression. 'Leizar I am sorry, but we need to make a confession. 'We know all about Dmitri and what he knows. There is no spy among us. We have been in contact with Dmitri for some time, and he told us the whole story about the Russian blackmail to get him to do what he did with your brother, and how they murdered his wife anyway.

'He wanted to help us in any way he could. So, we told him about what had happened with you and that you had returned to the shtetl. It was his idea to tell you the story about a spy.

'You see Leizar, we were worried that you seemed to have given up too easily. We weren't sure why, and we needed to be convinced we would not all live to regret it. You have to understand, we are a very tight team and what we're trying to do is covert. It depends on trust, and it fails when trust is broken.'

Leizar took this in. 'And you thought *I* had broken your trust?'

'Look at it from our point of view. We had trusted you, Leizar, drawn you into our movement, introduced you to people and given you open access to everything.

'And then… what? You disappear! And you disappear because some workers give you a little kicking one night when they're full of vodka. Do you see? We had to wonder if that was really all it took, Leizar? Or was there some other reason why you disappeared so swiftly?'

'A little kicking?' Leizar echoed, hotly. 'I couldn't walk!'

'You *said* you couldn't walk,' Edvard said, pointedly.

Leizar's amazement was turning to anger. He leaned toward Herschel, 'Just what are you accusing me of?' he shouted.

'We are accusing you of nothing,' said Herschel more softly. 'We want you to understand, your actions seemed odd, and so we had reason to *wonder*. It could have been that you used the opportunity of the beating to disappear because you'd got the information you wanted, and you knew you weren't going to get any more.

'Don't look at me like that, Leizar, also you walked out with my daughter, and she liked you. I thought you liked her, but… I don't know. The abrupt way you just went made us all a bit nervous. We had to consider, was there a darker reason?'

Edvard interjected, 'Leizar, we have been infiltrated before, but fortunately on that occasion we spotted it early. We have to be on guard, sometimes people don't turn out to be who they say they are. It could be they are here under false pretences to snoop around and gather information.'

'So you set me a test?'

'We spoke to Dmitri. He was certain you were honest, not an agent of the Tzar. He suggested this ploy. If you were really on our side, you would come back, to tell us what he had told you. That was why he hauled himself from his deathbed to do it. Because he was sure you would prove yourself to us, and we knew that if you were the man we thought you were, and you feared there was someone feeding information to the Russians behind our backs, then you would be compelled to return and warn us. That who we thought you were,' Edvard said, gazing at him intensely. 'And we were right.'

Leizar couldn't believe what he was hearing. His mouth had fallen open, and he had a heavy feeling in his stomach. He had been manipulated; he had been the victim of an elaborate hoax!

'This was all a trick? Why did you not just come to the shtetl, speak to me and my family. Find out if I was truly honest about the cause? A cause I have espoused all my adult life.' Leizar's voice was raised again, and he spread his hands in a gesture of openness. 'Are we not all friends who can trust each other?'

'It wasn't so simple,' Edvard replied. 'We *are* friends, but the work we do can be dangerous. We have to trust each other. So we had to be sure. Dmitri's plan offered us the way.'

'To be sure about me.'

'It was not only a question of trust. We needed to know that if you came back, you would stay, and forgive me, not run home if you get roughed up a little or…' He looked toward Herschel awkwardly. 'Things don't work out with a girl you like. Herschel saw great promise in your work, and the magazine and the movement is poorer without you. We need talent, Leizar. We need you.'

Edvard and Yitshok both leaned in to Leizar. 'He's right,' said Edvard, echoed by

Yitshok. 'We need you, Leizar.'

Although he was flattered by the praise, Leizar felt duped, and even worse that he had fallen for it. At first he had been half inclined to walk straight out again, but these last words lifted his spirits.

He leaned back in his chair and took a deep breath. 'Look, I am here, and although I am still smarting from the ruse you used to get me here, I want to assure you I am here to stay. This cause is in my heart, and I am more determined than ever to help it to come to fruition. He paused for effect and looked at each of them in turn. Never doubt me again!'

Herschel stood and with a smile, put his hand on Leizar's shoulder, 'Don't dwell on it, my boy. We are glad to have you back, especially with renewed determination and enthusiasm. I have taken care of the little matter of the rogue workers at the factory, Moshe will take you to buy provisions and return to your apartment, tomorrow you come to work as usual. We will talk more in the morning. And by the way, I know a certain young lady who will be very pleased to see you.'

Herschel was amused to see Leizar's eyes open wide at his last comment. Although nothing further was said, he gave Leizar a meaningful look, and then he left.

Leizar's thoughts were in a whirl. Did this mean there was still a chance with Chaya? He had not dared to think so.

Edvard and Yitshok explained that the magazine had put out two editions since he had been away, which Yitshok had edited himself. They discussed the writing of the contributors and reviewed the articles, and Leizar came up with various suggestions as to how they could have been improved. He got caught up with his customary enthusiasm when they started on the planning of the next magazine, until Moshe entered the room and cleared his throat loudly and ostentatiously.

'So sorry, Moshe, I got carried away.'

Leizar apologised to Edvard and Yitshok as well, even though they were both smiling; he shook their hands and took his leave.

Moshe helped him to buy food and groceries and carry them up to the apartment, which was much as he had left it, and he lit a fire in the stove to warm the place through. He went out and had a late lunch at a café and his mind was racing. He couldn't enjoy his food, even though he was hungry. He felt a lightness in his chest, and he was excited at the prospect of what lay ahead, and as much as he tried to suppress the thought, Chaya kept drifting into his head.

That night the dream returned, but this time there was another man watching the sex. He had no face, but he was very tall and strong. When he reached his climax, the faceless man grabbed the woman, who was screaming, by the hair and pulled her away. Leizar tried to hold her, but his strength was puny against the force pulling her. 'Don't let me go!' she screamed, and she started to wail, which got louder and louder until it hurt his ears. The wailing was taken up by other voices, all screaming and wailing in unison until they reached an unbearable crescendo. He awoke sweating and nervous.

All his emotions were whirling through his head. He lay on the bed, but he couldn't sleep, and eventually at six am, he got up, breakfasted and made a slow walk to the factory. He arrived too early, and it was not until eight am that Herschel and other workers arrived.

'Come, let's talk,' said Herschel, and they went into his office.

'I am so glad you returned, there is much to talk about, you are a thinker and you have a good brain. I have a problem and I would value your opinion. An American called Bonsack has invented an automatic cigarette rolling machine. It can roll more than 250 cigarettes per minute, at least 2500 per day, and they say it will get faster. Each cigarette rolled is perfect so there is no waste. I cannot ignore it because all my competitors will be buying them, and each machine only needs only one operator so I would be able to sell my cigarettes much cheaper and still make more profit.

'But it would mean the workforce would reduce radically and people will see they could lose their jobs. How do I handle it? I know you and the movement are strong advocates of workers' rights, and I support that, but if I don't move with the times, I will be out of business, and then nobody will have a job. How would you handle it?'

Leizar's mind immediately clicked into gear, and he was glad to have something to focus on.

Herschel continued, 'A firm in the USA who introduced these machines was the subject of massive riots when they laid off operatives. It was a bigger factory than ours, but in the end the workers smashed up the machinery and went on strike, trying to force the management to return to the old ways.'

'Hmmm... I can see the problem,' said Leizar. '20 machines would replace 100 workers. If you train 20 operators, with say, 5 overseers, it still means 75 people lose their jobs. Let me give it some thought and let's speak tomorrow.'

'You will come to my house tonight for dinner, and we can talk some more.'

Leizar's heart leapt at the thought of seeing Chaya again and his pulse quickened. He tried in vain not to show it, but Herschel had picked up the sign, and he smiled a knowing smile. Leizar returned to his workbench and was welcomed by the other workers, who expressed their sympathies about the attack. He also noted that two of the benches were empty. While he worked, he was deep in thought.

Leizar could truly see both sides of this problem. He struggled with it for a long time. Whilst his principles were screaming that the workers' rights should be paramount, and that jobs should come before profits to benefit the rich, he also understood that it would be worse if, through ignoring the advance of low-cost machinery, the product was overpriced in the market and eventually forced the closure of the factory, throwing *all* employees out of work. He felt that this example was at the heart the socialist principle. He worried about it all day. What if all the workers could benefit from the automation? Was there a way of keeping them all employed and incentivised to make it work?

At the end of the working day, Herschel and Leizar left together. On the way, Leizar was uncharacteristically quiet. He had mixed feelings. On the one hand, he was excited at the prospect of seeing Chaya, but also fearful and unsure of what her reaction would be. He was now aware that she had other admirers and that he could not bear to share her attentions with others.

They arrived at the house and they both went to wash up before dinner. Leizar was slightly disappointed that Chaya didn't appear, and even when they sat at the table, she wasn't there. Seeing the look on his face, Herschel smiled, 'Chaya is in her room, she will join us shortly.'

Herschel poured a glass of wine, and they wished each other good health in the traditional way, with a clink of glasses and *lechaim*. Leizar took a piece of the challa bread and a sip of the wine, 'I've been thinking about your problem,' he said. 'What is the demand for the cigarettes like? And how do you see it in the future?'

Before Herschel could answer, Leizar's heart skipped a beat. Chaya entered the room dressed in an emerald, green and white full-length gown, cinched tightly at the waist, with her hair piled up on top of her head in curls. She was more beautiful even than Leizar remembered. He felt his face reddening and worried that he was making a fool of himself.

Chaya seemed distinctly cool, 'Good evening father, hello Leizar,' and she sat down. In unison Leizar and Herschel raised themselves slightly from their chairs, 'Good evening Chaya,' they said together, and when they were all seated, Herschel answered Leizar's question, 'The demand seems to be enormous,' he said. 'I can easily sell everything I make.'

For a moment, Leizar forgot what he had asked, but he tried to gather his thoughts, 'Oh yes... of course.'

Herschel kept looking at him, but Leizar was distracted by Chaya's beautiful eyes which, as soon as he looked at her, she deflected to the table. Herschel broke into his thoughts, 'Well, why do you ask?'

Leizar felt unable to have a meaningful conversation. 'I would like to think about it overnight, if you don't mind. Can we speak at the factory in the morning?'

Herschel pursed his lips and nodded. He could see he would not get much sense out of Leizar right now anyway.

All during the meal, Chaya would not look directly at Leizar and only answered in short sentences when spoken to. By the end of the evening, Leizar wished he had not raised his hopes with her, because clearly she had other things on her mind.

Herschel could see what was going on, so he apologised that he felt very tired, and he was going to bed. He said he would see Leizar in the morning. He wiped his mouth on his serviette and left Chaya and Leizar sitting awkwardly in silence.

Leizar stood, 'Well, I must be going too, I also have a big day tomorrow, it was lovely to see you again Chaya.' He turned and made to leave, but Chaya intervened.

'Wait, Leizar! We should talk.'

Leizar paused. He had no wish to cause himself further embarrassment and pain if Chaya was about to explain why her future did not involve him. That would embarrass both of them. 'Please Chaya, there is no need to go into this any further. I work for your father and I know you live in a different world. Now I must go.' And he made for the door.

He picked his hat and coat from the stand on the landing and started down the stairs. He had reached the front door when he heard Chaya's voice again. 'No, my darling, please wait.' She had appeared at the top of the stairs. She had tears in her eyes.

Leizar thought he must have mis-heard. He turned as if in a dream and slowly started up the stairs again. Chaya held out her hand. 'Come, I can't bear to lose you like this.'

He cautiously re-entered the dining room, unsure of what was happening. Chaya was standing by the fire now; a single ringlet of hair had fallen and curled to the side of her face. Leizar thought he had never seen a face so beautiful. 'Have you found someone else? Is there a love back at the shtetl to whom you are betrothed? Leizar, have I lost you forever?'

Leizar gasped. What was she saying? He felt giddy and held on to the mantlepiece to steady himself. 'Why would you say that? I have no one.'

She came towards him, and they held each other tight as if to let go would mean they never embraced again. She put her lips up to his and they kissed deeply and breathlessly. Their bodies seemed to melt together, and she rested her head on his chest and they stood like that until Cook knocked on the door to ask if there was anything they would like before she went to bed. That broke the spell and they sat in chairs either side of the fire.

'Chaya, what is going on? I don't understand.'

'You left abruptly without even a goodbye, and I didn't hear from you at all. I was sure our relationship was over. I thought you would tell me tonight that you have plans with someone else.'

Leizar leaned across and took her hand. With a serious face, he looked into her eyes. 'But Chaya, when I was ill and I stayed here at your house, I saw another man attend you and Cook said he was *one* of your admirers. And Moshe said that you would break my heart. Truly you very nearly did! I thought I would be at the back of the line, just one of your admirers. My darling Chaya, I could not bear to share you.'

Chaya was smiling through the tears that had run down her face and that she was patting with her handkerchief. 'Oh Leizar. Of course, it's true I don't live in isolation, and there have been occasions when I have walked out with someone, but I have never felt the way I feel about you.'

'So, who was the man I saw arrive that night?'

She smiled, 'I also teach English, he was one of my students. Cook would not have known that, and I am sure she didn't mean to say that I have men coming and going all the time.'

Leizar felt as if his heart would explode. They stood and embraced again, 'Chaya, I am in love with you, I can't get you out of my mind, you are like the sun, the moon and the stars all shining to me at once. Is it possible that you feel something for me as well?'

She kissed him, this time with tenderness, a long lingering kiss, 'Leizar, I love you too, and I want to spend the rest of my life with you.'

'Then will you marry me?'

'Of course, my darling', she said, and they held each other again.

They talked long into the night, about children and families and plans to be together and how they would love and care for each other. Leizar resolved to speak to Herschel at the first opportunity.

In the early hours of the morning, he tore himself away and walked home, very cautiously. Looking behind and round every corner, but with a light-hearted spring in his step. He lay awake all night reliving the events of the day, in his usual way. He was astonished that his nemesis, Dmitri, had proved the catalyst for all that had happened. He was sure he was on the right path now, and unbelievably on that path with the love of his life… And she loved him!

He dozed just before the clock showed it was time to rise. He pinched himself to make sure it was all real and not another of his dreams, and he could not wait to start the day. He had also been giving Herschel's problem a lot of thought.

When he arrived at the factory, he went to speak to Herschel straight away.

'You say you could sell as many cigarettes as you could make.'

Herschel, smoking one himself, took a deep drag. 'The demand seems to be enormous,' he said. 'I can easily sell everything I make.'

'So, if you made a lot more, do you think you could sell them?'

Herschel quickly said, 'I could sell double.'

'I am thinking of something much bigger,' said Leizar. 'Let's suppose you were able to buy 50 machines. You could make more than 125,000 per day. You would be one of the biggest factories in Warsaw and the production would continue to increase.'

Herschel was thoughtful. 'Yes, but I don't have the money to buy them,' he said, and a gleam came into his eyes. 'But I am sure I could sell them because the costs would be lower, and even selling them much cheaper, I would make a lot more profit.' Then his face dropped. 'But I care about the people who work for me, and I don't want my factory smashed up.'

'Well, wait a minute,' said Leizar. 'Suppose you form a workers' co-operative?' With 50 machines you would need at least 50 trained operatives and maybe 10 overseers. You may also need a few people trained in the maintenance of the machines. As an incentive, you offer your employees the opportunity to be minor partners, each with a share of the profits which they would only retain as long as they were employed in the business. I think you could make it financially attractive to them and still increase the profits which if you wish, you could reinvest to buy more machines, improve working conditions or open another factory employing more people.'

'How interesting…', Herschel replied thoughtfully. 'So that way they would have an interest in the factory being successful under the new automation rather than opposing it.'

'Yes, but it doesn't stop there, you could work a night shift. You have 100 people. The machines don't get tired, so you could probably make another 75,000 at night. Everyone would be fully employed and incentivised, and you could pay higher wages.'

Herschel was taken aback. He took a deep drag on his cigarette and blew out the smoke. 'Well, I didn't expect anything so far reaching,' he said. 'The big problem is how to raise the money to buy the machinery, but maybe I can sell the idea to a bank or a financier. This needs a lot of thought. Leizar, you are an extraordinary young man.'

Leizar went back to work leaving a very thoughtful Herschel.

Leizar was pleased with the theory he had worked out and especially that Herschel had taken it seriously. He truly believed it could work, and it would stand him in good stead because his thoughts were more and more full of Chaya. He could not contain his excitement, and he planned to speak to her father about it at the first opportunity.

That night, Leizar could not sleep again. His head was full of Chaya, working out how to tell Herschel. How would he react? Would he be pleased, or angry that

Leizar might take away his beloved daughter? Where would they live? And above all, was it really true that Chaya had declared her love and wanted to marry him? Would she change her mind?

Then his thoughts turned to the factory and the scheme he had proposed to Herschel. He knew that had impressed him. Would Herschel pursue it? Where would he get the money? Could they convince the workers that it would also be good for them?

So many thoughts whirling around in his head.

Herschel called him into the office first thing, the next day. 'I want you to come home again tonight for dinner, so you can explain the scheme to Chaya. I have been thinking about it, and it is an audacious plan. It would be a massive step for me and her. We could lose everything, so I want her to understand what we are doing.'

Leizar's heart leapt. Yes! Tonight would be the night! Unbeknown to Herschel, he had ideas far beyond the factory plan. This would be the perfect opportunity to ask for his daughter's hand in marriage.

Leizar was thinking about it all day and as a result his production dropped, and he made the fewest cigarettes ever since he started, even since the first day. Avram noticed, when the other workers had left, he picked up one of Leizar's efforts and the tobacco fell out, the cigarette turned into a useless flat piece of paper.

'What is the matter with you? Are you not well? Your work today is rubbish.'

Leizar was dismayed and embarrassed. 'I'm sorry, Avram. I have so much on my mind today, really important things. I was not concentrating. Tomorrow I will make up for it, I promise.'

'Well, you'd better! First you walk out and go home, then you come back and your work is useless. Let me tell you, the boss listens to me. I know you have been sucking up to him, but you had better concentrate tomorrow. We can't have another day like this.' With that he took all of Leizar's production, tossed it all in the bin, and walked out.

Leizar's mind immediately returned to what lay ahead that evening. If all went well, he would explain to Chaya and her father, that he had some money to buy a ring and he felt he could afford a better place for them both to live even with sending the money to his family.

His thoughts were broken by Herschel, who called him to leave the factory together. On arrival at the house, Chaya answered the door herself, smiling and lovely, and welcomed them both home. Herschel noted the change in her from the night before, but he said nothing, and proceeded up the stairs. She held back and gave Leizar a hug and a little peck on the cheek.

All during dinner Leizar was stumbling as he tried to explain the factory plan to Chaya, because in his mind he was nervously planning what he would say to Herschel. He ate very little and they both noticed that he didn't display his usual appetite.

'Whatever is the matter Leizar?' she said. 'You've hardly eaten anything. Do you feel unwell?'

Although he knew she was teasing him, Leizar went quite flushed, not knowing how to answer. He shifted awkwardly in his seat and apologised saying he did not seem to be very hungry tonight. Chaya looked intently at Leizar as he struggled to explain the plan and how it would work. She caught on straight away, and could see the possibilities, but Herschel wanted to be sure she understood the size of the financial risk they would be taking.

'We owe nobody at the moment. We have a good business, and it pays for all our workers and for us. That would change and suddenly we would be in debt. The potential rewards are great, but so is the risk, and we would be staking it all on the plan of this young man.'

Chaya continued looking at Leizar. 'And tell me father, what would happen if we did nothing?'

'I believe eventually the industry will be mechanised, we will become a dinosaur and our factory will not be able to compete.'

'Then we should be grateful that *this young man* has come up with a unique pan for us, should we not?' I believe he is very special.'

This last comment was not lost on Herschel.

When the meal was finished Leizar asked to speak to Herschel alone, and it's fair to say that Herschel was not surprised. He had seen the change in his daughter, and he knew how close they were. Chaya had moped around after Leizar left and in truth, this was part of the reason Herschel had agreed to the subterfuge, to ensure the young man returned to the city with his record clear and all doubts about him dismissed. He had grown very fond of Leizar himself, he knew what was coming, or at least, he hoped for it.

Chaya brought the bottle of Krupnik, poured them each a glass and then left the room. She closed the door and stopped for a moment, tempted to listen outside, but after a slight hesitation, she knew that was dishonest and instead went to her room and waited.

'Well, my boy, what do you want to tell me? Is it about the factory and the machinery? We have a lot of planning to do.' Now it was Herschel's turn to tease.

Leizar took a large draught from his glass, and then a deep breath. 'N-No sir, I want your permission to ask Chaya for her hand in marriage.'

Leizar didn't stop once he had got going, and the words fell out of his mouth faster and faster as if he did not want to give Herschel a chance to say no.

'I've given it a lot of thought, I have enough money to buy a ring, and if I work really hard at the factory, I can earn enough to rent a better place to live.' He was gabbling now. 'I know I gave you all cause to worry about me, and I am so sorry, but I thought I had no chance with Chaya, I thought she wasn't interested in me, a poor boy from the shtetl, *but she is!*'

On these last words, his voice went up an octave as if he couldn't believe it himself. 'I really believe I can make her happy, and we can raise a beautiful family…..' He would have carried on if Herschel had not put up his hand and intervened.

'*Well,*' he said in a loud voice, so as to stop Leizar continuing his rant. 'First of all, you have my blessing. In fact, I was wondering when you would ask. I would be delighted to have you for my son-in-law.'

Leizar exhaled loudly at this. He had not even realised he'd been holding his breath.

'But it is not my decision to make,' Herschel continued. 'This is not like the shtetl: you must ask Chaya first. From the way you two look at each other, I think I know what the answer will be, but only then can we speak about plans for the future. So you had better finish your drink and go and speak with her right away.' He was smiling. He stood up, patted Leizar on the back and wished him *gazunte heit* - good health.

Leizar stood up so quickly, he knocked the chair over behind him, which clattered embarrassingly to the floor. 'I am so sorry, clumsy of me.' And he stooped to pick it up.

'Go!' shouted Herschel. 'Just go talk to her!'

Leizar hurried out of the door and went straight to Chaya, who, of course, knew exactly what they had been speaking about, but she still let Leizar go through the awkwardness of broaching the subject and asking her.

He had not had a bout of stuttering since the first night, but he had it now. 'My d—d-darling Chaya,' he started. 'I w-want you to s-sit down. I have something very susus-serious to ask.'

She saw that he had actually gone quite red in the face again, and she decided to put him out of his misery. 'Leizar, my darling sweet Leizar,' she said. 'The answer is yes, yes, of course it is yes! You know it is yes. It could not be more yes!' And she rose, fell into his arms and they embraced each other for a long time.

Eventually they disentwined and Leizar's breath was starting to return to normal. 'There is so much to think about now. Let's go speak to your father again. We can go tomorrow and buy a ring, and I have plans for where we can live. Then we have to go speak to my parents. And the parents must meet each other. Then we need the Rabbi and there is the ceremony to plan and book. Oh, my darling I know we will be so happy!'

Chaya was beaming at Leizar's overwhelming enthusiasm.

Herschel suggested that they could move in to the Eisenbaum home with him to start, and they could then take their time to find a home of their own, because there was plenty of room. They decided to fix a date for the wedding in the summer of next year. They talked for a long time about plans between now and then, letting Herschel know how they were in love, while they sat holding hands and stealing glances at each other.

Leizar went home that night with a heart bursting with happiness.

Herschel started work on Leizar's idea about the rolling machines. He needed a serious investor who could see the possibilities. After all, the idea of a worker's co-operative had never been heard of. But he would need to be cautious and circumspect for two reasons. One, he was a Jew, and two: if he disclosed his plans to too many people, it could get back to his competitors and they might beat him to it.

He arranged a meeting with his private bankers, from whom he had never borrowed a zloty.

He showed the figures of the profit that could be made from making 200,000 cigarettes per day with the prospect of even more as the machines got faster with no increased costs. Even after sharing profits with the workers, there would be plenty to share with investors, and repay the bank with handsome interest. The bank was so impressed, that they put together an investment syndicate from their clients, with guaranteed loans and a credit line to finance the whole operation.

Eventually Herschel and Leizar called a meeting of the workers to explain the plans. They were very suspicious. Why would the boss want to share his profits with them? It was unheard of and what was the catch? Herschel was pleased he had asked Leizar to help explain how it worked, because he was just a worker like them, and his enthusiasm for the possibilities rubbed off on them. They asked lots of questions, and Leizar went through the arithmetic of how they could produce many times the number of cigarettes for the same running costs, and not only would nobody lose their job, but they would share in the profits. In fact, they would each *own* a small share of the business.

Herschel explained the financial risk he was taking, having to borrow very large sums of money to buy the machines, and he feared that if they did not embrace the new machinery, competitors would, and they would get left behind.

It was a lot for the workers to take in. Leizar offered to stay behind and try to answer all of their questions after Herschel had left. Gradually the more receptive among them, mainly the younger ones, began to see the possibilities and warmed to the idea. Many questions were thrown at Leizar at the root of which was the question of trust. They were being asked to risk their livelihood. What would happen if it all went wrong?

Leizar was honest, explaining that it was not without risk, but they should also look at the risk Herschel was taking. It was a journey, and he was asking them to go along with him. The rewards could be handsome.

There was a lot of talking among the men, and Leizar let them continue. He walked among them, making positive comments and answering questions. In the end, such was the respect they had for Herschel, that he felt a large majority would go along with it. But as he left, he warned them that they should not divulge the plans to anyone, lest a competitor should get in before them. That would be disastrous. They all promised to keep the plans sacrosanct.

In the morning, Leizar would confirm to Herschel that the majority trusted them both. He thought that the doubters, of whom there were few, would come round, and the machines should be purchased.

In his normal way, he turned it all over in his mind as he lay in bed. He started to worry about how his parents would take it. They knew he had been seeing Chaya, but the last they had heard, it was not only over, but he had felt foolish at even thinking he had a chance with her. And then he had gone against their wishes by rejecting the marriage offered to him, and returning to Warsaw.

It would be hard for them to accept what had happened since, and how his life had completely turned around. And then how would they take the news that he and Chaya were to be married?

Already their old ways had been ignored. He could hear them now. *No professional shiddach macher, how do you know if you are suited? What about a dowry? And to a girl he hardly knows who lives in Warsaw!* This would be a hard job.

He would have to go to the shtetl right away to break the news and explain. But should he take Chaya, or would it be better to let them know about her first? Maybe they could get used to the idea before they met. He would not want them to be prejudiced against her.

The next hurdle was to arrange for the families to meet. The distance made these decisions really difficult. The options were: go to see his family alone and tell them all the news and all about Chaya, or take Chaya with him and rely on her to charm them, or take Herschel and Chaya together so the families could do some planning.

So, it could be one, two or even three trips.

Chaya and her father lived in another world from his family. How would that go? So many questions. He decided he would discuss it with Chaya tomorrow, and he finally fell into a fitful sleep.

The next day was *Shabbos,* so he went straight round to the Eisenbaum house in the morning. Chaya had a way of seeing things so clearly.

'Don't be so silly,' she said. 'I will go with you to meet your family. I know what life is like in the shtetl, you have told me so much. And whatever they say or think, I promise I will win them over.'

And Leizar believed she would. 'And then we can bring Papa back on another occasion, so they can make plans together.'

So, they arranged a carriage the next day. When they arrived, Leizar thought it best for Chaya to wait in the carriage at first. Although she had heard a lot about life in the shtetl, she was struck by the sheer rural feel of the place as she looked out. Wooden houses, straw roofs, a few people, mostly men, in traditional dress or work-clothes. The wind bringing a hint of the sweetish smell of traditional foods like chulent, tsimmes, and schmaltz herring.

Leizar walked straight into the house without knocking. He was surprised to see his mother sitting at the table while his sister Marcia was in the kitchen. Ryfke was shouting instructions. She turned when she saw him and started a fit of coughing. Marcia brought some water from which she took a sip and put her arms out to her son. She did not talk but continued to breathe heavily and noisily.

She was having trouble breathing and she could only talk between gasps of breath. Marcia explained that their mother had woken with this breathing problem this morning and she had been like it all day.

Leizar held his mother in his arms. 'Uma, I am so sorry you are not well, and I have brought Chaya to see you.' Ryfke looked up sharply at the mention of the name.

'Who?'

'Chaya, Uma you remember? I thought she was not interested in me, but I was wrong. Uma, she is the love of my life. Uma, I have asked her to marry me and she has said yes, and her father approves. Uma, we are to be married!'

This made Ryfke even more breathless, she was panting.

'How… can this be? We don't… know her. Nobody said you were… suited. Oh Leizar!'

'I don't want this to be a shock for you, Uma. Let's take it a step at a time, and we will explain everything.'

Ryfke was gasping. 'Don't try to talk now, Uma, she is waiting outside, I must bring her in, you must meet her.'

Marcia was also shocked at what she had heard. Her mother's sudden illness had frightened her, she felt very alone in trying to care for her, and the last thing she needed was an introduction to some woman from Warsaw. She had not said anything, but she stood wide-eyed, with eyebrows raised, holding her mother while

Leizar went to fetch Chaya.

Chaya entered the room with her beautiful smile beaming. She had chosen to wear a very simple long smock dress in grey with a scarf over her hair, but that did not hide her beauty. Marcia gasped.

Chaya walked straight over to Ryfke. 'Shalom Froy Domansky,' and she held out her hand, which Ryfke grasped before pulling nearer and giving Ryfke a gentle hug. Marcia held her mother protectively and Chaya smiled at Marcia, 'And you must be Marcia, I have heard a lot of good things about you.'

Marcia said nothing but undeterred, Chaya went on, 'Oh dear! I can see your mother is not well. Sit and let's have a look at you.'

She sent Leizar out of the room to make tea, and to Marcia she said, 'How long has she been like this?'

The truth was that, for all her shock, Marcia was a little relieved to have someone to share her worry with. 'I think she awoke with it this morning.'

Chaya felt Ryfke's brow which was a little hot, and her neck. She listened to her chest. Then to Marcia she said, 'Please bring a bowl of boiling hot water with eucalyptus if you have it. Also please make a drink with hot water, honey and lemon.'

Together they helped Ryfke inhale the steam, and then gave her the drink. Colour started to return to Ryfke's cheeks, and her breathing slowed. 'Thank you, Chaya,' she said. 'And thank you Marcia, I am feeling better already.'

Chaya said she should gargle with salt water and to drink plenty of the honey and lemon. She should do the inhalation three times a day, especially when she went to bed, and elevate her head when she slept.

Needless to say, Chaya made a great impression on Ryfke and Marcia. She helped prepare the dinner for the family, and by the time the children returned from school, they were all laughing together like old friends. Leizar was so proud of his future wife.

When Zelman and Duvid returned, they were stunned to find this beautiful woman in their house. Ryfke introduced her as if it was the most normal thing in the world.

'Zelman, Duvid and Moishe, come and meet Chaya. She and our Leizar are to be married. She will be our daughter in law!'

It was the turn of the menfolk to be shocked, although little Moishe ran and gave her a great hug right away.

Zelman beckoned to his wife, 'Come, we need to talk,' and he took her into their bedroom. 'This is the girl over whom he was broken-hearted? What has happened?'

Ryfke was still a little breathless. 'Oh Zelman, she is a wonderful girl. She has only been here a few hours, but already she made me better, and helped prepare the dinner. She is a *balabusta*. You will love her, and most important, Leizar loves her. They are perfect together.'

'But… but…' For once Zelman was lost for words. What about the *shiddach macher*. Who are her family, will we get on with them? And the dowry? Where will they live?' And his voice was rising again so it could be heard outside, '*What is going on?*'

'Wait, wait, calm down, have dinner, speak with her. They are so lovely together.'

During dinner, Chaya won Zelman and Duvid over with her personality and bright conversation. She wanted to know all about their lives and was very interested in the work they did with the children at the school. And little Moishe was besotted with her straight away. He jumped on her lap at every opportunity.

But at the end of the meal, Zelman felt it was time to get to the point and talk *tachlis*. 'So, you want to marry our Leizar?' he said, rather too bluntly. 'What do you know about him and his family?'

Chaya was unfazed, 'I know that I love him, and he loves me, we have spent a lot of time together and we have a similar view of life. I have met you all now, and you are even nicer people than I expected. I will support and do anything for my husband, and I know he will look after me.'

Zelman wanted to know if she was religious and if Leizar would continue to go to *shul*. How would they bring up their children?

Chaya explained about her father and his business. Leizar added that he was working at the factory, and they had great plans to expand the production. Chaya said they were observant Jews, and she would follow her husband's guidance in these matters. She went on to tell about the loss of her mother.

This was all going too fast for Zelman. 'Wait a minute. You make all these plans without us, without a *shiddach macher*, without anything?' He turned to Leizar, 'What is going on?'

'Upa, I am sorry I couldn't speak to you in advance, but please try to see, you will have a beautiful daughter-in-law, and we will make you both proud.'

'So, when and where is this going to happen and where are you going to live? We have a small *shul* here and our Rabbi can make some arrangements if the wedding is to be here. But what about your father, Chaya? We must meet and make plans. I suppose with my son's big ideas, you are intending to stay in Warsaw?'

Leizar said that he had discussed this with Chaya and that they thought the next step should be for the Domansky family to meet Chaya's father and then together, they could all discuss those details. She explained that her father had offered that they could live in his house to start with.

Zelman wanted to talk to his son, and Chaya wanted to get to know her future sister and brother-in-law. So, they naturally split into two groups.

Zelman poured Leizar a little schnapps. 'Do you know what you are doing, boychick? You haven't known her and her father very long, can you trust them?'

Leizar was thankful that his father didn't know about how they had all duped him with Dmitri. Before he could answer, Zelman continued.

'Last time we spoke, you were devastated by her rejection. Now, all of a sudden you are in love, you are getting married. Are you sure you are suited? This is *not* the way it is done.'

'Upa, you know I love and respect you and Uma above everything. You gave me life. But I have to live it my own way. I know these people. They are a good family, trust me. You will see when you meet. And, Upa, look how our family have taken to her.'

They looked over to the other corner of the room, where Moishe was sitting on Chaya's lap and there was a babble of noise. They seemed to be laughing and all trying to speak at once.

'Yes, she seems very lovely, and intelligent, but she is used to a good life. Leizar, be careful.'

Meanwhile Duvid and Marcia had a thousand questions for Chaya and she was answering each one with a smile and a laugh and sometimes a little anecdote about life in Warsaw. They were clearly enchanted with her, and Leizar's chest swelled with pride. He went over and gave them each a big hug. And when he said, 'You will all come and visit in Warsaw,' they were jumping up and down with excitement.

The time to leave was drawing near and Leizar and Chaya sat again with Ryfke and Zelman. Leizar took his mother's hand. 'So, can we send a carriage next week to collect you to come to Warsaw and meet Chaya's father? You will get on well with him, I'm sure.'

Zelman and Ryfke looked at each other and nodded; they were a little bewildered at the speed with which all this was happening. But with a little difficulty, Ryfke took a breath and drew herself up. 'And then after that, we will make a day for a celebration when the Eisenbaums can come and meet the rest of the family.'

On the way back, Leizar and Chaya felt delighted with the way the day had gone. The next day, they arranged with Herschel for the Domanskys' visit to Warsaw.

It was all very exciting, and both of the visits went well. The Domanskys were amazed when they saw the city and especially when they say how the Eisenbaums lived. Herschel had arranged for them to stay over, and Leizar and Chaya showed everyone round the city.

Leizar took them to see the factory and tried to explain his ideas for expansion, but his parents seemed bewildered by what they had seen, and he reminded himself that they had never set foot outside the shtetl.

They went to the office of the magazine and he introduced them to Yitshok and Edvard. They took tea with them, and they were proud to hear them say how talented their son was, and how lucky felt to have him back working with them.

Zelman and Ryfke had heard stories about the big city, but they had no idea they would encounter such hustle and bustle and constant noise. By the end of the day, Zelman was holding his head and when asked why, he said to Ryfke, 'How can they live with all this *shemozel* going on all the time? Everyone is in such a hurry, it's as if they are all late to get somewhere else!'

They got on well with Herschel who was a considerate host, and they were amazed at the idea of anyone living in a house with so much room. They returned to the shtetl in a dream, wondering what Herschel would make of it when he visited.

Ahead of Herschel's visit, the word had spread quickly that he was coming and that he was a big shot from the city, a *groisse knucker*. 'You know he owns a factory with a hundred workers *noch*' – and each time this was passed on, the number of workers was exaggerated so that by the time the carriage actually arrived, some people thought he might be clothed in pure gold. A crowd gathered quickly to catch sight of him.

Herschel knew he would be a bit of a novelty in the shtetl, and he wanted Leizar's family and friends to be relaxed with him. He certainly did not want to give the impression that he was a *Moishe Groisse*. So, he dressed very simply in an old tweed jacket and grey trousers with an open-necked shirt.

Quite a crowd had gathered to greet him when he arrived and Leizar left it to Zelman to introduce him round. Herschel was genuinely interested in all the people he met, asking questions, remembering names and who lived with whom. When it came to the family, he wanted to know how each one was related.

Eventually Ryfke called them in for tea with some of her famous *kichels*, and they started to make wedding plans.

When it came to the wedding ceremony, Chaya and Herschel had a discussion with Leizar before they left Warsaw. There was a problem which would have to be handled sensitively.

They wanted to have a beautiful ceremony in the Great Synagogue in Warsaw which could be attended by hundreds from the local community, but this threw up a logistical problem.

Although there would be plenty of room for all the Domansky extended family - the *mishpocha* - and there could be a celebration to follow, how would they get all the family and friends there and back? They were also aware that they wanted to avoid any sleight on the community where Leizar had been born and bred. They would not wish for anybody, least of all the Domanskys, to think they believed the little shul at Kawetschka was not good enough for them.

So, they were very careful how they approached it. When the conversation turned to the wedding itself, Herschel skilfully suggested it was important that both communities were properly included, and they way to do this was to have two ceremonies. One at the Great Synagogue attended by all the Eisenbaum friends and people they knew from business and the synagogue, together with the immediate Domansky family. This would be followed by another ceremony a week later at the shtetl, for everyone in the Kawetchka community. That would be followed by a big party to which everyone was invited.

Not wishing to embarrass Zelman, Herschel had told Leizar in advance that he would be happy to pay half the cost of the Kawetchka *simcha* as well as the Warsaw one. He suggested Leizar told Zelman that in private.

After much discussion about who would be invited to each one, and what everyone would wear, dates were agreed, and plans were started.

Ryfke was keen to get to know her new daughter-in-law-to-be, and they so she arranged for them to spend a few days together in Warsaw. This gave Ryfke a chance to talk about things like the *mikvah* ritual bath, and various 'women's matters' pre-wedding. She helped Chaya at the wig maker to design the *sheitels* she would need as a married woman, and of course Chaya was grateful for Ryfke's help in designing her wedding dress.

Over the weeks as the wedding approached, Leizar and Chaya spent a lot of time together exploring each other's opinion on matters great and small, and they found their views were very close regarding the rule of iron exerted by Tzar Nicholas II. Chaya was a good sounding board for Leizar and they worked together on many articles.

Leizar told her he was worried about his family. 'I take money to help out. Whatever bonus money I earn, I give to my father to help make ends meet, but I noticed when we were there, that things in the shtetl are not good. The people seem even poorer, and the houses even more run down. Upa said the taxes have gone up, and they all have to be even more careful of what they say and do. The Russians are always looking for ways to show the Jews who is the boss. '

Chaya nodded, 'I saw it too, it's a worry, and the truth is that even in Warsaw the plight of the Jews is not improving.'

'That's true, but the Russian oppression is different in the city. Although the Russians are cruel and overbearing, in such a large community as Warsaw where there are thousands of Jews, they can't control everything we do. That's why we can publish a controversial magazine and get away with it. In the shtetl you have to be very careful, they know everything you do all the time. Thoughts and words can get you killed, or worse.'

Chaya was learning about shtetl life, and what a big step it was for Leizar to move to the city. She thought he was very courageous to have returned, and it made her even more proud of him.

'And it's so frustrating that my father would never contemplate leaving. He gets very angry if the subject is raised. He says he has lived all his life under this regime, and it isn't so bad. Everyone knows everyone, and they support each other. If you behave yourself and pay your taxes, whilst you might still be subjected to the odd pogrom, you could still survive, study Torah and Talmud and feed your family. And he doesn't want to hear overt anti-Russian talk because he's seen what the Cossacks can do.'

CHAPTER 26

THE WEDDINGS, THE FAMILY, THE PLANS

The first wedding ceremony was beautiful. A *chuppah* in the Great Synagogue attended by everyone they knew in Warsaw. Leizar had bought his father a suit and a wing-collared shirt with a grey tie. He made him wear a fedora hat instead of the round *shtrimmel* and he had even trimmed his beard a little.

Chaya had bought Ryfke a lovely fuschia-coloured satin dress with a fur stole and she even got her to wear proper shoes with a little heel. Ryfke feared she would fall off them! The service was officiated by the Chief Rabbi of Warsaw, and the shul's *hazan* had a beautiful voice.

After the ceremony, there was a big celebration in the *shul* hall with every type of kosher food and wine. Although there was much dancing, segregation was observed.

Later in the proceedings, as was the custom, the new Mr and Mrs Domansky left to go to their room, and everyone knew the joining of these two people was about to be consummated. There was much nudging and winking as they departed, whilst the party carried on. Of course, they were both virgins and had no prior knowledge of how to behave, but they had talked about this moment many times and they both believed that their mutual love and respect, together with their wish to please each other would carry them through. And it did.

Chaya had talked it over with Ryfke and with some of the married women in the synagogue, and they had gone into some detail, so she knew more than Leizar,.

After a little wine, she took a sheet and laid it over the bed and they both nervously undressed. Leizar gasped at the beauty of his new wife's body.

Feeling awkward at their nakedness, they were bold enough to cuddle, feeling the warmth of each other's body. Chaya felt Leizar growing hard against her and gently took him in her hand. He gasped again. Then she took his hand and placed it on her breast, and they began to kiss passionately. She guided him to the bed and showed him how to please her with his hands and his tongue.

He licked and sucked at her nipples instinctively as they grew erect in response, and he was excited to hear her moan softly. She kissed his body, slowly moving down to his erect manhood. She caressed it with her tongue and was really surprised when Leizar could hold back no more and released his seed.

She recovered quickly and told him how manly it was to do such a thing and what a lot he was holding. She wiped him clean, and they had a little more wine, and although Leizar was embarrassed, it was not long before they were cuddling and touching again. Chaya was very aroused, and she showed him how to use his tongue and fingers inside her. A warm feeling was growing in the pit of her stomach, and she was moaning again with pleasure. Finally, she took his phallus and guided it into her. It hurt, but she expected it. She told him to push. But when he did, she could not help but cry out. He stopped for fear he had hurt her, but she was breathing very heavily and encouraged him to keep going until he was suddenly deeply inside her and they both reached an unexpected, but wonderful climax.

Leizar was completely overcome with love for his wife, but shocked when he looked to see a large blood stain on the sheet. He jumped up 'What have I done? What has happened? Are you in pain? I must get a doctor?'

Chaya smiled, she got up and discarded the sheet she had prepared for this. 'My darling husband, you have not hurt me, you have made me a complete wife. This is supposed to happen the first time. I love you, now come back to bed.' And they lay talking and caressing each other until they fell asleep. When they awoke, they made love again, and after breakfast they returned and did it twice more.

When Ryfke saw her daughter-in-law all smiles and giggles, she knew things had gone well. She gave Chaya an enquiring look, which she returned with a smile and a nod.

It was time for them to return to the shtetl and Chaya had arranged to go and stay with Ryfke and the family for Shabbas before the second wedding. She would arrive on Friday and stay overnight until the *simcha* on Sunday. That way she could assist with the arrangements and meet lots of people. Leizar would arrive Sunday morning with Herschel.

So the first time they would all meet that day would be under the *chuppah*. Chaya and Ryfke had become very close, and it helped at a time when she was missing her own mother terribly. She was looking forward to next Friday, but for now, she and Leizar waved her in-laws off.

The days flew by, and Leizar had a lot on his mind. Herschel had ordered the first shipment of the rolling machines which would arrive in a few weeks and of course, he was walking on clouds with his new wife, who only seemed to want to make him even happier. When the Friday arrived for her to go to the shtetl, he could not bear to be parted from her.

But Leizar had a *shteyn in zeyn shukh*. He could not forget that he had promised his dying brother something: to find a way to get the family out of Poland and into the USA. So far, he had done nothing about it. And this, he had *not* discussed with Chaya.

On Friday night he went to shul as usual, and he was asked if he would do tomorrow's reading from the Torah as a *mitzvah,* blessing for his marriage. Several men are normally given an *aliyah, c*alled up on to the bimah to witness a portion of the reading. This must be done in a strict order. First descendants of the tribe of Cohen, who were originally the priests, then the tribe of Levi, who were the carriers of the Ark, and finally, the rank and file of the tribe of Israel. The first to be called on this occasion was Menachim Cohain, a man whom Leizar had met before when he was called to the reading. He had heard that Menachim had managed to arrange for his parents to emigrate to the US. When he shook his hand and wished him *shkoyach -* respect, he quietly asked if he could speak to him afterwards.

At the end of the service, there was a short *kiddush,* wine and tidbits and in response to Leizar's question, Menachim said he would be happy to explain how he had managed the emigration, but it was not appropriate at that time in the synagogue, so they arranged to meet after the second wedding when things returned to normal.

Leizar and Herschel started off very early next day and arrived at the shtetl mid-morning on Sunday. Everything was buzzing. They were not allowed in the Domansky house where Ryfke, Chaya and Marcia were busy with clothes and hair. For this occasion, Chaya did not wear her wig so that she could be presented as if she was not married. Zelman had arranged for the men to have tea with his brother Shmuel at their house. Chava Devora had of course, laid out plenty of food, and they were made welcome.

The service was arranged for three o'clock in the afternoon and later, there would be a big party outside for everyone they knew. During the morning many of Leizar's Uncles and Aunts came to say hello and wish them *mazeltov*. They brought presents such as live sheep, dead chickens, a milk cow and much in the way of bed linen and household utensils.

The men dressed in their suits and formal shirts, clothing that had not been seen before in the shtetl except in pictures, and they looked very fine as they entered the little shul together at 2.30pm. It was already packed, and people were gathered standing in the corners and crowding around the doorway entrance. The shul had never been so crowded, there was a creaking of the wooden structures, and a buzz of expectant conversation. The women all wondering what the bride would look like on her special day, and the men talking about how Leizar would fare in the big city.

The Rabbi, the Chazan and other pious officials were on the Bimah, busy with preparatory prayers when the men arrived. Zelman was very proud to introduce Herschel, his new in-law or mechitten. There was much shaking of hands, wishing of mazeltov and cheek kissing. One of the officials, the shamas, came over and whispered in Herschel's ear and led him outside.

Although there was no music, the rabbi had a very strong voice and when he started singing a preparatory hymn the loud babble of conversation gradually subsided. The doors opened and with great solemnity, in walked the Khala, the bride, looking so exquisitely beautiful in pure white that even the veil covering her face for modesty could not hide her radiance, partnered by her father in black suit, wing collared shirt and tie and black fedora hat. His white beard contrasting sharply, but almost matching his daughter's dress. Behind them slowly walked Leizar's sister, Marcia, also looking lovely in a new long turquoise dress with a matching head-dress, and little Moshe Dawid in his own little black suit, with a turquoise handkerchief and tie. Although there was a great stir among the congregation at such a dramatic and beautiful sight, Leizar with Zelman beside him, had been placed with their backs to the door, strategically so they should not see the bride approach and Leizar steeled himself to resist the temptation to turn.

When they arrived at the chuppah, Herschel 'gave away' his daughter by passing her hand to Leizar who at last looked sideways at his beautiful bride whom he had not seen for a few days. Leizar conducted the traditional bedeken, lifting the veil and replacing it, and Chaya started the bride's customary walk circling her husband seven times. Only when she had returned to Leizar's side did the chazan commence the very moving and beautiful hymn of Mi Adir Al Hakol. 'He who is mighty above all beings, may he bless the bridegroom and the bride.'

Unusually at the conclusion of this hymn, there was a pause, and the rabbi sang the El Maleh Rachamim, a prayer for the departed in memory of Chaya's mother and Leizar's brother Mendel, both of whom were mentioned by name.

At the end of the service, Leizar broke the traditional glass by stamping on it with his foot and the place erupted in song, with everyone clapping and singing *simentov* and *mazeltov*. People started dancing around (segregated of course) and singing. It was a place of so much joy.

Slowly everyone went outside where long tables were groaning with food and drink. The rabbi said grace and the brochas over the bread and the wine, and everyone was given a piece of the challah and a small glass of wine with which they all toasted the bride and groom.

Two fiddles and a clarinet then started up and separate circles of men and women were formed, dancing slowly at first and then ever faster to a crescendo, at which point the bride and the groom were lifted on chairs and given a twisted white cloth. Leizar held one end and Chaya the other and they were effectively dancing on the chairs in the air without actually touching.

Eventually as people tired, they went to sit down, and the feast was started. There was more dancing and singing and eating and drinking. As the daylight started to fade, Herschel strode into the centre of the tables and the hubbub gradually died down.

'Bride and Groom, my very good new friends and all my new mishpocha,' he started. 'My thanks first of all, to our host and hostess Ryfke and Zelman, for providing a wonderful simcha to mark the joining together of my best beloved daughter, Chaya with your fine son and now my fine son-in-law, Leizar.' A little wave of laughter came when he said that.

'I know he is the product of the wonderful community of Kawetchka, and I thank you all for raising him into fine man he is today, a perfect match for my lovely Chaya. Together they make us all proud.' Everybody clapped and there was much loud cheering and raising of glasses.

The cheering was eclipsed by a massive explosion from inside the synagogue which blew the doors off. At the same time Herschel was surrounded by six fearsome Cossack horsemen with swords in their belts, drawing their whips from their boots. They struck Herschel down and rampaged over the tables. Although people ran from them, they were not quick enough, and many were injured. One of the horsemen went straight for the bride's table. Leizar put himself between the charging Cossack and his wife, thinking this might be the end for him. But instead the Russian turned his horse broadside on and unloaded a pig's carcase from his saddle. He dumped it, rotten and stinking on to the table in front of them.

The Cossacks left as swiftly as they had arrived leaving a trail of destruction. Slowly those who were not injured got up from where they had taken cover and returned to the tables to count the cost in injuries. Thankfully, no-one was killed. Herschel had been clubbed and whipped but nothing was broken. Zelman had been spared, as were Leizar and Chaya. There were some broken bones and much bleeding, and the long table with the food had mostly been destroyed.

The pig was the worst. People were disgusted, some refused to look. Women were covering their mouths from the stink. The Russians had defiled a Jewish religious occasion in the worst way possible. Ryfke went to Herschel who seemed to be the worst hurt. Together with Chaya, she took him inside to bathe his wounds, while the rabbi with Leizar and Zelman went to inspect the damage in the shul. The scene they were confronted with was awful. The Cossacks had entered the synagogue and planted a bomb.

The explosion had destroyed the bima and the ark containing the religious Torah scrolls and, in the place where the reading lectern had been was a massive pile of horseshit. The rabbi collapsed crying, Leizar and Zelman had to support him.

In the shtetls and small rural communities, it was not unusual for the Russians to target gatherings and celebrations to keep the Jewish population subjugated. But this was surely the most spiteful attack anyone had witnessed. The women took care of the injured, and the men worked all night to clear up and clean. Eventually the family and some close friends returned to the Domansky house and Shmuel took Herschel to his house where Chaya could bathe and dress his wounds properly and in private.

This time the wedding night for Chaya and Leizar was not a night for love making. They stayed awake long into the night talking. The promise he had made to his brother was weighing heavily on Leizar's mind this night, but he felt he could not yet share it with Chaya, whose family were well established in Polish society. Instead they talked a lot about how Herschel would feel in the morning, and how they could help him. This was the first time he had personally been subjected to the Russian cruelty, and it shook him to the core. Chaya was proud of Leizar for protecting her, and they both thanked God that no-one had been killed.

CHAPTER 27

Chaya became pregnant very soon after the weddings, with the baby due in the spring of 1895. She blossomed, and to Leizar she looked even more beautiful.

Leizar followed up on his contact with Menachim Cohain, who explained that he had been introduced to an 'agent' in the nearby town of Wadowice and this man had arranged the whole thing. The Russians were stopping people from travelling across states, and made it very difficult to leave. The taxes they collected were valuable and they would not let them just walk away. This was especially true if they wished to leave the country. But he said that if you had the money, the British and German steamship lines were taking many Poles to the UK, US and elsewhere. It was expensive and a hard journey, but it could be done.

When they had arrived in New York, he received a postcard from his parents, saying they were well and had been registered, but he had no idea whether they were housed or how they were living, and he had no way of finding out. He would wait until they wrote again, hopefully with an address. Menachim said he had heard what happened at the wedding and at least they would not be subjected to disgusting, hateful treatment like that. Leizar managed to get the name of the agent and determined to follow it up.

Lena was born in the spring, a beautiful and healthy baby. Herschel had arranged for Ryfke and Zelman to come and stay with them as soon as the waters broke, and

Chaya was grateful to have her mother-in-law with her. She had a long but uncomplicated delivery and Ryfke, Zelman and Herschel were proud grandparents, although the episode was tinged with a little sadness because it brought home to Herschel and Chaya how much they missed his wife and her mother. Herschel was besotted with the little one and couldn't leave her alone. He surprised everyone by singing Yiddish lullabies to the baby, who appeared to be looking at him in disbelief, although Ryfke explained that a new-born baby can hardly see at all.

He generously told the Domanskys that he would provide transport for them to come visit as often as possible.

The first delivery of the rolling machines arrived, and it was with great excitement that they were eagerly unpacked and examined by Herschel, Leizar and two of the men who had been studying how they were to be put together and maintained.

After the initial scepticism toward the announcement of the co-operative system from some of the workers, they were now all won over and enthusiastic to see these new machines that were going to make them more money.

When they arrived from the docks, it turned out that the packing crates had had a rough journey across the seas and the machine parts had not all arrived in perfect condition. Advice would be needed from the manufacturer on how to repair the damage, and although everyone was disappointed that there would now be a delay while Herschel wrote to the supplier and received advice, this seemed to heighten the anticipation. Alongside that, though, the rumour mill started working overtime.

Would they actually work at all? Had Herschel been duped, after having paid all the money up front? Or had they, the workers fallen for his talk of co-operatives and shares when he never intended to do anything other than close the factory?

It took several weeks, but eventually they received detailed instructions and there was a great cheer on 'start-up day' when they got them going, and started to experiment with how they were to be used. It took a while to get the hang of it, but when they were going, everyone was astonished at the speed with which they could produce perfect cigarettes.

Over dinner that night Leizar was ecstatic. He could see that his big plan could work, and he congratulated Herschel on having the vision to see how the investment would pay off.

'There will be an industrial revolution all over the world,' said Leizar. 'Automation is coming, and workers will be scared of it. They will be in fear of losing their jobs, but what we have demonstrated is that they don't have to. It's just that their jobs will change, and the result will be greater productivity, which will create more wealth. My concern is that this wealth must be shared and not go straight into the pockets of the ruling classes.'

Chaya looked at him with a knowing grin, 'That's quite a speech, Mr Domansky,' she said with not a little pride. 'But I don't think the Russians would agree.'

'You're wrong, Mrs Domansky, we must all work to change things. Many of the Russian proletariat can see that the system is rotten, and it cannot survive much longer. In the West they have seen this coming, and things are changing. We must also work to fuel the fire of change.'

Herschel enjoyed these ideological discussions with his son-in-law and his daughter. His admiration for Leizar had continued to grow, and he was thankful he still had them under his roof, at least for now. He leaned back and lit a cigarette. He took a long drag and blew the smoke out.

'We've taken a very big step, but things were happening in Warsaw before you arrived. You know who our Mayor is, Sokrates Strynkiewicz? He's made a lot of advances in the city. We now have a horse-drawn tramway, and they are beginning to install telephone lines. Only a local system so far, but it has massive potential for fast communication. A sewer system and water supply network is also being worked on, so there is a lot happening. Alas, this has all been paid for by higher taxes on the people, so the Mayor does not quite share your vision Leizar, but he is a forward thinker.'

In one way or another, Leizar had been so blinkered while he'd been in the city, that much of this was news to him. 'I'd like to meet Strynkiewicz,' he said, and Herschel smiled.

'Well, word of our automated factory has got around, especially about the workers co-operative we have formed. You may like to know that Mr Strynkiewicz is coming to the factory tomorrow, together with a reporter from the local press. So prepare for some publicity, we cannot hide. But a word of warning, Leizar. You and I will need to be careful what we say. There is always the danger of jealousy when this gets into the newspapers, and we must be aware of it. Let them talk to the workers, and we will keep pointing out how good it is for their future.'

The mayor and the press were at the factory for some time the next morning, and the interview went really well. It appeared in the local newspaper and was well read. In spite of their circumspection, many people wanted to see the factory, and in the aftermath of the article, Herschel had to post security guards 24 hours a day as a precaution.

CHAPTER 28

MINNA IS BORN AND LEV ARRIVES

The news had spread a long way, and one morning, a visitor arrived at the factory asking for Leizar. He was clearly a Russian, dressed as he was in all black leather with a Russian style double cap on his head. He had dark hair, a bushy moustache and just a trace of a small beard on his chin. His leather jacket was buttoned right up to his neck in the Russian style, and he wore glasses with a thin round frame. He looked quite young, but in spite of that he had a serious face.

He introduced himself as Lev Davidovich Bronstein. He said that he had travelled from Russia and staying in Warsaw for just a few days. He had heard about the workers co-operative and the machines, and he had come to see for himself. He had read that it was Leizar's idea, and he would very much like to talk to him.

Herschel could see that the visitor was more interested in Leizar than himself and put that down to the two of them being close in age, although Leizar was probably a year or two older. It was when Lev mentioned that he heard of Leizar's work with Edvard and the movement, that Herschel's ears pricked up. A Russian here in the factory and asking about the movement… He pulled Leizar to one side.

'Leizar, be very careful. You don't know this young man. He could bring a lot of trouble to us. Maybe he is from the Duma, we could lose everything we have, and worse, end up in prison.'

Leizar was already wary. His experiences in the past had taught him not to trust anyone he didn't know, but there was something about this intense looking young man that chimed with Leizar. 'Don't worry Papa, I am not stupid, but I want to Leizar had demonstrated the machines to Lev, he walked him to the front door, and he left. Leizar returned to Herschel's office. 'He wants to have a chat and there is something very curious about him. He is Jewish so I have arranged to meet him at the synagogue later and find out more. I will be careful, I promise.'

When they met at the Great Synagogue, Bronstein explained that his family were Jewish, from Ukraine. They lived in a small village originally, but they had recently moved to Bereslavka, which had a large Jewish community. He went to school in Odessa, and he had studied the works of Marx. Apart from Russian he spoke English, French and German and he was a fervent believer in the development of communistic principles to create a fair society throughout the Russian lands, and eventually the world. He and his compatriots were completely committed to the cause.

He had heard of Leizar, Edvard and Yitshok and the work they were doing in Poland and when he had heard further of the workers' co-operative, he'd been interested to know more, and this was one of the reasons why he'd decided to spend some time in Warsaw.

Leizar was impressed to find that word of his activities had spread, and inspired Lev to travel to Warsaw. He was very impressed with the serious nature of this man, and he found they were very close in their political views. They talked for a long-time exchanging thoughts and idealisms. Leizar suggested Lev come home with him and have dinner with the family tonight.

He could meet Chaya and Herschel, and the next day, he would take him to meet with Edvard and Yitshok. He found that Lev was not a man who smiled much, and he had an intense stare when he was listening. But he was clearly pleased to be invited and they left the synagogue and walked to the Eisenbaum house.

Herschel was guarded, even though he trusted his son-in-law's judgement. He knew he would not have invited Lev to the house unless he was sure he posed no threat. But Chaya was gracious and welcoming. They sat down to a typical Eisenbaum meal with wine which Leizar thought was especially delicious, even though it was punctuated by cries from the baby which caused Chaya to leave the table. But Lev did not eat much. He was more interested in talking than eating. His questions were intense and searching and his gaze fixed intensely upon whoever he was speaking to. Consequently, they were all rather wary of the man.

The next day they went to the office of Yitshok and found him working away editing an article which had been written by Leizar himself. He was delighted to meet with Lev, especially when he heard of his background and that he had travelled all this way, in part, to meet with them. He sent a boy to inform Edvard, who arrived a little later. Once again, the conversation was intense and far-reaching, but Edvard was especially intrigued by this young man, who seemed to have a comprehensive understanding of left-leaning governance, but was surprised at the iron grip the Russian aristocracy had on the Polish people.

The time passed quickly and when Lev eventually apologised, explaining that he was leaving Warsaw shortly, they were quite disappointed. They resolved to keep in close touch via the post and Lev said he would submit some articles for the magazine. It's fair to say that all three were extremely impressed with this young man and felt that they had met someone of real substance, but they could not help feeling there was something special about someone who would travel all this way to see a factory.

Later that year Chaya delivered another beautiful little girl – Minna had arrived.

CHAPTER 29

THE PLAN TO EMIGRATE

The 'stone' in Leizar's shoe continued to nag away at him. He wanted to know more about emigration, so he went to Wadowice to meet with the agent. Although Menachim had written to him in advance, Leizar was surprised to find that he was a vicar in the local church. Leizar was also somewhat taken aback at his appearance. He was very short, only came up to Leizar's shoulder, and Leizar himself was not a tall man. He had a completely round, moon-like face with thick bushy black hair, a black moustache, and a curly short beard. His eyes seemed too big for his face, which gave him a wild stare and his body was almost as round as his face, giving the impression of one of those roly-poly toy dolls that will not fall over. He wore a black cleric's robe and although he sported a white collar, it was rendered invisible in the folds of his neck. When he spoke, his voice was incongruously high-pitched.

His name was Pyotr Borin: he said he worked as an agent for the Beaver Steamship Line, a subsidiary of the Elder Dempster line, one of the UK's leading shipping companies and yes, he was able to arrange papers and transport out of Poland.

Emigrants had to travel overland to Hamburg in Germany, where they would board the ship. It was possible to buy a through ticket from Warsaw to the United States and the cost was 75 US dollars. Leizar had known it would be expensive, but this was around three months' wages per person.

Pyotr said to be careful and discreet in their dealings; recently an agency had been charged with persuading would-be migrants to leave their homes, cheating and stealing from them along the way. There were many unscrupulous agents, and when they were thrown into jail, their 'client' migrants who were already in transit were left to their own devices. No one knew what happened to them.

Pyotr said he had facilitated the emigration of many Poles, but added that it was not an easy trip and very expensive. He gave Leizar his name and address and suggested he think about it and let him know if he wanted to proceed.

As the months passed, this knowledge started to eat away at Leizar. He had only spoken to Herschel and Chaya about living in Warsaw, and he was now earning a salary which ideally would permit him to save for, and eventually buy a house for his young and growing family. He already had a very tidy nest egg put away.

But remembering his promise to Mendel, and indeed, that he now had children to consider, he began to wonder if instead, he should take his brood to America, where they would be safe, and treated as equals. If he could get a job there, then perhaps in time he could bring his parents and their family to follow. They would be truly in the land of the free, where opportunities existed for everyone prepared to work hard. Most importantly, he would fulfil the vow he had made to his brother, adding some meaning and hope to a senseless, pitiless, pointless death.

Chaya did know of Leizar's vow and that he had gone to meet with the agent, but they had not really discussed it fully. It was easy for her to see what was on Leizar's mind, though, and it troubled her greatly. So, before Leizar's return she went to speak to her father.

Herschel listened carefully and without comment as Chaya explained about the vow and the agent, and his frown deepened when he heard that Leizar was on his way back after speaking with the man. As was his usual way, he sat smoking a cigarette and saying nothing.

'I will not allow it!' he said eventually. 'You can both forget this nonsense. You are my only child; I will not lose you and my grandchildren. Look what happened at the wedding. I could have died. Would you want that to happen, and you were in some far away country? When I am dead and buried, then you can think about this *mishigarse!*'

He didn't raise his voice, in fact he was speaking quietly, but somehow this gave his comments more gravity, and left no room for discussion. Chaya resolved simply to leave him and wait to see what Leizar said when he returned.

He arrived the next day and Lena was waiting for him, as she always was. She ran up and gave him the biggest hug and kisses. 'Daddy, I love you best of all!' she said. It was the most wonderful welcome home.

He picked her up and went to look for Chaya, who was busy in the kitchen with little Minna toddling around her and getting in the way. He scooped up his younger daughter and carried both girls together. When Chaya was ready, they bathed their daughters together in the big tub and, smelling beautifully clean, they both fell fast asleep in bed.

After dinner Chaya and Leizar retired to their bedroom and Chaya told him of the conversation with her father. Leizar listened intently, 'Of course, I can understand his reaction and I would not expect anything different. Perhaps we should wait, but I know he is a very thoughtful man and I will discuss it with him tomorrow.'

It was after work the next day that Leizar approached Herschel before dinner. He was relaxing in his big, winged armchair and smoking a cigar. He offered Leizar the other chair and a drop of whisky from the decanter by his side.

'Herschel,' said Leizar, as he declined the whisky and sat in the chair opposite, 'Chaya told me she spoke to you. It is true that I went to find out more about the possibility of emigration, but she and I have not discussed it yet. I have been thinking a lot about it and asking myself if I am happy for my children to grow up under the regime here. I want them to have opportunities to fulfil their potential, which this regime will not allow.

'Also, I made a vow with my brother Mendel before he died. Maybe things will change here and perhaps I can have some small influence on that with my writings, but if it happens, it will take a very long time. I have also been thinking that we must take account of others who will be affected, I have my parents and all my family in Poland, and very importantly, of course, we have you. I have been turning all these things over in my mind, and Chaya explained your reaction, which I completely understand. I hope you know that I have developed enormous love and respect for you, and I want to assure you that we will never do anything without your blessing.'

'Leizar, you are a fine young man, and I am lucky to have you for my son-in-law. I am grateful for what you have said, believe me when I say it is a great comfort to me'

Leizar was nodding along until the conversation took an unexpected turn.

'But I have been thinking a lot about it since Chaya told me. Let's have dinner and relax and tomorrow we will have another chat.'

When they went to bed, Leizar told Chaya what her father had said. They were both puzzled. Herschel was a deep thinker and they wondered what was on his mind.

Again, it was after work and before dinner that Herschel asked Leizar to come and sit with him. 'I have been thinking about this all night, and it is not as simple as I first thought. We live in changing times, and I must take everything into account. I hope you don't mind, Leizar, but I would like to talk with my daughter, after which you and I can speak together.'

This intrigued Leizar all the more, but of course, he agreed, left the room and told Chaya that her father wanted to speak to her. It had to have something to do with emigrating, but he could not guess further than that.

Chaya looked lovely in a printed taffeta long dress flounced out with petticoats, her hair done in plaits down her back. There was a soft swish when she walked into the room and sat opposite her father.

'My darling best beloved daughter.'

He used to start this way when she was a little girl, whenever he was about to say something she may not like. 'As we know, things are changing in the world. I am sure there will be an uprising or maybe even a revolution in Eastern Europe. The proletariat are becoming stronger all the time, and eventually I think the Russian rule on the one side and the Austrians on the other will be overthrown.

'I have a wonderful business now, mainly thanks to your Leizar. People all over the world are smoking an enormous number of cigarettes. The demand is insatiable. I could still sell double or treble what I am able to produce.

'Leizar knows all this, and he can see it coming. He is your husband, and you have a young family. They are your first priority now. Whatever happens, I will be alright. But Leizar has his parents and his brothers and sisters to consider, and they are not in such a great position. I also know the vow he made to his dying brother weighs heavily on him.

'He is wonderful man, your Leizar, and whatever he decides I know he loves you and respects your opinion, so you will discuss it together. I just want you to know you should not see me as a responsibility. I will thrive now, under any regime.'

Chaya was shocked at his candour, and a tear rolled down her face at the realisation that he was giving her freedom to go with her family, and maybe never see him again.

'And even more than that,' Herschel continued, 'should you decide on a campaign to help other family members emigrate, I can easily provide the finance, and I would be proud to do it. So never doubt my love for you, my best beloved, your father is always here.'

She flew to his arms and hugged him tight, 'Papa,' she said, between sobs, 'You are my father, we are blood, and you are without Mama. I can never leave you.'

He stroked her hair gently and made shushing noises, eventually he said, 'Sometimes we have to make hard decisions, my darling. You must think of your husband and your children first. Wherever you are, I can visit, and it won't be long before the new telephone system will allow us to talk frequently. Now go get your husband and let's talk together.'

Leizar was shocked when Chaya told him. 'Your father is truly a great man, and whatever transpires, we must never forget that he has such love for us all, that he is prepared to let us go. I must speak to him right away, then I will tell you both about the agent in Wadowice.'

They entered the room together to see Herschel puffing away and smiling, but Leizar did not sit. 'Chaya told me what you said, and only a great man could be so objective as to consider what may be good for his family at his own expense. I am in awe at your ability to put your understandable emotions to one side and remain objective.

'I meant what I said, and I would never go against your will, and neither would I go against the will of my wife. She and I must discuss it at length. We make all decisions together, there is a great deal at risk and a lot to consider. And I am in awe that she is your only daughter, and these are your grandchildren, and yet you would be prepared to let us go.'

Herschel smiled, 'Leizar, in the short time we have known each other, I believe a mutual love and respect has grown between us. You have a duty to make your family safe and give opportunity to my lovely granddaughters. They deserve to grow up free. This part of the world is changing and who knows what it will be in the future. You must take them all to the new world. Maybe one day, I can join you there, but I have the money to help you. I know that your love for Chaya is without bounds and I trust you with her, the most precious thing in my life.'

Leizar welled up when he said this, and he stood and went over to hug Herschel. 'You are truly a great man. You see things so clearly.'

Chaya's tears were running now, and she was dabbing her face with a pretty lace handkerchief. She went and sat on her father's lap, kissed and hugged him tight. Leizar took her hand, and they went to their room.

'What a man your father is! I was truly moved by his clear-eyed reaction and indeed his generous offer of finance. Now we have the biggest decision of our lives.

'I told him he is a truly great man and I believe it to be so. But this is a lifetime decision we must make together, there are so many factors to take into account. Your father unselfishly leaves his own emotions to one side and trusts us to decide what is best for the family on the same basis. He has shown us that clear thinking is necessary, and emotions can cloud the issue.'

Chaya was already crying, her body slumped in the chair while she patted her puffy eyes with her handkerchief, as if to give the lie to Leizar's words. 'Oh! Leizar, how can we possibly do that? I would have to leave my father, whom I love with all my heart, and you would leave your parents and all your family and give up the magazine and your role at the factory. On top of all this we would be going to a place we know nothing about.'

They talked all night and turned it over in every way. Herschel's reaction had made it all a reality, and by the morning it was clear that they had to take it seriously. Leizar would find out as much as he could from his contacts through the shul and the community, and they would take some time before they could decide. Chaya would talk further to her father.

Leizar found that Menachim was not the only person in Warsaw who had used this route to escape the country. Indeed, once he started to talk among the community, there was no shortage of people with experience or rumours of the system, and they were very prepared to gossip about it.

He found that many Jews had emigrated out of this region, with the vast majority going the United States. But there were others who suggested different solutions to oppression, some of which he was very aware, and others not so much. Some Hassidic Orthodox Jews, who looked to protect Judaism, tried their best to isolate themselves away from hostility and outside forces by making their homes unwelcoming to Jews and Gentiles alike. They lived a communal life where only a few worked, the men studied Torah and Talmud, and the women cooked and brought up the children.

Zionists on the other hand promoted mass migration to Palestine, while socialist Bundists sought to unite all the Jews in Eastern Europe in the class-based fight for economic reform. Others believed that assimilation into mainstream culture was the best response.

Leizar decided to go to the shtetl and discuss it with his parents. He knew he would have a hard time convincing his father to leave the land of his birth, in spite of all the degradation and atrocities that the community had suffered. But Herschel's words rang in his ears. 'The children should not be denied the chance to live in peace with equality of opportunity.' He knew he would face his father's initial stubbornness and that it would be a fight. But he equally knew that after the first reaction, Zelman would begin to see sense. However, that did not mean he would bend to it.

CHAPTER 30

A CHAT WITH ZELMAN

He arrived at the shtetl at lunch time and as always, Ryfke was delighted to see him. The children were at school with Zelman and straight away Leizar could see something was different about his mother, but he could not put his finger on quite what it was. She seemed extremely happy to see him and started singing as she went into the kitchen to put food on the table, which he helped her prepare. She continued singing quietly under her breath as she worked. She looked lovely in a long blue shift dress with her natural hair pinned up. She did not need to wear the *sheitel* when at home with her family. The house was warm and the fire was burning cheerfully.

They sat down to a simple lunch of bread, pickled herring, and a Russian salad, with tea and lemon in the traditional glasses drunk through a sugar lump. 'Well, my darling, I know you have been doing some great things in the city, but I have some news too.'

Leizar was intrigued. Clearly his mother was busting to tell him something. 'I am expecting another baby!' She said it and just sat back to see his reaction, which was exactly as she expected. Surprise at first and then a dawning delight. His mother was in her mid-forties which was quite old to have another child, but not that unusual. 'Yes,' she continued, 'Isn't it wonderful that *Hashem* (God) has blessed us again.'

After the initial surprise, Leizar realised that this news would not make what he had come to talk about, any easier. 'Uma, it is wonderful to see you so happy, but you are no spring chicken you know, you must be very careful.'

'Yes, yes, I know all that, but Hashem would not have let this happen if it were not a blessing. Are you not delighted? You will have another little brother or sister.' Leizar's stern face broke into a smile. 'Of course, Uma, a new baby is always a blessing.'

Leizar's plan was to speak to his mother first and see if he could convince her of the wisdom of the plan and enlist her help with his father. They chatted for quite a while about the new baby, speculating on whether it would be a boy or a girl, and suggesting possible names. Eventually, Leizar felt he should broach the subject.

Of course, the concept of emigration was not new to Ryfke and would not be so to his father or any of the family. They all knew of Mendel's legacy in this regard, and that Leizar had inherited it by way of the vow. However, they had only ever spoken of it in an abstract, 'what if' sense. To be confronted with a concrete plan that was actually deliverable and could be funded was something quite different.

Leizar explained that he was thinking he would go alone in the first instance. With the help of Herschel, he could afford to make an initial trip to establish links for accommodation and work and then come back for his family. Once they were settled, he could send for his parents and siblings and maybe others of the wider family too. It was the most incredible opportunity.

'Oh Leizar! Your father will never go for this. This is our home. All our family and friends are here, and we all look out for each other. How can you think of taking away our family and our lovely grandchildren? And with a new baby on the way too. We had to learn to live with the grief of losing a beautiful son who did nothing wrong, and then you want that we lose you too? Moving away. Must we always lose? You have to forget about this for now. Don't even mention it to your father. He has not been well, and I fear for him if you tell him this.'

This was indeed a problem for Leizar. Although his mother was very traditional in her outlook, she was also a very perceptive woman and could usually see the bigger picture. Also, he knew he was her favourite, a fact which he hoped, would help him to reason with her, but it worked against him when she thought of losing him. On the other hand, he thought his family may have got used to him being absent from the shtetl, so perhaps this would not be such a wrench. He had to admit that from his side, he would miss his family terribly and he knew, Chaya would miss her father.

He tried reasoning with his mother all afternoon, and by the time the family were due home from school, he did not think he had moved her much.

First home was Moshe, who came running into Leizar's arms with a big hug and lots of kisses. Marcia came in starving hungry, and he got a quick kiss before she sat at the table and inhaled the snack Ryfke had prepared for them. Duvid followed, delighted to see Leizar. He wanted to know all the news and was a little put out that Leizar was clearly holding something back. Finally, Zelman came through the door. Leizar was surprised that his father seemed to have aged in the short time since he saw him last. His face seemed more lined, and his beard was turning grey. But as always, he was delighted to see his first-born son, of whom he was, justifiably, very proud.

Leizar waited until dinner was finished and the children had been put to bed. Ryfke, Zelman, Duvid and Leizar sat at the table. Zelman could feel the atmosphere was a little tense. 'Well, my boy, I can see you have something to say. What have you got to tell us?'

'Upa, you know about Mendel's plan to move the family to the US, and my vow to him to do everything I can to make that dream a reality……' Zelman cut him off. 'Yes, yes that *mishigarse* rubbish, don't tell me with all the great work you have been doing, you have spent time thinking about that?'

Leizar always found it hard to control his reactions when his father was dismissive in this way. It never failed to get under his skin. 'Upa, just listen please!' He tried to explain about his conversation with Menachim and his meeting with the agent. Also, the conversations with others in Warsaw, and that he had found out that this was a route being used by many Jews. But Zelman did not want to hear it. In fact, the more Zelman realised that Leizar had done some work to find out about it, and that it was a real possibility after all this time, the less Zelman wanted to face up to it. And his method was to get angry and not let Leizar speak.

But Leizar was now a father himself and no longer the boy Zelman used to control in this way. He faced up to his father, which was something Duvid had never seen. To Duvid, Zelman was the master of the house, and his father must be right, simply because he was his father.

Ryfke was starting to be tearful. 'Please listen both of you!' she shouted. 'There is another young person in this room, not even born yet. Do not shout and scream in front of him. Also, the other children – you think they can't hear you?'

Zelman stood, '*Hak mir nisht kayn tshaynik,*' he exclaimed. Leizar took a deep breath, 'Sit down Upa,' he said very firmly. 'There is much to discuss.'

Zelman sat down rather heavily, his face slightly red and his eyes wide at being directed by his son. Leizar went on to explain that he not only wanted a better life for his parents and all his family, but that they should also think of the little ones. What chance did they have living in the shtetl under the current regime? And what about the grandchildren? Leizar's children could have a free life with the opportunity, each of them, to fulfil their talents. Why would Zelman deny that to them?

Zelman took a deep breath. He started rather quietly, but his voice gradually grew to a crescendo. 'This life may not be much, but it is all the life your mother and I have ever known. And it is not too bad. If you behave yourself and you pay your taxes, you can keep clean. Everyone thinks they can change things, socialists, communists, Zionists, but the Russians have the power. They will always be the winners.' He was shouting again now, 'And let me tell you boychik, nobody will change that!'

As Zelman's voice got louder, so Leizar's became softer. 'You may be right Upa, but if I am correct, then the children would not have to worry about that. They would be safe in the land of the free!'

It seemed that the wind had gone out of Zelman's sails. Leizar seized his chance, 'Let me explain the financial arrangements.'

'Oh!' Zelman seemed to wake up again, his voice full of sarcasm, 'There are financial arrangements? Of course, we have plenty of money, I forgot!'

Leizar explained about the 75 dollars per person, which infuriated Zelman all the more. 'Oh, is that all just 75 dollars? You seem to have forgotten. We are poor people. We don't have enough to feed us and keep us all warm. Maybe you didn't notice, with your fancy life in Warsaw!'

Ryfke had explained to Leizar before, he should recognise Zelman's pride. Although Zelman was grateful for the money he contributed, he hated that he was dependent on it.

'No, no Upa, I spoke with Herschel. The factory is making huge profits with the automatic machines. He has offered to pay for us all to take this trip.' Zelman threw his hands up in the air dramatically, 'Oh my rich *mechitten*. Of course he can pay for anything! He can pay for everyone to do this, and when they go, we don't even know what happens to them. Is he taking the trip?'

'No, no, Upa. He has his business here, he'd stay with it.'

But Zelman was standing again and banging the table this time.

'*Men zol zikh kenen oyskoyfn fun toyt, voltn di oremelayt sheyn parnose gehat.*' It was one of his favourite sayings: if the rich could pay people to die for them, the poor would make a decent living. But he was just getting started, and he went on, at the top of his voice, 'Don't you dare think of taking any more of our family away from us. Stop with all this and carry on doing what you are doing, and we should all be well!' He turned to Ryfke.

'Now don't you give him any chance to *farmisht dein kopf* with this *mishigarse.* He went on and on and in the end Ryfke could stand it no more and she ran into the kitchen with her hands over her ears. Duvid put his arms round his mama. He hated to hear their papa shouting. It happened sometimes when he had come home late, and the schnapps had taken its course. Zelman had a bad temper and would sometimes chase the children around, banging the table if they said the wrong thing – but he had never struck out at any of them, and if he lost his temper, they would often find a sweet under their pillow when they went to bed. He usually slept it off and was fine next morning.

But Duvid worried for his mother, who seemed so much smaller than his father. Although Zelman was not a tall man, he was very strong and could look fearsome with his bushy beard. Today he was shouting louder and thumping the table. When he was like this, it was best to keep out of his way. So Ryfke went to the children to kiss them goodnight, and Leizar and Duvid went to bed.

The next day Leizar went to see Shmuel, who was always easier to talk to than his father and he was surprised to find that his uncle was aware of the agency route for emigration. He said he had been speaking to 'some people' who had tried this route. It was not as easy it sounded.

First of all, the shipping lines were only selling steerage tickets, and as there were no reserved berths, they could sell as many as they liked for each ship. Some ships were leaving with more than a thousand people standing in steerage, the bigger ships had far more and two thousand was not unheard-of. That meant the refugees were treated like cattle and it was standing room only with no proper facilities. The ports of departure were in Germany and Holland, so the travellers had to get themselves overland to those ports. There was now a railway from Warsaw to Hamburg, but it was very expensive, and some people had travelled by wagon or donkey and not made it, and others had even tried to walk.

Shmuel had heard of people setting out with valid tickets who didn't make it even to the port of departure. If they made it to the port, the Companies were obliged by the US authorities to give each refugee a medical and various inoculations before they were allowed to board. Some family members were considered too sick to travel and not allowed to board the ship with their families. Others had fallen ill at sea and then been turned away at immigration in America; forced to sail back to Europe.

So, it was not easy. Not to be deterred, Leizar said, 'Yes Uncle. Tell me what is good that comes easy? If it was easy everyone would do it. But there are successes aren't there? Many of them? And in the land of equal opportunity, we can work hard and be free and happy without the fear that someone will take away what we have?'

'Leizar,' said Shmuel, 'of course many people are using this route, but you must recognise it is not a guarantee of success. You must also remember that the America is taking not only refugees from Eastern Europe, but also from many other countries, Ireland, Asia and the Far East. People are pouring in. Then there is the language. The one language we have never learned is English and that is the one we would need.'

Leizar explained that he had the backing of Herschel and he had offered to finance a number of people. He was thinking of making the journey himself first, and then once he had established himself, he would send for Chaya and the children, or go back for them, eventually arranging transport for other family members who wanted to come.

'Well,' said Shmuel, 'It's a huge advantage to have Herschel and his finance behind you, but there are still big risks involved. Anything could happen. You are in the hands of people you don't know, and you have to trust them. They want the money in advance. You could lose your family and not meet up with them again. It is a dangerous and treacherous route, and there is also the threat of bandits, especially if people find out who you are, and that a rich man like Herschel involved.

Then you have the problem of your parents. Zelman will never leave Poland. The only time he even leaves the shtetl is when you take him to Warsaw. The children are still young. But you are right, our people deserve the opportunity not to have to live like this, and I don't know what our world will be like if there is an uprising. Herschel is a very wise man. He can see this, and that is why he encourages you even when it takes away his own loved ones.'

Leizar was very thoughtful. 'Perhaps, if I can get my family safely to America, and establish us there, then maybe over the years, I can persuade Upa and the family to come and join us? I could even arrange for others to come over when they are ready? Duvid may want to come soon, and what about you and your family? Maybe when Upa sees the life we could have over there, perhaps even he will change his mind?'

Leizar went to the school to speak with his father. Zelman had calmed down since the night before, but Leizar was still met with a cold reception. Zelman's face was serious, he decided to try emotional blackmail. 'You know you upset your mother last night, and she did not sleep for worry about you? No matter what a big man you think you are, you are still her little boy. How can you do this to us with a new baby on the way?'

But Leizar's face was also set stern. He was not going to change his mind. In fact, after his chat with Uncle Shmuel, he was all the more determined. After they spent an hour talking, Zelman could see he would get nowhere with Leizar, so he finished the conversation in his typical style. *'Kleine kinder lozn nit shloffen, grosse kinder lozn nit leben.'* little children don't let you sleep; big children don't let you live - he turned away from his son.

Nevertheless, when Leizar returned to Warsaw, he was excited. He knew he had upset his parents greatly, but he was equally sure this was the right thing for his family, and what's more, he thought he could establish a way to 'rescue' many others from the oppression under which they lived.

CHAPTER 31

Leizar could not wait to talk to Chaya and start planning. Of course, he also needed to discuss plans with Herschel. Leizar was half afraid that Herschel's generous offer to fund emigration for 'a number' of people may have been a bit rash. He had not spoken to him about it since. Would Herschel come through with that offer? Especially since it meant he would not see his daughter and his grandchildren. Would he have second thoughts?

Leizar rushed into the house, and he was delighted to find that Minna was now toddling. She managed the distance from her mother to her father and only fell on her face twice. But unabashed, she got up smiling each time, with her arms out to him. She would have made it, if Lena had not run into the room, straight to her father and knocked the little one flying out of the way which made her cry.

Leizar gathered them both up in his arms with big kisses and cuddles, and carried them over to their mother. He gathered her in too; a family hug. Chaya was often surprised at Leizar's strength. It was a family trait. Short, but very stocky and extremely strong of body and mind. 'My darlings, I am so glad to see you. I feel like I have been away a long time, but papa has had a good trip and I must talk to Mama.' He whispered to Chaya 'I have so much to talk to you about.'

Chaya smiled, took the children and helped him off with his coat and hat. 'And I am so pleased you returned safely, I always worry when you are away. Now go and wash up and relax. I will tell my father you are home, and cook will prepare some dinner. When you are ready, I will pour you a whiskey and you can tell me all your news.' Chaya had realised immediately that Leizar would want to speak to her before sitting down to dinner with Herschel. Once again, Leizar thought how lucky he was to have a wife who was not only beautiful, but intelligent and sensitive.

Chaya put the children in their bedroom with lots of toys, and strict instructions to Lena to look after her sister, which was a bit of a challenge because Minna was developing the Domansky physique: short but very strong, and quite capable of overpowering her sister.

'Chaya, I have spoken to my parents and my Uncle Shmuel and I have done a lot of thinking. First let me ask, have you spoken to your father any further about his generous offer to fund emigration?' Chaya shook her head. 'No, there has been no mention of it since last we spoke, but he would not have made such an offer without thinking about it, and for sure, he would never go back on his word. You can count on it.'

Leizar took a draught of his whiskey, and it was starting to make him feel much more relaxed. 'Good, I must speak to him about it. My darling, I am absolutely convinced that this is the right move for us, and I know how to do it. Just think, in a few months' time, we could all be living the American Dream! With nobody telling us what to do! And above all, our girls can grow up learning English in an American school. And maybe graduate to college and become professionals, if that's what they want.'

She wanted him to explain in detail about his parents' reaction, but her face darkened a little when she heard that Ryfke was pregnant. 'I must go to see her,' she said. 'She is not a young woman to have another baby now.'

She was not surprised at his father's reaction, but it did worry her that they would be leaving their parents and siblings behind, not to mention Leizar's uncles, aunts and cousins.

Leizar started to explain his plan, that if her father agreed to finance it, he would travel first and establish himself. Find a place to live, and maybe the chance of a job if he was very lucky. Then he would return for Chaya and the children. That way he would know all the people who were important and how to navigate any potential problems on the way. He would buy 'kosher' tickets from a reputable steam ship company to ensure their safety.

They were interrupted by a loud scream from the bedroom. They both ran in to see that Lena had tied Minna's hands up with a dressing gown cord and she was, busy painting colours on her sister's face. Both the girls looked up and laughed when their parents burst in and Leizar and Chaya ended up laughing too. They cleaned up and went down to dinner where Heschel was already waiting. 'Well, my boy, what news of the shtetl?'

Leizar went through the plan again, after first explaining the reactions of his parents and his Uncle Shmuel. 'Upa will come round, he said. 'He is very upset, but I think he knows in his heart of hearts, that this is the right thing for us. It hurts me to hurt them, but it does not need to be forever. In this day of steam ship travel you can get to America in a couple of weeks easily, so if we are established, we can send for them. Maybe Papa, you could even come visit?

All of this was said between mouthfuls of delicious chulent with fresh bread. The children started to get restless, so Chaya took them to their room with some lokshen pudding for a treat and got them ready for bed.

It gave Leizar the opportunity to tactfully ask Herschel how he felt about the funding now that they knew the cost. Herschel's face grew quite serious and Leizar feared bad news was coming. 'We left that a little open, didn't we?' said Herschel - without waiting for an answer, he continued, 'Look, you know I am making really good money now. I can sell my cigarettes many times over, and I am buying another six machines. These are a modified version which are, believe it or not, much faster. What am I going to do with my money? You, Chaya and the grandchildren are the most precious things I have. And I would not be in this position if it was not for you. So, we must work together on this, you find the safest way to do it, and I will provide the money.

Again, Leizar was astounded at the generosity and clear headedness of his father-in law.

'I have also been thinking. You do not need to work at the factory. You can draw your salary and continue to work on this plan. You must speak to Edvard and Yitshok. You have not written for the magazine for a while, and I have spoken to them. They know of your idea, but I they do not want to lose you and I am sure they will try to convince you to carry on writing. I have opened an account with Western Union which will enable me to wire money to the United States. I will also establish a fund in your name here which you can draw on. It will be sufficient to fund the tickets and travel for your scouting trip, and for the family to follow. After that let's see how it goes.'

Chaya returned and they all drank some tea and Herschel continued talking. Herschel drew his chair closer to them both, 'Look, my darling and best beloved daughter, you and the grandchildren are the only family I have, and one day whatever I have that I can retain from the Russians, will be yours. It is because I love you all so much that I want you do this. The only thing I cannot give my grandchildren here is the respect of others and the opportunity to succeed. You can give them that. Yes, I will come visit God willing, so we will not lose touch. And if we can manage to finance others to do the same – then we will.'

Chaya started sobbing again, and even Leizar had a tear in his eye, but everything Herschel said made sense. 'I will start tomorrow to find out the best and safest way and I hope to take the first steps soon. I cannot tell you how grateful we are. Without you it would not be possible. I hope I can become half the man you are.'

Their lovemaking that night seemed very special. Leizar had stayed up for a final drink with his father-in-law and when he entered the bedroom, Chaya was completely naked, her long hair hanging loose past her shoulders and just covering parts of her breasts. She put her arms out to him and coming into them was like coming home. It was soft, warm and protective. Not a word was said but she kissed him deeply and with her whole mouth and tongue, urgently but also tenderly. Leizar was almost ready to explode. He lifted her, put her gently on the bed and almost ripped off his clothes, his manhood proudly erect.

She took him in her hand and pulled him on to her. He kissed her again on the mouth and then her neck, and shoulders. He cupped one breast and felt the nipple come alive. He kissed and caressed it until she moaned with pleasure. His lips travelled slowly, gently touching her other breast, her belly and finally the soft fur of her womanhood. Chaya felt that familiar heat at the very centre of her being. She could not contain herself; she was filled with desire for him.

She took control and seized his erect phallus. She guided him to her mouth and turned him so that he could continue to caress her outer lips and then with his tongue deep inside her, she gasped. They could both wait no longer. She opened her legs and he pushed inside. They made rhythmic passionate love to each other and burst into climax together.

Afterwards, they lay back on the bed mutually exhausted. It was perhaps the best love they had ever made, as if it might be for the last time. He held her in his arms and with a warm and secure feeling, she fell asleep.

But Leizar's mind was racing. He felt energised and charged with the job ahead. When Chaya was fully asleep, he gently eased out of bed and went to smoke one of Herschel's cigarettes while he turned it all over in his mind. He was excited to think that in a few months, they could be in America. But despite that, his thoughts kept returning to Herschel's comment about their future inheritance. Strangely, it had not occurred to him before that Herschel would not carry on forever, but he now realised, their future could be very bright.

They made love again in the morning, this time more like old lovers meeting again with each knowing the pleasure of the other and finished just in time before the bedroom door burst open and two little girls came to jump all over them. After the family breakfast, it was time for Leizar to go and speak with his colleagues at the magazine.

Edvard and Yitshok were angry when he told them of his plans. Yitshok stood, 'What do you think this is here? You think you can just come and go as you please?'

Edvard was also standing, 'Leizar, we brought you here to help the movement, and when you walked out, we took you back, not just because you are a nice fellow, but because you are talented and the whole movement and the magazine need your help. How can you let us down again You are making a mistake. If you want to help change things you should put the people above your own ambitions. This capitalist democracy of the West, it will never last. It just means some people can get rich at the expense of others. What sort of equality is that?'

Yitshok was pacing up and down now. He went close and put his face close to Leizar's 'Leizar, you are doing real work here, that will help us change lives for millions of people. You have a special talent, and you are already well known and well-read here in Warsaw. What can we do to convince you to stay?'

But Leizar was immovable. 'I am sorry, but I have thought long and hard on this. I have discussed it with Chaya and with Herschel. I have to say I have not entirely forsaken my socio-communist feelings and the capitalist principles do not sit entirely well with me. Before when it was only me, I would not have countenanced it, but I must think first of the safety and prospects of my wife and children, and also of the vow I made to my brother.'

Edvard and Yitshok tried everything to find a way, and their frustration did not seem to dissipate. In the end Leizar said he must leave. He said he would keep in touch, and maybe the magazine could be published in the US, and he could continue to write.

They told him they had received a letter for him from Lev Bronstein. He immediately opened and read it.

'My dear friend Domansky,

When we met, I felt we had a lot in common, so I thought you might like to know what has happened since. I have met and married Aleksandra Sokolovskaya, a member of the party and we have been working together writing and distributing printed leaflets and revolutionary pamphlets. Alas, I was arrested along with 200 members of the union, and I am now awaiting trial in Moscow. A new party has been formed, the Russian Social Democratic Labour Party (RSDLP) and I am a member of it. They want me to change my name – they say it is too Jewish.

The old party was decimated by arrests, and it had split ideals. Some were arguing that the party should focus on helping industrial workers improve their lot in life, they are not so worried about changing the government. They believe that societal reforms will grow out of the worker's struggle for higher pay and better working conditions. Others argue that overthrowing the monarchy is more important and for that a well-organised and disciplined revolutionary party with military backing is essential.

I believe the latter is the pressing issue and there is a newspaper 'ISKRA' based in London that has been helping to express and distribute those sentiments. They want me to join them and write for them. I would value your opinion.

Well, my dear friend, do write and tell me how goes the world with you. Perhaps we will meet again when we can further the cause.

Your friend
Lev.'

Leizar was impressed that Bronstein had taken the trouble to write to him, and especially that he was seeking his opinion. He determined to keep in touch.

But first he wrote to Pyotr Borin, the Russian cleric, outlining his plans for emigration of his family. He asked for details of the cost and the timetable for the return trip for himself, and then the cost for the whole family later. He sent the letter by special courier – it was possible to pay for a rider to take a letter by hand to another part of Poland, it was expensive, but Leizar could not wait for normal post, which would take many days to be delivered and returned. He arranged for the courier to wait and return with a reply.

When the rider returned the next day, Leizar excitedly opened the envelope. Pyotr said he would write to the shipping line and ask for a special quote for the journeys that Leizar described. If the quote was acceptable, he thought it could happen quite quickly because there were ships leaving every few weeks. He would write again as soon as he heard. Leizar was rather disappointed. He was impatient to make plans, and he thought he would get a quote right away, but he understood, and wrote back to tell Pyotr to use the same courier for speed as soon as he had information.

Leizar enjoyed being at home all day with Chaya. He was able to play with his children and visit his other uncles and aunts in Kawetchka, some of whom still harboured disapproval due to his leaving before the funeral of his brother. 'I can forgive, but I can never forget,' said one older aunt.

But they knew that he was a success in Warsaw, and many had met Chaya and the children and had a soft spot for them. Leizar did not mention emigration. He knew their minds were completely locked in the shtetl and they would not be able to appreciate the opportunities he could see for the future generations.

Three days later, he received a letter from Pyotr. It was possible to arrange the train journey to Hamburg and passage on the RMS Megantic, out of Hamburg to Glasgow in Scotland. The ship would lay over for 5 days to reload and travel onwards to New York. If that was sufficient time for Leizar, he could re-board the same ship, or if not, he could wait for the next vessel, which would probably leave two weeks later. There would be an overnight stay in Hamburg on the way out and Pyotr could arrange a bed for the night, but he could not guarantee any accommodation in Glasgow, where Leizar would have to fend for himself. For the full trip they would need 200 dollars.

The cost to travel with his wife and children on a one-way basis later would be a further 100 dollars for each adult and the children would be 75 dollars each. Of course, this would not be payable until they were ready to leave.

Pyotr told him there would be many questions for him at immigration in Glasgow. Refugees from Eastern Europe often stopped over there, but the authorities were anxious not to import criminals trying to escape justice. He said the shipping line would give him the name of a contact who could help in Glasgow.

It was a great deal of money and Leizar did ponder whether he should try to find another quote. There were cheaper berths available, and he was paying a premium to travel with a reputable company. Maybe they should just take a chance and all go together? That would save 150 dollars. He discussed it with Herschel.

'Leizar, thankfully we can afford it. Every decision you make should be on the basis of the safety and welfare of your family and yourself. You are all more precious than gold to me. Do not make any decision on the basis of cost. So, go make arrangements, I am behind you.'

So it was that Leizar paid the 200 dollars and four weeks later he was on the train from Warsaw to Hamburg. He had written to his parents to say he was going to make the trip to explore the possibilities and he would contact them again when he returned. In any event, he would be in touch with Chaya through the office of the shipping line.

He had been warned only to wear old clothes and carry a battered suitcase. There were bandits who would attack anyone who looked like they might have something worth stealing. On arrival at Hamburg dock, he was shown to a run-down apartment block which had once been painted white but was now a very dirty grey streaked with black. He was directed to a room on the first floor. There were four beds and virtually no other furniture, bare walls with cracks, and uncovered floorboards. There was a smell of body odour, and the place looked like it had not been cleaned for a long time. The other three beds were occupied by three other men, none of whom looked that savoury.

He said hello in Yiddish, which was received with grunts, he sat on the bed and looked around, thankful that it would only be one night. He decided to keep his suitcase with him at all times. There was a knock on the door and a very large woman with an enormous chest and hair tied back tightly, entered with a tray. In German she said her name was Helga and here was food for them. Leizar was given a plate of cold sausage, sauerkraut and bread.

He had not anticipated that his conscience would be tested so early. Clearly the food was not kosher, and he had no idea what may be in the sausage. But he was hungry, and he realised that on such an adventure, kosher food would be impossible to find.

The only hot drink was coffee which Leizar had never tasted and frankly didn't like, but he had a small bottle of schnapps which made it palatable. Each of his room companions seemed very wary of each other, and there was very little talking, they ate their food and one after another laid down on the thin, bare mattress. Since the bedding looked as though it had been unchanged over many visits, Leizar kept all his clothes on.

There was very little sleeping amid the noises of the dockyard, the rather stale smell of the room and the noise of the other occupants, so he lay awake most of the night. At 6.00am they were given more sausage and bread with coffee and told to get ready to board the ship. He was more than ready to get out of there.

His ticket was Zwischendeck, between decks. This was a tiny open deck in between second class and steerage. Only a few people had been allocated that space, which meant the steerage passengers walked past them, squeezed past the ship's machinery and were directed down steep stairways into the enclosed lower decks. Steerage would be their prison for the rest of the voyage. He was grateful to Pyotr for arranging this for him.

The line of passengers proceeding down to the hold was astonishing. It seemed never-ending, and Leizar could not believe the ship could accommodate so many. Uncle Shmuel had warned him that since there were no designated berths in steerage, the shipping lines were unscrupulously making money by overselling the space.

They crammed as many people into the hold as they could. The journey for them would be miserable.

Each of the Zwischendeck passengers had been allocated a deckchair and a cover. This was to be their accommodation for the trip. Eventually the ship was loaded. The engines had been idling, but the power required to pull away into the River Elbe created massive noise, vibration and smoke. The big steamer seemed to heave herself away like a big beast that had been sleeping and did not want to move.

As they pulled out towards the mouth of the river things quietened down and Leizar realised that what he thought was the prime position on the in-between deck, was the first place to receive the smoke from the funnels when the wind blew it back.

Chaya had packed some food in a separate bag for which he was grateful, but it did not last long and in the evening he was hungry. The food onboard seemed to consist mainly of cold sausage, cheese and sauerkraut. He gave little thought to what may be in the sausage, and there was only coffee to drink, but at least he wouldn't starve.

He had found two other men from Galicia with whom he struck up a conversation, and they agreed between them to try and rehearse the questions they would be asked at immigration in Glasgow. Luckily one of them spoke some English.

He said his name was Avram Groisse and he would also be travelling on from Glasgow to New York to meet his brother who had made the trip some months before, so he had some idea of the questions.

The obvious ones were: name, age, occupation, nationality. And then, had they ever been in prison and importantly, how much money did they have on them? They had been told to say they had about 25 dollars. It was important to appear that they could support themselves for a while, but at the same time not to make themselves a target. They must learn the questions and answers in English.

The journey from Germany to Glasgow would take about seven days and the seas were not too rough. However, that did not prevent a great deal of seasickness and throwing up, not all of which went over the side. For that, Leizar was grateful he was on the open deck. The stench emanating from steerage below them was putrid. He made a mental note to make sure that, when he made the trip with Chaya, they were placed on the in-between deck and to tell her to pack more food for the children.

They pushed out into the North Sea, past Amsterdam and on day three they saw a port city which they were told was Antwerp. The next day they entered the English Channel, sailing past Southampton before rounding the 'toe' of England at Plymouth and following the coastline up towards Wales. Day six took them into the Irish Sea past Liverpool and the Isle of Man before arriving a day ahead of schedule at the Firth of Clyde. It took a long time to negotiate the sea traffic along the Clyde, so it was late afternoon by the time they arrived in Glasgow.

The city was alive and buzzing. There were buildings as far he could see, and the atmosphere was smoky. There seemed to be a haze over everything. The big ship had to be very carefully manoeuvred past paddle steamers and ferries into the dock and tied up. Leizar was very excited. He was about to set foot in Great Britain!

Passengers were asked to disembark, which was easier said than done. The first and second-class passengers formed a line down the gangway that led into a chained-off enclosure with a sign saying 'Immigration.' And there it stopped. The mid-deck people would be allowed to join the end of that line next, but it moved very slowly. It was starting to get dark by the time Leizar and his newfound friend, Avram Groisse even got on to the end of it. He doubted that the steerage people would get off that night at all.

After hours of standing in line, Leizar felt tired, hungry and irritable. He presented himself in front of two uniformed officials. They sat at a makeshift desk made out of packing cases and they were clearly not happy to be dealing with a big shipload of immigrants so late in the day. In front of them was a big ledger in which they painstakingly recorded details of each person. They compared each entry with the ship's manifest, in which was recorded the names of all those on board. One official was smoking a pipe from which he would blow a great cloud of smoke every now and then.

CHAPTER 32

GLASGOW

Although Avram had helped him learn the English Questions and Answers, he did not warn him about the Glaswegian accent which to Leizar's ear, made the questions all but unintelligible. He made out the first question 'Name?', which sounded like 'Neeehm?', but the officials clearly did not recognise 'Leizar' and wrote 'Louis Gombank' They checked it against the manifest and couldn't find it, so they just ticked another name. Leizar saw their mistake, but thought it better to keep quiet.

Avram had warned him that people could get turned away if their answers were not satisfactory, but Herschel had previously advised Leizar to pack several boxes of cigarettes for just such an occasion. When it came to 'oakyewpee-shun', a word that had to be repeated several times before Leizar understood it was 'occupation', he had rehearsed the answer 'cigarette maker' and with that he opened his bag and gave a box to each of the officers.

The atmosphere changed immediately. Suddenly he was the friend of the officers and they filled in his form without much reference to him, slapped him on the back and off he went.

He managed to find Avram and together they went into the offices of the shipping line to see if they could find Pyotr's promised contact. Alas, they found the door firmly locked. So, they determined to walk into the town to see what they could find.

The ship had arrived at West Port docking station, and in a few steps, they found themselves at the end of Argyle St, a main thoroughfare. There were still plenty of people about and there was a constant buzz of background sounds, together with some bright flashes that occasionally split the night from the shipyards, where the welders were working nightshifts. The city had a grey, smoky feel and smelt of coal, wet moss and soap.

Following a sign for the Central Railway Station, they walked up High Street until they came across The Bell Inn and after a couple of whiskies, they found the patrons very friendly. When people realised they were refugees just landed from Eastern Europe, they were full of helpful suggestions, most of which they did not understand at all. So they resorted to sign language, and pictures they drew for each other on a piece of paper.

The landlord kept pointing at them, and then at the ceiling. They could not guess what he meant. Avram said perhaps they think we have arrived from heaven? And Leizar looked carefully at the ceiling, thinking there must be something up there he had missed. The other customers in the pub, seeing this unfold, could not stop laughing. Eventually, the landlord took Leizar by the arm and showed them both upstairs to where the pub had a couple of rooms that they could rent. He wrote the price as ten shillings a week, and after he had converted it to dollars, they could see it was very reasonable. They decided to stay there until they could get their bearings. He was even prepared to take their dollars and change some into Scottish pounds. All this was explained with a mixture of pidgin English, hand signs and drawings.

They deposited their suitcases and each using the sink in the corner of their room, washed some of the grime off from the journey. There was a knock on the door, and Leizar opened it to find a short lady of generous proportions, with grey hair tied back in a bun and a barmaid's apron over a grey dress. She had knocked on Avram's door too and greeted them both with the German 'Guten Tag, ich bin die Vermieterin' (Good day, I am the landlady.) Mein name ist Rosie Bell.

Although her German was a bit stilted and formal, and she got some words wrong, it was close enough that Leizar and Avram could recognise what she was saying due to the similarity between German and Yiddish.

She beckoned with her head and asked them in a mixture of Glaswegian English and German, to follow her downstairs again. She had laid out two hot dishes of haggis with neaps and tatties. The Landlord, whose name was Bryan Bell, showed them how to pour whiskey over the haggis and after the rubbish served up on the ship, it smelled like heaven. They looked at each other. Not a word passed, but they both knew the kosher world was far behind them. They tucked into it, even though they had no idea what they were eating.

While they ate, with the help of Rosie, they explained their separate plans. She seemed to be warming to the use of the language and she apologised, saying that she had learned German at school and had not used it since. They both apologised to her that they could not speak English at all.

Communication improved as Rosie became more fluent, and they explained that they had onward tickets to New York. The ship was leaving in five days, and they both wanted to be on it. Bryan smiled, and his wife translated that there were many ships leaving Glasgow for New York. Everyone seemed to want to be in America these days.

Leizar explained that whilst Avram was joining family there, his own plan was to establish himself in New York and shortly to return to Warsaw to collect his family. That would mean another stay over in Glasgow. Bryan said, via his wife, that as long as Leizar paid his way while he was there and sent him a deposit when he was ready to return next time, he would make both the rooms available for him.

They had a few drinks downstairs with the locals, and decided to go to bed and explore Glasgow the next day. The truth was that Leizar could not wait to get into a clean bed again and sleep properly. Bryan showed them to their rooms again, which seemed like luxury compared to what they had experienced lately. Each room had two beds and a sink. There was a shared toilet and bathroom between them. There was even a small gas fire. Leizar was impressed. He considered this an incredible stroke of luck.

Before going to bed, he wrote to Chaya to let her know he had arrived safely and told her the good news that he was settled with good people and looking forward to the onward trip to New York in a few days. He let her know that they could even arrange a good stop-over for all the family next time. He said he would return for them as soon as he could.

They woke early next day to the delicious smell of bacon wafting up the stairs. Rosie suggested they tried 'the works' with eggs, bacon, sausage, black pudding and fried bread. But they were shocked to find that most of it was the meat of the pig, which of course, was forbidden to observant Jews. But Avram had pointed out to him that he had already eaten food which was not kosher, and that they would have to continue to do so. Leizar tried the bacon. It was delicious, so on this morning he enjoyed a big breakfast, which set them up well for the day.

They explored Glasgow, mostly walking and taking care to avoid certain areas that were considered dangerous for various reasons, not the least of which was an outbreak of bubonic plague. Bryan and Rosie told them that because Glasgow was growing so fast, and people were pouring in, this was leading to poor sanitation. The city was rife with rats, and there had been an outbreak of plague carried by the vermin. They should be alright if they kept to the cleaner parts of town.

The city had just built its first subway, and they could ride it on a circular route from near the docks down to Buchanan St and through Govan and West St back to the docks. This was their best mode of transport.

Leizar and Avram called in to the shipping office and made sure they had a reserved place on the ship when it departed. Things were falling into place beautifully. The shipping office also had a courier service, so Leizar wrote again to Chaya to tell her he would soon be on his way, and it would not be long before they could start thinking about their new life in America. He told her he was very pleased that he had made the journey as far as Glasgow because he had learned a lot that would hold them in good stead for their main journey together to America. He mentioned Avram and said in a few days' time he would be making that very journey with him.

When they returned to the pub, Rosie said there had been an immigration officer asking to see Leizar's documents. With Rosie's help, Bryan explained this was not unusual. It was a requirement that all hotels and guest houses had to report the names of their guests, and sometimes the authorities liked to check up on them. So Leizar let him have the document he had received when he disembarked. It didn't worry him, and he went to bed that night and slept soundly.

The next morning, he had enjoyed the cooked breakfast again and he had also got used to the tea made with milk and sugar. He was finishing his second cup when two men in uniform walked in and asked the landlord for Louis Gombank. As soon as he heard the name he came forward and tried to explain his name was actually

Leizar Domansky.

The language was a problem, so Rosie was called to assist. They gave Leizar to understand they wanted to talk to him, and he should go with them. Leizar was apprehensive, but he trusted Bryan who was clearly indicating that Leizar should not argue with these men. So, he got his coat and with one of the men either side, they walked him to another part of the city, to a building marked 'Police.' He knew what that word meant.

Leizar was becoming more worried by the minute, he had a terrible sense of foreboding. But he could not think of anything he had done wrong. They put him in a locked room and left without saying a word. There was nothing much in the room, just bare walls and a table with four chairs. He sat on one of them turning everything over in his mind from the time he left Hamburg.

When they returned an hour later, they were accompanied by a third man. dressed in civilian clothes, tall and thick set with black hair and a heavy moustache. He addressed Leizar in Russian. 'Good morning, Mr Domansky, we need to have a chat with you, and I am here to translate, my name is Rudi Vostok.'

Leizar was relieved that at least he could now communicate. 'Why am I here? I have done nothing wrong?' This was communicated to the uniformed men and translated back.

'These gentlemen are from two organisations. The one on your right is from Immigration Control and the other is Mr William Melville, Superintendent with the Special Branch of the police. They want to ask you some questions.'

Leizar had no idea who Mr Melville was, nor had he ever heard of the Special Branch, but he knew the words 'immigration' and 'police' well enough. He was a little relieved when Vostok added, 'They think you may be able to assist them with their enquiries.'

'Am I in trouble?' asked Leizar, his voice a little shaky.

'Just answer the questions please,' Melville said, via the interpreter, taking the lead. 'Is your name Leizar Domansky?'

'Yes.'

'Then why on your immigration document does it say Louis Heller, a passenger who was not listed on the ship's manifest?'

Leizar explained it was a simple mistake and although he knew the officer had written the wrong name, he did not want to trouble him to correct it. He had also seen the officer tick the wrong name on his schedule.

'Did you arrive on the RMS Megantic from Hamburg?'

'Yes.'

'Are you originally from Warsaw? In the Russian Empire?'

Leizar explained that although he had been living in Warsaw, his home was actually a small village in Galicia.

'Do you know someone called Lev Davidovich Bronstein, a leading figure in the Communist movement in Russia?'

'Yes, he visited me in Warsaw.'

'Do you know someone called Edvard Abramovski?'

'Yes.'

'Do you know someone called Yitshok Peretz?'

'Yes.'

'Have you written articles for the subversive magazine Haskalah?'

'Yes.'

Leizar was beginning to realise where this was all leading, but how did they know so much about him?

'Are you the brother of Mendel Yaacov Domansky?'

'He was my brother, yes.'

'Was he hanged as a convicted murderer?'

'Yes, but...'

Melville raised his voice and cut him off in English. 'We will ask the questions. Mr Domansky, I am arresting you under the Immigration Act 1898. I have grounds to believe you are a subversive and an anarchist. If you do not have a lawyer, one will be provided for you.'

And with that they all walked out, leaving Leizar alone in the locked room. He was completely shocked. Thoughts of the terrible miscarriage of justice against his brother crept into his mind. He was left in the bare room which just had the wooden table and four chairs. The door had a small peephole, but he could not see much of what was happening outside. There were no windows.

After a couple of hours, the door opened, and two uniformed officers entered. Without a word, they took him out and bundled him into a carriage. It was a short ride to Duke Street Prison where he was thrown into a cell on his own.

Leizar was sick with worry. Surely this could not happen again – this was the United Kingdom. Although no-one seemed keen to talk to him, the experience was made worse because he could not communicate, except through signs. Later he was given a meal of bread, cheese and ham. He tried to eat, but the bile kept rising in his stomach and in the end, he just left it. The cell had a wooden bench with a thin mattress which served as a bed. He wearily laid down, feeling so terribly alone in a foreign country where he did not speak the language and beside himself with worry.

It was not until the next morning that a man arrived announcing that he was the lawyer assigned to his case. This man did not look like a lawyer. He wore a brown tweed jacket with stains down the front, green tweed breeches and a flat cloth cap. He had no hair on his thin face and he was forever wiping his runny nose with a rather unsavoury looking handkerchief. Fortunately, he spoke fluent Russian and introduced himself as Gyorgy Berkov.

Leizar was quick to tell him that although all he had, accidentally entered the country under a false name, written for a banned publication and was the brother of a man hanged for murder, none of those facts added up to him being a subversive anarchist. He was only stopping over in Glasgow en-route to America, to where his whole family wished to emigrate. He guessed that he had come to the attention of the authorities because of the mistake on the immigration form, which must have led them to investigate his background in Poland. He explained everything truthfully to Berkov, including the unfair trial and conviction of his innocent brother. Leizar quickly realised that there was more to Berkov than met the eye. He wrote everything down in English at the speed Leizar told it to him in Russian.

Berkov explained that he was an immigration lawyer and had represented many arrivals from Eastern Europe. The western world was becoming very concerned about the socialist views gaining ground everywhere. Many publications had found their way into the hands of various paranoid government officials, who had become convinced that there were plans to overthrow the British government and perhaps with that, the rule of law.

They believed this was already happening in Eastern Europe and the West was on its guard. Last year there had been an anti-anarchist conference in Rome attended by Heads of State from many countries. William Melville was a leading figure in what was considered to be the guard against anarchist infiltration into the UK, and he had travelled to Glasgow, where the ports had been identified as an entry point for subversives from the east.

The mistake on the name at the port of entry had been very unfortunate. They were watching all the entries very closely, and Berkov confirmed that that had probably led to the investigation. A new organisation was being formed between western countries in the fight against international crime and subversive activity. It was called Interpol, and the police departments of many nations had signed up to it.

Berkov closed his notebook and stood. 'The problem we have now is how to convince the authorities that you are not a threat when they have this evidence against you.'

'But surely, they can see that I want to *leave* Poland and travel to America, and why would I do that if was a subversive who wanted to overthrow its government?'

'Look, it is my job to represent you. Unfortunately, by your own admission, you are, or have been a political activist. I am afraid Melville is conducting a bit of a witch hunt. He *wants* to find subversives. But I know a lot of people here. Let me speak to the authorities and come back tomorrow. I will try to find the ear of the right person to convince you are just passing through.'

That night Leizar tried to sleep on the wooden bench with a rough blanket and insects crawling over him. He had been given some sort of very salty porridge and he was shivering from cold and fear. This was all truly awful.

He lay awake most of the night. In the dark, the place was never quiet. Inmates were moaning, at least one was crying and every now and them a piercing scream would break out.

In the morning, another bowl of the horrible, cold porridge was pushed through the hatch in the door with some tepid, grey tea. He was so hungry; he would have eaten anything. Eventually, Bryan arrived. With signs and drawings, he let Leizar know how sorry he was to find him here, and assured him that he would soon be out again. He also brought a letter from Chaya. The letter contained news that was at once wonderful and worrying. Chaya was pregnant!

How could this all be happening at once? Leizar wanted a big family and would normally have been ecstatic at the news, and he could imagine all the family's *mazel-tovs*. But from his current viewpoint, in a filthy Glasgow gaol, his mind immediately went to his faltered emigration plan. How long would he be locked up? Would he miss the next ship out anyway? And with Chaya pregnant, should he abort the onward journey? Perhaps, when he was let go, he would have to return to Warsaw, and they needed to revise their plans. She said she was only eight weeks pregnant, but she had been to the doctor and she was sure. That would mean a wait of more than a year before the baby arrived and was old enough to travel with them.

Gyorgy arrived in the afternoon looking grim. 'They say they are going to try you for subversive activity and illegal immigration. The first problem you have is money. I have to tell you, I have no experience in this sort of thing, and you will need a good lawyer. It is expensive.'

Leizar's face dropped. He had been hoping Gyorgy would convince them that he was not a subversive and allow him to travel out of the country so that he would cease to be their problem. He had thought he had given Gyorgy sufficient ammunition to mount a good argument.

'This is terrible.' Leizar started to tremble, and his voice started softly as if he was talking to himself, and then gradually increased in volume until he was shouting. 'I can't stay in this place, and I *have* to be on that ship in two days' time. My wife is pregnant. What is going on, Gyorgy? I have done nothing. You must get me out of here!' By now he was shouting loudly and banging his fist on the table. The guard came running in, but Gyorgy convinced him everything was ok. Just bad news from home.

'Leizar, you must calm down. This will get you nowhere. Can you raise some money? If we can move quickly and hire a top lawyer, maybe you won't have to suffer this for long.'

Leizar took some deep breaths. He sat on the chair and put his head in his hands. 'I must write to my father-in-law in Warsaw. I believe there is an account at a bank in Glasgow from which I can draw some money, but I don't know which one.'

'How much do you have?'

Leizar was hesitant, remembering the warning to say he only had twenty-five dollars.

'You don't want to say, right? Come on Leizar, I am trying to help you, not rob you!'

He could see that he had to come clean and have faith that Gyorgy was honest, 'I have one hundred dollars.'

'Good, that will cover the initial fees of my firm. But you may need more.'

Leizar was thoughtful now, 'The letter must be sent right away by hand courier, but even then it will be several days before we get a reply.'

Gyorgy smiled. 'There is a quicker way. We can make use of the telegram system. My office has a machine, and we can find the address of a post office in Warsaw. You will have to restrict yourself to a few words, but we can get the message across, and a reply within a few hours.' Leizar had heard the word 'telegram' before, but he had no idea how the system worked.

'Here, write the name and address of who it is going to and a short message.'

He gave Herschel's name and address and then the message which Gyorgy shortened and rewrote in telegram speak. '*Trouble in Glasgow stop don't tell Chaya stop I will write separately stop what is name and detail of bank to draw money stop.*'

But despite this progress, Gyorgy's face took on a grimmer look. He sat down, sighed, and looked at Leizar, with apprehension. He took a deep breath. 'I do have to tell you there could be another complication. If we cannot convince the prosecution to drop the charges, then the trial may not take place for a long time.'

Leizar felt the hair rise on the back of his neck. His eyes narrowed as the words sunk in. 'What do you mean, a long time?'

'Justice moves slowly here.' Gyorgy was quick to add, 'I am not saying this is what *will* happen. Hopefully we can get you out of here in a few days.'

Leizar repeated, emphasising his words slowly, '*What... do... you... mean, a long time?*'

'The worst way, it could be several months. I have to tell you the best and the worst. If they drop the charges, you are out in a few days. If they go to trial, then we apply for bail and you are still out in a few days, but...' He hesitated. 'If the court decides there's a risk of you not returning for the hearing, and factors in that you are an immigrant with a desire to leave the country, then they could decide to keep you here.'

The prospect of being incarcerated in this hell hole for months was more than Leizar could bear to think about. He stood and raised his voice again. '*NO, NO, that cannot happen.* I have money, I will pay anything. You must get me out of here, and if you cannot do it, send me someone who can!'

Gyorgy seemed startled at Leizar's change of attitude. 'Alright, I was just preparing you for the worst. We will not let that happen. It is very unfortunate for you – for us - that anarchism and subversion amongst immigrants is such a hot subject here right now, and the government are so focused on finding show cases as a deterrent to others. We will not let this be one of them, though, I assure you.' He picked up the telegram message and left.

So that night Leizar composed two letters.

To Chaya, he wrote:

My darling sweet and beautiful wife. I cannot tell you how much I love and miss you and the girls. Wonderful news that you are expecting another. I wish I was there to hold you and share it with you. Alas, things have not gone so well here in Glasgow. Please don't be alarmed, but there was a mistake on the entry forms that has led to me being arrested. The worst of it is that there may well be a trial and it may not come up for several months. That would mean that I would have to alter our plan for me to go on to America. But I may not be able to return for some time. Don't worry, I have a good lawyer and I am sure I will be acquitted. I am writing separately to your father for advice.

It leaves us with a dilemma, my darling. If we wait until my release and I then travel home to return with you and the girls, it may be two or three months before I can do so, by which time you will be four or five months pregnant, and I remember that you are usually quite uncomfortable by then. Would it be prudent to make an arduous trip at that time? If we put it off until after the baby is born, then we would have to wait until he or she is old enough to travel, so we are talking about at least a year or more, and I fear that, with the political circumstances in Europe, it might not be so easy to make the journey then.

I want you to know that I remain convinced that we should move the family to the USA, but I would not do anything that would cause pain or discomfort to you. So have a think about this and let me know how you feel about the next step. My feeling is to put off the whole thing for now. The circumstances are just bad luck (not the baby, of course). We can try again next year, and if not then, you know me, I will find a way.

I am sending this by courier, who will wait to collect a reply and deliver it back to me. Never doubt my love for you all and that we will be reunited soon. Kiss my darling girls for me.

Forever, Leizar

To Herschel he wrote:

Dear Herschel

I will include detail in this letter that I have not shared with Chaya. You will understand why, so I rely on your discretion. Firstly, another big MAZELTOV! You are expecting your third grandchild! Another mitzvah. How lucky we are.

I have to tell you that things have not gone so well here…

He went on to explain all the events leading up to his arrest, including the actual charges and how they had come about, and that he was now incarcerated with little hope of release for several months. He explained the dilemma regarding their emigration timing and asked his advice. Also, that he would have to hire expensive lawyers and hoped that he could call on Herschel's generous offer to provide funds, even though they had not been intended for this purpose. He said he had paid for a special courier to carry the letters, and asked Herschel to write back by return in the same way.

Gyorgy came to see him next day and brought a gentleman whom he introduced as Maynard Campbell, QC. Leizar was quite taken aback at the appearance of Mr Campbell. In contrast to Gyorgy, who looked disordered and thin, Mr Campbell was neatly dressed, in control, and very large indeed. He wore a three-piece suit, the waistcoat of which was suffering badly from the strain the buttons were under, a wing-collared shirt with a black, tightly-knotted tie and a bowler hat which he removed as he entered the visiting room, revealing a few strands of white hair and a large face with a ruddy complexion. His voice had a deep resonance which filled the room.

'Mr Campbell is one of the finest barristers here in Glasgow,' said Gyorgy. He is well versed in matters of immigration and well known to the judiciary and the bar. I have explained the detail of the case and Mr Campbell would like to ask a few questions.'

Leizar realised that if he was going to spend more time in Glasgow than he'd expected, he would have to try to master the English language and he was aware that the Scots had their own version of it. But for now, Gyorgy had to translate. Campbell was most concerned about Leizar's writings and especially the death of his brother, but he seemed satisfied with Leizar's explanation of events. He said he would need twenty pounds deposit and signed and witnessed statements from any independent witnesses to the trial of Mendel, as well as from character witnesses, and from Leizar's employer and father-in-law. He agreed to take the case on.

Ten days went past, during which Leizar became more depressed. Gyorgy visited once a week, which was a highlight, but he had no news, simply saying that Mr Campbell was working on the case and that Leizar need to be patient because things moved slowly, but that he was sure there would be a good outcome. As expected, he had not been successful with the bail application. He had a visit from Bryan and Rosie, who brought him some food, for which he was very grateful. He was losing weight due to the disgusting slop provided by the prison. He asked after Avram and was not surprised to hear that he had left for America on the day arranged.

Eventually, the courier delivered the replies to Leizar's letters. He smelt the letter from Chaya to see if any of her scent lingered on it, and then tore it open with great excitement.

Chaya wrote:

My beloved husband, what a shock to hear you have been arrested, but surely when they know who you are, they will realise their mistake? I have discussed the situation with my father who is most concerned, and I have given it much thought. Leizar, I think there is only one option. If you are going to be unable to return for several months, then I will come to you with the children. Already I cannot bear the thought that you are locked up and I am not there when you need me. I can book passage for myself and the girls and be with you within a few weeks. As you know, I am quite capable of dealing with the journey now, but you are right, maybe a few months further on, it would be more difficult. That way we will all be together and as soon as you are cleared, we can continue on our way to America.

I will contact Pyotr right away to book a passage. Keep in good cheer, my love, and I will be with you soon. With all my love always, your Chaya.

Herschel's letter was more detailed. He wrote that he had set up an account with Western Union in Glasgow, which contained £100 and established a credit line, so that whenever the balance dropped below £25 it would be topped up again to £100. Leizar could draw on it and he gave him the details. He was not happy about Chaya travelling on her own, but he could not dissuade her from so doing. She was very headstrong. However, he would make sure she was properly booked in decent accommodation from Warsaw to Glasgow. He had considered sending someone with her, but Pyotr advised against it as it might cause further complications at immigration on arrival with a man who was not her husband, at the same time as her husband was incarcerated.

Leizar was surprised at Chaya's positive and very practical solution. What a wife he had! What other woman would come up with such a plan and be prepared to initiate it right away? But he was very worried that she intended to make the voyage, pregnant and with two young children. His first reaction was to tell her not to do it. If anything happened to his beloved Chaya or his children, he would never forgive himself. It would be the end.

He turned it over and over in his mind, but the more he thought about it, the more he could see that it might be the only way he could get the family out of the country in the foreseeable future. Knowing Herschel, Leizar was sure he had gone through the same thought process too. His love for his daughter and his grandchildren knew no bounds, and yet he seemed to have come to the conclusion that this was a plan that would work. Also, of course he knew, as Leizar did, what a formidable lady Chaya was, and how determined she would be having made up her mind. Indeed, even if Leizar told her not to do this, he doubted that it would stop her.

So he replied to both letters in reassuring terms and gave them all the immigration tips he had picked up. The in-between deck, not to look too affluent, how to register on arrival, everything he could remember. He said he would let them know immediately by telegram if there was any chance the charges would be dropped. He also explained that he seemed well-represented already with a solicitor and a well-known barrister, who had asked for them to gather statements from everyone they could think of who might support his character and especially from independent witnesses to the trial of his brother.

There followed weeks of living like a criminal in ragged clothes with little opportunity for personal hygiene and food which was not worthy of the name. He saw Gyorgy from time to time, but he had no further meetings with Mr Campbell. Gyorgy explained that it was his job to liaise with the barrister, and Campbell was advising every step of the way. Although their application for bail had been turned down, Campbell thought they may have another chance when his wife and children arrived, as he could mount a convincing argument that the risk of Leizar absconding was now greatly reduced.

Chapter 33

Chaya's journey

Herschel travelled to Wadowice to meet with Pyotr, in order to be sure the arrangements were perfect. Pyotr advised that Beaver Shipping had altered their schedule and most of the steamers were no longer going to the USA via Glasgow. He had been informed of a German line, the Hamburg-America line that had a ship, the SS Deutschland, that was still scheduled to dock in Glasgow. The options were for the family to travel with Beaver to Southampton, and then by train to London and on to Glasgow, or to buy tickets direct to Glasgow with the German line. He pointed out that the language issue might not be such a problem on a German ship. Most people who spoke Yiddish, were able to understand German.

In response to Herschel's question, he said that first and second class passages were always booked many months in advance and the cost for the three would be several times the extortionate price they were already paying. So, reluctantly, Herschel bought tickets, making sure that they were for the Zwischendeck.

Clearly, it would be easier for Chaya to travel direct and Pyotr said there was a voyage in three weeks. He told Pyotr to go ahead.

Chaya had much to prepare. She went to the shtetl to break the news to Zelman and Ryfke who took it very badly. Although Chaya had won their hearts long ago, the news that Leizar was in prison awaiting trial, brought back the terrible memory of their other son, Mendel. They were even more concerned to learn that Chaya was going to make the journey with their grandchildren whilst she was expecting another. They felt that they were losing their family, one by one.

Chaya packed as much as she could carry. Her pregnancy was starting to show, and Lena was a good girl, who would help as much as she could, but Minna was still only three years old and often wanted to be carried. Although it was a different shipping line, Leizar had warned her about the food, so she took as much as she could carry of the things that the children would eat.

Herschel came to see her off at the train station and the first part of the journey to Hamburg went smoothly. The children both fell asleep.

The ship was due to leave the next day, so she was put in the same apartment block that Leizar had occupied. This was hard for Chaya. It was dirty and she had to share with two German women. Coming from her comfortable life in Warsaw, she had expected that this journey would not be easy for her or the children, but now she was confronted with the musty smell and the dirty conditions, she had to steel herself. She tried to remain positive, at least she had a bed which she shared with the children. It was a little bit cramped, but that didn't stop the children from sleeping after they had eaten some of the food she had packed for them.

She hardly slept herself, so early next morning, she was ready to leave. The woman brought some of the German sausage, cheese and coffee and Chaya was able to get some milk for the children. She had the same guilty feelings as Leizar, but she ate the *traif*. Embarkation started right away.

Chaya waited in line with the children for an hour before she got to the front and was invited to come forward. The steward addressed her gruffly, in German, 'No man?'

'No just me and my two children.'

'Hebrew?'

'Yes.'

'Ok, you come with me.' And he took her across the main deck and down two flights of steps to the steerage hold.

'Wait a minute, I have a reservation on the in-between deck.' The steward looked at her and shrugged. Chaya drew up to her full height, which was not very high, 'I want to speak to your boss. I have two young children and I have a reservation for the in-between deck, not down here.'

She showed him her tickets. He gave them a cursory look and shrugged again. 'Hebrew women at the back here.' He said indicating the very back of the ship's hold, where there was a door leading to a separated part of the ship.

Chaya was not a person who gave up easily. She was used to being heeded by the people around her and she held her ground. Minna was starting to cry, seeing her mother was getting upset. The steward went away and left her standing while he showed two other women to the aft steerage. With the children around her, Minna crying and Lena asking what was going on, Chaya was pleased when a seaman in uniform approached. He was wearing a naval cap with the insignia of the shipping line, and he had an impressive beard. At last she would speak with someone in authority.

He spoke in German. 'You have a problem?' Chaya explained that she was travelling with two children and her reservation was for the in-between deck. She would be happy to pay to upgrade if necessary.

The officer seemed to lose interest while she was speaking, 'Well, I am afraid there are no reservations in third class, and we are instructed to keep women separate from men, and Hebrews together in one place.'

Chaya was now very angry, and her voice had risen several decibels. 'This is terrible, it is not what I paid for,' she was shouting now, and her raised voice brought the two women out who had passed her. 'You want to get off?' said the seaman. This was a culture shock for Chaya. Here, everyone was being huddled together and treated as if they didn't matter, and she was being treated no different to everyone else.

One of the other women spoke to her in Yiddish, 'Oh! What beautiful children! We are in the same position as you. Look, my dear. You will be better off with Jewish people; we look out for each other. Also, you need some privacy with your two little ones. Come with us, it's only a few days.' Chaya's instinct was to dig her heels in further, it was on the tip of her tongue to say, 'Do you know who I am?' but she had the children to think about, and it seemed she had little alternative. She doubted they had much in common, but the two women seemed very nice. How bad could it be for a few days? So, she agreed.

Entering through a wooden door towards the back of the ship, she saw quite a large space. There were further makeshift doors leading to large dormitories each with about 10/15 beds. Very few people had yet boarded, so there seemed to be plenty of space available. The two women introduced themselves as Becky and Rita Levack. They were sisters. Chaya explained her circumstances and that she was travelling alone with the two children. They could see she was expecting a third.

Becky and Rita looked at each other, it was clear to them, that Chaya came from a different social class. Even her downgraded clothes were of the finest quality, and the way she spoke set her apart. But they knew the journey would be even worse for her with the two small children and one on the way. Despite the differences, they wanted to help.

'My, you are so brave,' said Becky. 'Don't worry we will look after you,' said Rita, 'And we will help you with your adorable children.' Chaya was grateful and decided to choose two beds near the sisters and stay put.

Becky and Rita were not twins, but their ages were very close, 25 and 26 years. They both had dark red hair cut into a short bob and they wore the plain black clothes of the Hasids. They had no sheitels, so she supposed they were not married. They were going all the way to New York where they would meet up with their family who had made the trip last year and Chaya was surprised to find they were Galician from another small shtetl. Chaya actually felt buoyed by the thought that she had some friendly support. During the argument with the seaman, she had felt very alone.

They were able to choose any bunk beds they wanted. Chaya got a double bunk, the lower for herself and the top for the children who thought it was great fun to be up high. Becky and Rita had beds next to hers. The Hebrew-only, steerage part of the ship was filling up very quickly; it was not long before all the beds were taken, and yet women were still coming in. They were told they were too late for a bed, so they would have to make do with the floor and they were given a mattress. On each bed was a mattress filled with straw, and a life jacket which had to double as a pillow.

Chaya left the children playing on the bunk and went with Becky and Rita to inspect the bathroom and find out where they would eat. She was in for another shock. In the bathroom/toilet there were six cubicles, each one was exceedingly narrow and short, and instead of a seat there was an open trough, in front of which was an iron step and behind it a sheet of iron slanting forward. On either side wall was an iron handle. There was no evidence of toilet paper and there were two small basins with a hot and cold tap, but the hot did not work.

There was a large room beyond that with wooden benches and shelves where they were to take their meals. This room was unisex, and the men entered from the other side. Being below the water line, there were no windows or ventilation. Suddenly the engine noise, which had been there all the time increased to a mighty crescendo, so loud it was impossible to talk over it, and the ship began to shake violently. Bits of wood and utensils were shaken off shelves and fell to the ground. The ship was pulling away.

Later, when the engine noise had settled down, Chaya took the children to the eating quarters, and found it was crowded with people. She stood for a while with nowhere to sit, until a man in a thick woollen trench coat and long hair tied in a ponytail told everyone on the bench – which was already full, to move up closer, and with the children on her lap, Chaya managed to squeeze in.

Lena seemed to think this was great fun. She was talking to everyone and asking questions. Some didn't understand her Yiddish, but she seemed to think they must be deaf, because she would just say the same thing even louder as if that might help them understand. Chaya tried unsuccessfully to quieten her down and hoped she and her girls would not catch anything from the rather unsavoury looking people she'd been forced to squeeze up to.

Six large women came in carrying huge baskets with stale bread, and enormous kettles and pots with boiled potato soup. The children were very hungry, but she had little success in getting them to eat the tasteless soup. Thankfully, 'ponytail man' told her there was a small facility on the main deck where she could buy some food and drinks for the children when she could get to it.

The voyage was the most awful experience for her. When the sleeping quarters were full, with no ventilation, the smell pervaded everything. She tried to get the children out on to the open deck, but they had to run the gauntlet past the men's quarters and step over people sleeping on the floor. There was much sickness, and Chaya found it impossible to sleep for all the coughing, sneezing, and moaning. She heard a lot of rustling, which was explained one night when she saw a rat scurry across the floor. She had to stop herself from crying out for fear of waking the children. Some people became very sick, and one person even died. They had no idea what happened to the body.

Each day became more difficult to bear, the toilets were filthy and difficult to use, For the first few days they were not cleaned at all. On one occasion a six-year-old girl was seized with violent stomach cramps. The doctor ordered a hot bath, but when he found there was no hot water, he ordered a cold bath. Becky went to help the mother and the little girl, but she said the cold water ran out so thick and filthy it was not fit to use. There were no towels, so they had to use a sheet.

Chaya thanked God for Becky and Rita. Without them, she wondered if she would have survived it. She soon realised she lived in a world where her background would count for nothing, and she must learn to fit in. The sisters looked after the children and played with them when she struggled through the scattered humanity to get to the main deck. And they kept her morale from failing by telling her what a wonderful life they would have when they all arrived in America, and urging her to keep in touch with them. Most of all, it mattered that they were just there, and that they cared what happened to her and the children.

Also, there were other children for Lena and Minna to play with. They soon made friends, despite the mixture of languages. Some of the children on board spoke Russian, a few spoke Yiddish and the rest almost entirely German. But they all managed to communicate. Initially, Chaya worried that the girls might catch something from them, but Rita told her not to be so silly and children were far more resilient than she might think.

When they were not playing however, there were often tears, especially from Minna, and cries of 'I want to go home.' The beds were filthy, and every night, Chaya had to strip them and clean off the bugs, but still they all got bitten during the night. But the girls actually seemed very robust. They might go to bed crying but they woke each day with new expectations, ready to see their new friends.

Apart from the odd trip to the deck to buy food for the children, they had not seen daylight since they boarded, and Chaya was worried what effect all this might have on her pregnancy. But she felt alright, and she had adapted to the roll of the ship very well.

On the eighth day, a steward came to tell them they would be docking in two hours, and to get themselves ready for disembarkation. Although she was exhausted from the lack of sleep and poor food, Chaya now had to stand in line while the first and second class passengers disembarked. It took two further hours before she found herself in front of the immigration officials. Leizar had warned her in his letter about how to answer the questions in English, but the Glaswegian accent was as impenetrable to Chaya as it seemed hers was to them.

In answer to the monosyllabic question 'Neeehm?', they could not deal with the name Chaya at all, and she became Janie Domansky. Minna became Minnie and Lena became Leah. But Chaya made sure they ticked the correct names on the manifest. She stumbled through the other questions and was eventually allowed through, largely because Minna was crying, and Lena was moaning that she was hungry. The ship was due to stay two days in Glasgow, so Rita and Becky had disembarked, and they came running up to Chaya. 'We must keep in touch. In case we don't see you before we leave, here is the address of our brother in New York.' And they hugged and kissed each other and the children.

This all took place outside a dockside pub and it was observed by a group of six dockers who had just finished their shift and were sitting drinking pints of ale. 'More fucking refugees, look at 'em. I don't know why we let 'em in,' said one. 'Aye, God knows there's not enough food to go round now,' said another. 'Two little bairns and another on the way, they breed like rabbits.'

The dockers seemed to be winding themselves up and the comments got louder deliberately, so Chaya could hear. The sisters departed, and one of the men stood up and came forward with his glass tankard half full. 'Fuck off back to your own country! We don't need you here!' And with that he threw the remains of the beer over Chaya.

The men were all gesticulating angrily toward the little family group, and the beer was dripping down Chaya's face. She was completely shocked, and both the children were crying. But somehow it sparked her determination. Wondering what sort of country she had arrived in, she gathered up her belongings and took each of the children by the hand.

With the two girls in tow, a knapsack on her back, carrying a suitcase and obviously pregnant, Chaya literally *shlepped* herself to The Bell Inn where she almost fell through the door with exhaustion. Via Gyorgy, Leizar had told Bryan and Rosie she was en-route, and they were expecting her. Bryan rushed forward to help, but Chaya's face went white, she took one look around the pub, and then everything seemed to be spinning, she collapsed in a heap on the floor. Minna started crying, Lena started shouting, 'Mama, Mama!' and the whole place erupted. Men and women crowded over Chaya, and Bryan was unsure whether to call an ambulance. Luckily an efficient looking lady, small and slim with short blonde hair raised her voice above everyone else. 'Alright, everyone get back and leave us alone. I am a midwife, and I can see this woman has fainted, she needs time and space to breathe.' She spoke with the voice of authority, so everyone stepped back.

'Landlord, bring me cold water and a wet flannel.' From her bag she took a small clinical thermometer. After the cold compress had been on her head for a few minutes, Chaya came round and the midwife gave her the water, which she drank greedily. Both of the children were crying now, and the midwife spoke softly to them, but with that authoritative voice. The children did not understand a word that she said, but they were bright enough to realise that she was helping their mother and she wanted them to step back quietly.

To Chaya she said, 'Hello dear, I am Mary Dunbar, and I am a midwife.' Chaya did not understand, but the tone of Mary's voice was reassuring, and she picked up the name. Rosie appeared and translated for Chaya, and Bryan sent one of his boys to fetch Gyorgy, who arrived ten minutes later. He introduced himself to Chaya in Russian and explained that he was a solicitor helping her husband.

Chaya asked for more water and gathered the children up in her arms. 'What happened?' she said and, 'Where am I?'

Mary answered and Gyorgy translated. 'You're in a pub called The Bell Inn. The landlord seems to know who you are. You have just arrived with these two little bairns.' (Gyorgy had trouble with the word 'bairns') 'And you passed out because you are dehydrated. Drink as much as you can and let's get you sitting up.'

To the landlord she said, 'Bryan, is there somewhere the lady can lie down quietly for a little while? She is clearly very pregnant, and I would like to examine her.'

To the children with Gyorgy's help, she said: 'Now you are two lovely little girls. How pretty you both look. Mummy needs a little quiet, so if you are going to stay with her, can you be as quiet as little mice?' The children nodded, and Rosie took them by the hands.

Chaya was grateful someone was taking charge, and everyone seemed kind and caring. Mary did a clinical examination of Chaya and pronounced that although she was unable to take blood pressure, she had listened to the foetal heartbeat and as far as she could tell, the baby was well, but Chaya was in a state of exhaustion and needed rest. She suggested Chaya presented herself at the Glasgow Royal Infirmary where Mary worked, and she would have a doctor check her over properly. 'Don't worry, it's a voluntary hospital, you won't have to pay,' she said.

Rosie had stayed in the room. 'Now, you just relax there my lovely, and I will take the children downstairs and give them a good meal. I have some nice chicken pie with chips and if they finish that all up, there is jelly and ice cream. And I will send a nice meal up on a tray for you and the baby. You are eating for two now you know, and you look as though you could do with it.' Minna and Lena's ears pricked up at the mention of ice cream, which was a very rare treat at home, so they were happy to go with Rosie.

Chaya's sense of relief was enormous. After all she and the children had been through, to be lying on a bed with the children off her hands for a while and someone who cared about her bringing a proper meal. Her eyes welled up with tears and she started sobbing. She was desperate to see Leizar, so she asked Gyorgy to try to arrange a visit for her that afternoon.

Chapter 34

Morris is born and the Accusation

Feeling much better later that afternoon, Chaya washed, changed and put on a little make up. She washed and changed the children, who were very excited at the prospect of seeing their father, but she had to explain that papa was not able to come to them because he had to stay with some people for a while. Gyorgy ordered a carriage and within a few minutes they were outside the prison. Chaya looked up at it. She saw a large, grey forbidding building, five stories high, built of black stained stone with hundreds of small, barred apertures that served as windows with no glass. The entrance was through a very narrow, but heavily armoured wooden door.

Nevertheless, there was a shock in store for them when they were led into the visitor meeting room.

It was a large room, with blank wooden walls and a low ceiling. There were benches laid out for visits, but they were all empty. Chaya, the two children and Gyorgy were shown in by a burly prison officer who, when they were seated, stayed by the door with his arms folded.

Leizar was led in by another officer, he was in handcuffs, and he looked terrible. He had lost weight, his face looked drawn, and he was slightly bent over. He had on a prison shirt with no collar and very worn and faded and breeches with marks all over from previous wearers. His hair was cut very short.

The children were stopped from running to hug their father and could only blow him kisses, and the same went of course, for Chaya. Leizar was a proud man, a serious man who set high standards for himself and demanded the same from others. He could not bear to be humiliated in front of his wife and children as if he was a petty criminal. At first tears came to his eyes, and he kept looking down, that the children should not see his shame. But as their hour together progressed, the shame was replaced by anger. This was not his fault, and it was time this terrible wrong was put right.

He did not expect Chaya's pregnancy to be so obvious. She was now 24 weeks but looked as she had at 40 weeks when she was previously expecting, and although she underplayed the detail of her dreadful journey, he was at first ashamed for her, and then overcome with love for this woman who had endured so much to be with him.

Now Chaya had arrived, Gyorgy said he would speak to Maynard Campbell to see where they were with the case. If, as he originally advised, the case did not come up for months, assuming he was acquitted, Chaya would not be in any state to travel to America. So, they would have to wait in Glasgow and travel with the young baby sometime next year. That would mean living at the Bell Inn for a long time.

Maynard had always advised that he would make another approach to the court when Leizar's wife and children arrived, and maybe the judge would believe he was not likely to abscond and grant bail. He would also approach the prosecution. Now that the whole family was here, maybe if he could convince them of Leizar's innocence and persuade them to drop the charges altogether. But Gyorgy took care not to raise expectations and advised that this was a long shot, but was worth a try.

Gyorgy knew that Maynard had received the letters from Leizar's friends and family in Poland to support his good character, and that would help.

They agreed he should speak with Maynard tomorrow, and report back after he had spoken. The children could not understand what was going on at all. They just wanted their father to come home with them. They were tired and getting tetchy, so they all blew kisses and had to wait while Leizar was led back to his cell and the other door was then opened for the family to depart.

Gyorgy helped Chaya to the hospital for her check-up which thankfully went well, and the doctor said that considering what she had been through, she and the baby must be very strong.

That evening, Rosie helped Chaya to feed the children and they ate up hungrily at the promise of more ice cream. They bathed them and put them to bed in nice fresh clean linen. Chaya thought it was wonderful to see them clean and smelling of soap. Very quickly, they turned over, kissed their mother goodnight and closed their eyes. Chaya took her food in the pub together with Rosie and Bryan. They already knew about Leizar and with Rosie's help, she explained the plan for tomorrow. There was only one visit allowed for each prisoner, but he could see his lawyer at any time. So, Rosie suggested she invite her sisters two children round so that Lena and Minna could play with them while Chaya visited Leizar. Tomorrow was Saturday and there was no school.

After the best dinner Chaya had eaten for a long time, she had a bath and went to bed with a slight feeling of guilt that whilst she was tucked up in a warm, clean bed her husband was suffering inedible food and cold, filthy conditions. However, she was so exhausted that she fell quickly into a deep sleep.

The next day, Chaya was grateful for the exclusive time to visit Leizar, even though this time the room was full of other visitors. They were able to exchange stories and update properly on everything that had happened since they last saw each other. Leizar was pleased to hear that Gyorgy was speaking to Maynard about the possibility of release, and they decided that if that were to happen, they would continue their journey to New York right away while Chaya could still travel. She said Gyorgy thought that now his family were here, and affidavits had been received from Poland, there was a chance the charges could be dropped. Leizar told Chaya to ask Gyorgy to find a shipping line with availability in the next few weeks and enquire the cost of a second-class family cabin to New York in case they needed it. Their hour was up too quickly, but she left with a positive feeling. Perhaps from this point things would start going their way.

She visited Gyorgy's office the next day. He told her that Maynard was meeting with the prosecutor and hoped to have some news later. He said he would be glad to enquire about the availability of berths on ships leaving for New York but advised that it would be prudent to wait for news from Maynard first.

She was on tenterhooks for the rest of the day but although Gyorgy had promised to contact her as soon as he heard, nothing was forthcoming, and she went to bed that night disappointed.

But that only heightened her excitement when he turned up at the pub during breakfast the following morning. She could hardly contain herself while he ordered tea and toast after which he said, 'I have good news and bad news. The prosecutor will not drop the charges completely, but if Leizar will plead guilty to a minor charge of perverting the course of justice and giving a false name, these can be dealt with by way of a fine which can be set off against the time he has already served in prison, and Leizar will be released. Maynard explains that this is their way of accepting that he is not a risk, and the original charges are inappropriate, but they will save face and ensure that he can't make a case against them for false imprisonment.'

Chaya's face broke into a wide smile. This seemed the perfect solution. 'However,' Gyorgy continued, 'The bad news is that Leizar will then have a criminal record in the UK, and I am afraid the US authorities would refuse him entry to America.'

This brought her down with a bump and she slumped back in her chair. 'But that is so unfair!' She exclaimed. 'They accept he has done nothing wrong, and he is innocent of the charges, and yet he has to plead guilty. What sort of justice is that?' Gyorgy explained that the UK authorities were not concerned with the consequences of the deal. The fact that it may preclude the family's plans for America was nothing to do with them. Maynard suggested that they request a meeting with Leizar that afternoon and meet at the prison when he would advise them on their options.

The children found their mother very distracted all morning and when she heard the time of the meeting, Rosie again offered to look after them.

Later that day, when Leizar was led into the visiting room, Chaya, Gyorgy and Maynard were already seated. Maynard broke the news to him, and he reacted badly. The Domansky temper showed through, and he was shouting. 'The *momzers!* How can they do that? I will never agree. I have done nothing wrong. *A meesa meshineh oyf zey.* You tell those *momzers* I will fight them all the way!'

The prison guards quickly ran to subdue Leizar, but Maynard prevented them from taking any action and indicated that Leizar needed to calm down so that they could sensibly discuss their options. He said they did not have to accept the offer, and the case would proceed to trial. The implications of that were the delay before the trial date, several months, the cost of fighting the case, and in Maynard's view a

70% chance he would be acquitted. However, that meant there was a 30% chance he would be convicted and then he might face several years in prison. Along with that option, assuming acquittal at trial, they would have to wait anything up to a year before Chaya was able to travel with the new baby. The other option was to accept the offer, be released right away, and establish a life in the UK instead of America.

The latter was something they had never considered. Why not live in the UK? Chaya and Leizar looked at each other. Maynard said if they wanted time to think about it together, he could ask for an extension to the visit on the grounds that he had to discuss trial strategy with his clients. The lawyers stepped outside, made sure Chaya could stay, and left them to think about it.

In their usual logical manner, they turned over the options and thought carefully, trying to leave emotion out of it. Maynard's advice did seem to be the better of the options. If they stayed and fought the case, it was by no means certain Leizar would be acquitted, and if convicted, it would mean a long spell in prison. Even if Maynard could convince the court to grant bail, it would be a long time before the case was heard and even if he was then found not guilty, the baby would be due, and it would be a long time after that before they could travel. Then there were the girls. They needed stability in their young lives. They had already been uprooted from their home and brought to a place where they could not even speak the language. It was important to establish a new permanent home so they could arrange schooling and where the children could feel safe and secure.

If they accept the offer, Leizar would be released straight away, and they could start planning. Perhaps the first decision would be where in the UK they wanted to live. They could stay in Glasgow if they wanted, or move to another part of the UK, maybe even London and Leizar could find some work. They would be in no rush, because Rosie and Bryan at the pub were happy to have them live there for the time being and the rent was reasonable. Leizar's pride would not allow him to rely on Herschel's money for long, but for the time being they were not under any financial pressure.

When Maynard and Gyorgy returned, Leizar wanted to know if they could trust the authorities. 'You must understand that where we come from, I would not believe them whatever they said. If we agree to this deal, can we be sure it will go the way you say, and I will be released with no further charges? And will the judge understand that I am pleading guilty to something I did not do? '

Maynard sat back in his chair which caused such a strain on the buttons of his waistcoat, that Chaya thought there was a danger they would pop and shoot off like bullets. His deep voice resonated in the small room, and he felt the need to keep his advice impartial and balanced. 'It is important to appreciate that the British legal system is entirely independent. Nobody can defy the ruling of a judge.'

He put his thumbs in his waistcoat, which made the strain on the buttons even greater and continued, 'Point one, on the agreement between the sides. The prosecution has agreed to this deal and jointly we will put it to the judge. But he is not bound to accept it. Having said that, he could hardly insist that the original charges must stand, because it would be open to the prosecutor to offer no evidence and if he allows the new charges to be put, you will plead guilty and therefore a trial would be avoided anyway.

'Point two, sentencing. The judge has guidelines on the penalty for the reduced charge, but he is free to depart from them if he sees fit. The guideline penalty for the charge to which you would plead guilty would be a fine. It would be normal in sentencing for the judge to take account of the days you have spent in prison, and it is open to him to set those days off against the fine he has sentenced you to because you have already been punished. So, we would expect the result to be immediate release with no further penalty. I would go as far as to say that it would be very unusual if things did not work out the way I have described. But I cannot give you a guarantee.

'Point three, would the judge understand this is purely an expedient? Well, you *did* enter the UK under an assumed name, didn't you? Even though the mitigation for that was a lack of understanding of the language. The fact that the prosecution has dropped the other charges infers to the judge that they do not have evidence to make the charge stick. But you are completely exonerated of that charge, because it was never put to you.'

Gyorgy smiled when Maynard stopped talking. He was sweating from trying to keep up with what had turned out to be an expert barrister's opinion from a leading QC.

Leizar, of course, had not expected such a detailed and careful response. He looked across at his wife, who nodded imperceptibly. He thanked Maynard and said he understood. He said they had made up their minds, please would Maynard accept the deal on his behalf.

Maynard said he would go back to the Procurator Fiscal right away, but they had to wait a few days for it to be ratified before a Judge and consequently Leizar could be released. Gyorgy and Maynard left and Leizar and Chaya instinctively moved to hug each other but were restrained by the guard. 'Never mind, my love,' said Chaya in a few days we will be able to hug to our hearts' content, and I cannot wait.'

Three days later, Gyorgy arrived in the pub again at breakfast time. He told Chaya that all had been agreed and there would be a court hearing that afternoon as a formality, where the new charge would be put to Leizar, he would plead guilty, the judge would pronounce sentence which, all being well, would result in Leizar's immediate release. He asked if Rosie would again look after the children so that Chaya could attend the court, and hopefully return with their father. She agreed readily.

Chaya had never seen the inside of a court and it was quite intimidating. The judge's seat was set on high, and barristers and solicitors were seated deep in the well of the court. The defendant was placed in a stand behind a chest-high wooden wall on the other side of the well, but level with the judge. There would normally be a jury at one end and the public gallery where she was sitting was opposite where the jury would have been. There was much mumbling until a loud voice shouted, 'All rise!' and the judge entered. After that the proceedings were quite swift. The judge invited the clerk to put the new charge to the defendant. When asked, 'How do you plead?' Maynard and Leizar both stood, and Maynard's voice boomed out, 'Guilty, my Lord.' The judge pronounced sentence almost immediately, which was exactly as Maynard had described, and he told Leizar he was free to go.

Gyorgy signalled that Chaya should meet him at the front door in ten minutes. He and Maynard went down to the cells from where Leizar would be released. When he saw them, he gave Gyorgy a big hug and with some restraint firmly shook the hand of Maynard. In Yiddish he said, 'Thank you so much', and waited while Gyorgy translated. 'I must now learn to speak English. You have not only kept me sane and freed me from that hell hole, but my wife and I are now excited about our new plans to become British citizens. I cannot thank you enough.'

They all met Chaya at the front door, and of course, Leizar and Chaya were hugging and kissing like newlyweds. Having thanked the lawyers yet again, they boarded a hansom cab back to the pub.

There was a great deal of euphoria when they arrived. The children were so excited, they ran squealing 'Papa' and jumped into Leizar's arms. They nearly knocked him over. He had lost a lot of strength. But they had missed their father and would not leave his side.

Leizar gratefully accepted a single malt whiskey offered by Bryan, and went to his room to unwind and freshen up and as a special celebration, Chaya helped Rosie and they made a special meal of roast lamb with wine and brandy.

The children were allowed to stay up late, and neither girl would leave Leizar's lap, as if they were scared he would go away again. After they eventually went to bed and Leizar had kissed them both good night, he and Chaya could not wait to retire themselves. Having said good night to Rosie and Bryan, they again acted as if this was the first time for both of them. They were undressing each other with passion and urgency as soon as the bedroom door shut and they made love, first with a hunger borne of long absence, and then with great love and tenderness. Leizar was reticent the second time, worrying about the pregnancy, but Chaya reassured him that after what she had been through nothing could hurt the tough little baby she was carrying.

Leizar wrote to Herschel and to his parents. He apologised to Herschel that money had been spent unexpectedly on legal fees, and now quite a bit would go on accommodation at the pub until they could work out what they were going to do. But thank God they were all safe and well now and able to start planning again. He told both their parents not to worry, that it was all a misunderstanding, and he was reunited with Chaya and the children, and she was fit and well and carrying their third grandchild.

He said they were living comfortably and now they had a chance to think about it, they were pleased about the decision to stay in the UK, where there was a strong government and the rule of law applied, and most importantly if you worked hard, everyone had an equal opportunity. He told them he and Chaya were trying to learn English and of course, Chaya sent her love. He borrowed a little of Rosie's watercolour and used it to attach a handprint from each of the girls to both letters. They were thrilled that their grandparents would see them.

They decided they would not do anything in a rush and Rosie and Bryan had become friends as well as landlords. Bryan said he needed some help in the pub in the evenings and if Leizar would collect glasses and wash up he would offset that against his rent until he could learn English and get a better job. Lena was enrolled at the school where Rosie's sister's children went, and Chaya looked after Minna and studied during the day. Within a few months, they were all able to communicate in a sort of pidgin English, with accents that were a mixture of Glaswegian and Eastern European.

It was in November that year that Chaya started contraction pains and with no dignity whilst she was helping in the kitchen, her waters broke. Rosie helped her upstairs and after an hour with the pains coming quite quickly, they sent word to the hospital, who said they would dispatch a nurse as they had no midwives available.

The nurse turned out to be a newly qualified young girl who had never delivered a baby before, but at least she had brought some equipment. A Pinard horn - a sort of trumpet for listening to the baby's heartbeat, a birthing stool, and a bag containing various bandages and smelling salts. But she had no idea how to proceed. Rosie also had no experience, but luckily, since this was Chaya's third, she at least could take charge.

In between contractions she told the nurse to lay out her equipment while Chaya lay on her back on the bed. She told her to warm the olive oil and gently rub it on her stomach and genital area. She told her to check the amount of dilation and when she was fully dilated, Rosie and the nurse helped Chaya on to the birthing stool. She told the nurse to fetch some clean cloth and sit in front of her, and without any fuss, she pushed her newborn son into the world. She instructed the nurse to cut the cord and clean the baby who announced his arrival by starting to cry immediately. Rosie took the child and handed him to his mother, where he latched on to her breast and started feeding happily.

After Chaya had made sure the placenta was delivered, Rosie helped the nurse clean up and called Leizar, Bryan and the children. Leizar was delighted to hold his newborn son and the girls were fascinated that they now had a little brother.

They all had a hold and a little cuddle with the baby, and after the initial euphoria had subsided, Chaya told them all to go out and asked the nurse to put the baby down because she needed to rest. Leizar started to think about how he would go about the *bris milah* – circumcision - and the *Pidyon Haben,* the ceremony for offering up the first-born son. He would need a rabbi and a *mohel,* a specialist in religious circumcision.

Bryan went with Leizar to register the birth. They had decided to name the baby Morris and that was the name recorded on the Birth Certificate, but when Leizar returned, in typical Domansky style, they changed their minds and decided to call him Monty, so that was how he was known everafter. And of course, being born in Glasgow, Monty was automatically a British citizen.

Bryan said he had heard of a Jewish community on the South side of Glasgow, and he thought they met in a prayer hall in Oxford Street. Leizar walked there next day. He did indeed, find a discreet house that had been converted into a synagogue. The door was unlocked and on opening it, he kissed the *mezuzah* according to custom. A young man was seated at a desk in the hallway and when he saw this asked straight away, 'You are Jewish?' He welcomed Leizar and started talking like a machine gun. 'I am Rabbi Cornbloom and I have recently been appointed by the United Synagogue of Scotland which was only formed a year ago. This is the start of what I am sure will be…' Leizar stopped him.' In his pidgin English he said, 'I sorry… English is poor speak Yiddish? Or German? Russian?'

The rabbi switched to Yiddish straight away. 'Oh! I am sorry,' and then he repeated what he had said and went on to let Leizar know there was a fast-growing community of Jewish immigrants and that this very pseudo synagogue was the centre of it. He told him when the services were and said he would love to meet Leizar's family.

That gave Leizar the chance to have a say. He explained his circumstances and especially that he had a new baby boy. 'Mazeltov!' exclaimed the rabbi who was certainly not what Leizar would have expected the leader of a Jewish community to look like. He was dressed in a worn tweed jacket over a striped shirt that could have been his pyjamas. He had long, black, shoulder-length hair tied back in a ponytail. On his feet he wore plimsolls. Had it not been for the man's *payot,* long sidelocks and the *kippah* skullcap, Leizar would not even have thought he was Jewish.

Rabbi Cornbloom showed Leizar through to the back room which was quite large and used as the synagogue. There was a small ark containing the Sefer Torahs with a small *bimah,* a pulpit, in front of which was a desk for reading the Torah. In front of the bimah were chairs laid out in rows. The rabbi explained there was no certified mohel in Glasgow yet but he, Rabbi Cornbloom himself, was skilled in the technique and he would be pleased to conduct the ceremony, and also to officiate in the Pidyon Haben. He would also arrange for some of the community to attend to make up the ten-man *minyan* required for the ceremony to proceed.

Leizar had mixed feelings. Rabbi Cornbloom was a far cry from the image of every rabbi he had ever come across and he was not sure he should trust his precious son to him. So, he invited him to come and meet with his wife and children. The rabbi said he would be delighted and could attend that very evening, but Leizar had to apologise and say that he should be aware that they were renting rooms in a pub and there was no kosher food. 'Don't worry,' he replied 'ff you have some dried fruit and nuts, and maybe some tea, that will be fine for me.'

Leizar walked slowly back to the pub, breathing deeply and wallowing in his freedom. He stopped to look in some shops and bought a bunch of flowers for his wife. When he arrived, he found everyone doting on baby Monty. Chaya was delighted with the flowers and Rosie was very happy to take the baby and put him down to sleep so that Chaya and Leizar could have a chat.

Chaya smiled when she heard about the unconventional young rabbi and was delighted to hear she would meet him that evening.

Rabbi Cornbloom scored a big hit with Chaya and the children loved him, he went down on the floor and played games with them before he met baby Monty, who seemed intrigued by the Rabbi's *payot* when he held him. Even Rosie and Bryan liked him; they had never met a rabbi before.

In the event, Leizar needn't have worried about the *bris*. On the eighth day after the birth, they were able, through the rabbi, to invite several members of the Glasgow Jewish community and as Leizar said, this might have been the first *bris milah* ceremony to be performed in a pub. Rosie and Bryan were fascinated, and the rabbi was happy to involve them in the ceremony. It all went off very well and they invited everyone to return three weeks later for the *Pidyan Haben* party. On that occasion other patrons of the pub were welcomed and included in the party too.

CHAPTER 35

SHMUEL AND FAMILY IN BERLIN

It was not long after their daughter Molly was born that Zelman and Ryfke wrote to say that Ryfke was pregnant again. She was expecting in the summer. Leizar thought this was not only too soon, but also it dangerously late in life for his mother. He wondered if his parents were trying to replace the children they had lost, but Chaya told him not to be so stupid, and to wish them mazeltov, which he duly did. In their exchange of letters, Leizar was constantly telling his parents they should come to live in the UK. Why stay in a country where Jews were second- or third-class citizens and crippled with taxes and pogroms? But it made no impression on his father.

Leizar was going to the synagogue every Friday and Saturday and the community were delighted to find their new member could do the *leining* or readings from the Torah. He quickly became very popular, and he and Chaya had many invitations to family homes for shabbas dinner.

Leizar's English had improved greatly, and he was able to start writing again. Through his newfound friends he became aware that the democracy in the UK, although it offered freedom and opportunity, was far from perfect. Only men were allowed to vote, and women were still pretty much chattels of their husbands – not something that Chaya could ever accept. There was a general election that year but as an immigrant, he could not vote. The election was won by the Conservative and Liberal Union party led by Lord Salisbury. This was the first election contested by the new Labour Representation party. In spite of not being eligible to vote, Leizar took a great interest in the political campaigning, and he was impressed that although they were defeated at this election, there was now a serious political party that represented the rights of workers. He was also impressed by a young journalist who had been elected to the House of Commons for the first time. Although this young man was a Conservative, Leizar was fascinated by the power of his election speeches. Winston Churchill's views on self-determination and freedom of expression made a big impression on him.

There was no way Leizar would ever convince Zelman to leave Kawetchka. He said that whatever the situation there, it was his home, and he would never leave. However, Leizar also corresponded with other members of the family, and he was surprised to learn that his Uncle Shmuel was thinking of emigrating with his family. Shmuel had spoken to Herschel, who had agreed to sponsor them. However, Shmuel said in his letter that he had been speaking to a lot of people, and he thought it may be better to go to Germany. As a Yiddish speaker, he could understand German, and all his family would be able to communicate right away. Also, he had children of school age, so their education could continue quite smoothly.

This gave Leizar a lot of pause for thought. Germany was effectively ruled by Kaiser William II and in recent years the Chancellorship was given over to the Social Democrats by way of a democratic vote, and that was a growing trend. It seemed that Germany was a more democratic and a fairer society even than the UK.

Later that year, he received a letter from his brother Duvid. He had been speaking with Shmuel and wanted to go with him to Germany, and he said his sister Marcia had been thinking about it too.

As usual, Leizar discussed everything with Chaya. He had been working in the pub, and was now able to serve behind the bar, but they had no other ties in the UK, and they could see the merit in what Uncle Shmuel was saying. They were yet to make a decision on where to live permanently. They had thought they might go to London where they heard opportunities were greater than in Scotland, but Leizar was starting to think that Berlin may be a better option, especially because he would have family there.

Whilst they were listed as aliens as far as the UK government was concerned, an immigrant could apply for naturalisation after three years of habitation. They both felt it would be very important to become British citizens, which would automatically then cover Lena and Minna and of course, Monty was already British. That would give them the option of travel to Germany or wherever they wanted, and they would have the automatic right of return if things did not work out.

So, in 1902 they applied for and obtained, naturalisation papers which allowed the family to obtain British Passports, of which Leizar was extremely proud. The passport was an impressive document stating that 'His Britannic Majesty... Requests and requires... Etc...' There was no photograph, but it was signed by the Secretary of State. Leizar had never held a passport at all, so this was particularly precious to him. It was valid in all European countries, so it would allow entry and exit to and from Germany.

The following year he heard that Shmuel, Duvid and their families had successfully made the trip to Berlin. They wrote that the German immigration authorities seemed welcoming of refugees who were fit and able to work. They had found some rented rooms and it seemed they would have their pick of jobs. Germany's economy was booming. Industrialisation was happening very fast, and factories were looking for operatives. At the same time, farming was also expanding at a rapid rate. Shmuel said people said they were living in the *gründerzeit,* the good times. Workers were able to join unions and there was even some collective bargaining for wages and conditions, the average weekly wage was 500 Marks and there was plenty of overtime pay for those who wanted it.

Leizar was now very interested and noted that Shmuel and Duvid would also not experience the language barrier they had encountered. He told Chaya that as soon as Uncle Shmuel told him he was settled, he would make a trip to Berlin to see for himself what life was like there.

It did not take long before Duvid had a job in a steel factory – hard and hot work, but well paid and Shmuel had been hired outside the city, as a farm worker. This suited Shmuel. He was used to working on the land and he still suffered pain from his injured leg if he remained seated for too long. The children were enrolled in a school in Freidrichstrasse and both families were renting apartments nearby.

Leizar made the trip and was impressed with what he found. The Social Democracy in Germany seemed already to be much closer aligned to his way of thinking. They seemed further down the road to equality of opportunity than even the British. A great deal of power was still vested in the big industrialists, but workers had a voice, and bosses seemed to appreciate the value of a staff united in the success of the business. He had learned that the British were a very subtle lot. They talked a lot about freedom of speech and self-expression, but pressure could be brought to bear on anyone too outspoken and censorship was practised covertly.

He stayed for three days with his brother Duvid, which brought back memories of when they'd shared a room back in the shtetl. Duvid introduced him to his landlord, Ernst Schultz, a smartly dressed man in a relaxed way, with almost white hair, a moustache, and a monocle in one eye. Leizar would have guessed his age around mid-50s. He wore a chequered tweed suit, stiff white collar and tie and rather incongruously, a bowler hat which was a little too small, so that his hair stuck out at the sides. Duvid said that his brother was thinking of moving his family over from Scotland.

Over a beer, Ernst explained that Germany was moving fast, not only industrially, but in terms of freedom of speech and workers' rights. He showed Leizar a copy of *Berliner Illustrirte Zeitung*, (BIZ) a weekly illustrated magazine published in Berlin.

He said it was the first mass-market German magazine. It was extremely popular and it pioneered the format of illustrated news magazines. There was nothing like it on the market. Ernst was a friend of the business manager of the publication, David Cohn, and when he heard that Leizar was a writer, he suggested he introduce them.

So, on the second day, curious to understand the character of the written press in Germany, Leizar and Ernst went to the offices of the magazine and met Mr Cohn, a short dumpy man with gravy stains down his tie. He was smoking a cigarette which never left his lips and the ash dripped down his shirt front. He proudly showed Leizar some recent copies of the magazine and Leizar was surprised at the breadth of the content covered, and the fact that it was clearly left-leaning in its views.

They had a long conversation and David explained that the magazine was owned by Leopold Ullstein, a self-professed Marxist. Ullstein had invested in the latest equipment such as photo-offset printing - he believed BIZ was the first publication to print photographs inside the magazine - a linotype machine and cheaper paper, making it possible to sell the magazines for only 10 pfennigs an issue. Ullstein had developed it into a modern news journal with a specialised staff and production unit for pictures and a fully maintained photo library.

When he heard Leizar was a writer, and had worked with Yitshok Peretz he was very impressed. Also, that he was living in Scotland and originally from a shtetl in oppressed Poland, and he had strong Marxist views. They spoke for many hours exchanging political and economic views, each from a different perspective. At the end, David said that if Leizar decided to join his family in Berlin, there was a job waiting for him.

CHAPTER 36

Leizar was very thoughtful on the journey back to Glasgow and could not wait to share his thoughts with Chaya. The next day after the girls had gone to school, and Monty was asleep, they were able to have a serious chat. He described every detail of his trip and Chaya in her intelligent, practical way listened intently and very seriously. They had a thoughtful discussion and decided to give it the 'overnight test' and see how they felt in the morning.

However, although he did not really admit it to himself, Leizar missed having his extended family around, not to mention his parents, there was no-one in Glasgow and at least in Berlin he would have his Uncle and Aunt, his brother and his cousins.

But the next day, Chaya had some news for him. She was pregnant again, ten weeks gone. She said she knew before he went to Berlin, but she didn't want anything to stop him going. Of course, Leizar was excited, but it rather took the wind out of his sails and then his face dropped. Cheila knew her husband well. She read his face perfectly, the mixture of surprise and excitement at the news, and yet knowing she had upstaged him. This was why she had not mentioned it last night.

'That is the good news, but we have done this before. Last time I had to do it on my own. Let's list the pros and cons,' she said, in English.

'On the plus side, there is no real language barrier in Germany, although Yiddish is not the same as German, but it is widely understood there. And it looks as if you could get a job doing what you love, writing - and with an organisation with similar views to your own. You have family there. We are British citizens so we would need a travel visa, which would be readily available for us. We do not have any firm ties here. Minna remembers her Yiddish so German would be easy and the children can probably go to school with their cousins. Germany has a stable democracy which is left-leaning. The economy is booming and there would be good opportunities for our children when they are older. And if anything went wrong, we would have the right to return to the UK. Now you say the minus side.'

In his musings thus far, Leizar had not thought much about the downside. 'Well, the first thing of course is the baby. If we are serious about moving, then it would make sense for it to be before it becomes too uncomfortable for you. Although I can tell you this journey would be a lot less arduous than the previous one, and we would arrive as British citizens.

'We are established here, although we do not own anything. But we have made some good friends and the whole family can speak English even if it is heavily accented. We don't yet have anywhere to live in Berlin, but I can speak with Ernst. He may have another apartment and if not, I am sure he knows someone who has. Let's sleep on it again,' concluded Leizar. 'And tomorrow you can write to your father – I will write to my parents and also Uncle Shmuel and Duvid. They can find out about accommodation and schooling.

The responses from their parents were surprisingly positive. Herschel knew that the German economy was booming, and their industrial revolution was moving fast. He kept in touch with Ryfke and Zelman, so he was also aware that some of Leizar's family had moved to Berlin. He thought it would be a very good move for them if they could find the right accommodation and be happy in Germany. He was delighted that another grandchild was on the way and advised that they either make the decision quickly or wait another year until the baby was born, but he thought it would be better for them not to have a babe in arms to contend with on the journey. It would also be an opportunity for them to rent their own home instead of living in the pub. He said they should ensure they bought cabin class tickets for the journey, though.

The letter from Ryfke and Zelman was also positive. Their new baby had arrived safely, another little sister for Leizar. This one was called Sayde. Marcia was now the oldest one at home and a *shiddach* had been arranged for her with the grandson of Joseph Galitzer, the unofficial doctor. Joseph wanted to be a properly qualified doctor, so they had plans to move to Warsaw where he could study. That meant they wouldn't be seeing much of them. Again, it occurred to Leizar that as his parents' children were moving away, they seemed intent on replacing them. That would leave Moishe 13, Harry 3, Molly 2, and the new baby Sayde.

Zelman and Ryfke thought it was a very good idea for Leizar and Chaya to move to Berlin to be with their uncle and cousins over there. Much better than being stuck in Glasgow in rooms over a pub.

Uncle Shmuel had spoken to his landlord, Ernst, who also owned the adjacent block to the flat they were renting from him. There was a two-bedroom apartment available, which Ernst thought could be made into three bedrooms if Chaya had another boy. And Duvid had spoken to David Cohn at the magazine, who said that if Leizar took on a sub-editing job and wrote a regular column which was well received, he would take him on the staff and pay him 500 marks to start.

The whole thing seemed to be falling into place and Leizar said the move to Germany seemed *beshert* (fated, or destiny).

And so it was that he booked a second-class cabin for the whole family on the North German Lloyd (NGL) line ship, Wilhelm der Grosse, a well-appointed steamer leaving for Hamburg in eight days. This was not the fastest route. It would take three days at sea, and then four hours by train from Hamburg to Berlin. The quickest route was by rail to London, then across the English Channel from Southampton to Rotterdam and then train to Berlin. That way the whole journey could be done in a couple of days. Leizar was sorely tempted because he had never been to London, but Chaya, very sensibly pointed out, they were travelling with three children, Lena 9, Minna 7, Monty 4, and one on the way, so the simpler sea crossing made more sense.

Rosie and Bryan were sad to see them go as were the rabbi and Glasgow's Jewish community. They all wished them well and said to contact them if they needed anything. Rosie and Bryan said they would always be welcome if they wanted to come back. They were there at the quayside to wave them off, and there were a few tears.

The journey went quite well, although the children got very bored during three days at sea. Chaya was expected to entertain them while Leizar engaged in conversation with other travellers. She managed to find some children's' books written in German which she was able to read to them. The theory was to get them used to the language, but they soon became bored with that and wanted to play. There were quite a few Germans on board, and the others were mainly British, so the children found some friends around their own ages to play with. Also, Leizar had no problem with communication and as everyone found out, Leizar could talk!

They arrived in Hamburg and went through immigration easily, showing their British passports and visas. The next challenge was to find the train station and book themselves through to Berlin. They were *schlepping* quite a lot of luggage. Leizar had two large suitcases and in spite of his protestations about her condition, Chaya had insisted on managing two more. The girls had smaller cases, and they all had knapsacks. When they arrived at Hamburg Hauptbahnhof station, they found there was quite a queue to book tickets, and the station was crowded. Monty was tired and wanted to be carried and the girls were hungry. Leizar was starting to get angry with everyone, he told the family to sit on the floor and look after Mama, and he would join the queue for tickets.

There were three queues for tickets and as they neared the counters they got quite tightly funnelled together. Leizar felt someone handling his knapsack. He turned round quickly just in time to see a man with long hair and a grey coat making his way through the crowd away from him. A woman behind said, '*Ich glaube, er hat dein geld genommen,* I think he took your money.'

Leizar was furious. 'Stop that man!' he shouted. No-one moved. He ran after him roughly pushing people out of the way. The man tripped and Leizar was on him. Like most of the Domansky men Leizar was short but very strong. It turned out to be a young boy about 16 or 17 years old. Leizar held him down until the police arrived and took him away. They wanted Leizar to make a statement and took Shmuel's address in case they needed to contact Leizar, but now he had lost his place in the queue and had to start again. It was only later when they were on the train that he wondered why no one had helped him and Chaya explained that he had shouted in Yiddish, so although the German people would have known what he was saying, it was clear that they were not in a hurry to help Jews.

In due course, they arrived at Berlin Potsdamer Bahnhof station in the centre of Berlin which was a place such as they had never experienced. There seemed to be people everywhere. All hurrying to be somewhere else. Carriages, horses and just people on foot. It was the first time they had seen the new motor cars. The German company Daimler had started production and it seemed they were very popular. They seemed to come quickly from all directions, and one had to be careful crossing the street.

They hired a carriage to take them to Friedrichstrasse which was on the East side of the city where they eventually arrived tired, hungry and exhausted, at the address of Uncle Shmuel. The family had been watching from the window, and on their arrival they all ran out to greet them. They were helped inside, welcomed and given a meal. The children were excited to meet their cousins, and they all went off to play, all except Monty who was fast asleep. This left the adults free to drink coffee and talk. Shmuel and Duvid had taken the day off work and although they were very tired, Chaya and Leizar wanted to see their new home which was literally next door.

When they entered it is fair to say, they were quite crestfallen. They had not been told that it was in a very poor state of repair.

The street was all apartment blocks which were terraced together. Each building had four floors. There were two shops on the ground floor of their building, and then two apartments on each floor above. So, six apartments in all. Shmuel and his family had one on the first floor, Duvid on the second, and Leizar's was on the third floor.

The front door was in between the shops, behind which was a hallway that gave access to a steep staircase leading up to the floors above. The wooden staircase creaked as you walked up, and the walls were painted a sort of dark turquoise which was flaky in parts. It was lit by a single gaslight on each landing. Chaya did not find it easy to walk up the stairs and they would clearly become an issue as the pregnancy progressed.

The internal wooden door to their flat had once been white but it was now dirty and flaky and when they entered inside the apartment it was no better. There was a small lobby with a door on the left leading to a tiny kitchen with a coal fired stove and a table and chairs. The whole flat had uncovered stone floors, and the walls were very much like the landings outside. A bedroom led straight off the kitchen with a large iron framed bed and the same dingy combination of stone floor and a single gas light. There was a door returning to the hallway. Another door led to another large bedroom with two beds, one of which was broken and sagging in one corner. There was a chest of drawers, and a brown painted wardrobe. Next to this room was a bathroom/toilet. There was a metal bath, which needed a good clean, a butler sink and a couple of small tables. The décor, if you could call it that, was much the same.

Seeing the dismay on the faces of Leizar and Chaya, Ernst said, 'Look, this apartment is very cheap, you won't find anything cheaper in Berlin. And you are next door to your family.' At this Uncle Shmuel took charge. 'Come Ernst, Leizar, Duvid, let's go and talk.' So Chaya returned to Chava Devora while the men went to Duvid's flat. He invited them to sit, and Shmuel took control. 'Ernst, my very good friend,' he started, 'This is not fair. The rent you are asking is similar to what you are charging Duvid and myself. And this apartment is a disgrace. It is simply not worth it.'

Shmuel moved in close to Ernst. 'Listen Ernst, you will have three good tenants here, who will pay the rent regularly and look after your properties. We do want to all be together, but my nephew and his family cannot live in that disgusting place. So, if you want to keep us as tenants, you have to do something.'

This conversation went backwards and forwards, and they talked for nearly an hour. At the end of which Ernst agreed that if they would do the work of redecoration, he would supply all the materials and buy new furniture.

Leizar was delighted, because the accommodation itself was perfect, and he was sure that once, Chava Devora, Chaya and Duvid's wife, Esther got involved, it would look beautiful. And when they told the women what had been agreed, they immediately started exchanging ideas on what they would do with it. Colours, drapes, floor mats. They couldn't wait to get started.

For tonight it was agreed that they would stay with Esther and Duvid, who would sleep in one room with their two boys, and Chaya and Leizar could have their bed. They would put up the collapsible bed for the children in the same room. The women set about making dinner for all of them.

They all woke early next morning, determined to start their new life. The next step was the school. It was very nearby, just across the road in the opposite block. They had left all thoughts about keeping kosher far behind, so after breakfast of German sausage, bread, cheese and coffee – and some milk for Monty, they took the children to meet the head mistress. She seemed very kind and said she could see a likeness in the children with their cousins. She would be very happy to have them in the school and they could start tomorrow. They were very excited to be in school all day with their cousins – much better than when they were in Glasgow. Monty was a little confused as he really did not speak German nor Yiddish and could not understand what was being said. Even Minna had some difficulty, but Frau Schmitt said not to worry. With Berlin growing at a rapid rate, many of the immigrant children were not fluent in German when they started, but they picked it up faster than their parents.

Leizar had an appointment with David Cohn at the magazine, and the other men had gone to work, so he left the women to plan the renovation of the apartment. He doubted the wisdom of Ernst in allowing them free reign to order what they wanted and charge it to his account.

'I hope he doesn't regret it,' he said to Duvid. 'It's a bit like letting children loose in a sweet shop. Knowing our wives, they could have a great time ordering and buying materials and furniture, all of which they can charge to Ernst.'

Leizar became aware that Duvid was making strange faces and kept clearing his throat. 'Whatever is the matter with you?'

At which point all three wives entered the room, they had been in the doorway behind Leizar, and Duvid had seen they were listening.

'Oh! Children in a sweet shop, eh?' Chaya looked from one to the other, and whilst Leizar had a broad grin on his face, Duvid had gone quite red. 'Well, just you wait and see.' And with that they all trouped out again.

The meeting at the magazine went well, and Leizar agreed to David's terms. As he had no other commitments, they agreed he could start the next day. Leizar already had a few ideas for articles which they discussed, and David asked him to do a regular column and start with the story of the Workers' co-operative he had set up with Herschel and how it had worked.

When he returned and learned what the wives had ordered, he thought Ernst might not have reckoned on the sort of money the women were spending. However, as he said to himself, Ernst probably should have known better than to allow three Jewish women to go shopping with no limit on the budget.

The goods started to arrive and with them, the bills. After he got over the initial shock, Ernst was true to his word, and settled all the accounts.

They decided that the women would work on the apartment during the day, and the men would do the heavy stuff when they returned from work and at the weekend. It did not take long before the place started to come together. They painted all the walls in white and light colours, bought rugs for the floors and new furniture throughout. They all worked hard and would not let Ernst see the finished product until it was complete.

A week later, they were pleased with what they had done. It was looking great, and they invited Ernst in for coffee. When he saw it, he had to admit, they had turned it into a very desirable property. His expression turned very thoughtful, and he said, 'I think I could get a lot more rent for it now!' He was shouted down by everyone in no uncertain terms.

Leizar found Berlin very agreeable. They had a nice home which was exclusively theirs for the first time ever. They had family all around and later that year, Chaya gave birth to their fourth child, Jacob. Uncle Shmuel and Duvid had not yet joined a Synagogue, but Leizar felt the need to do so, especially with a new son. They went to meet the rabbi of the New Synagogue on Oranienburger Strasse. It was a magnificent building of Moorish design with a large, gilded roof that could be seen from miles around. Leizar introduced himself and asked if the Rabbi was available.

Whilst they waited, they took in the size of the place and concluded that there must be a very large Jewish congregation in the area. A door opened and a large man dressed in a long white shift ducked as he came through. He was wearing a soft white hat with a sort of pommel on top and he had a short dark Van Dyck beard. His face broke easily into a smile as he introduced himself as Rabbi Lipschitz.

Leizar explained that they had just arrived in Berlin from Glasgow, and it turned out that Rabbi Lipschitz knew Rabbi Cornbloom; they had attended the same yeshiva together when they were younger. Rabbi Lipschitz was very interested in the Domansky family and their background from Poland. Of course, when he heard Leizar could do the *leining* from the Torah, he was delighted. Even in such a large community, there were not many who could do it accurately. He explained that Berlin now had over 110,000 Jews and the synagogue could seat 3,000. He wished Leizar *mazeltov* on the birth of his son and, yes, of course, they would supply a mohel for the circumcision and say a blessing in the synagogue for little Jacob.

Leizar found Berlin an interesting blend of old and new. Wherever you looked the city seemed to be in a hurry to change from one to the other. Unter den Linden, a beautiful street lined with linden trees was the centre of the city. It ran from the Brandenburg Gate, past the statue of Frederick the Great to the Royal Palace. The Gate was impressive. Two hundred feet high, surmounted by the Chariot of Victory. He enjoyed walking down it, as he did whenever he went to *shul*. He could not help but wonder what his grandfather, or even his father from the shtetl would have made of it.

Elsewhere the air smelled of dust and the ground was riddled with construction pits. Here a house was being torn down, there the skeleton of a new one stood nearly twice as high as the old building. It was a city on the move.

During the day, nobles, townspeople and the simply curious strolled along Friedrichstrasse. They would stop to admire the city's first electrical interior lighting at Café Bauer or try a cool pale ale at the Pschorr Brewery's beer palace, or maybe even take in an operetta at the Apollo Theatre. It was an exciting city of contrasts and growing very fast.

Leizar found his initial discussions on editorial content with David Cohn at the magazine to be very open and helpful. 'Berlin is quite an open-minded society now. I believe you have come across the Haskalah movement before, well it is very much alive and thriving in Berlin, and as you know, the word means 'Jewish enlightenment.' At the same time, David went on, there was no problem openly discussing the ideology of Marx, who was of course, German.

'Leizar, you have made a very good start, and I must say I am very pleased with the way circulation has increased after your first articles. Your column is controversial and challenging.'

So, things were going very well. Through his readership, Leizar had also started a discussion group which met once per month and quickly became oversubscribed.

When Jacob (Jack) was old enough to attend school, Chaya let it be known that she could teach English, Russian and Yiddish and she soon had a business working from home as a language teacher. At this time, Germany was attracting people from all parts of Eastern Europe, and with immigration at a very high level, there was a great demand for language tuition. The Domansky families had settled well in Berlin and were very happy for several years.

CHAPTER 37

UNREST AND SADNESS 1910-1913

Letters from Poland told them that Ryfke continued to have babies against medical advice. Faye was born in 1904 and Chava in 1905. Moishe Dawid was now 19. He had his father's talent for mathematics, and was helping out Zelman by teaching at the school. That meant Ryfke had five children at home, aged between five to ten. Marcia wrote that this was a constant worry. She was in Warsaw and could only rarely return to the shtetl. Each time she could see this was too much for Ryfke and she was struggling. She discussed it with Zelman and her brother Moishe, but she was unable to get much of a reaction from them.

The Domansky families saw massive progress in Berlin during these years, especially among the Jewish community. Jews were rising to positions of respect and high profile in industry, commerce and politics. In banking, many Jews were in senior management positions and also in teaching and the arts. Despite large scale immigration, the Jewish population of Berlin remained small – less than 1%, but as in generations before and since, they began to be disproportionately represented at a senior level in many professions.

This began to work against them. There had long been an unease in the Aryan population, concerning their perception of Jews. The old German elite watched resentfully as these new Jewish up-and-comers gained standing in Berlin society. The resentment was perhaps stimulated by the rather lavish synagogues, with their gold painted domes standing out like beacons.

Strains of anti-Semitism crept into society. The Anti-Semitic League had been openly founded in Hamburg and anti-semites who were part of the *völkisch* movement stated that Jews could never be properly assimilated into German society. This was a growing rumble under the surface in Berlin.

It was not only the Jews. Immigrants from other cultures were flooding in and taking jobs in industrialised Germany, which began to suffer growing pains. The indigenous Berliners eyed all this suspiciously and began to push back. By 1912 Berlin's population had grown from 835,000 when the Domanskys arrived, to nearly two million.

The Domansky families began to see the effect of all this in their daily lives. There were not many Jewish children at the school, and occasionally there would be some bullying. In bars and cafés, and sometimes even in the street, Shmuel and Duvid had heard themselves referred to behind their backs as *Judenschwein* (Jewpig), and Minna came home one day and said a child in her class had said her parents told her Jews were *untermenschen,* subhuman.

Leizar, Shmuel and Duvid arrived at the synagogue one Friday night to find the word Judenscheiss (Jewshit) daubed on the front wall in large red letters. A crowd had gathered outside, with everyone expressing their revulsion that a holy place of religion could be defiled in this way. Of course, the Domanskys had seen it all before. 'Come,' said Leizar, 'Let us get buckets and water and between us all we will clear this in no time.'

The rabbi stood with arms folded across his chest and tears in his eyes. 'How can they do this? What have we done to them?' But the workmanlike approach of the Domanskys led the congregation to get on with it, and in a short time the disgusting daubing was gone.

It was that year that Herschel wrote to let them know that Ryfke had passed away. Zelman was full of grief and Herschel knew that Leizar and Chaya and the family in Germany would want to know right away. They knew her health had been failing, but it was still a hammer blow to Leizar and Duvid to hear that their mother had died.

As soon as the men returned home from work, they got together with their wives to discuss what to do. Clearly Leizar and Duvid had to make the journey back to sit shiva and support their father; they would miss the funeral of course. Shmuel, not being a blood relative, was not required to go, and it would be impossible financially and practically for the children to go. Chaya and Esther were worried about Zelman being left with young children. How would he cope?

They found a ship leaving Hamburg next day for Warsaw. They booked a second-class cabin and wrote to Zelman, Herschel and the family to let them know they were on the way and would be there in a few days. Ships were able to travel faster than 12 years ago, and the journey time was now four days. However, assuming they stayed only two nights – which would mean they could sit shiva for three days – they would still be away for almost two weeks. They both got permission from their employers, and they were on the train next day to Hamburg.

Herschel met them when they arrived in Warsaw. He was delighted to see Leizar and excited to see the photographs he'd brought of Chaya and the children. In fact, there was one picture of Chaya on her own with the four children around her, that reduced him to tears. 'I'm sorry,' he said. 'She is the image of her mother.' And he touched her image in the photograph with tenderness as if somehow, she would feel it.

He called his mind back to the present. 'I am so sorry about your mother, Leizar and Duvid. I wish you long life. Come here.' And he put his arms round the shoulders of both men.

'Everyone advised her to avoid having more children, but you know how stubborn your parents could be. Of course, when I heard the news, I went to see them straight away.'

'How was our father?'

Herschel tightened his lips and gave them a bland look that said a lot. 'He is not good, but you will raise his spirits now you're here. Moishe Dawid is a comfort to him, but the house needs a woman to look after the children. He told me there were complications with the birth of the last child Chava, and Ryfke had never really recovered.'

Duvid wiped a tear from his eye, and Herschel continued. 'He said she had been spending a lot of time in bed and not eating well. It's good of you both to come right away, your father will be buoyed by the support of his sons. Let's go straight there.'

Expecting a journey that would take the rest of the day, they were astonished to find Herschel had bought one of the new motor cars. It stood outside, big and shiny. 'Jump in, I can drive you straight there, and it will only take two or three hours.'

They arrived to find Zelman in a bad way. He was sitting at the table, still in his nightshirt, with his head in his hands. His hair and beard were unkempt and looked unwashed. Leizar and Duvid went straight to him. His face lit up, and he stood and hugged them both as if he would never let them go. At the same time as if the dam had broken, he burst into great, sobbing tears. His chest heaved and fell, with tears of pain running down his cheeks.

They let him cry it out for a while, saying nothing, and then gently, they sat him back down at the table. A bowl of chicken soup stood in front of him, untouched, and he held his head in his hands and quietly continued to sob. Herschel went outside to give them a little privacy.

Zelman was not alone, Marcia had come from Warsaw, Moishe was there, but the children were at school. 'Papa, eat your soup, I made it specially.' She motioned to Moishe to stay with his father, she wanted to talk to Leizar and Duvid.

She took them into the kitchen, wringing her hands she said, 'Papa has been like this since it happened.'

'Tell us about it,' said Leizar.

'I came to the shtetl when I heard she was bad. I knew they couldn't manage on their own. The doctor warned them both not to have more children, but they wouldn't listen. You know what they were like. Mama's health got worse after Sayde was born. The births were not easy and each one took a great toll on her.'

'But Papa couldn't see it?' Duvid said, incredulously.

Leizar put his finger to his lips, 'Shhhh.' He did not want his father to hear.

'She was lucky to have survived the birth at all, and thank God the baby is alright. Mama haemorrhaged badly and didn't stop bleeding for several days. The doctor prescribed complete bed rest. After several days it did stop, but she was pale and ate very little. She became stick thin and even a short walk would tire her out.'

She started crying, 'Mama was never the same. Papa woke up one morning to find the bed soaked in blood. We sent Harry to get the doctor, but by the time he arrived, Mama was gone.'

They returned to Zelman, who had perked up a bit.

'Papa, we came as soon as we heard, I am sorry we could not be here sooner.' This was Duvid who was having trouble talking at all.

There was an awkward silence and Moishe said softly, 'The funeral was awful, and we sat shiva only one night, Papa wanted to wait for you both to arrive.'

Leizar nodded. 'Yes, now we sit as a family. Have you arranged the rabbi and a *minyan* for tonight?'

Marcia looked at her brother and smiled, 'Leizar, by now everyone in the shtetl knows you are here. There will be a houseful tonight and every night.'

Herschel had been sitting outside in the car. Now he came in. 'If it's alright with you all, I would like to stay for one night to join the prayers and memorial to Ryfke. I am sure someone will put me up for the night, and I will return to Warsaw in the morning.'

They hardly had time to finish off bowls of Marcia's chicken soup. A delicious meal in itself, with the *lokshen* and *kreplach* pasta, *matzo* dumplings, carrots and little pieces of chicken. They each had two bowls, except Zelman, who just pushed it around the bowl.

People started to arrive for the *shiva*. The immediate family sat on the low chairs, and there was a babble of conversation, mainly focused on Ryfke, and what a wonderful person she was. It enabled Zelman and the family to let out some pent-up feelings by talking to others, which was what the *shiva* was designed to do. The rabbi arrived and prayers were said. Zelman and the brothers all said *kaddish* for their mother, after which the women started to distribute glasses of tea, apple strudel and *kichels* they had brought to the shiva house.

Each night of the *shiva*, prayers were said before a packed houseful of people, and everyone was able to pay their respects to the whole family. Zelman kept saying how wonderful it was to have his two oldest sons there, and how Ryfke would be looking down with pride. He insisted that within the memorial prayers, the name of Mendel was also added. The Aunts and Uncles brought food for the *shiva* family, and they all said they would pop in after the *shiva* period to help Zelman, Marcia and Moishe with the children.

Zelman had seemed somewhat better with people around him, but when the shiva was over and everyone had left, knowing they would be leaving the next day, caused his spirits to sink again. Marcia said she would stay as long as she could, but she must return to her husband in Warsaw. They were all worried that with the best will in the world, they could not rely on the occasional 'pop-in' from their aunts. How could Zelman and Moishe cope with the family on their own?

Leizar, Duvid and Marcia were completely torn. Moishe, recognising that they were all feeling guilty to leave them, was valiantly saying that he would take responsibility with the help of his aunts and uncles. But how could a young man in his early twenties, who had to work during the day, handle that? Zelman was completely out of it. He lay on his bed, and he had hardly eaten anything.

There was a loud knock on the door. It was Aunt Clara. She strode across to the table and put her handbag down firmly, as if it was her talisman. As Leizar had found, she was a formidable lady with very strong views she had no qualms about expressing in the most forceful terms. She was quite a large lady which made her all the more intimidating.

Wearing a brown tweed coat with her *sheitel* tied up in a bun, she smelled of trees and grass. 'Right!' she said loudly, and she certainly had gained everyone's attention. 'Someone has to take control here. What do you think you are doing? You can't leave your father in this state, a man who has lost his wife trying to take care of children who have just lost their mother.'

'But…' Moishe was cut off before he could say more.

'What, you can take care of everyone? Who are you, Moses? You talk directly with *Hashem*? You need looking after yourself!' She turned to Leizar and Duvid, 'Oh yes, you must return to Germany, you are the big shots, too good for the shtetl. And then Marcia, 'And you! What sort of daughter can leave her family like this?'

They were all speechless. Clara continued her rant, 'Go, go! Get on with your lives. We will survive. I will look after this family.' She put her arms round Moishe and took him into the other room. 'Don't worry *tuttele*, Aunt Clara is here. I will come every morning before breakfast. I will feed everyone and get the children off to school. I will take the baby back with me. And I will cook and make sure Zelman is eating. I can do it all.'

With that, she went in to Zelman and told him that he could not grieve forever. He had a family to look after. She got him out of bed, and made him eat some soup.

Leizar smiled to himself. 'You wouldn't want to cross Aunt Clara.'

But he was relieved that she had taken control. Although he felt guilty about leaving his family in this state, he had no doubt Aunt Clara would pull up trees, if necessary, to ensure they were well. Eventually she left, with the baby, closing the door loudly behind her and saying she would be back early in the morning.

Zelman had gone to sleep, and they gathered round the table again.

Leizar and Duvid explained the situation in Germany, saying what great opportunities there were, even though there seemed to be an undercurrent of envy relating to the large-scale immigration. If only they could persuade Zelman to join them with the family.

Leizar could see that things had not changed much in the shtetl, and they still lived in fear of pogroms. Marcia said that in Warsaw the socialist political movements were gaining strength, but this seemed to be tightening the grip of the Russian overlords in the countryside. He asked Marcia and Moishe if they thought there was any way they could persuade their father to agree for the family to leave Poland. They both pursed their lips and shook their heads sadly. Marcia said, 'Believe me, Leizar there is no chance at all, especially now; he will never leave the place where his wife and son are buried.'

They were all silent for a while until she continued, 'But I have been discussing it with my husband, Joseph. He says that when he is fully qualified as a doctor, he would like to practise in another country.'

Moishe spoke quietly, almost as if he was ashamed of what he was about to say, 'You know I am so torn. I too, would like to emigrate, but if Marcia goes, then Upa and the children would only have me to lean on. Aunt Clara can't run the family forever. Seems like I am stuck.'

He had tears in his eyes, and with a deep sigh, Zelman brought them together in a group hug. There was really nothing more to say. What Moishe had said was true, and yet it was so unfair on him. Before they went to bed, Leizar and Duvid stayed up late trying to think of a solution, but there seemed to be no answer.

In the morning they spoke with Aunt Clara, which only started her on another rant, saying that they should come back and take care of their family. But even she softened a little when they reminded her that they had their own wives and families, and their first duty was to them.

In the end Leizar and Duvid stayed an extra day, but they had to return. They told Moishe they would write, and try to find a way. For the time being they were sorry and grateful that he would look after their father and siblings, and they would all work on finding a solution. 'Keep trying to convince Upa,' Leizar said to Marcia. 'Just one little "Yes", and we will find a way to get you all out.'

And so they left with great feelings of guilt. The sight of Zelman standing at the door wringing his hands and crying openly would become seared in their memory.

CHAPTER 38

The contrast on their return to Berlin was unbelievable. Having been away for two weeks and spent a few days in primitive quietness, the hubbub of people, electric trams and motor cars seemed even more marked. The two new hotels which had been under construction had now opened: the Esplanade and the Excelsior, each with 600 rooms. Ladies in grand hats walked arm in arm, and Berlin seemed even more vibrant.

Chaya, Esther and the children were of course, delighted to welcome them back. The wives were relieved, it had been a big worry for them to be away so long. They were distraught at the description of how they'd had to tear themselves away from Zelman and the family. Chaya's concern was plain to see, 'There must be some way we can arrange for the family to come here. We can find the money, I am sure. My father will help.'

Leizar and Duvid grim-faced, both shook their heads. 'Papa will never leave the place where his wife and son are buried. He wouldn't leave before, so there is no way to persuade him now. That means that Moishe and the children are stuck there too. It is very hard, Chaya, but I have to say I am glad that we have our family with us here.'

But other things were changing in Germany too. The next day Leizar went to work at the magazine and David Cohn called him in to the office. 'I wanted to talk to you about how things are going here in Berlin,' hHe said, between slurps of tea through the sugar lump.

'Socialism seems to be gaining more strength and maybe we have been an influence in that. In the recent elections the socialists recorded 75% of the votes, and the Social Democrat party now has control of the Reichstag.'

Seeing David's serious expression, Leizar responded, 'So, that's good, isn't it? Things are moving in the right direction. What's the problem?'

'There are two problems. You are aware of the growth of anti-semitism and of resentment against the success of the immigrant population. This may be a type of socialism we did not want.

The second problem is the Kaiser. He sees the way things are moving and these proletarian and socialist ambitions do not suit him. I believe he is determined to maintain his grip. Think it through.'

Leizar's mind had been full of other things. But thoughtfully he said, 'Well as Emperor, he is head of the armed forces, he controls foreign policy and appoints the Chancellor. He is in complete control of the largest economy in Europe.'

David interrupted, 'Yes, and he sees workers' groups becoming more powerful, demanding more equality and rights. His power is slipping. While you were away, the tram workers went on a militant strike. Instead of negotiating, the Kaiser and the Chancellor instructed that at least 500 workers should be gunned down.'

Leizar gasped; having just returned, and been so distracted with family problems, he had not heard about this. 'What? Five hundred people shot in broad daylight? *Oy gevalt!* How can this happen?'

'The whole of Berlin is shocked. People are frightened. There were bodies in the street. I think they did it as a show of strength. It was an outrageous and very dangerous move. Leizar, Berlin is becoming a dangerous place for Jewish supporters of equality.'

Cohn's update was truly frightening and when Leizar returned home, Chaya ran to meet him. 'Did you hear, Leizar? Did you hear what he did, that *momzer*? He shot good people because they want a different life.' Leizar held her and stroked her hair, the three children joined the family hug. Lena said, 'Papa, we don't want you to work at the magazine anymore, it's too dangerous.'

It all gave Leizar much to think about in bed that night.

When he went to the office of the magazine next day, David was waiting for him.

'Look at this.' He showed Leizar an article he had just written

Yesterday in the Reichstag, August Bebel, a Marxist politician, made a speech - condemning the dreadful attack on a civilian protest. He said that the conflict the Kaiser was causing in the country, culminating in this monstrous act was being closely watched internationally, and that speeches the Kaiser had made recently were being seen as threatening, and even war-like. He was rebutted by the Chancellor, who said that Germany needed to show its strength to the world. Babel said that the Kaiser was hurtling down a route would end in disaster. He said that the world was watching.

The article went on to express the need for freedom of expression under democratic rule and urged the people to show their solidarity against this oppression.

Leizar read this with great concern, his brow was furrowed, and he was biting his lip. This was a dangerous article, and things were moving too fast. The words of his children were ringing in his ears. 'Are you going to publish this?'

'Of course, that is what we are here for. This could be the time to break through, the German people have the support of the world.'

Leizar worked quietly at his desk for the rest of the day. He had not recovered from losing his mother, or from the helpless guilt of leaving his brother to cope. And now there was this.

When he returned home that evening, Chaya showed him a letter from Herschel.

My dearest Leizar and best beloved Chaya, I have been watching the news closely and I am worried for your safety. The Kaiser has been provocative and threatening, and the Russians always react. I don't like the way things have been going between Germany and Russia. If war should break out, it would result in massive destruction and death on both sides.

Leizar - your Uncle Yossel, Auntie Clara and their family have decided to emigrate to London, and I think you should consider leaving Germany with the family. You were very wise to become British citizens and as such you have the right of return. I urge you to use it.

Give my wonderful grandchildren a big hug and kiss from the grandfather. I miss them terribly. Lena must be nearly 19, a young woman, Minna not far behind, and even Monty and Jack are growing up fast. Remind them of their grandparents from time to time, and keep them safe.

With all my love
your loving father and father-in-law.

Chaya could hardly wait until he had finished reading. 'What are we going to do, Leizar? If there is truly a war, then surely Poland will be in the middle of it. What will become of my father?'

Leizar's face was grim. 'We have already uprooted our family twice, and we have not really had much chance to settle anywhere. We moved here for a better life, and to give our children better life chances. But I have to say, thank God we are all British and we can easily travel back.'

He took her in his arms, 'My darling, we must protect our family. That is our first priority, but let's watch and see how things progress. Maybe it will settle down, and your father is the most perceptive man I know. He will make the decision that is right for him, whatever happens.'

But as the days passed, the rhetoric worsened between Germany and Russia, and the atmosphere in Berlin seemed more volatile. Lena had made up her mind. In her usual dogmatic way, she said they should leave Berlin right away and go to live in London. Minna was not so sure and Monty, who saw himself as German, did not want to go anywhere. Jack just didn't want to leave his friends.

A few weeks later, a letter arrived from Uncle Yossel in the UK.

Dear Leizar and Chaya,

We have heard what is going on in your part of the world, and we are glad we made the decision to come here. It is a wonderful country, so green and peaceful.

When we arrived, we were introduced to an organisation called The Grand Order of the Sons of Jacob. It was a set up to assist Jewish refugees and help them to settle in London. This organisation owns large multi-storied houses in Ladbroke Grove, West London, and we were offered an apartment for which we pay very little rent. The idea is that we can live here until we can find our feet. It is comfortable.

As a master tailor, I have now got a job with one of the fashion houses in Central London and I earn a good wage.

Leizar, there are great possibilities here. Jobs are available and it is possible to buy houses on the outskirts of London at very reasonable prices and there are societies that will lend you the money to do so.

If you and the family returned to the UK and we all work hard we could club together, and buy a large house between us. That way we would all be together under one roof. What do you think?

Love to you all
Uncle Yossel

Leizar had to take it seriously. As always, he turned it over in his mind before discussing it with Chaya.

There was a great deal to consider. The children, for a start. Lena was 19, a lovely young lady working in a cosmetics shop speaking fluent German. She had probably forgotten her English altogether. Minna was 17. She had inherited the Domansky poor eyesight, and she wore thick glasses. She worked in the kitchen at the Excelsior hotel. German was her only effective language. Monty was 15 and just finishing school. He only spoke German. Jack was 11. All the children would have to learn English if they returned, but thankfully, it would only be Jack whose education was interrupted.

After a few days, Chaya had grown used to the idea, and she was very much in favour of the move. 'The only downside is the language,' she said. 'We are all British and we should live in our own country. We've made a nice home here, but we don't own it, and Uncle Yossel is giving us an opportunity to become property owners. The girls will find work. I can teach languages; you will continue to write and Monty will adapt - after he has finished complaining! We will all help Jack to settle and finish his education. I don't want to live in a country where they can shoot five hundred innocent people.'

Leizar smiled, it was typical of Chaya. Once she had made up her mind, she was so positive.

They had a family conference with Shmuel, Zelda, Duvid and Esther. Shmuel and Duvid could both see that it was highly likely the Kaiser would take Germany to war with Russia, and they were all equally shocked at the recent atrocity. They could see the wisdom of getting out of Germany.

Uncle Shmuel was pulling his beard thoughtfully. 'We have been thinking what to do, but it's not so easy for our family. We are not even naturalised Germans, so technically we are classed as refugees. I think Yossel got into England just in time. I hear they are turning away boatloads of refugees now. The risk is so high for us. We could end up stateless.'

Duvid seemed keen to get out. 'If there was a way, I would rather go to America. I think they take refugees willingly and they are a long way from Europe. It's very attractive and to be fair, Leizar, but for a bit of bad luck, it is where you would be now.'

But there was also the cost. Leizar and Chaya were pretty sure Herschel would finance their journey back to England, and might also help them with the property purchase. But they could hardly ask him to finance the journeys of eight more family members to America, a far costlier trip in the first place.

It was in Feb 2014 that Leizar eventually agreed with Chaya and they came to the conclusion that their family should return to the UK now. He explained to his uncle and his brother that when they arrived, he would try to find a way to get their families out too, but that he had to protect his wife and family first. It was hard to say, hard to hear, but they came to terms with it.

And London with Uncle Yossel and the family sounded very appealing. Since he returned, Leizar had been writing to Zelman and the family in Poland to keep them updated. Due to the remote location of the shtetl, he knew they would only have heard rumours about what was happening in the world, and of course he begged his father to make the decision to leave. He received no reply, and was unsure if his letters had even arrived.

But when Leizar wrote that they had decided to move to England, and that he could still try to get the family out of Poland to join them, he received a reply at last. Zelman wrote:

My wonderful, big shot son, who leaves his father and his family and takes away his grandchildren.

First of all, nothing will happen. I am an old man and I have heard all this talk before. It will all blow over. Second, I want to make it clear to you. I would rather hack off my legs than leave our home here in Kawetchka. My wife and my son are buried here. You think I would leave them?

My boy – you are the one who leaves. You have done enough leaving for all of us. Me? I am staying here.

Give my love to my grandchildren, who don't even know me!

With love from,
Your Father

Although Leizar knew this was designed to play on his guilt, it still got to him, as Zelman surely knew it would. So the family were stuck there. Poland was likely to become involved in a war between Germany and Russia, and all night, every night, he thought about his father and Moishe struggling to look after the younger children.

But Marcia wrote that she had managed to make contact with their old Aunt Yentl. She did not live in the shtetl. She had met a man many years ago and moved to another part of Galicia altogether. They had not seen her since they were children. Her husband had passed away and, according to old Jewish custom, she had recognised her duty to look after her brother and his family. She had moved back and was now running the household in Kawetchka. Leizar smiled when he thought of how many times Aunt Yentl had told him women were not just for housekeeping, and he played out in his mind, how it would be when Yentl started quoting Torah and Talmud at Zelman.

There was a ship leaving Hamburg for Grimsby in three weeks and Leizar was able to book a second-class cabin for the whole family. The journey by ship was much shorter to the eastern side of England and they would only be on board for one night. They would proceed by train to St Pancras station in London, a journey of only 5 hours, ando in two days they would be in London.

They had mixed reactions from the family. Lena had changed her mind and flatly refused to go. 'Why would I leave this vibrant city, with so much life. Why? To go back to that *farshtinkeneh* place like Glasgow, all grey and miserable.'

But Chaya knew the real reason: Lena had a new boyfriend.

Minna was more sensible, and she was quite excited at the prospect of learning another language and living in a country that had an Empire across the world.

Monty and Jack only knew Germany, so it was going to be a big wrench for them to travel and live in a country they knew nothing about. Leizar reminded Monty that it was the country of their birth. Chaya worked her persuasive magic, and by the time she had finished with them, three of their children were excited at the prospect.

She didn't do quite so well with Lena, who started making arrangements to live on her own after they had left. There followed an almighty row with her father, which ended up with Lena digging her heels in even further. Leizar decided this was a battle to fight another day.

Chaya wrote to let her father know their travel arrangements and said that she would be back in touch when they arrived in London. She hoped that one day, he would come and visit them. Leizar wrote again to his father, and they both wrote to Uncle Yossel.

Yossel replied straight away. 'We are so excited to hear you are coming. Don't worry, we will arrange everything for your arrival. You can catch the LNER railway from Grimsby which will take you to the London Underground Station at St Pancras. Ask for the Metropolitan line train to Hammersmith station. I will meet you there. Send me a telegram when you know which train you are on from Grimsby, so I can work out the timing. Make sure you have some English money.'

At the magazine, David Cohn was not happy when he heard they were leaving. 'Look, Leizar, I understand that you are British citizens, and you want to return home, but you also have a responsibility here. You can't just walk out.'

'I am sorry, David but my first responsibility is to my family.' Leizar felt very awkward. He knew David would have to work twice as hard.

David did not let him off the hook. 'But it's not your only responsibility. Look, we all agree that Germany has entered a period of social and political unrest. The government and the Kaiser seem on a collision course, and yes, perhaps a war may be approaching. That creates a most important time for journalists. We must provide information and views. The magazine is very influential in shaping the thinking of ordinary people and you, my friend, have quite a following. You also edit the magazine.'

There was a pause before he continued, 'Look, I gave you work when you arrived in Berlin, and I think you owe it to me and your readers to ensure the magazine does not suffer.'

In the rush to come to a decision and the speed of implementing it, Leizar had not thought this through, but he could see that Cohn had a point.

'But I have the opportunity to remove my family from danger, and I have young children, surely you can see that I have to put my family first?'

Another pause, longer this time, after which Cohn leaned towards Leizar in a conspiratorial manner: 'I have a suggestion. Through the magazine, I have contacts in America. There is a Jewish organisation that raises funds through wealthy Jews in the U.S to help Jewish refugees. I know your uncle and your brother want to go to America. If you stay on here until I can find a replacement for you, I will see if I can arrange for finance and help to get them there.'

David had clearly given this a lot of thought. He had not come up with such a proposal off the cuff.

Leizar hesitated, 'You could really do that? You could arrange for them to get out?'

'Look, I can't promise, but my contacts in the US have helped many people. You know me, Leizar, if I say I will do something, I will move mountains to make it happen.'

'You give me your word on that?'

'Yes. You can send Chaya and your family to London, and you could join them later. The arrangements for Shmuel and Duvid's families should be under way. You may even see them leave.'

This addressed one of the demons in Leizar's head. He was very guilty that his family could get out of Germany whilst Shmuel and Duvid's families seemed stuck. 'Let me think overnight, and we will speak tomorrow.'

As always, Leizar sought Chaya's counsel. When she heard it all, she became very thoughtful. 'Well, he has a point about you letting down the magazine and all the readers. And he did employ you straight away when we came here, which enabled us to pay our rent, and put food on the table. We do owe him something.'

As always, Leizar was thankful he had an exceptional wife who could be objective about such a thing. His heart reached out to her.

'I know you feel guilty about leaving your uncle's and your brother's families here when we leave, and if he can find a way out for them, it would be a *mitzvah*. But I don't like the idea of leaving you here indefinitely.'

He remained quiet while she was thinking.

'Of course, I can make the trip to London with the children. Compared to the journeys we made before, it will be easy, but I don't want you here if war breaks out.

Another pause.

'Why don't we do this?' she said thoughtfully.

'Tell him you will stay until he finds a replacement editor, for a maximum of three months, but ask him to confirm with his contacts that funds can be found for Shmuel, Duvid and their families to travel to America. If he cannot confirm it, you will leave. And we need confirmation from Uncle Yossel that we have accommodation in London.'

Leizar looked at her with deep love in his eyes. The plan was a good one. 'I can advertise for my replacement straight away, and even with a handover, I should be able to join you before the three months are up, and while I am here, I can make sure all goes well with Shmuel and Duvid's arrangements. I will speak to Cohn tomorrow.'

Leizar knew it: this solution should work. His satisfaction at getting there was tinged with disappointment, though, because he, too, had been excited at the prospect of going to London.

Leizar was surprised when after a week, Mr Cohn called him in to his office. 'Well, good news! There are quite a few organisations who receive donations from wealthy Americans to assist Jewish refugees fleeing to America. I happen to know Felix Warburg, who heads up the American Jewish Joint Distribution Committee as well as the Hebrew Sheltering and Immigrant Aid Society. They specialise in sending funds to Central Europe to assist families like yours. Felix's brother is Max, who runs MM Warburg bank in Hamburg. They distribute the money through Hilfsverein der Deutschen Jüden to ensure the recipients are genuine. I will put your uncle in touch with them right away.'

Leizar was impressed. 'Thank you, that's wonderful. I have advertised for a new editor and will interview applicants next week. Of course, if I find someone suitable, they will have a second interview with you. If you are satisfied, then I'll arrange a handover period to ensure the magazine remains well supported.'

It was falling into place.

'Chaya will take the children to London, and I will stay on here until the new editor is installed and working well, but my maximum stay will be three months, and my expectation is that it will not need to be that long.'

There was tremendous excitement in all three families.

Chaya and Leizar had much to do to prepare for their departure. The first job was for Leizar to make sure all the family were in line, especially Lena. He called a family meeting.

'You are all clever, and I know you have been following what has been happening here.'

Mainly to Jack, he said, 'There may well be a war in Germany. Many people would be injured or die. And that would be dangerous for us all. As Jews, we are usually the first to suffer but we are lucky because we are British citizens and so we can't be refused re-entry to the UK.'

Straight away Lena said she was not going, and this got right up Leizar's nose!

'Now you listen to me!' Leizar raised his voice. 'You will do as I say, young lady. Do you think I would allow you to remain here and maybe be killed or worse?' Lena turned away; they were as stubborn as each other. In the style of his father, Leizar was now shouting at the top of his voice and thumping the table. 'While you are my daughter, you will listen to me and have respect. Do not test me on this!'

Lena had not seen her father like this, and he was formidable. In his anger, he had knocked the utensils off the table, and the water jug had smashed on the floor. The others shrank slowly out of the room, not wishing to be involved. All except Chaya, who was also a bit shocked at the strength of Leizar's reaction. Softly she said, 'Leizer *liebchen,* go speak to the children, Lena and I will clear up in here, and then I'll have a chat with my Lena.'

Chaya made some tea and after clearing up, she sat down with Lena. She knew that her daughter had the same temperament as her husband. If you told her she could not do something, then she wanted it all the more.

So Chaya started off by drawing a verbal picture of life in London. 'Lena, darling listen to me. We are not going to Glasgow, we are going to London, the biggest and most progressive city in the world. It is the centre of fashion and highlife for teenagers, especially beautiful young ladies. There are night clubs, cinemas and the young people called Bright Young Things. Lena, you will be a star there.'

Gradually, she could see Lena coming round so she tempered the vision with some reality. 'Don't get me wrong, it will not be easy at first, but we are a very strong family when we all pull together, and we will establish ourselves very quickly.'

'But Mama, I have forgotten my English, how will I get on?'

'Darling, Lena. I am there for you always. I will help you and you will be speaking like a Brit in no time. You are beautiful, and you will love it. I know you have a new boyfriend…'

'Oh! Don't worry about that Mama, he has been seen with another girl. I don't care about him. He can rot in hell for all I care.'

Chaya smiled. It seemed now as though she had been pushing against a half-open door.

She put her arms out and held her daughter tight, 'Now go and give your father a hug and tell him you love him.'

That still left Chaya worried about Lena's reaction when she heard that her father was remaining in Berlin for a while, but oddly enough, when the time came, she did not react to it.

With some sadness, they started to prepare for the departure of all the family except

Leizar. Minna and Monty were not at all happy with the arrangements; they knew his work at the magazine was controversial and they worried that it might make him a target. 'Don't worry, *kindele*, I can look after myself, and as soon as I have found my replacement, I will be with you.'

He was more worried that they had a lot of luggage and how they would handle it without him. 'You look after your Mama and your little brother, and don't let her *shlepp* too much.'

To Monty he said, 'You are the man of the family, make sure everyone is safe, and let me know as soon as you are settled.'

They tried to pack things in a way that could be managed between them. Everyone had bags and suitcases to carry, and the night before departure, Leizar and Chaya made love for the last time in Germany. It was tender and beautiful and afterwards they lay talking for a long time. Neither wanted to be parted. Leizar's mind went back to the journey to Glasgow.

'Chayale…' It was the first time he had used the endearing form of her name. 'I thank God every day that I found you. Not only the most beautiful woman in any room, but with a beautiful mind. A wonderful wife and mother. If I could, I would want you to see yourself through my eyes, only then would you realise how special you are.'

She leaned over and kissed him full on the lips. A lingering long, loving kiss. 'My darling Leizar, it will not be long before we are together again in London. That is very exciting…'

Leizar interrupted. 'I think of my journey to Glasgow, and how it all went wrong. Take care my *liebchen,* and send me a telegram as soon as you are with Uncle Yossel, so I know you are all safe.'

'Don't worry about me and the children. We will all be fine. I am used to these journeys now, and I have been through far worse travels than this.'

What Chaya didn't say, and what had not occurred to Leizar at all, was that Jack was actually a German citizen, born in Berlin. Was Chaya going to have trouble with immigration in London?

They left early next day and there were lots of tears all round. Leizar and the other Domanskys waved them off until they were out of sight. He took a deep sigh and was grateful that his relatives remained for now. He was not alone.

It turned out that Chaya and the children had an uneventful journey. Arrival at immigration in Grimsby was much more organised than when she had travelled to Glasgow. She was questioned about Jack, and she had to see a senior immigration official, who explained that Jack was actually a lucky boy. He would be classed as 'British by Descent' as both his parents had been British citizens at the time of his birth. In due course they would be able to apply for a British passport for him and he would effectively have dual nationality.

Chaya was very impressed with the transport system in England. The train to St Pancras was comfortable, they had a compartment to themselves, and the underground system was incredibly far reaching. She got somewhat confused by the different coloured lines, but they found their way to Hammersmith, where they managed to meet up with Leizar's Uncle Yossel whom she recognised due to the family likeness. He had the same stature as Leizar and Zelman – short and stocky with a very serious face. He wore a large black greatcoat and a round brimmed hat, with a cigarette in his mouth which he only took out to greet her and the children, which he did in a rather gruff voice.

'So – you made it! All on your own and without a man!'

Chaya bit her lip. The inference that a mere woman might have more difficulty with a simple journey was anathema to her. She made a mental note to set Uncle Yossel straight in due course, but she looked at Lena and Monty, who had both been slighted by implication. Especially at Lena, who was about to let Yossel know what she'd thought of the comment. Chaya jumped in loudly... 'Yes, how lovely to see you Uncle Yossel. This is Lena, Minna, Monty and Jack. Leizar sends his love and hopes to be joining us soon.'

Yossel had hired a taxi to take them to Ladbroke Grove, which afforded them the opportunity to see that part of West London. To Chaya everything looked rather old and dirty. It looked older than Berlin, but just as busy. More motor cars and people everywhere. They were all very excited, although Uncle Yossel did not crack his face.

Jack laughed out loud. 'Look, look at those funny men on their bicycles with pointy hats on.'

'They are policemen.' This was Lena who remembered them from Glasgow. 'And you had better behave yourself or they will come and arrest you!'

They all laughed; it was certainly not like Berlin.

The roads seemed to have no logical order, and Chaya wondered how people found their way around. They passed through Notting Hill and turned left into Ladbroke Grove and they were all struck by the hustle and bustle of the place. Yossel explained that here they were almost in the centre of London. They pulled up outside one of the high terraced houses. Four floors plus a basement.

Clara was already standing on the pavement as they arrived. In contrast to her husband, she wore a big smile that lit up her whole face. 'Welcome, welcome, how lovely to see you all.' Chaya introduced the children and everyone got big hugs.

The house was huge, and Yossel had arranged for Chaya and the family to have the top floor. They were used to stairs and to their surprise, they found that the rooms were also large with high ceilings. Their floor had three bedrooms, a small kitchen and a separate bathroom and lavatory. It was sparsely, but adequately furnished and the décor looked a little old, but it was not bad. The place was fairly warm and well-lit with electric lights.

Clara was keen to show them their new home. 'I hope it is large enough for you all, I have been through and cleaned it, so it should be ready, but I am sure you will want to make it like home. Remember it is only temporary.'

Chaya decided she and Leizar would have the largest room, but the second was still pretty big and she allocated that to the girls. The boys could share the third room, which was still a decent size. Of course, a row broke out immediately. Monty was the most vocal 'Why should they get the biggest room, with the best view? We are the men, and we should get preference over girls – that's the way things are!' He deliberately said this in German to be more assertive.

Although Lena was the most vocal and would normally be the first to fight back, Minna could be more convincing when she wanted to be. People did not want to argue with Minna.

Because her eyesight was bad, even with her thick glasses, she went right up close to people when she spoke. On this occasion she turned to Monty and with her face only a few inches from his (they were both around the same height – short) she spoke very quietly, but forcefully, and she was quite heavy for her age, which could also be rather intimidating.

'You don't want me to lose my temper do you, little brother? Because you know what happens when I lose my temper!' Monty seemed physically to shrink. And Lena, on seeing this, piped up.

'Now be a good boy, and go to your room, before you get into trouble.' She would have built it into a famous Domansky row, but Chaya jumped in, 'Stop it you two! *I* made the decision and that's it.' Monty huffed and puffed, he got hold of Jack and walked him into their room as if it was the last place in the world he wanted to be.

Chaya turned to Clara and Yossel. 'Thank you so much for arranging this for us. I apologise for my ungrateful children. We will soon settle down. The place has great possibilities.'

'You must be tired and starving hungry. Yossel went out and bought some shopping for you; as soon as you are ready, come down to us, and I will make some dinner.'

Yossel and his son Simon appeared with all the luggage, and they left the family to sort themselves out.

Chaya looked in the larder and found they had all the essentials, while the children started to unpack and fight over who was going to have which bed. Clara made them a lovely roast dinner with chicken, potatoes, and vegetables, and jam pudding and custard for dessert. The children had never seen custard before, but they loved it, and Monty and Jack had double helpings each, after which Jack promptly fell asleep in the chair. Chaya apologised that they were all tired from the journey, and they had an early night.

Chaya wrote a telegram and a letter to Leizar. The telegram just let him know they had arrived safely, and said there was a letter on the way. In the letter, she explained that Yossel had met them as arranged and they were all settled. The flat was adequate and Clara had made them dinner. She asked how things were going in Berlin and when he thought he could join them.

She put out the letter ready for posting and went to bed. She missed Leizar's touch and the feel of his warm body next to her, but she was exhausted, and she slept soundly.

The whole family was up early next day, and they made some plans. Chaya would seek out Clara, and they would go shopping. Lena and Minna would look for English lessons and Monty would look after Jack and at the same time look for work.

It only took a few days for them to settle, and thankfully Chaya had enough money to see them through for a while. Yossel and the family were a great help.

Chaya found her English came back to her straight away, and Lena seemed able to get by, except that when they tried to speak, they found people had difficulty understanding them because of their accent, which was Glaswegian mixed with Eastern European. Minna remembered a few words, but Monty and Jack of course had nothing at all.

Chaya was not keen on the way some men were looking at her girls, but the girls loved it. They were both quite attractive and got a lot of attention. Chaya made a mental note to have a word with them to be careful.

Leizar wrote back:

My dearest, darling wife,

What a relief to hear you all arrived safely with no incident. Very interesting to hear about Jack. It only occurred to me after you had left that Jack was a different nationality from the rest of us, and I was worried about what would happen at immigration.

I am glad to hear that the apartment is adequate, although I am not sure what you really mean by that word. I hope it will be comfortable for us all, and you have Yossel and Clara if you need anything.

I am afraid things seem to be getting worse in Europe. Our stringers tell us Austria is claiming Bosnia as its own territory and so is Serbia. With Germany growing stronger, Britain has decided to align with France and Russia in the event of a dispute – 'The triple entente,' they call it. And the Kaiser doesn't like it at all. He feels surrounded.

I keep reading the words of my father in the letter he wrote. Am I abandoning him? What will become of them? What can I do? I feel so helpless, my darling.

But I know I have to live with this guilt, and you and the family are my first priority. I believe war is becoming more than a possibility, and I am determined to get out of here as quickly as I can. I already have some applicants for the job.

Keep in close touch with me, give the children a big hug and tell them to look after their mother, I hope they do not fight too much. And tell them it wouldn't hurt them to write too.

I love you all so much,

Your husband and father,
Leizar

Chaya helped her children with the language, and they settled down very quickly. London seemed to be full of young people, and the whole family loved the markets and the vibrancy going on all around them.

But it was not until July 1914 that Leizar hired his replacement and handed over editorial control of the magazine. David Cohn was very reluctant to let Leizar go. It became clear that if there was a war, Germany would be at the heart of it, and he felt it was a very important time to report on international developments. But a deal was a deal, and he knew the family were already in London. 'You can send me articles from London, you know. It would be good to get a different perspective. Leizar, I am sorry to see you go. You are a very talented young man, and if you ever return to Germany, there is a job for you here.'

Leizar thought this was very unlikely, but he thanked David. 'We will try to keep in touch. You have to work out how to live without the Kaiser in charge. I have enjoyed working with you, David. Shalom Aleichem.'

Leizar travelled back to Britain at the end of July to join the family. Two weeks later, Austria sent Archduke Ferdinand to Sarajevo to negotiate the land dispute and demonstrate Austrian authority in the area, whereupon he was murdered by Gavrilo Princip, a member of a Bosnian nationalist group called 'The Black Hand'. This effectively sparked the First World War.

Leizar arrived at the house in Ladbroke Grove like a conquering hero. Everyone was out on the pavement to meet him, and he was almost buried under the affectionate hugs of all his family. After all the excitement died down, and he had unpacked, they once again sat down to dinner, all together, as a family. Chaya and Leizar kept stealing glances at each other. They were all reunited again. Over dinner that evening, he tried to explain what he perceived was happening in Europe.

'The bad news is that many had hoped that this would be a local war between Austria, Germany and the Eastern European states, but it is escalating very quickly. I think the Kaiser sees this as an opportunity to expand his territory, asserting his authority in Europe by defeating France swiftly, and this could bring Britain and Russia into the war.' He smiled at his children. 'I think your father got out of Germany just in time.'

They all started to fire questions at him, 'What does it mean for us if Britain enter the war? We thought we came here to get away from it.' 'What will happen to Zeider and the family?' 'What about Grandpa Herschel?'

Leizar did his best to answer, but he had to say that, honestly, he didn't know what the consequences would be. Like everyone else they would have to watch the news. The question about Zelman made his stomach tighten, but he said the family should be alright. They were in the country, and if there was fighting, it would be in the cities. He wished he felt as confident as he was trying to sound.

After dinner, when Chaya and Leizar were alone, he could see she had something on her mind. They sat on the edge of their bed. 'Alright, my beautiful wife. Tell me what else I should be worrying about,' he said with a smile.

She turned to face him, 'Leizar, you're right, I did not want to worry you on your first night, but there is something that has been on my mind.'

He took her hand and she continued, 'With the onslaught of war in Europe we should think about our plans. We have some money put by, but it is all in German marks. The war with Germany is bound to involve Poland and especially Warsaw. My father's business could be shut down, and the banking system may be disrupted. The rent for the apartment is subsidised, and it is very reasonable, but we have six mouths to feed. I have to tell you I am really worried about money.'

Leizar did his best to reassure her. 'Starting tomorrow, I will be out there, and I'll find employment. We will need to change the German marks, little by little. The exchange rate is very bad now, but I am sure it will improve. And I think we should discuss this with the older children. I don't want to worry them of course, but they are old enough to understand. As soon as their English is up to it, there is no reason they can't look for work and help out. Give it a little while, and things will look much better.'

After warm and tender lovemaking, Leizar held her in his arms, 'Now I know I am finally home.' With that he turned off the light, and they slept in a cuddle.

But try as he might, Leizar could not find a publication that was hiring journalists, especially one with left-leaning views.

Chaya and the children had no experience of being so short of money that they had to worry about food, and Leizar's pride would not allow him to ask for help from Yossel. Chaya suggested she could find work as a waitress, but London was beginning to focus on the war effort, and she had no experience to offer. After a few weeks, money was really running low and Chaya had to feed the family on very little. They had to be frugal with the light and heat which operated on a meter.

It was Minna who came to the rescue. Without her parents' knowledge, she spoke to Lena and Monty. 'This cannot go on,' she said, 'The family will soon be starving and the three of us are fit and strong and able to work. I am going to speak to Uncle Yossel and find out what we can do, we should be prepared to do anything to help the family.'

This was received enthusiastically by Monty. 'Yes,' he said. 'Mama and Papa have always looked after and provided for us and now they need some help. This is our time.'

It has to be said that Lena was not so keen. 'What sort of work can we do? Our English is not so good, and we have no experience of anything.'

Monty huffed, 'We have to be prepared to do anything it takes. At least you two can speak and understand English. I have to learn, unless I can find a job with German people – and I doubt that in the middle of this war. Let's see what Uncle Yossel says.'

So that evening when Yossel returned from work, they sneaked down and asked if he had any ideas where they could look for work. 'We will do anything,' they said.

'Anything?' replied Yossel. 'Well, you might be in luck. The place where I work has been turned over to making Army uniforms and kitbags. They need thousands of them, and we don't have enough machinists. If you really mean it, I can take you in to the workshop, and tell the boss that I will train you on the machines. You'll pick it up quickly and when you are productive you will have a regular weekly wage. You don't need any language skills and we can all interpret for Monty if he needs it.'

They had a hard job persuading their father that they should go to work in the factory. He thought his children could do better than that. But in the end, it was Chaya, once again, who persuaded Leizar to 'look the other way'.

At first Yossel found it very difficult to convince his boss, Manny Gold, that he should employ German people, but Yossel explained that they were all British citizens who had been living in Germany before the war.

'Manny, these are good people, relations of mine, they need the work and I guarantee they will work hard for you. You need the production, and I will train them. Give them a break.'

Manny looked at the three of them, they did look keen, and he relied on Yossel to keep the factory going. 'Alright,' he said, 'I will give them a try on this basis: they will not get a penny until they are able to produce whole garments. If they can do that then I will pay half a crown for each complete garment that passes quality control; fair enough?'

Yossel was grateful on their behalf, but Lena, who understood everything that was said, was not happy, To Yossel she said, 'Who the hell does he think he is? We should work for no money? He can take his *farshtinkener* factory and shove it up his arse!'

They all crowded round Lena, who was ready to walk out. They all tried to convince her that this was better than they had hoped, and it would help out their parents when they needed it.

Manny saw this going on and walked over. 'Alright,' he said. 'Three shillings per garment, that's my last word!'

This was a lifesaver for the family. Monty was the quickest and was soon producing at least three garments a day. He worked without stopping. He brought a sandwich from home and ate it by the machine.

Minna was also productive, but her eyesight meant she had to look closely and go a little slower, but she also was soon producing garments and earning some money.

Lena applied herself to the job at first, but she never really got the hang of it and although she did produce a few garments, they kept getting rejected for poor workmanship. Being Lena, she argued with quality controller, and called him a 'schmuck.'

And the more the others tried to coach her, the more irritated she became. There were days when she could not get out of bed, and would turn up late, or maybe not even turn up at all.

In the end Manny spoke to Yossel, 'Look Yossel, she's getting on my nerves. She's producing nothing and taking up a machine, and she thinks she knows best all the time. I have to replace her.'

Yossel had no defence, everything the boss said was true.

Monty thought Lena was secretly pleased to get the sack. When Leizar found out, it was the subject of another big Domansky row. But still, Lena never went back.

'Well, don't think you are going to laze around here all day while everyone else works to keep you. You go out and find a job. I don't care what it is, but you earn something to contribute.'

She did get a part-time job in a chemist's shop as an assistant, but it didn't last. Lena just didn't want to work.

However, Minna and Monty between them were bringing in around £3.10s per week, enough to feed the family and pay the rent on their own. Chaya and Leizar were so proud of them. Lena didn't seem to care.

Yossel told Leizar that he had not yet joined a synagogue, but he knew there was one nearby, in St Petersburg Place. So Leizar took a walk and was amazed to find one of the most magnificent and beautiful synagogues he had ever seen, just a short walk from Ladbroke Grove. It was an impressive stone structure from the outside, and even more beautiful when he entered, with an intricately carved bimah and massive stained-glass windows. There was a plaque indicating that the foundation stone had been laid in 1877, by Leopold de Rothschild.

Leizar knocked on the door of an office. It was opened by a young man with a wispy black beard and thin round spectacles, wearing a kippah. He explained that his family had recently arrived in the area, and asked if it was possible meet the rabbi.

The man had a studious look which changed by the time his glasses had slipped down to the end of his nose. He pushed them back up, just before they fell off altogether. 'Welcome, Reb...?'

'Domansky.'

'The rabbi here is Rabbi, Professor Sir Herman Gollancz, you may have heard of him?' Leizar shook his head.

'Sir Herman attends the synagogue only on Shabbas mornings, but you may not know that this synagogue is the jewel in the crown of the British United Synagogue movement, so we have two rabbis, Reverend David Klein is the acting minister, and he is here. I am sure he would be delighted to meet you.'

'That would be wonderful, if he can spare a few minutes, thank you.'

While they were waiting, Leizar and Yossel took the time to look around. The Torah ark was on a raised platform and approached by sweeping marble steps. Eight massive marble columns supported the high curved roof and the large bimah was placed in the centre of the floor away from the ark itself. Leizar thought it was the most beautiful and spiritual place.

Reverend Klein seemed quite young. He wore black rabbinical robes with a kippah on his head. Unusually for a rabbi, he was clean shaven with hair slicked back. He walked towards them in a very determined manner, as if he was late for something. As he neared them, he extended his arm in front of him, ready to shake hands. He also talked in the manner he walked, quickly.

'Welcome to London and welcome to our beautiful synagogue, Chaim tells me you have recently arrived with your families, how wonderful, I am David Klein, the acting minister. Come, let's go to my office, I will make tea.' This was all said in one breath, while he was shaking hands with each of them.

When they were sat in his office, Leizar and Yossel introduced themselves, explaining that Yossel and his family had been here a little while, and Leizar only a few days, although his wife and children travelled several weeks before.

'Tell me about your families,' said Reverend Klein, 'and where you have travelled from. I would like to know about you.'

Together they explained their backgrounds. Klein was very interested, he wanted to hear the whole story. Leizar went through the family history, starting with life in the shtetl, the pogroms and poverty, through his time in Warsaw and the workers co-operative, meeting his wife, all the traumas in Glasgow, their journey and life in Berlin, and ending with their arrival in London. Yossel had come directly from Poland, and they both considered themselves lucky to have got their families out before the war. Klein was very impressed. He fired questions at them like a machine gun until they both felt quite exhausted.

'I am keen to meet your wives and families,' he said. 'I am sure you would like to hear a little about the synagogue and the Jewish community in the UK?'

They found they had to concentrate hard, because the information came at them quickly. 'The synagogue can seat eight hundred people, which we consider to be very large, but of course, in Eastern Europe you would have had larger ones.'

'Yes, but never one as beautiful as this.'

'Thank you. The United Synagogue movement is the largest Jewish religious body in the UK and this synagogue is regarded as one of their most treasured. We have a resident choir led by a chazan with the most beautiful voice, who also officiates at the services.' He drew a breath. 'Where are you living? Is it far from here? Can you walk to shul? We would love to see you.'

Before the rabbi could continue, Leizar said that the family would very much like to join the shul and would be attending for shabbas service.

'Wonderful, may I suggest you leave the family names with the secretary? When you become members, we will try to allocate numbered seats for you all, as soon as they become available. We are an Ashkenazy community and I take it you all read Hebrew, or does anyone need a little help?'

He was very interested to hear that Leizar was competent at *leining* and would be very happy to take part in shabbas morning services. Reverend Klein thanked Leizar and said he looked forward to meeting the rest of the family this shabbas. There would be a kiddush afterwards and they could meet some of the congregation. And then suddenly he was gone, leaving them to show themselves out.

Leizar and the family attended Friday night service and again Saturday morning and they were amazed at the professionalism and beauty of the service. They had never experienced a resident choir before, and together with the chazan, who had the most beautiful voice, this was unlike anything they had ever witnessed. Leizar and Yossel could not help thinking back to the rudimentary little shul in Kawetchka, and Leizar wondered what his father and grandfather would have made of what he was witnessing now.

Leizar, Yossel, Monty, Jack and Simon sat downstairs while the women were upstairs during the service. There was quite a crush when all the women descended and a loud babble of noise as all the men went to greet them.

Leizar and Chaya hung back for the kiddush after the service, which took place in the hall attached to the synagogue. The Ladies' Guild had provided a magnificent spread of food, sweetmeats and nibbles, and they were offered wine, whisky and grape juice. Sir Herman Gollancz himself led the prayers for the food and wine and broke the challah bread, which was the signal for everyone to start eating.

He was a very impressive figure with piercing bright blue eyes. He wore long white robes with a white and blue tallis on top, and a soft, white rabbinical hat. But his most striking feature was the luxurious red beard that reached down to his breastbone. Leizar and Chaya were introduced to him.

'Oh yes! I heard that you have all recently arrived, welcome to our community.'

'Thank you, I must say we are very impressed,' said Leizar. 'We have attended synagogues in Poland, Germany and Glasgow, but never a shul of such beauty, matched by the impressive conduct of the services.'

Sir Herman had a way of looking intently when he was listening, which Chaya found a bit unnerving, as if he could see right into your soul, but he seemed very interested in Leizar's background and wide experience, from the shtetl to living in Warsaw and then Glasgow and Berlin; his interest intensified after Leizar said he was a journalist.

'Follow me,' he said, and took Leizar by the arm over to where two men were talking. He tapped one of them on the shoulder.

'Leo, can I introduce you to a new member of our community, a journalist with a very interesting background. Leizar Domansky, this is Leopold Greenberg, the editor of the *Jewish Chronicle*, the most influential Jewish publication in the UK.'

'How do you do?' said Leizar, using the quintessentially English way of greeting, and while they were shaking hands, Leopold Geenberg indicated the other gentleman.

'And this is my very good friend Joseph Cowen, President of the English Zionist Federation.'

Sir Herman was called away to meet someone else, leaving Leizar to speak to the two men. They were both extremely interested in Leizar's background. Mr Greenberg gave him a card and suggested he call in to his office on Monday.

Leizar left the shul very excited and bought a copy of the 'JC' as Greenberg's paper was known, on his way home.

The headline was '*BRITAIN HAS BEEN ALL SHE CAN BE TO THE JEWS; THE JEWS WILL BE ALL THEY CAN BE TO BRITAIN.*'

The children had gone on ahead and Chaya had linked arms with her husband, 'Well! Weren't we lucky to be introduced to the editor? I think this is *beshert* – meant to be, Leizar - this is an opportunity!'

Leizar nodded thoughtfully, 'Well, who knows? Maybe it will lead to some work, but in any event, we have met some very influential people.'

Leizar had worked out his route, and the next day he took the underground to Holborn and arrived at the offices of the *Jewish Chronicle* at 9.30am. He was shown to Mr Greenberg's office and offered coffee. He could not help but compare these very civilised working conditions with the dingy, gloomy place in Warsaw where he'd worked on the original magazine.

Greenberg's office was sparsely furnished, with just a large desk behind which he sat, an upright chair in front for Leizar, and a green filing cabinet in the corner. There were two telephones on the desk.

'Thank you for popping in,' he said. 'I understand you have a background in journalism, and you have lived in Eastern Europe. Let me tell you a bit about this publication.'

He explained that the paper was wholly against Russia's treatment of Jews in Eastern Europe, but now that Britain and Russia were allies, he had to tone down the criticism. The paper was also fiercely supportive of the establishment of a Jewish State. Finally, he said, 'Forgive me, I am very direct, would you submit a column on life in the shtetl?'

Leizar nodded slightly, 'Just one column?'

'I don't know you. Perhaps you are Hashem's gift to newspapers, but perhaps you are not. Let's see it first. If it is acceptable, maybe we could have a regular column moving on to life in Warsaw, and then Berlin and so on.'

'Since you are direct, I hope you will not mind if I adopt the same approach. What do you pay?'

'Well, you would be a freelance contributor, I will judge the merit of each article, and pay what I think it is worth. It remains your copyright, so you can negotiate if you think I am undervaluing it. I can't print without your permission, and the column will bear your name.'

It was not quite what Leizar had in mind, but it was an incredible stroke of luck to be introduced to the main man, and have a chance to show what he could do.

'Thank you, I will work on the first article. What is your print deadline?'

'We publish every Friday, so if you can get it to me tomorrow, I can look at it and, if I can approve, it will go into the paper this week.' He stood and shook Leizar by the hand, 'Would you like to have a look round?'

Leizar nodded vigorously, 'Yes please, if you have the time.'

He opened the door and gestured for Leizar to follow as he walked. 'The JC is a weekly newspaper printed on site. So the first stop is the print room.'

They entered through large double doors and Leizar saw that the word 'room' was a misnomer; this was an enormous space, filled with massive machinery. Leizar was awed by its size and dazzled by its beauty.

They walked to the far end. 'I don't know whether you are familiar with the way we do the typesetting. You need to have good eyes to do this all day.'

Ten operatives sat laying out the small type by hand. Greenberg continued, 'Each letter or digit has to be selected with tweezers and laid onto the "set." When each line is complete, it is locked into place. Of course, there are many sizes of type, including the very large ones for headlines.'

The truth was that printing at the magazine in Warsaw was rather rudimentary and nothing compared with this. Greenberg went on to show the massive print machines. 'The set gets proofed to ensure it is accurate with no mistakes, and then it gets loaded into the machines. Each machine had two or three 'minders' who load the ink and paper. They have to oil and cool the machines which can print ten thousand copies an hour. As you can see, we have five of these machines, and we work twenty-four hours a day. When we hit the final publication button, the papers are bundled and loaded into the vans for delivery by van or train up and down the country.'

To say Leizar was impressed would have been a massive understatement; he smiled inwardly as his mind went back to the introduction of the cigarette rolling machines, which had seemed a revolutionary step into automation at the time. He followed Greenberg out to the entrance. 'Of course, there is lot more to it, we have the press room, the photography department, artwork, all sorts of activities that go to make a national newspaper.' He smiled at Leizar's obvious amazement. 'Impressed?'

Leizar had tightened his lips and was shaking his head. 'Truly, I have to admit I have never seen anything like it. By comparison, our little magazines in Warsaw were nothing. I am proud to be offered this opportunity. I won't let you down.'

'Thank you for showing me around.' He shook Greenberg's hand again, and left feeling elated.

On the way home, he used what little money he had to treat the family to a bar of Cadbury's milk chocolate, and Chaya saw right away that it had been a successful meeting. He would start work on the article straight away.

CHAPTER 39

WWI 1914-1918

After dinner, Chaya, Leizar, and Monty crowded round the wireless, anxious to hear how the war was progressing.

'The Germans have advanced on two fronts. Through Belgium to France in the west and together with the Austrians they have moved east into Poland, where they were opposed by the Russians.'

Chaya gasped when she heard this. 'I wonder if they reached Warsaw. I hope papa is alright.'

'Shhh! We need to hear.' This was Monty, and the wireless was crackling somewhat, so he turned up the volume.

'On the Western front the Germans have been halted at Marne and the two armies are deeply entrenched, with neither making much progress. Both sides have suffered heavy casualties, and the weather is not helping. They have torrential rain.'

Leizar turned the volume down. He was grim faced. 'Yes, we have to worry about them all. I am screaming inside about my father and the family in Kawetchka. I need to know how they are.'

Leizar had written many letters, and received no replies. He was doubtful that any of them had even arrived.

But two days later, Chaya received a letter from her father. The envelope was dirty and the corner looked as if a dog had chewed it. They opened it with excitement and trepidation.

To my best beloved daughter, and her clever and devoted husband.

It is very difficult to correspond these days, and I did receive one of your letters Leizar, although it seems you wrote another which I have not had. So, I write in the hope that you will get to see what I have written.

I don't know what you are hearing about the progress of the war from London. I am sure propaganda slants things. Here is an update from here.

Warsaw has been a place of much fighting, and the Germans are in control now. I have closed the factory and moved out to the country, where it is fairly quiet so far. Life seems to be going on more or less undisturbed, except we see a few German officers from time to time, but they don't really bother us, they look around, make a few notes, and leave. There is nothing here for them.

But I visited the shtetl, and I am very sad to tell you that Zelman is not doing very well. He mourns the death of Ryfke very deeply, he doesn't eat much, and he is quite frail. Your Aunt Yentl is there, and she is a godsend. She runs the household like a military academy and looks after them all. The children still go to school, but I'm afraid Zelman is not involved. She bullies him and Moishe, and makes them eat. I fear to think what would have happened without her. We have a lot to thank her for.

They all send their love to you all, and Aunt Yentl says she hopes you are studying Torah!

I said I didn't think there was much chance of that.

Anyway, my darlings, how are my lovely grandchildren? Lena and Minna must be all grown up, and Monty too, I guess. It sounds as if you are getting along alright with Shmuel and Duvid and the families. I hope the war doesn't touch you there.

Keep writing. The odd letter does seem to make it through.

With all my love,
Papa.

It was not what Leizar wanted to hear. It was not a surprise to hear that his father was still grieving, but he was encouraged that Aunt Yentl had taken charge. He thought she could defeat the Germans on her own!

The big shock came in May 1915 when the sirens sounded in London. Minna and Monty were at work, when the loud whining of the sirens pervaded everything, while at the same time the room went dark. Leizar and Chaya looked out of the window and a vast object cast a shadow that blocked out the light.

A massive airship appeared over the house like some big grey behemoth. It was so low over the building that they could see its fat underbelly moving slowly and quietly with a threatening, sinister hiss.

Jack came running in very frightened, and Lena followed close behind. They had heard that the Germans were using these Zeppelins, but the reports suggested they had only been sighted in East London. The appearance of one so close was truly frightening. 'Papa, what is it?' shouted Jack. 'Is it going to eat us?'

Leizar and Chaya did their best to remain calm for the sake of their children, but they had heard that the Zeppelins could drop bombs and use machine guns. They could see the men in the carriage at the centre of the belly crouched over mounted guns. They could easily kill them all from there. Chaya held Jack, while Lena stood in wide eyed amazement at the massive size and threatening nature of the thing.

It passed slowly over the house and then they began to hear the sound of explosions Thankfully, their building was not touched, but this was followed by the buzz of airplanes, and from the window they could see the flares of small fires.

The whole air raid took about twenty minutes. Jack was frightened and crying, and Lena was shaking, and although their parents tried to comfort them, they were scared too. More importantly, where were Minna and Monty? Had they been caught up in it?

It stopped as suddenly as it had started and after another twenty minutes, the all-clear sounded and Leizar ventured out on to the street. Buildings were damaged and some windows were blown out. People were shocked. The war had finally reached them.

He returned to his family. 'Monty and Minna must still be at work. Pray they are alright,' was the first thought he shared with Chaya. 'There is quite a lot of damage out there, maybe it's not so good to be on the top floor.'

Lena was now in the huddle with Chaya and Jack, and they slowly released each other. They went down to the ground floor. Clara was on her own and terrified. Yossel and Simon were at the factory. She was glad to see them.

Gradually they realised the horror was over. Clara made tea for them all. 'If there is another raid, can we come down here with you?' Leizar asked. 'At least you have some shelter.'

'Of course, of course, it's better we are together.'

They drank the tea gratefully, and the worry over the family at the factory grew stronger. After an hour had passed, Leizar put on his coat. 'I can't sit here while we all worry ourselves sick. I'm going to the factory. I have to know what has happened.'

'No, Leizar, no!' Chaya cried at the top of her voice. 'You don't know if there will be another raid, and you may be caught up in it.' She stood in front to stop him.

Thankfully, just then, the front door opened and Minna, Monty, Yossel and Simon all walked in. Chaya was so relieved to see them and hugged them both tightly. 'Thank God; we were so worried about you. What happened?'

Monty explained: 'As soon as the sirens sounded, all the workers from the factory ran down into the Underground station. There were hundreds of people down there, all crowded onto the platform, but at least it seemed safe from the bombs. We stayed there until we were sure it was clear, but I have to tell you, people were terrified.'

'Thank God you are home and safe,' said Chaya.

'Yes,' said Leizar. 'What a good idea. The Underground is a good place to shelter.'

Monty was smiling, 'I think many people are going to be there all night in case there is another raid. But Minna was nagging us so…'

Minna interrupted, 'I wasn't nagging! *You* were the scared one.'

'So, we decided to risk coming home because we were all were starving.' Monty was laughing now.

Yossel chipped in, 'It's all very well for you to make jokes. You should see it out there, buildings and houses damaged People are frightened, what have we done to deserve this? We should all go to shul and thank Hashem we are safe.'

Clara made dinner for them all. As always, there was soup that only needed to be warmed up, and a chulent to follow.

After dinner they tuned in to the news on the wireless again.

'London was subjected to its first air-raid today. 42 Zeppelin airships and a number of German airplanes attacked the capital mainly to the East. The ground artillery easily shot down the airships which made very large targets, although one Zeppelin was reported to have made it as far as West London.

The Army has erected barrage balloons which force the Zeppelins to stay at high altitude where they are at the mercy of the wind and cloud conditions and cannot pick targets. Our scientists have invented an incendiary bullet which can be fired from an ordinary rifle. The bullets will be deployed all over the country and they are very effective against the Zeppelins, which are filled with a helium gas. They are easy targets, and explode when hit with these shells. Once again, British inventiveness leads the way.

On the Western front, the allied army has launched a successful attack against the German defence lines at Champagne. In the East, Russian troops are engaged in heavy fighting in Eastern Prussia.

The Prime Minister wishes to thank everyone for their quick reaction to the raid, whilst at the same time, extending heartfelt sympathy to those who may have suffered losses. King George wishes me to tell you that his thoughts are with you all, and he will be speaking directly to you tonight. On behalf of the British Government, we assure you that we are with you, and we have complete confidence in our heroic servicemen. Britain will prevail. God Save the King.

And with that the National Anthem was played, and the family solemnly stood to attention.

The war had suddenly become very real for Londoners. There were other raids reported and the government broadcasts continued to pour scorn on them, saying they were largely ineffective, and that our defences could deal with them.

Leizar had submitted his first article to the JC newspaper, and it had been well received, even though the war had overtaken interest in almost everything else.

But Leizar was welcome at the offices of the newspaper, and it was not long before he heard reports from other parts of the country which were not so encouraging. The barrage balloons were helping, yet some of the Zeppelins got through and when they did, they seemed invincible. Massive great blundering things that moved slowly, wreaking havoc and destruction. They were indiscriminate and often blown off course by the wind, but the results were terrifying.

Thankfully, the family had not seen much of this in West London, but Leizar worried that it was only a matter of time. The government announcements were designed to placate, but as the war progressed, despite the propaganda pouring out on the BBC, it started to become clear that the war was not going so well and the Germans were making advances on land, while their U-boats wrought havoc at sea.

Lord Kitchener launched a massive campaign to encourage men to help in the war effort by joining the military. The 'Your Country Needs You' poster was everywhere, and Monty felt he had an obligation to help the country of his birth. They had just finished dinner and listened to the daily wireless report. He thought now was the time. 'Papa, I want to sign up and help defeat these *momzers,* it is not right that we come here and when the country is in trouble, we don't offer help.'

Jack piped up, 'Yes, so do I. I'll come with you.' Although Monty was approaching his 18th birthday, Jack was only 15, and small at that. He already had the Domansky eyesight, and wore thick glasses.

Chaya's heart jumped. She and Leizar had discussed the possibility that Monty might say this. It was a topic of conversation between Chaya and everyone she knew with teenage sons. Young men were being sent home badly wounded, and many in a coffin. They wanted their boys in the safety of their own home. Jack, of course, was much too young anyway.

She glanced at Leizar and saw that he was winding himself up. His face was set, his lips tightened, and he was slightly flushed. He stood up by the table. *'Enough!'* he shouted very loudly. 'You live in my house, and you will abide by my rules.' He looked across at Monty and thumped the table. 'I will not allow this. Boys are dying out there.' His voice subsided a bit. 'Let the others go and get killed. We can help by working hard, producing uniforms and clothes for them to wear.'

He turned to Jack, 'And as for you, little man, go and tidy up your room, put your things away, it is nearly bedtime for you.' He thumped the table again. 'And that is the last I want to hear about it.'

Chaya was relieved that he had dealt with it so firmly. With Minna and Lena, she cleared the table and brought in tea for them all.

But Monty was not happy. He would not go against his father, but he knew boys of his age who were signing up, and it did not sit well with him.

The JC was now publishing articles and first-hand reports from people and families in Glasgow, Liverpool and elsewhere including the East End of London. The major cities, docks and industrial heartlands had been under attack. German airplanes were backing up the Zeppelins, but although the bi-planes had machine gun mountings, they were not very effective at dropping bombs. However, there were rumours that large bomber aircraft had been developed which were much more accurate.

Leizar kept all this to himself, but Chaya knew he was worried. "We left Germany to escape the war, and look, it has followed us here. What do we do now? How do we escape this time?"

It was a question to which Leizar had no answer.

Then came an announcement on BBC radio.

His Majesty's government announced today, that Parliament has passed the Military Service Act. All single men between the ages of 18 and 40 are liable to be called up for military service unless they are widowed with children, ministers of religion, or unless they are medically unfit.

Monty had now just passed his 18th birthday. A few days later, he received a letter telling him to report to the British Army recruitment centre at Holland Park. Although his parents were trying to think of ways to get him out of it, Monty was pleased to be called into action.

By this time, Monty's English was pretty good, and when they realised he was bilingual in English and German, he was assigned to a training camp in Chiswick where he was given a medical and taught to be a soldier. At the end he was assigned to General Woollaton of the Royal Army Medical Corps as a translator.

Very few letters were getting through, but Leizar received bad news from his Aunt Yentl.

Dearest Leizar, Duvid, Shmuel and all the family

It is with great regret that I have to tell you that Zelman passed away, olav ha-shalom. To be honest, it was a mitzvah that he died, because he was wasting away. I want you to know that I did everything I could for him, but after Ryfke went, he just didn't want to live anymore. I wish you all long life.

The effect of the war has been terrible. The Russian army has been fighting the Austro-Hungarians and Kawetchka is no longer a place where anyone can live.

Both of those armies did terrible things. Houses were destroyed and atrocities committed against people you know, more dreadful than I can tell you.

So, a few days ago, with Moishe Dawid, and the children, we put all our belongings on a cart and, using our donkey and horses, we planned to escape overland. But just when we were on the point of leaving, Zelman's heart gave out, and he passed away in front of us. I helped Moishe and we quickly buried your father, and left with the children. I am sorry to bring you this bad story, but we marked the grave, and we had to move quickly.

There were a lot of families walking, and many fell ill or were forced to stop on the way, but thank God, we have managed to get to Vienna; the journey took several days. Some of my late husband's family live here, and they have taken us in, so for the moment, we are all safe. But we are in hiding. I may not be able to write again, so keep well and safe in these terrible times.

Moishe, Harry, Molly and Sayde all send their love, and hope to see you when all this madness is over.

Love from
Your Aunt Yentl

Although Leizar had been half expecting bad news about his father, it was hard to hear that he had died in these appalling circumstances. As he read the letter, tears came into his eyes.

Chaya was reading the letter over his shoulder. She gasped when she saw the news and Leizar put his head on her chest, she cradled him and held him close. 'I am an orphan,' he said. 'And what will become of Aunt Yentl and Moishe and my other brother and sisters? Harry would be fifteen, Molly, thirteen and Sayde twelve.'

Although Lena and Minna only had vague recollections of their grandparents, and Monty and Jack, none at all, they were sad for their father when they heard the news.

That night before dinner, the family gathered, Leizar said the *kaddish* prayer for his father, even though they did not have the full *minyan* of men present. He had torn his shirt in the traditional way and for once dinner was eaten in comparative silence.

They had no time to properly mourn; life had to carry on amid all the destruction and restrictions.

Minna continued to work with Yossel at the workshop where the demand for military uniforms had increased. Lena and Jack were at home and Leizar found it difficult to sell his written articles because all the papers were preoccupied with the war. So again, they had to survive on very little money.

Monty had written that the death and injuries he had seen near the front were unimaginable. Death was all around, but almost worse than death, were the terrible injuries. Men with missing limbs or worse, those who had to have limbs amputated, often with no morphia available. Men with open wounds and scared young boys who did not want to die but knew they were going to.

Some of the patients were German and Monty's job was to interpret. He was also called to the officers from time to time to interpret letters or messages received in German. He was billeted with the doctors and medical ratings, so he was spared the soldiers' daily privations.

Leizar told all the family to try and lose their accents quickly. They were often mistaken for Germans and even when they lapsed into Yiddish it sounded like German. With the country at war with Germany and bombs destroying homes, local people quickly became anti anything German.

Indeed, the family were surprised to find quite a few German families living in

London. The local baker was German, as was the butcher and it was a bit of a shock when they found the butchers window broken one morning and the baker's shopfront daubed with 'German pigs go home.'

When the news came that a German U-boat had sunk the passenger liner RMS Lusitania off the coast of Ireland and over 1200 civilians had died, anti-German feeling accelerated and there were riots in London and Liverpool.

One evening Minna was leaving the workshop with Uncle Yossel when a bath-full of dirty washing water fell from above, completely drenching them. They ran off to cries of 'Dirty Germans.' When they returned home like drowned rats, it was all Chaya could do to stop Leizar from going to retaliate.

Instead, he wrote an article for the London Evening Standard, which they published under the headline:-.

'WE ARE ALL ON THE SAME SIDE'

'With Britain at war with Germany, it is not surprising that anti German feeling is running high. My family have suffered abuse because some of us have German accents. But we are British!

As British citizens living in Germany before the war, we escaped and returned. Our menfolk are on the Western Front risking their lives fighting with the British Army, and there are many like us.

And yet because we have an accent, we suffer verbal and sometimes physical abuse. I know of many families who are getting caught up in the anti-German animosity.

The article went on to explain that many of these families had already suffered persecution in Germany, and in other countries, and among them are even heroes saving the lives of British servicemen on the front line.

This prompted many 'Letters to the Editor' some of which were published. Leizar was hopeful that it may have pricked the conscience of some, who would not be moved to write, because almost without fail, those who did were not supportive.

One letter was headed 'Once a German – always a German.' So, the family had to be very careful – they all had accents of one kind or another.

The wireless was left on all day to catch news updates and in early 1918 they heard that Germany had been pushed back on both fronts and the allies' blockade of German ports was leading to exhaustion and starvation. Also, two million American troops had been drafted into the war effort. Commentators felt that the Germans were no longer able to continue the war. Shortly afterwards it was announced that the United States had been approached about an Armistice. The German surrender came in November 1918 and six hours later the guns of the first World War fell silent. It was the 11th hour of the 11th day of the 11th month.

Chapter 40

After the war - Lena and Minna

On Armistice Day 1918, the London streets were full of people celebrating. Strangers were hugging and kissing each other. It had been a bloody war. Over 20 million people had died and 21 million were wounded. Many families were grieving for men and boys who went away to fight and did not return.

The Domansky family were relieved when Monty returned fit and well. He felt a bit of a fraud because although he was near the front line, he was never involved directly in any fighting, and yet he was treated as a hero.

However, their celebrations were cut short when Chaya received news of the death of her father. She was completely devastated. She had not heard from him for some time, but that was not surprising during the war, and Poland had remained the scene of heavy fighting on the Eastern front.

The letter was from Moshe Vasilinsky, the man who first contacted Leizar and introduced him to Edvard and the Polish movement. It was addressed to both of them, and they read it together.

Dear Chaya and Leizar

I hope this letter reaches you and finds you both well. I managed to trace you through the British Consulate.

I am sorry to be the bearer of such terrible news Chaya, but I have to tell you of the passing of your dear father, Herschel. As you know I worked with him for many years, and he was a giant of a man in every way. I can hardly believe it myself.

Chaya dropped the letter, her eyes filled with tears and great globules ran silently down her cheeks. Leizar tried to comfort her, but she began to sob. He tried to nestle her head against his chest, but she pulled away, racked with pain. Leizar stroked her hair and held her as best he could, but she pushed at him as if his arms would magnify her desolation. He could not bear to see her suffering, and felt helpless.

This went on for some time, during which not a word was said, and the only sound was Chaya's weeping, but gradually, she began to gain control. She sat upright, and started to dry her tears.

In between sobs she said, 'Perhaps… I should never have left him… I was not there when he needed me.' She started to beat her chest.

'And… he never really knew his grandchildren. Lena was only five and Minna two when we left. And Jack and Monty never met him.' Leizar had picked up the letter. Chaya dried her eyes and they read on.

There was terrible fighting in Poland, and Warsaw was taken and retaken by the Russians and then by the Germans and Austrians. You may remember my wife, Gitte? She was killed in the attack on Warsaw. Just like that, life snuffed out. I have to thank your father for my own life. He forced me to flee with him.

We managed to arrive at a place called Przemvsi to the East of Krakow in Galicia. The Russians originally occupied the area but were beaten back by the Germans and the whole place was ransacked. We were taking refuge in a house that suffered a direct hit. I was badly injured, I have lost my left leg and my left arm, but I am afraid your father didn't make it at all. He died instantly. I don't think he suffered any pain.

Chaya's tears were flowing again, but this time she allowed Leizar to hold her.

The factory in Warsaw was destroyed and even the Magazine office was smashed up.

I have no idea what had happened to Edvard and Yitshok.

What will happen to the Polish people now? The Russians are in charge again and there is death and destruction all around. I am so sorry Chaya, and I wish you long life.

Your friend Moshe Vasilinsky

Of course, Chaya was inconsolable. Since the death of her mother, she and her father had been closely bound together until she married Leizar.

'Now I am also an orphan.' And she ripped her clothes. 'I always thought I would see him again, and we would be a family once more, now he is gone forever. Oh Leizar, I feel that part of me has died.'

Jack was the first to return, followed by Monty and then Lena and Minna. They could all see that something very bad had happened and they tried to comfort their mother. They had never seen her so distressed. When they were all together, Chaya and Leizar explained what had happened. Although they understood their mother's grief, only Lena had any memory of Herschel and that was very vague.

Chaya sat *shiva* and Rev Klein said prayers for her father. She was grateful for her family and friends from the synagogue who visited during the awful, lonely week, to be of comfort to her as she sat, the sole mourner.

Lena

There was a massive shortage of virtually everything after the war. All manufacturing plants were crying out for staff, and since so many men had not returned or been seriously injured there was a very high demand for women to replace them.

So, Lena tried again at the clothing workshop, although she was less than enthusiastic. They were no longer making uniforms, but demand was very high for men's clothing, for those men who had returned, and this time Manny knew it would not be so easy to replace her. Unfortunately for him, she knew that too, so she got away with producing garments that often had to be finished by others.

Leizar and Chaya both felt that it was time Lena was married, but of course there was no *shiddach macher* now and the emancipation of women was under way. The Domansky girls were at the forefront of that. The other problem was a shortage of men of the appropriate age. However, Lena was a very attractive young woman, and Leizar asked around at the shul. Mrs Grunwald spoke to Chaya. She had noticed Lena and suggested they arrange a date with her son Sidney.

Chaya spoke to Leizar. 'He is not exactly a match for Lena, 'she said,' He's fat, and he has a cast in one eye. He didn't go to war because of his eyesight.'

'Look,' said Leizar, 'there are not many young men around, and unless we push her, you know she'll sit at home for the rest of her life. He seems a good man from a good family.'

When it was suggested that she meet him however, Lena's hackles rose, 'No, I won't go. I don't want a man in my life.' And Lena had never seen Sidney because she rarely went to the synagogue, so she had no idea what he was like.

Leizar decided to be masterful. 'When you live in my house, you will do as I say. Now out of respect for me and your mother, at least go on this date with this young man. You may like him and who knows where it might lead.'

As usual a big row followed, and the rest of the family got involved. Minna knew the Grunwald family and was about to shoot her mouth off, as she so often did. 'Oh – not Sidney….' Leizar raised his voice and cut her off. 'Don't interfere young lady!'

Leizar would not be beaten, he insisted Lena at least meet the man and after she had tried everything, Lena, finally agreed, but only because she had no other options.

Alone with Minna, though, she wasn't stubborn and defiant; she was upset. 'What am I going to do?' she asked, with tears in her eyes. 'I don't want a man; I'm happy at home. Can't you talk to Papa?

Minna's eyes rolled, 'Just go along with it, how bad can it be? It's one date.'

The parents arranged for them to meet at a restaurant in Notting Hill. Sidney wore an ill-fitting 3-piece suit that looked like it had been made for someone else. The buttons of the waistcoat were under enormous strain to contain his belly and when she arrived, he looked at her with his good eye.

When Lena saw him, her face dropped. He stood up and went to kiss her on the cheek – she flinched. He had taken a table at the rear of the restaurant, and when she reluctantly sat, she found herself wedged in the corner.

The waiter presented the menus and Sidney tried to make conversation, 'Your father says you work in the clothing trade, what do you do exactly?' He was bemused when Lena didn't answer. She had a glazed expression, she wasn't listening, and all she could think about was how could she get out of there. There was silence for a few seconds. Sidney cleared his throat pointedly.

'Oh, oh, sorry,' said Lena. 'I was miles away. Do you mind if I use the ladies room?'

He stood up and she squeezed past him. She stayed in the toilet as long as she dared, but she couldn't face going back into the restaurant. She noticed a window near the lavatory so, being Lena, a creature of action and impulse, she climbed up on the toilet, opened the window, and jumped out. She ran all the way home.

When her parents asked why she was back so soon, she shrugged, 'Well, I met him, that cross-eyed, stupid *shmerel*. I did it because you forced me. I was polite, but it didn't go so well and we didn't really get on with each other.'

But the next day, when Leizar found out what had really happened, he hit the roof!

It was Saturday and after the morning service, Grunwald sought out Leizar. 'That daughter of yours is crazy!'

Leizar thought he was upset that the date didn't work out and started to apologise, 'Well, it seems they didn't hit it off…'

But Grunwald cut him off. 'You don't know what she did, do you?'

And he proceeded to tell Leizar that his son had waited in the restaurant until it seemed there must be something wrong with Lena – maybe she was ill. So, he asked one of the waitresses if she would go and see if she was alright. How foolish he'd felt when the waitress told him that Lena wasn't there, and that the window was open, so she must have jumped out.

He was so embarrassed. 'Who does a thing like that?' said Grunwald. 'Only a crazy person. You'd better do something about that girl before she does something worse. I expect an apology at least.'

When Leizar told her, Chaya couldn't believe it either, and another massive row took place in the Domansky household. Leizar was shouting at the top of his voice and banging on the table. He kept saying, *'Du farkirtst mir di yorn!'* - You'll be the death of me, and 'You have no respect!' He kept shouting and shouting, until he could no longer catch his breath and Chaya made him sit down.

Lena was crying and kept saying, 'You don't understand.' Over and over.

'Look what you are doing,' this was Chaya, 'Do you want to make your father ill?'

She sat down next to Lena and took her hand, 'Whatever happened, it's very embarrassing for the whole family. I don't know who was right and who was wrong here, but you can make amends. Just go to Grunwald and say you are sorry. That will be the end of it. Do it for me and your father.'

But, having inherited the Domansky stubbornness she said she would rather stick a pin in her own eye than go and apologise. She wouldn't do it, and they could not make her.

------------*------------

Minna

The clothes that were worked on in the workshop were designed and cut out by tailors in another building and the pieces were delivered in large bundles for sewing and pressing. Minna had been seeing one of the tailors for some time, and one day when they were alone in the kitchen, she mentioned it to her mother.

'Yes, I thought there may be someone in your life now. I've seen the way you have been a bit distracted lately. So, what is his name?'

'His real name is Leopold, but everyone calls him Lou.'

'And you're quite keen on this Lou, aren't you?'

Minna was pleased she had confided in her mother, 'Yes Mama, we have been spending some time together. He is a good man, very kind, and I like him a lot.'

'Well,' said Chaya, 'your father and I would like to meet him. Next Friday night, why don't you ask him if he would like go to shul with your father, and then they can both return for Friday night dinner with the family.'

Minna was delighted and she excitedly told Lou the next day.

But he was somewhat apprehensive. 'I don't know, Minna. That's a big step. Suppose they don't like me. I am bound to say the wrong thing with my poor English and my accent, people don't always understand me. And with all your family, your brothers and your sister?'

'Don't worry, Lou. Monty and Lena already know you, so they won't be surprised, and my parents are lovely; we all have strange accents.'

'How should I dress? What should I bring?'

'Wear what you would normally wear for shul. You will meet papa, and spend some time with him, and then when you walk home, you will meet my Mama, who is the softest, most wonderful lady. They are going to love you.' She replied. 'You don't need to bring anything.'

Lou rolled his eyes, '*Frum dein moil tsu Gott's erin*' – from your mouth to God's ears. 'How do you know?'

'Because I love you, and if they know that, they will love you too!'

This was the first time the word 'love' had been used between them, and Lou's face went red.

On Friday after work, Minna brought him to the synagogue and introduced him to her father. Of course, she had to sit upstairs with the women, which gave the men an opportunity to exchange a few words in between the service.

But there was a problem. Lou was also an immigrant and although he spoke English, his accent was so heavy that Leizar could not understand him. Leizar kept saying 'pardon' and 'what did you say?', and it swiftly became embarrassing. It wasn't only his accent; Lou rather mumbled his words, too.

So, Lou would mumble something and, in the end, Leizar would nod or shake his head, hoping that Lou would accept that as a response, but once or twice Lou gave him a funny look when Leizar got it wrong. He thought Lou must think him quite rude and wondered how Minna managed to communicate with him.

The solution was that they found they could converse easily in Yiddish. Lou was also a short man, but still not quite as short as Minna. He was a little overweight and he was a chain smoker.

Leizar thought he looked quite a bit older than the 25 years Minna had said. After the service, Leizar took care to introduce him in Yiddish only to those people he knew could speak the language. Lou got on well with them.

Leizar went home ahead, leaving Lou and Minna to follow slowly. Chaya was waiting at the door, anxious to know what he was like and before he had taken his coat off. 'Well?' she asked.

'Well, he's no oil painting,' said Leizar. 'But let's face it, our daughter doesn't see too well, so maybe it's a *mitzvah*, and he seems like a good man. He is a master tailor, and he earns a good living.

'So what is wrong with him?' asked Chaya, who knew when her husband was holding something back.

'Well, it's the way he talks. In Yiddish he is fine, but in English nobody can understand him!'

Just then, Lou and Minna arrived, 'Welcome and good *shabbas*, Lou, come in, take off your coat, Minna will show you where to wash your hands, then come back and sit with us.'

Chaya had prepared a traditional Friday night dinner, chopped liver, chicken soup, roast chicken, followed by lokshen pudding. Leizar poured wine and they tried to make him feel at home.

Lou ate well, but the conversation was quite comical. Minna, Lena, Monty and Jack spoke German, not Yiddish. Normally it was possible for a speaker of one language to understand a speaker of the other, but when Lou spoke it was only in his heavily accented English and Yiddish. Lou's understanding of English was very good, but when he spoke that language, they couldn't understand a word he said. So, the conversation was very stilted. The family would ask him a question in English, and Leizar would ask him to explain his reply in Yiddish, some of which would be picked up by the family, but often misunderstood, and Leizar would then have to fill in the missing details for them in English. Lena and Monty saw this coming, because all the factory workers had this problem with Lou; they thought it was very funny, and although they tried not to, they couldn't help suppressing a laugh whenever the conversation went wrong. At one point they both had to make an excuse and walk out of the room until they could compose themselves.

Lou explained that his family was Hungarian and of course he could speak his mother tongue, but that could only be understood by Hungarians, or people who spoke the language. He knew that he was often misunderstood in English, but he hoped that, in time, he would lose some of the heavy accent. All this was said in

Yiddish.

'So, tell me more about your family, Lou,' Leizar said – also in Yiddish. 'How did you come to be here on your own?'

'Well, we lived on the outskirts of Budapest, where we had a small farm. Taxes were very high, and we had to pay to the government in Vienna. Believe me, it was a struggle. I worked in the capital, where I learned to be a master tailor. I have no brothers or sisters, and my parents couldn't afford the cost of emigration, but they scrimped and saved, and got the money together for me to come to the UK on my own. I wouldn't have come, but they said they would follow. I have written many times, but so far, no reply.'

Chaya was making sympathetic noises, and Leizar interjected, 'So you made the journey alone?'

'Yes. The ship docked at Grimsby, and I came to London. When I arrived, I couldn't speak any English, but as a master tailor, there were many jobs available. I got the job at the factory where Lena, Minna and Monty work and now I am their only tailor.'

'How does that work at the factory?'

'Well, they have a designer who draws sketches. I make all the patterns from the designs and cut out all the parts for the machinists to make into garments.'

'So, the factory could not operate at all without you?'

'They would have to find another master tailor, but I work very hard, and I keep them going.'

The meal was finished, and Lou said in English, 'Sankyou, ze food voss delisss…..' He struggled over the word delicious, and Minna finished the sentence for him. Again, he had gone red in the face.

'Poppa,' Minna continued, 'Lou has something to discuss with you.'

Leizar and Chaya could see what was coming, so Chaya ushered everyone out of the room, and poured them each a glass of schnapps.

Lou asked Leizar's permission to marry Minna. It was a formality really, because if Minna wanted to marry him, she was of an age where she did not need her father's permission. It was a matter of respect, though, and Leizar appreciated it. Of course, he readily gave his permission, and called all the family back in. With a glass in his hand and a smile on his face, he said.

'Lou has asked to marry your sister, Minna, and I have given them my blessing, so you can all wish them mazeltov.'

Chaya poured kosher wine for everyone, and although it was not a big surprise, they all crowded round with questions about when and where and how.

Lou bought Minna a lovely diamond engagement ring, and the wedding was booked at St Petersburg place in six months' time. Chaya and Minna got busy with dresses and planning, and Lou became a frequent dinner guest at the Domansky home. Everyone tried very hard to help him with his English pronunciation, but to be honest, it didn't help that all the Domanskys had strange accents too.

It was a most beautiful ceremony with the choir backing the chazan and the rabbi reading the vows, and there was a party at home afterwards. Only the less religious members of the community were invited, because it was not possible to keep the men and women strictly segregated. Lou earned a good wage, and they moved into their own apartment.

Lena

Lena was a problem. She had become a compulsive gambler and each week she would squander her wages on horses or dogs. She would put bets on with a backstreet 'bookie's runner' and occasionally she would win, but then lose it all back again.

Eventually, her boss at the workshop could stand no more of her nonsense and poor workmanship, and he said she should find another job. That was all it took for Lena to throw the cottons and bobbins she was holding on to the floor and storm out.

She went straight to the bookie to place another bet. And while she was there, she asked what he would pay for a runner in the Ladbroke Grove area where she knew he was not represented. He put her on commission only, so there was no risk for him, and she started work for him the next day.

Leizar and Chaya worried about her constantly. She was always in trouble, often placing bets herself with money she didn't have.

'We must find a way to marry her off.' Leizar said, 'She's an attractive young woman. If we can find an older, responsible man who can take care of her, maybe he can keep her on the rails.'

'Yes, you are right,' Chaya said, dubiously, 'But that is easier said than done. Men like her and she is attractive, the problem is she doesn't like them, and it always ends in tears.'

Leizar shook his head, 'We've got to do something. She can't carry on like this forever, and we never know what she'll do next. She needs a firm hand. I am going to speak to the rabbi tomorrow.'

'This is not a difficult problem.' David Klein had shown Leizar into his office and they were sipping tea in the traditional way, through a sugar lump. Kids today think they know everything. Lena is a lovely girl, and she would make someone a beautiful wife. It should not be too difficult to find such a man in our community.'

Leizar slurped the tea and lit a cigarette. 'But you don't know her, she is so head-strong.'

'Yes, yes, I heard what happened with the Grunwald boy.'

He sat thoughtfully looking at the ceiling. After a few moments he said, 'Leizar, if you can't persuade her to meet some possible *shiddachs,* then I'm afraid as her father, you are going to have to put your foot down.'

Leizar raised his eyebrows. 'That's easy for you to say.'

'There is a shul member who is very eligible. Do you know Morris Binstock?'

'No.'

'I will introduce you this shabbas. Morris is a trader from Manchester. He is a lovely man, and he is quite well off. He has a business in Westbourne Grove and a very nice big house in Notting Hill. His wife passed away a couple of years ago and I know he has noticed Lena when she was in shul. He asked me about her. Morris is a young 39-year-old, and he has two daughters. I've met them, and they're lovely. Maybe Lena could benefit from the influence of an older man? It's a good *shiddach,* Leizar, and Lena would be set for life, she would want for nothing. Will you at least meet with him and see what you think?'

Leizar finished his tea and thanked the rabbi. On the way home, he didn't know what to think. Would it be possible to persuade his problem daughter to marry a man like this? If he was wealthy as well as handsome, perhaps there was a chance.

But he knew better than to try to second-guess Lena.

So of course, he went home to discuss it with Chaya. In her normal way, she was very practical. 'We don't know the man, and we don't know his daughters. Why don't you meet with him and have a chat? You will need to tread carefully. On the one hand he needs to know what a *matzeer* he is getting with our beautiful daughter. On the other hand, he should understand what he would be taking on. His life would change radically. Lena would see to that.'

'Oh! That's all I have to do?' said Leizar sarcastically.

'No, actually and importantly, you have to see if he and his daughters would be good for our Lena.'

So, after shul, Leizar took Morris for a coffee, and they got on really well. Morris was a handsome man, tall with a military style moustache. He was smartly dressed in navy blazer and grey flannel trousers. He said he had lost his wife to the Spanish flu epidemic at the end of the war; it had been a very difficult time for him and his daughters.

'I grieved for a long time,' he said. 'I hardly ventured out of the house, except to go to shul. But my daughters have pulled me round and made me see that I have to get on with my life.'

Leizar nodded, 'I know a thing or two about grief.'

'I noticed Lena in shul, she is a beautiful young lady, and I did ask the rabbi who she was. I would love to meet her, Leizar.'

Leizar nodded. 'Look, I must be honest, it may be that you hit it off with her straight away, but I have to tell you she can be difficult. She is my first-born daughter, and of course I love her with all my heart, she is lovely, and she has a quick, bright mind, but she can be very headstrong.'

'Yes, yes, I did hear she could be difficult, and I heard what happened with Grunwald. I like a strong woman and I would like to meet her. Maybe she needs an older man to exert a steadying influence?'

To himself Leizar thought, 'You have no idea,' But out loud he said, 'Tell me about yourself.'

'Well, I had a trading company in Manchester, but after my wife passed, we moved to London. I bought a large house in Notting Hill, and opened a haberdashery shop in Westbourne Grove. The shop does very well, there's not much competition, and it's starting to get well known in the area.'

'And your daughters?'

'They are 15 and 13, and everybody who meets them says they are lovely. Of course, like you, I am biased. But they miss their mother, and they need some female influence as they grow up.'

'Let's not get ahead of ourselves,' said Leizar. 'Let's see if she wants to meet, and if you get on together.'

'Yes, I just want you to know, that if it did work out, I would look after her and be a guiding light. She would want for nothing.'

Later, Leizar discussed the meeting with Chaya. She had great reservations.

'We are talking about Lena. She doesn't have a maternal bone in her body. She doesn't want any man in her life, let alone a 39-year-old with two daughters.'

'But,' said Leizar, 'this is a quite handsome man, well dressed, distinguished, and well off. There is a lot to like here. She has not met anyone like this before.'

Chaya could see that an older man may be a good influence and perhaps more able to handle her, especially if she, in turn, knew she would be able to afford the nice things in life.

Taking account of how contrary their daughter was, they knew that she would push back against any suggestion from them. If this was to happen at all, it would have to be her decision. So, they decided it might be best to ask Morris to invite the Domanskys to his house without any mention of *shiddach*. Just a casual invitation as someone Leizar had met at the synagogue. That way Lena could see how well he lived without any pressure. If that went well, he could ask her out and maybe she would be influenced by seeing what the good life looked like.

So, it was arranged for a week later, and they persuaded Monty to take Jack to the ex-servicemen's club, so it was only Leizar, Chaya and Lena who arrived at Morris's house in Notting Hill. It was huge, with wide marble steps leading up to the impressive polished front door. Leizar pulled the wrought iron handle which rang the bell and Morris welcomed them in.

Chaya thought he looked very handsome. He wore a light brown, two-piece suit with a dark brown waistcoat, from which dangled a gold watch chain. His bow tie matched the waistcoat and the silk handkerchief peeping out of his top pocket.

He showed them into the dining room, which was warm and tastefully furnished. The table was laid for four and Morris apologised that his girls had been invited to their friends for lunch, but said they should be back afterwards.

Plates of chopped liver and egg and onion were already on the table and as Morris poured wine, he complimented Chaya and Lena on their dresses and said how pleased he was to welcome them all to his home.

The dinner, cooked by his maid, was excellent, and they all ate well. The conversation flowed freely, and Morris made a point of trying to engage Lena in the conversation; but she was typically uncommunicative, offering monosyllabic answers.

After dinner, they retired into the lounge, where there was a roaring fire and two settees facing each other with easy chairs at either end. His daughters arrived, chattering about their friends and what they had eaten for dinner. Morris introduced them, and somehow, they seemed to click with Lena. They took her to show their bedrooms and talk about clothes and make-up and surprisingly, Lena actually seemed to get on with them.

Bearing in mind his stilted conversation with her, Leizar and Chaya were surprised when a few days later, Morris asked Lena to have dinner with him and she accepted. Maybe their plan would work.

They saw each other on several occasions over a couple of months, and Lena even willingly attended shul on Saturdays. Eventually Leizar was delighted when Lena told him she had decided to marry Morris.

This was quite different from Minna and Lou, who had been very respectful, and asked his permission, even though they had not strictly needed it. But it was typical of Lena. She had made up her mind, and when Leizar asked if she was sure she said, 'You don't understand Papa, I am marrying Morris – that's it.'

The Domanskys invited Morris to their house for another Friday night dinner and they all drank to the health of the engaged couple. Of course, Lena was delighted that the ring Morris bought her was much bigger than Minna's.

The next day they went to the synagogue and booked the wedding for July that year. Morris told Lena she could have whatever style of wedding she wanted, and Lena decided on full 'floral and choral.' The shul would be decked out in flowers and there would be a full choir. There would be a big catered reception and a party afterwards at the Binstock house. Chaya and Lena started to plan the wedding dress and the guest list. It was very exciting.

But two days later, just as Leizar and Chaya thought things were going so well, the front door slammed and Lena stormed in with 'No, no, no – I am *not* marrying him!'

They were astounded, 'But why? You seemed so happy. What has happened?' asked Chaya.

Lena sniffed, 'He is a pig. And his daughters don't like me, and I tell you something, I don't like them either.'

The conversation went back and forth. Chaya took her into the other room. 'Lena, it's normal to have reservations at this time in your life. You have found a good man, and not only that, but he is also handsome and wealthy. Tell me what has happened.'

But Lena was not in a mood to be reasoned with. As usual, when she had made up her mind, she was immovable. No matter how her parents tried, it only made matters worse.

Minna tried talking to her, which resulted in Lena throwing a hairbrush at her, 'You don't know how I feel, get on with your own life!' she shouted.

This went on until late into the evening until Lena locked herself in the toilet and refused to come out. In the end they had to accept that the wedding seemed to be off.

Leizar spoke to Morris the next day. Of course, he was devastated. He said he had detected that all was not well between Lena and his daughters, but he thought it would pass. He said that his relationship with Lena had been going well, and he felt it would be strong enough to overcome a few bumps in the road. 'I need to find out what has happened. I must speak to the girls.'

He called at the Domanskys, the next day. 'You won't believe it, Leizar. I spoke to them. They have been talking to their friends and they worked out that if I married again, and something happened to me, Lena would benefit, and it would dilute or even take away their inheritance. She would be their step-mother, and she would be in charge of the house and the business.'

'So, they've been doing all they can to put Lena off?' said Leizar. 'And believe me it doesn't take much.'

'What can I do to resolve this?' Morris said. 'What do you think, Leizar? Will she come round?'

Leizar was not going to let this opportunity pass by. Morris was perfect for Lena, there wouldn't be another chance like this, and he felt he had to make it happen.

Chaya spoke to Lena again and did all she could to persuade her daughter, but with Lena, the more they tried, the worse it got.

Leizar was shaking his head and clenching his fist in frustration, 'This is not right.' He said to his wife. They had tried everything, and they sat in the kitchen in the evening sipping tea. 'She can't play with people's lives like this. *We* know what's best for her, and this time I am determined to make it happen.'

He thumped the table, 'It's time to be firm with her.'

Chaya raised her eyebrows and gave him an old-fashioned, sideways look. Leizar very rarely spoke in this tone of voice, and she knew he could be even more stubborn than her daughter. She was not looking forward to the conflict.

Chaya told Lena her father wanted to talk to her, which might not have been the best approach. He sat her down and started with, 'Now look, you are being very silly…' That was like a red rag to a bull!

Lena stood straight away, 'Don't you accuse me of being silly. It's my life and I won't live it with that pig and his *farshtinkene* daughters.'

Leizar sighed and tried to keep his voice very even and controlled, 'He is not a pig, he is a very handsome and wealthy man.'

He told her he understood why the daughters were upset about the inheritance and explained that Morris could make a will so that they did not lose anything if he married Lena.

That made matters even worse, 'What? she screamed. 'You mean I should live with the pig and if he dies, I get nothing!' she shouted. 'Over my dead body.'

Leizar could see he would get nowhere trying to be persuasive. He changed tactics.

He also stood and raised his voice, 'Well, my girl, you *will* marry him, and you *will* love and cherish him. On this occasion we know what is best for you, and if you love us, you will do this and make it work.'

Chaya could see they were on a collision course. 'Lena darling, we have loved you and looked after you all these years, and now we want you to do this for us. We may not be around for ever, and you are a mature woman, you should not still be living with your parents. Morris is a lovely man; you can make it work.'

But Leizar's hackles were up; he stepped in front of his wife and was visibly shaking. He grabbed a china urn and smashed it on the floor. Red faced and shouting loudly. '*This* time you *will* listen to me. This is *my* house, I am *your* father and you *will* marry Morris.'

Lena was visibly frightened; she had never seen him this angry. She started crying. Leizar kicked the chair over 'That is my final word!' and he walked out of the room.

So, it did happen, and it was a forced marriage. Leizar would not relent, and Lena had no support from any of her family. Although her mother would put her arms round her, and say words of comfort, she remained firm on what Lena had to do.

Eventually, Lena saw that Leizar was completely unyielding and very angry. And so in the end, she went through with it, although she cried all the way through the wedding ceremony.

CHAPTER 41

The 1920s had started well for the family. Two weddings and two daughters married, and two eligible young men still at home. It was a time of high employment. Jack was now working in the workshop along with Monty and Minna, and they were busier than ever trying to fill the demand for new clothes.

In fact, there was a very high demand for all consumer goods. Full employment meant people were starting to earn good money with little to spend it on, and this created opportunities.

So Monty and Jack decided to make some children's clothes at home and sell them in the markets that were beginning to flourish around London. They would work evenings and weekends, and on Sundays they went to sell their produce.

They took a small stall in Berwick Street market in London's West End. It was mainly a fruit and vegetable market, but very near their workshop. There were a few stalls selling clothing and they had some really cute coats and jackets for young children. People loved them and they had no trouble selling them, but the rent on the stall was high and made it hard to make a decent profit.

Also, the West End was full of crooks. On the second Sunday morning they were approached by two shifty looking youngsters. 'Want yer stall protected guvnor?'

'Get out of here,' came Monty's response.

'It'll only cost a pound and we'll make sure it doesn't get set on. There's a lot of crooks round 'ere, y'know.'

Jack and Monty stood firm and sent them packing. It turned out to be a bad move. Later that day the stall was overturned, and their lovely clothes were trampled in the mud.

They put up quite a fight, but they were soon overwhelmed by four thugs who took all the money they had made that morning. 'Should 'ave paid for protection,' one of them shouted as they made off.

The boys returned home with black eyes and bruises, no stock and no money. When they told their parents, Leizar said, 'You can't pay these *momzers*. What do you think, if you pay them, it will be the end? No, next time, they will want two pounds, and them more. Once they've got you like that, you will never have any peace.'

They had to think again. They were convinced they could sell these little coats easily to make money, but where and how?

Later that year Minna became pregnant, and with expert help from Chaya, delivered a little boy they called Simon. He was the first-born son and the first grandson, so after the *bris*, there was a *Pidyon Haben* and a big party. The new grandparents were so proud, and Leizar took to pushing the pram around the neighbourhood, loving the way people would stop and 'goo-goo' over the baby. 'Yes,' he would say proudly. 'This is my first grandson.'

Morris suggested that Leizar open a haberdashery and trimming shop in Ladbroke Grove. There was a clear demand for quality trimmings and Morris could show him how and where to buy it from the wholesalers in London and Manchester. There were plenty of empty shops, so Leizar took his advice. He found a shop at a reasonable rent and opened his first business. The family were all proud to see the sign go up over the shop, bearing the Domansky name. It worked well for the family, because he also stocked some of Monty and Jack's children's clothing.

The atmosphere in London was hotting up. People were anxious to forget the horrors of war, jazz nightclubs were opening up and of course, Lena was a frequent patron. Morris was not so keen, but he knew that if he didn't go, she would go on her own, and goodness knows what that would lead to. They became quite well known around the London nightclub scene.

Leizar received a postcard out of the blue from Lev Bronstein, addressed to 'My good friend Domansky.'

Dear Leizar

I met a man called Pyotr Borin, a party member. He told me you had gone to Berlin, and I obtained your address in London from the shipping office.

I hope this letter finds you well, and I thought you might like to know how it goes with me and the movement. I served some time in prison, but on release I joined up with the Red Army and you may have heard the civil war was successful from our side, and together with comrade Lenin, and backed by comrade Stalin, we finally overthrew the rich bourgeoisie.

I am proud to tell you, Communism will prevail in Russia, and everyone will be equal at last.

Please write to me with news of what is happening in the UK.

Salutations,
Lev Bronstein

Leizar was intrigued to receive this letter. It occurred to him that he had never really known much about Bronstein. He wrote as if he was influential in Russia, and he had clearly gone to a lot of trouble to trace Leizar in London.

Leizar had been following the civil war, but in its aftermath, he had been shocked at the aftermath – or at least, what the press said about it. If the Western media could be trusted, it seemed that that Lenin and Stalin were effectively weaponizing their brand of communism, and that far from being liberated or empowered, the proletariat were just being subjugated all over again.

In Leizar's view, this was the opposite of the original socio-communist plan. It sounded as if Stalin was even more forceful than the Tsars, and intended to create a police state.

Chaya counselled Leizar not to respond to Bronstein's message. 'This is dangerous,' she said. 'Who is he, this man? What does he want with us? You never know who will see these things and jump to conclusions. Don't make our lives any more complicated.'

He took her advice and never wrote back. And a good job too, because the type of radical Communism developing in the East was increasingly seen as a threat to democracy in the West.

In the United States, General Palmer had declared the Red Scare. And the government had been raiding the headquarters of radical organisations and arresting thousands of suspected radicals. Several thousand aliens had been deported.

Although not so severe, the British government was also alert to the threat and suspects had been arrested. Chaya's advice was well founded.

To Leizar's satisfaction, however, the purer form of Socialism was now a growing trend all over the world, and he was delighted when, in 1924 the first UK Labour government was returned under Ramsay MacDonald. Trade Unions were springing up and the power of the workers began to be harnessed. Meanwhile the vote had been extended to working class men. Women had also succeeded in getting a vote, but only if they were over 30.

Jack and Monty became aware of the large street markets in the East End of London where the Jewish and Irish immigrant communities were establishing themselves around the docks. They decided to check them out. Their experience in Berwick Street had frightened them off, but now it seemed that the East End markets were offering a wide range of goods, and since they were largely populated by immigrants, perhaps not so dangerous. So they decided to investigate to see if opportunities existed.

Sunday was said to be the big market day, so they got up early and got on the underground from Ladbroke Grove to Liverpool Street. When they exited the station into Bishopsgate, they couldn't believe how busy it was; crowded with people of all colours and creeds.

They walked to Middlesex Street which was the beginning of the market known as Petticoat Lane, a name they were told originated from the old brothels that existed there since the 1700s. They were astonished at the size of it. Many times bigger than the one in the West End. Hundreds of stalls selling everything from clothing to food, cosmetics, toys, everything imaginable. Many of the stall holders were Jewish.

They jostled along with the crowds to Brick Lane market, just off Middlesex Street but still part of Petticoat Lane. It was not so busy, and you could buy pets and live animals there, such as budgerigars, cats and dogs. Stripe Street was another part: packed with stalls selling domestic goods, crockery and glassware and then they walked round to Houndsditch, where there were mainly wholesale warehouses not open to the general public.

Stall holders were more than happy to explain how the market worked. It was open every day except Saturday, but Sunday was the big day. The best place to trade was in Middlesex Street itself, but unless you were there every day, it was very difficult to get a pitch. Stalls could be hired from the Market Controller and there was no form of regulation. So Sunday traders just had to arrive very early. They had to line up with their stalls at the Aldgate end. At 6.00am the Controller blew a whistle and the traders had to run with their stalls, to claim a pitch at the other end. They were told that this led to many rows and fights over the best pitches. But, everyone said, it was worth it.

So they were determined to give it a try next week. Of course, unlike some of the regular stallholders, they had no car or van to deliver the goods to the market and yet they knew they had to be there long before dawn. One thing about Domansky men, they were not lazy. In fact, if hard work was the only criteria for making money, they would have been very rich.

On the way back on the tube, they were excited, 'Ok', said Jack, 'we'll take rails of clothes on the underground, that's all.'

'That's no good,' said Monty thoughtfully. 'On Sunday the tube doesn't start until 6.30, that's far too late. We will have go late on Saturday evening and sleep rough somewhere.' Jack didn't like the idea, but he couldn't come up with an alternative.

So when Saturday came round, they put all their produce on mobile rails. Chaya gave them a package of food and drink and waved them off. This time they took the train straight through to Aldgate, arriving at 11pm. They found the office of the Market Controller, although of course, it was all closed up, but there was quite a bit of cardboard strewn around. They went into a corner and laid down plenty of the cardboard to make somewhere to sleep, and they covered themselves with the clothes from the rails. After eating a beigel and some cold tea, they both dozed off.

Surprisingly, they both managed to sleep until they were wakened at 4.30am by a policeman prodding them with his truncheon. 'What 'ave we 'ere then?' he asked.

They explained, and thankfully the copper realised they were not tramps and he was quite sympathetic when they explained what they were doing.

He spoke in quite a kindly tone, 'Well, you'd better get going. Tell you what. I'll take you over to meet Sean Rafferty, the Market Controller. You need him.'

Monty and Jack realised they had struck lucky. There were already a few people waiting to speak to Mr Rafferty, but the policeman ignored them and went straight into the office. The copper and Rafferty clearly knew each other well, and after the officer explained that these boys had slept outside all night to get a pitch, Rafferty was very helpful.

They hired a stall with wheels, and they were set and ready in position by 5.00am with many others. Due to their lucky break, they were at the front of the queue. When the whistle blew, they ran for all they were worth and managed to get a pitch about halfway down Middlesex Street. They set up the stall, bought some hot tea and by 9.00am the market was packed with people. It was amazing, and by the end of the day, they had sold most of what they had brought. There were no fixed prices, so they could charge whatever they thought the customer would pay, and there was animated bargaining all the time.

Monty was in the midst of serving customers when a young boy approached the stall with a man and woman in tow. Chaya would have described the boy as a raga-muffin, rather dirty trousers, shirt and waistcoat and a battered cap on his head. The adults, however, were clearly not connected to him, they were quite smartly dressed.

Monty was astonished when the boy started showing the little coats and selling to them as if he owned the stall.

Monty went to stop him, but Jack was curious to see what would happen. The boy certainly had 'the gift of the gab' and didn't stop talking. Eventually it seemed the customer was interested in buying one of the coats.

The boy sidled up to Monty '*Vi fil?*' – in Yiddish it meant 'how much?'. Fortunately, those words were the same in German and Monty caught on straight away. '*Ein funt,*'he said - a pound.

This exchange was said very quietly, but the customer didn't look like he would have understood it, in any case. There was a bit of haggling and they agreed at a price of one guinea, or one pound and one shilling. The boy took the money, the customer took the coat, and the boy went to Monty for his one shilling 'over.' The boy explained that there were a few like him in the market and they worked purely on 'overs.'

He said they were all freelancers, they didn't work specifically for anyone, and they would try to stop people walking by, engage them in conversation, and find out what they were interested in. They were great salesmen and would tell stories to the customers about how they knew somewhere they could get a great deal and a big discount.

For example: 'You want to buy a coat for the little girl? I know this stall holder has the best in the market, but he has to sell all his stock today. Come and have a look, I can get you a great discount.'

The stallholders didn't mind because it cost them nothing, they made extra sales and the customers felt they were getting special treatment. Some days the boys could make quite a bit of money, but other days they didn't cover the cost of their fares.

The market finished at 2.00pm and Monty and Jack had made a lot of money, beyond their wildest dreams. They were absolutely exhausted, having been up virtually all night. The adrenalin had kept them going, but they started to feel it now, and they both fell asleep in the train on the way home.

When they arrived, they couldn't wait to tell Leizar that they had made as much money in a few hours as they both made working for the whole week at the workshop. Leizar and Chaya were full of pride. Leizar gave one of his rare smiles, 'Well done to both of you. You deserve it after what you did. Come here,' and they had a group hug.

Chaya broke off to say, 'And I've made a lovely dinner for you, come – let's eat.'

But Leizar knew they boys could not do that every week, staying out all night and sleeping rough, and they had been lucky to find the kindly policeman. Another one might have moved them on. Also, he was intrigued to hear what was going on in the East End of London where the Jewish immigrant community was largest.

So, the next day Chaya looked after the shop, and Leizar went to the East End. He sought out the Market Controller. The boys had told him he was an Irish man called Sean Rafferty, so he introduced himself and explained he was the father of

Jack and Monty.

Sean remembered the two boys very well, 'Aah yes,' he said, in his broad Irish brogue, 'the wee lads that came up the night before, didn't they? To get a good pitch.'

Leizar suggested he buy Sean a coffee, and when they were seated, he leaned across and lowered his voice conspiratorially, 'Sean, I don't know if you have kids, but as you can see, my two boys are hard workers.

'Oh yes, I can see that, sir.'

'And they're prepared to do whatever it takes, but as their father, how can I stand by and see them knock themselves out every week like this?

'You see, they don't have a van, so they work all week at the factory, they make up stock on Saturday, and then they have to sleep rough on Saturday night to be in time for your whistle on Sunday morning, because the underground doesn't start early enough on Sunday. Is there any way round it, Sean?'

Sean knew how hard it was for immigrants to make a living in London and he had taken a liking to Monty and Jack. 'Well sir, between you and me, there are a few young boys I sees sometimes– 14 or 15-year-olds. I think they could be paid to position the stall on Sunday.

'There's a school, Thomas Buxton, in Commercial Road; a lot of Irish boys go there, and I think they would do it for the right money. The families know me, so you could trust 'em.'

'Sean, I really appreciate that, I'm going round there now.' And he slipped a pound note into Sean's hand.

'Ooh, thank you very much, sir. I'll keep an eye on yer boys, so I will, don't you worry.'

So Leizar walked to the school which was quite nearby and asked for the Headmaster. He explained what he wanted and that he would be willing to pay a good price as a bit of pocket money for the boys. He found the Head very co-operative. 'There are boys in the school already who are doing this sort of thing, and I have no objection to boys taking on a job outside school as long as it doesn't interfere with their lessons.'

The Head suggested that Leizar put a notice on the notice board, and then wait until break time. He gave Leizar paper and crayons which he used to draw up a notice saying he would pay five shillings for two boys to do a job every Sunday morning very early.

Then he waited, and it was not long before he was inundated with offers. He chose two of the boys, who looked bigger and stronger than the rest and explained what they had to do. He arranged for them to meet Jack and Monty at the Controller's office at 5.30 am next Sunday.

Feeling pleased with himself, he went for a walk around the area, and he came across the famous Tubby Isaacs fresh jellied eel stall. This was a delicacy he had never heard of, and after a taste of the spongy slippery product, he vowed he never would again.

Then he walked over to Houndsditch where he attempted to enter the Houndsditch Warehouse Company, a massive wholesale warehouse stocking all sorts of products including haberdashery and trimmings. He was not allowed in without a business card to prove he would be purchasing on behalf of a business. The warehouse sold goods at around 30% less than retail prices, and they did not charge purchase tax.

It was clear to Leizar that some of the market traders were simply buying stock from the Houndsditch and selling it for a marked-up price on their market stalls. This could be a great resource for his shop. He resolved to return with a business card. The day was certainly an eye opener.

That evening he told his sons about his day. They were surprised and impressed that he had spent the day in the East End and Monty was delighted when he told them about the two boys who said they would set the stall up for them. Jack was a bit sceptical, wondering how reliable they would be, but he perked up when Leizar said he had arranged for them to do a 'trial run' next Sunday and meet the boys.

As soon as they were alone, Chaya gave him the biggest kiss and cuddle, 'Leizar, I am so proud of our boys, but I am even more proud of you!' she said. 'In one day you have solved so much for them, I am a lucky woman to have you.'

Monty and Jack enlisted the help of Minna and Lou after work and on Saturday to make up more stock, and which they put on the rails after dinner and left. They stayed overnight in the same place so they would be ready at 5.30am. Sure enough he two boys arrived at 5.15am, ready to work.

They said hello to Sean and introduced the boys, who Sean already knew.

'Right,' said Sean, 'this is what we do. If you are happy with these lads, then you give me a month's rent for the hire of the stall. Then the boys can set it up every week at this time.'

He went outside and blew the whistle, and all four ran with the stall and the stock. They got a great pitch again in Middlesex Street.

They made it clear to the boys that they were to get the stall in place every week at this time. They should try to be first in the line. They were to hold the pitch until Jack and Monty arrived with the stock at 7.30am. They told them they would trust them to find the same pitch every Sunday, and explained how important it was to get on or near where they were today. They paid them, thanked them, and let them go home.

It was another very successful trading day, even better than last week, clearing more than £20, most of which was pure profit.

So, when the next Sunday arrived, the brothers were nervous. Would the boys let them down? Could a couple of schoolboys really handle it? Getting up while it was still dark, and then running with the stall as soon as the whistle blew, to find the best pitch.

They caught the first tube train with yet more stock, and on the way, Jack said, 'This is never going to work, is it? I don't think Papa has any idea. A couple of kids. I wonder what we will find when we get there? We may have to find the pitch ourselves this time.'

Monty nodded, his cigarette permanently in his mouth and ash dripping down his front, 'It's worth a try, and we've got the Market Controller on our side. Let's see what happens. We may have to sleep there every week in future.'

They worried all the way to Liverpool Street station, and then anxiously *schlepped* the rails through the streets which were already getting crowded.

They arrived in Middlesex Street, relieved and delighted to find the stall in position and in an even better pitch, but they were shocked to see the two boys standing by the stall, looking battered and bruised. 'What on earth has happened?' they said, almost together.

The boys explained they had had arrived early and got the best pitch they could, but another stall holder arrived late. He couldn't get a pitch anywhere in the street, so he told them to push off, this was his pitch. They weren't going to be pushed around, and they described what had happened.

Eddie, the bigger of the two, smiled and explained, 'He was a big bastard, so he was, but he was mostly fat. Mickey and me, we both box at school. Mickey is a champion. He represents London.'

Mickey interjected, 'He probably thought we would be a pushover, mister.'

Eddie continued, 'So, he pushed Mickey into the stall, and he when he fell over, started to shout and tell us to bugger off, but he never got it out, because I kicked him straight in the balls.'

'Then one of his mates turned up and started weighing in,' said Mickey, but I was up off the floor in double quick time, and while he was staggering around holding his privates and telling his mate to see to us, I hit him with my best haymaker on the side of the head.'

Eddie laughed, 'You should have seen it. He didn't know what had hit him. Then they both came for us, and they landed a few blows, but we were getting on top when my dad arrived with one of his mates. They didn't fancy a scrap with all of us, so they tried to run off, but Mickey tripped up the first one, and the other fell over him. It was quite comical.'

'By this time a crowd had gathered, and they were marched off to the Controller's office. They are now banned and can never trade in the market again,' said Mickey.

'He thought because we were young, he could push us around. But he made a mistake,' said Eddie.

The brothers were very impressed, and they could see that, although they were still at school, both the boys were taller than them, and well built. While Jack set up the stall, Monty took the boys for a cup of tea.

Over tea with milk and hot apple strudel, he said 'Look, we're really grateful for what you did today.' He reached into his pocket and gave them each a shiny half-crown.

'Wow!' said Eddie, who seemed to be the spokesman. 'We would have taught him a lesson anyway, but thanks.'

Monty realised that he had picked two great allies, and they could become very important. 'Ok, this is the deal, if you can get a really good pitch every week, then our takings will be better. We want you to share in it.'

Monty knew that would really grab their attention and it certainly succeeded. 'So, listen carefully; we will pay you, either ten shillings or a half per cent of the takings, whichever is the greatest every week. Last week that would have been worth one pound to you.'

The boys couldn't believe their ears. This was a fortune. 'Wow!' said Michael again. 'That's like a week's wages!'

Monty was on a roll. 'That's not all. Today's pitch is really good, thank you, but if you can ever find an even better one, say right at the start of Middlesex Street, then the stall would take even more money. On that basis you would earn even more, maybe make that up to two pounds.'

The boys both smiled, 'Don't you worry mister, you're gonna get the best pitch.'

Monty offered his hand, 'Let's shake on it,' Then his face went serious. 'But remember, if you ever let us down, that will be the end of it. I'm sure there are lots of young men at the school who would like to earn this sort of money.'

He left the boys to finish their tea. 'See you next week!'

The boys couldn't believe their luck. But it was a shrewd move by Monty because every week after that they were guaranteed the best pitches and the boys made a lot of money too. From then on, the word had spread, and the brothers, aided by their helpers, became quite well-known among the other traders.

The East End was full of characters and the brothers got to know a lot of them. The most colourful were the auctioneers and though they didn't have much time, when things went a bit quiet, they loved to take turns watching them perform, selling mostly homeware, and they would shout to attract attention, then they would take some of their products and verbally 'build them up to the sky' while a crowd developed. They would say a top price which 'I am not asking today, because we are selling off the last few,' and then they would shout, 'Not a pound each, not ten shillings, not seven and six, I tell you what, for one day only… five shillings each. Only a few left. Who wants one?'

Of course, five shillings was the price they'd wanted all along, and often these traders would have 'plants' - friends in the crowd who would start things off by appearing to buy first. It was a great skill, and entertaining to watch.

Leizar would go with his sons occasionally and buy some stock for his shop from the Houndsditch, and sometimes Lou would go with him. Between the market and the wholesalers, they could buy almost everything the family needed much cheaper than in the shops of West London.

After a while, the Domansky boys started to become quite well known in the area, as 'Little Monty and Jack.' They could sell as much as they could make, so it wasn't long before they gave up the work in the factory and went flat out all week making up stock for the stall. Lou was cutting patterns and was still able to keep the factory going, and Leizar's shop was making a profit, so the family income was good, and it wasn't too long before Minna gave birth to her second child, a little girl called Rita,

So, the first half of the decade had gone well for the family.

However, in the mid-20s, after the relief of the end of the war and the euphoria that followed, cracks began to appear in the outlook for Great Britain and her allies. The war debt was enormous, and the pound was devalued, which immediately made essential imports such as food much more expensive. With prices rising in the shops, workers were demanding more pay, and management had no idea how to handle the new empowered trade unions. This led to the General Strike of 1926, and Communists infiltrated the trade unions, seeing that this could be a route to overthrowing capitalism.

<hr />

Lena remained a problem. She helped out by working in Morris's shop, but she was taking money from the till and losing it gambling. The daughters hated her, and she hated them. The way they saw it, although Morris had protected them in his will, Lena was taking the money now and it was disappearing before their eyes.

The way Lena saw it, she was trapped. She wanted her independence back. She hated Morris and his daughters, and she would not let him near her sexually. They slept in separate rooms.

One day a policeman walked into the shop, 'Are you Mrs Lena Binstock?'

'Yes,' she replied, wondering if she was about to be arrested for something.

'Mrs Binstock, I have some bad news, I am afraid your husband was involved in an accident, he was knocked down by a car.'

Lena didn't bat an eyelid. 'Good', she said, 'How badly is he injured?'

The policeman removed his helmet, 'I am sorry to tell you that he was killed outright.'

Lena responded right away. 'Pity it didn't happen sooner!'

As he had promised, when the will was read, most of Morris's estate went to his daughters with only a small fund for Lena. Although the value of the shop had been eroded by Lena's gambling, there was still a substantial inheritance for them and in particular, the house. Of course, that meant Lena had to move back in with the family. Thankfully the rooms in the apartment were large and they split one of them in two so that Monty and Jack could have one side and Lena the other. None of them were very happy about it.

Later in 1926 Monty told his parents that he had met the girl he wanted to marry. Rachel Green lived with her parents in Park West, a block of high-priced luxury flats at Marble Arch, in London's West End.

He had met her in the market one Sunday and was struck by her beauty. Monty knew he was punching above his weight with a girl from a plush apartment in Marble Arch, and on their first date he asked with some trepidation where she would like to go for dinner.

Rachel turned out to be very modest. 'Monty, I would like to go anywhere you enjoy.'

This was an open goal for Monty. 'OK, he said, have you heard of Blooms in Whitechapel?' When she said no, he went on, 'Well, it's very famous and all the East Enders go there, but it's not posh.'

To his delight, she didn't mind a bit, so they went together to sample the delights of a salt beef sandwich on rye.

They had to queue outside for a while as there was no such thing as a reservation, and the owner came round with slices of wurst to keep them going while they waited. Once inside, they sat in a booth and ordered a chopped liver starter followed by sandwiches and lemon tea from the waiter, who wore a grubby white apron with a money belt round his waist. Rachel had never been in an establishment like this. They had to pay before they were served, and the waiter took the money and put it in his belt. Monty explained that the waiters were all self-employed, and they had to buy the food from the kitchen and sell it to the customers. This was to stop thieving.

She was even more surprised when the chopped liver arrived, and Monty asked for some bread. The waiter leaned across the plates of the people in the next booth and took a handful of their bread which he gave to Monty and Rachel. The people at the other table looked at the waiter in amazement; he shrugged and said, 'They want bread!' as if that explained it.

The restaurant was packed, and the food was delicious. Monty told her that it was said to be the best in the world. Surprisingly after that, she was besotted with him, and they had a short but intense courtship.

He brought her home to meet the family and she scored a hit with Chaya straight away. She was quiet – which was good because the Domanskys were noisy – but she was also kind and very attentive. She got on well with all of them. Leizar thought she was lovely, 'Surprising what a salt beef sandwich can do!' he said.

The Greenbaum family had come over from Holland before WW1 and shortened their name to Green. Leizar and Chaya were invited to their apartment in the posh part of town. They were very impressed as they entered the prestigious block which of course, was purpose built with a revolving glass entrance.

They were greeted by a uniformed concierge who escorted them to the Greens' apartment. Leizar whispered to Chaya, 'I wonder what my father from the shtetl would have thought if he could see us now.'

Leizar was rather uncomfortable in the plush surroundings, but his ears pricked up when he heard that Rachel's father Solomon had retired from the diamond business. Never one to be backward in coming forward, after drinks and canapes, in front of Rachel and Monty, he went to sit next to Solomon and blurted out, 'So what are you going to do for my boy?'

There was a sharp intake of breath from Monty, and Chaya tried to kick him under the table. Fortunately, Solomon and Anne, Rachels mother, were mild mannered people and saved the embarrassment by deliberately misunderstanding.

'We will be proud to take care of all the wedding arrangements, said Anne.' It took the wind out of Leizar's sails, and he knew from the look he received from his wife, that he'd better not say what he'd really meant.

Rachel's parents arranged a lavish wedding which would take place in January 1927 at The Assembly Rooms in Central London with two hundred guests, of which they allowed the Domanskys fifty.

That got right up Leizar's nose. 'Why should they have three times more than us?' he shouted to Chaya when he heard.

'Because they're paying for it, 'she said. 'Now you'd better calm down over this or you'll spoil the day for Monty, Rachel and everyone.'

Remembering Herschel had paid only for the closest Domansky family, and they had organised a separate function for all their friends and family, he harrumphed and sulked away, mumbling, 'They've got more than three times our money.'

When the day arrived, it turned out to be a spectacular wedding. Leizar had gone along with everything, and only put his foot down by insisting that the wedding ceremony was conducted in their synagogue at St Petersburg Place, which did not meet with any resistance when the Green family saw how beautiful it was.

When it came to planning where the young couple would live, there was no room in the Marble Arch apartment and, in any event, Rachels parents made it clear that even if there was, there would be no question of the couple moving in with them. Monty would have been dead against it anyway.

So, it meant they would move in with the family in Ladbroke Grove and the place was now getting very crowded. Lena had to give up her room for them, and Leizar and Chaya carved off a piece of their own room for Lena. She was not happy!

Monty decided that the name Rachel was a bit of a mouthful, and he shortened it to simply 'Ray.' After all, Monty was really Morris and Jack was really Jacob. Why should anyone be known by their real name?

And it was not long before Ray became pregnant. Their first-born son, Arnold was born a year later and the second child a daughter, Rosetta a year after that. They were all squashed into the little room, and the babies, cute as they were, disturbed everyone's sleep. Something had to be done.

Although Leizar still had a strong belief in the need for a more equal society, he did not agree with the totalitarian approach of the Communist party, and there was a growing mood of dissatisfaction about workers' rights. He was writing consistently for the *Jewish Chronicle* and other papers, and as always, his strongly stated views stirred up some deep reactions.

Toward the end of the decade, people had less money to spend, and this was depressing everything. Shops and markets were suffering, and restaurants were closing.

On the other hand, there was a stock market boom: brokers were effectively creating debt by allowing investors to buy stock and only pay 10/20 percent of the value. This had driven the markets to an unsustainable level in the second half of the decade and in 1929 the US market crashed. Millions were wiped off investment values overnight.

All this had a knock-on effect on the family. People were not quite so free with their money, which affected takings in the market and the shop.

It seemed as though everything was slowing down, and an air of depression replaced the optimistic atmosphere of a few years ago.

CHAPTER 42

THE 1930S – ANOTHER SADNESS

There was a great deal of political and economic unrest in Great Britain and all over the world.

Unemployment was rising, and demand for products was falling fast. The work at the factory had slowed and Lou feared for his job, now that Minna was at home with the children. Petticoat Lane was still busy, but Jack and Monty were not able to get the prices they had before, and there were outbreaks of anti-Semitism from far-right organisations who, as in past history, blamed the Jews for the depression.

The National Unemployed Workers Movement was set up by the Communist Party of Great Britain to demand better unemployment benefits and work for the unemployed. In 1929 they organised a Hunger March on London. After the US stock market crashed, world trade slumped and by the end of 1930 Britain had more than 20% unemployment.

———————※———————

Jack had met the love of his life, Helen and they also decided to get married. The family was growing rapidly. Lou struggled with the name Helen, he just could not pronounce it, so instead called her Lainchen and oddly that name stuck, so that was how she was known.

There were now far too many people for the apartment in Ladbroke Grove. It was a problem. They'd converted every space into sleeping quarters and even the living room had become a bedroom by night, but they were all living on top of each other, and there was very little privacy. This led to tensions which caused massive family rows, with Chaya and Leizar acting as referees. Something had to be done.

Ray's sister-in-law, Celie had inherited property, which included the Marble Arch apartment where she and her husband Harry lived. Ray and Monty were over there for tea when the subject came up. 'We can't carry on living as we are,' said Monty. 'You understand about property in London, what can we do?'

Celie and Harry explained that it was a time of great contrasts, although there was less money around, house building was booming. Houses were being built in suburban areas at an unprecedented rate. 'We just bought some houses in Acton, West London. They're really cheap. Have a look, you've got good incomes, and you can borrow money to buy. That's what we do, and it's a really good investment. The prices will go up, and you can make money tax free.'

When Monty told Leizar, he liked the sound of that. They went to meet with an Estate Agent introduced by the Greens. Leizar wanted to know how it worked.

'Well, there are not enough people buying, and this has driven prices down. Interest rates are low, and it creates a great opportunity for people who have a good income. I can show you houses where the mortgage repayments would be less than the rent you're paying in Ladbroke Grove.'

So, to split the costs, Leizar and Chaya together with Jack, Lainchen and Lena bought a three-bedroomed house in Acton, West London, and Monty, Ray and the children, together with Minna, Lou and their children bought another one close by. They still had to split bedrooms, but it was luxury compared with how they had been living, and it brought some independence.

In the 1930s, radio came of age and the families were able to hear news as it became available instead of waiting for the next day's newspaper. This also meant that organised entertainment was broadcast, and the Domansky families would crowd round the radio, or wireless as they called it, after dinner and listen to comedy and music piped right into their living room.

It made everyone much more aware of what was going on in the world, but alas, there was not much good news. Anti-Semitism was again on the rise. In Europe, large scale unemployment was rife, and times were tough for people. The Domanskys were always interested in what was happening in Germany where they still had family, and the news from there was very grim. The humiliating defeat in WW1 was still fresh in the minds of the German people, and they were looking for a champion.

BBC news reported that a new political party had been formed, which was gaining popularity. National Socialists, or Nazi for short. They had a charismatic and radical leader, Adolf Hitler. His powerful speeches were broadcast all round the world. He blamed much of the world's problems on Communists and Jews and his propaganda was very aggressive.

The British government was worried when, in 1933, President Hindenberg appointed him as Chancellor, and then died shortly afterwards leaving Hitler with great power. He abolished the role of Chancellor and declared himself Fuhrer of Germany.

Leizar was worried, 'We still have family in Germany and Poland. This *meshuggener* is whipping things up again, and we know what the German people are like, do you think there could be another war? If things go from bad to worse, what will become of our families and friends?'

The propaganda coming out of Germany also spawned anti-Semitism elsewhere. Sir Oswald Mosely was the founder of the British Union of Fascists, who were in support of Hitler.

The *Jewish Chronicle* reported that Mosely was holding rallies and demonstrations in the predominantly Jewish areas of East London, and that fights were common in and around the Petticoat Lane market area.

One Sunday Monty and Jack were on the stall when the market went quiet. A line of black-shirted men spread across the width of the market, carrying wooden clubs and cricket bats. Visitors had crammed onto the pavements behind the stalls, but the stall owners faced them down. Their leader was a big man holding a club in one hand and patting his open palm with it. They stood facing each other for a minute or two until the leader just shouted one word: 'Right!'

At this signal, they started shouting obscenities, and overturning stalls. Monty and Jack joined the rest of the stall owners trying to repel them, and they got beaten for their trouble. Eventually the police arrived, and the black-shirts disappeared, but they noticed not one arrest was made.

It left a terrible mess with stock strewn all over the street. Slowly and in some cases, painfully, all the stallholders helped each other, but much was ruined.

The next day, the papers reported it as follows:

Oswald Mosely and his British Union of Fascists attacked stall holders in Petticoat Lane yesterday. A mob of some fifty men clad in their black-shirted uniform deliberately provoked the many Jewish market traders, who retaliated. Fights broke out and there were several injuries. The police attended eventually, but no arrests were made.

'You stay away from that market now,' said Leizar when they returned home. This time they didn't argue with their father, but they were not going to be beaten by a bunch of anti-Semitic thugs. It made them even more determined, and when Lou heard, he was incensed. 'I am coming mit choo, next veek, unt bringing some friends, big bull vuns.'

So, they continued to work in Petticoat Lane on Sundays, and although there were skirmishes, because the stallholders all had support, the Mosely followers didn't turn up in numbers again. Young Jewish men were determined not to be intimidated. Of course, though, this ruined the trade in the market. People kept away. Trouble was bubbling under the surface all the time.

It came to a head in June 1934. Mosely organised a rally of over 12,000 of his Fascist supporters in Olympia, many of them in their uniforms. This caused consternation and anger among many, especially the Jewish community. When they heard about it, Monty, Jack and Lou joined many of the younger synagogue members who went to disrupt the meeting. The police were there in force, trying to keep the two sides apart. But the event was deliberately provocative and the anger and violence it provoked ensured that it got maximum publicity; as a result, the Fascist message began to spread.

———✳———

In the following year, Chaya became ill. It started with a shortness of breath and sometimes she found it difficult to speak. The local doctor said she had a virus and prescribed aspirin, bed rest and a hot toddy at night. But it got worse, and she started complaining of pains in her chest.

She had never really been ill. It had always been Chaya who looked after everyone who was feeling poorly. Leizar was fussing round her all the time, trying to make sure she was warm and comfortable, which only seemed to make her irritable.

After several worrying days, he was relieved that her chest seemed easier. Her breathing had almost returned to normal, and she sat up in bed and ate a good portion of soup with lokshen and pieces of chicken. 'Thank God you are feeling better. Some colour has returned to your cheeks.' He gave her a hot toddy, and they both went to sleep.

When Leizar woke the next morning, she was still asleep, which was very unusual for Chaya, who was usually up early, whether she was ill or not. He kissed her gently on the cheek, but she didn't stir and Leizar had the shock of his life. She seemed cold and still.

He ran out of the room in his pyjamas and raised Jack and Lena. 'Quick, quick, help – it's mama – she's asleep, and I can't wake her up.'

Jack ran to Minna's house, and she came running. She took one look at Chaya and told Jack to run to the phone box and call the doctor, 'Tell him it's urgent and come quickly,' she said.

Lena ran to the other house to get the rest of the family. An hour later, when the doctor arrived, Chaya still had not moved. Leizar had a pain in the pit of his stomach. He was sitting watching her, rocking back and forth. Lena and Minna were in the room with Leizar.

The doctor simply felt her neck for a pulse. He turned to them and quite brutally just said 'Well – she's gone. Nothing I can do.'

Leizar screamed and the girls started to cry. Then Leizar seemed to lose control. He ran out of the room and downstairs into the street, still in his pyjamas.

Every now and then he would let out a loud scream like an animal in great pain.

He ran down the road screaming, and neighbours came out of their houses. Jack and Monty ran after him and when they eventually caught up, he had collapsed in the street.

They got him up and although he was shaking, they helped him back to the house where the doctor stood waiting. The family were frightened. Leizar was gasping for breath, and he had gone red in the face. He didn't stop shaking. The doctor gave him a sedative which caused him to slump on the bed where Chaya still laid. The scene was horrific.

The doctor left some tablets and said to give him one every four hours to settle him down, but they couldn't leave him lying next to Chaya. Every now and then he would look over at her, touch her and scream.

Tears were coursing down his cheeks now. Jack, Monty and Lou managed to lift him between them and get him into Lena's room. They were all sobbing, and very frightened.

Oddly, it was Lena who took charge. 'Minna and I will stay here with Papa - Jack and Monty, you have to call the synagogue and make arrangements for Mama. We can't leave her here like this. They will tell you what to do.'

The shul secretary was very good, she swung into action and talked them through everything that had to be done, and all the arrangements were made.

During the next few days, Leizar seemed to shrink physically. He wouldn't eat, and he kept calling out for Chaya. 'Don't leave me, I'm coming with you.' He would shake and sometimes emit a whining noise, but he wouldn't speak. The family made sure he was never alone.

The shock of Chaya's sudden death changed Leizar substantially. Minna and Lou took him into their house while the family dealt with the formalities, so that he didn't see the body being removed and he stayed with them that night. The synagogue was a great help, but the whole family were traumatised.

The funeral and the shiva were awful. Leizar needed more medication to cope and for several days he would suddenly break into tears, sobbing. And this would often start the girls off. It was a terrible time for the whole family.

Leizar's personality underwent a change. He had never smiled much, but now he became very stern and quiet, hardly talking to anyone. He was also more reactive to everything that was going on around him. He was short-tempered with the children and told everyone to keep them away from him. The house was full of tears. Chaya had been the fulcrum of the family and her passing had left a massive hole.

————————✳————————

The Battle of Cable Street was organised by Mosely and his British Union of Fascists in October 1936. He let it be known that a march would take place of three thousand Fascist supporters in their black-shirt uniforms through the East End of London. It was designed to be deliberately provocative, especially to Jews.

When Leizar heard about it, he was incensed. It seemed to motivate him, that he had something to vent his anger on.

He became very agitated as if this was a personal affront directed at him and his family, and he was not short of compatriots. The whole Jewish community became very enaged, and plans were circulated by word of mouth that they must not let this happen.

The march was planned for the following Sunday, when Jack and Monty would normally have been manning the stall. Leizar told them to speak to as many people as they knew in the area and to garner support.

Leizar's pent-up rage had been building and was starting to emerge. Recently he had been having dreams and reliving the past hurt and indignities that had been heaped upon himself and his family over the years. The rabbi told the family that it was good to get him to talk, to let out his feelings.

He would tell anyone who would listen about the huge injustice and tragic death of his brother Mendel, including the horrendous execution. Then on to the disgraceful pogroms, the horrible attack and the crippling of his Uncle Shmuel, the murder of Ada Ochter, the desecration at the wedding; the attack on him in the alleyway in Warsaw; the death and destruction of Herschel and his Polish friends, culminating in the loss of his life partner and the light of his eyes, his beloved Chaya.

The anger with which he related these stories was shocking to those who heard them. He had not spoken much about his previous life, and a lot of this was new, even to his own children.

But his real rage was focused on the Fascists, who once again wanted to denigrate Jews. He whipped up feeling among many synagogue members, and on the day of the march, they joined the throng of people determined to oppose the demonstration.

Jack, Monty and Lou knew this would be a worse confrontation than the previous one, and when Leizar said he was going with them, they did all they could to stop him. They didn't want their 63-year-old father anywhere near the violence. They enlisted the help of the Minna, Lena and Ray, but Leizar steamrollered the lot of them. All his pent-up rage was coming out, and they simply couldn't stop him. He had made up his mind.

Around 100,000 local residents had petitioned the Home Secretary, Sir John Simon, to ban the march because of the likelihood of the violence it would incite. He refused, quoting the people's democratic right to demonstrate, but he told the petitioners that there would be a strong police presence to ensure it passed off peacefully. On the day, people had travelled from all over the country to join in, and it was estimated that 20,000 anti-fascist demonstrators turned out, to be met by 7,000 policemen, including mounted police.

The Domanskys stationed themselves behind a barricade that had been constructed across the road in Whitechapel to stop the march. The police attempted to clear the blockage to allow the marchers through, but the crowd fought back with rocks, chair legs and rotten vegetables. Even the contents of chamber pots and other projectiles were thrown at the police.

Leizar was one of the most violent. He managed to pull a policeman off his horse, whereupon he was immediately arrested and taken away.

The battles went on all day, with the police trying to clear the way for the Fascists to continue their march, and the community determined to stop them. Eventually the marchers gave up, leaving the anti-fascists to riot with the police.

Jack and Monty were desperate to find out about their father. They were told that Leizar had not suffered any serious injury and had been taken to Aldgate Police Station. In a way they were pleased, because his early arrest meant he had been removed from further trouble, but now they had to get him released and take him home.

It wasn't so easy. The police station was packed with people who had been arrested, and they had to wait for hours to speak to the desk sergeant. Leizar had been put in a holding cell with many other people who had been arrested, some of whom were Blackshirts. That had provoked him further and he was apparently causing trouble.

The sergeant was well aware of Leizar. 'Oh yes, the little bloke. I'll be glad to get rid of him before we have to arrest him for something else. He's been charged with affray and disturbing the peace, so we can release him into your custody, on police bail, sign here please.'

In response to their question about what happens next, the sergeant said he would have to appear in the magistrate's court in due course. For now he was free to leave.

Leizar showed no remorse when they got home to Acton. He said he wished they had let him at the '*Black shirted momzers, a double meesa mishineh oyf zey.*'

A few weeks later he appeared in court, pleaded guilty and was fined one pound. He nearly made it worse when he told the magistrates that if he had managed to get to the Blackshirts, they would be charging him with a bigger crime.

So now they had a father with a criminal record.

CHAPTER 43

WW2 – 1939/1945

In 1937, Lainchen gave birth to a lovely little girl they called Hetty, and this seemed to start a chain reaction. Two years later she had another little girl, Rita, and Minna gave birth to Joe. Rachel had another little girl, Jeanette and a year later, not to be outdone, Minna had another little girl, Sheila.

The family was growing rapidly, and now even the new houses were too small. So Jack decided to move out with his family. Leizar encouraged him to look outside London and he found a nice semi-detached, three-bedroomed house in Northolt, a nice, quiet, suburban place.

Once again, the rumblings of war were worrying everyone. The Japanese were at war with China, and in addition to his self-styled title of Führer, Adolf Hitler had declared himself commander-in-chief of the German armed forces as well as German war minister. Civil war had broken out in Spain and Hitler had sent the Luftwaffe to bomb areas of Spain seemingly in support of the socialist Republicans.

Towards the end of the year, Hitler was conspiring with the Austrian government to unify Germany and Austria.

The girls had worked together and prepared a meal, so that all the family could come together for Friday night dinner, and after the little ones had gone to bed, Leizar took the opportunity to speak to them all.

'The news is bad,' he said. 'And we've seen this before. The Germans are acting even worse with this *meshuggener* Führer. What a surprise! In his poisonous speeches who does he blame for the economic depression? Oh yes, Jews!

I believe war in Europe is very likely, and if that happens, I think there is a fifty-fifty chance that Britain would get dragged into it.'

'Iss a vorry! said Lou. 'Unt here ve haf de also the anti… ant..ss….'

Minna helped him out with the missing word. 'Anti-Semitism.'

'Yes, yes', he said, frustrated with himself. 'But iss a vorry for all Chews, no?'

They discussed the situation long and hard. In the end when the ladies were yawning, Leizar summed it up. 'At least we are in England with a democratically elected government and the highest respect for the law in the world. There is nowhere we can run to, so we must put our faith in our adopted country.'

As the year wore on, it became clear to all nations that there was no stomach for war in Great Britain, and the government seemed prepared to do almost anything to avoid it. In 1938 the British Prime Minister, Neville Chamberlain signed the Munich Agreement with Hitler.

He was praised as a hero because many people in Britain felt that, although it gave way to many of Hitler's demands, it would avert another war - and they had not fully recovered from the last one.

Leizar didn't agree. He wrote in his article under the headline:

NEVER, EVER, EVER… GIVE IN

Bullies only understand one thing STRENGTH. Our Prime Minister thinks that he has made a deal with the Fuhrer. He has not!

All he has done, is to show how quick we are to give in.

I have lived in several countries, often under oppression, and I can tell you first-hand, you must meet strength with strength, or they will think they can walk over you.

This agreement gives away parts of Czechoslovakia which are not ours to give, and where Germany have already moved in their troops. Britain led France and Italy to agree and because the Germans have already taken what they want, now the pressured Czechs accede part of their country.

This is like the school bully, who takes a ball in the playground and threatens the owner, and for an easy life, the others let him have it. You know what happens next? He comes back and takes the bat, the other balls, and everything.

This is a bad move by the Government. It may look good now, and I just hope it still looks that way as time passes.

Leizar was right, it was not long before Hitler wanted parts of Poland and Hungary, and when those negotiations stalled, he simply invaded Poland in 1939, which was the start of WW2 and Britain was in it.

Leizar could see that this war would be fought in a different way. Airborne conflict would be paramount. Since WW1 there had been massive advances in munition and explosives, Messerschmitt and Stuka had developed highly manoeuvrable fighter planes and bombers, and the RAF were proud of their Spitfires, Hurricanes and the famous Lockheed bombers from America.

The front page of the *Daily Mirror* screamed.

HITLER PLANS TO INVADE FRANCE AND BRITAIN!!

In September 1939, the government decided that, as a precaution, as many women and children as possible should be evacuated from London and other big city areas, to safer locations in the country.

There followed a massive logistical operation. The British government asked people in rural areas to come forward to take in women with very young children and older children on their own.

Leizar wrote:

EVACUATION!!

The government's proposed evacuation of women and children from the cities to the countryside is a very sensible move.

Anyone who thinks this war will be anything like the last one is sadly mistaken. Although many people died in 1914-18, the fighting took place in mainland Europe and there was no land fighting in Britain.

And although we suffered destruction from aerial attacks, many people are not aware of the incredible advances in air power and munitions on both sides. Hitler has ambitions to rule all of Europe. The fighting, bombing and destruction in our beautiful cities has the potential to be many times more effective and dangerous.

They will target city centres and industrial hubs, and if that happens, they are not places for women and children.

We have the best trained military in the world, backed up by our well-equipped and brave Royal Navy and Air Force. Together with our allied nations, I am sure the Germans will be repelled, but be aware that air attacks will not be so easily contained this time, and the power of the munitions is many times greater.

I urge you to keep your family as safe as possible. If you live in or near city centres, or military, or sites of strategic importance, do not hesitate to send your loved ones to the country.

And if you live in a rural area, please help by offering to share your home with evacuees. We are all in this together.

The whole family were made aware of the force of Leizar's determination and leadership. He insisted very loudly, that his grandchildren be sent to a safe place right away. Acton was almost in the centre of London, which was bound to be a prime target for the Luftwaffe. He warned his sons and son-in-law, 'You are all of an age where you could be conscripted to fight, God forbid. But if that happens the girls would be left alone with the babies.'

But they argued with him, 'The children are very young, and their mothers want to stay. We think we will be alright here.'

Leizar grew very frustrated with them. This was not the first time in his life when he had a clear understanding of what was likely to happen whilst others, who did not have his experience of how bad things could get, thought he was out of touch with reality.

The only one who agreed right away was Monty. His children, Arnold and Rose were of an age that they could join the evacuation from their school, and most of their school friends were going. Rachel was worried, though. 'I don't know Monty, how can we send them away to people we don't know? How do we know how they will be treated, and maybe...' she added, with tears in her eyes, 'we may never see them again.'

But Monty was convinced. He also said that Rachel should take Jeanette away to the country as well. The government had said there would be facilities for mothers and babies, and he wanted all his family safely out of danger. She would not go against her husband, so reluctantly she agreed.

They were contacted by the school who would be co-ordinating everything, and received instructions on how to proceed.

So, on the appointed day Monty took Arnold and Rose to Paddington Station. He had told them that they would be going with their school friends to stay in a lovely place in the country, but they thought their father was going with them on the journey. Rachel had packed a knapsack for each of them with all the things on the government list, a gas mask, a change of underclothes, night clothes, plimsolls spare socks, toothbrush, hairbrush, comb, towel, soap, face cloth handkerchiefs and a warm coat. Being a Jewish mother, she also made sure they had plenty to eat.

They had to wear a label on a piece of string round their necks, bearing their names and the name of the school. They were quite excited when they arrived at the station and saw all their friends and teachers they knew from school. There was a constant babble, and they didn't stop talking about the adventure they were going on.

But then, their father took them to one side and explained that he would not be going with them. It came as a shock. They both stared at him as if they were being betrayed.

Arnold found his voice, 'You mean you are sending us away? Why Dad, what have we done?' His eyes were filling with tears, and Rose started crying.

'We don't want to go, we want to stay with you. Does Mum know?'

'Don't cry, look, you will be with all your friends, and you will be in a nice place with nice people. The war is coming, and you will be safe.' Monty was not good with this sort of thing, and the children were crying openly now. They felt abandoned.

'But…. What are we going… to do? We will be on our own,' Rose said, in between sobs. What have we done that you want to send us away?'

Monty realised that he should have explained all this before, but he had wanted to avoid the trauma, and truly he feared that the family would try to talk him out of it.

Monty loved his children, and would never have hurt them for the world, but he didn't know how to handle this. He wished now that Ray was with him. He decided it was best to be firm.

Unfortunately, that made matters worse. 'You won't be on your own. You will have your friends and your teachers. Now buck up both of you, we are sending you to a place where you'll be safe.' The train whistle blasted, and the station was filled with smoke from the engine.

'Now, it's time to board the train, so off you go.' And he pushed them up the step. Tears were streaming down their faces now, and they were really scared. One of the teachers came along and helped them into the carriage.

The whistle blasted again, there and with as massive hiss of steam which drowned out all words, and multiple loud chuffing sounds, the engine began to heave the train away, leaving their father standing waving on the platform, but they wouldn't look at him. They were very frightened.

The teachers passed among the children with words of comfort and encouragement during the journey, but the Domansky children were snuffling and crying most of the way. Rose turned out to be the stronger of the two, and it was she who started to comfort Arnold. Some of the children had brought games to play with their friends, and for a while that helped take their minds off the ordeal.

Eventually they arrived at Swansea station. They were told not to forget anything, step down carefully on to the platform, where they were marshalled out of the station and along into a big hall nearby, packed with people.

The children were told to line up together down one side, and the teachers organised ten at a time to go up on the stage. The local people chose the children. they wanted as if picking a pet to take home. It was demeaning for the children and did nothing for their confidence.

Rose and Arnold were in the last group and by then there were only four adult couples left. One lady chose Rose and said she only wanted one, but Rose wouldn't let go of Arnold's hand. She started crying, and the lady's husband came forward, put a hand on her shoulder, and said they would take them both.

The lady was quite plump with grey hair tied up in a bun. She wore a heavy tweed suit and brown heavy shoes. But she had a kindly face, and Arnold thought it looked nice when she smiled.

The man, by contrast was small and thin, not much taller than Arnold. He wore a tweed jacket and grey trousers with a tweed cap on his head and a pipe in his mouth, which was not lit.

He told the children to follow and led the way to where their car was parked. It was a rather old Austin Seven, known as the Baby Austin, and it looked pretty run down. But actually, Rose and Arnold didn't mind, the Domansky family were never in a position to have a car of any type and they were not used to being in one.

The lady told the children to get in the back. They were scared, holding each other's hands really tightly, and Arnold hit his head on the roof as he tried to get in.

Before they started off, the lady said, 'Now look you.' Rose and Arnold looked at each other. They both thought she spoke really funny.

'We are Mr and Mrs Morgan, and we live on the Gower Peninsular. That's about two hours outside of Swansea.'

She had a soft voice with a strong Welsh accent, and said, 'Now you will be staying with us at our-'

'When can we go home, please?' Rose interrupted.

'Well, you have to stay until it's safe where you live. We don't know how long that will be. But this is a lovely part of Wales, don't you know, and you'll find it very different from where you live. We're in the countryside with very healthy open air. You'll see farms and sheep and all sorts.'

The car had reached the outskirts of Swansea, and the children noticed how the scenery was becoming green.

'Now, we live in a nice house, and you will each have your own room, and you will be going to our local school. There are some house rules that we will explain when we arrive.'

Arnold blurted, 'Do you have any children?'

'No dear. We have no children of our own, but we do have a dog.'

Mr Morgan was driving, and the children thought it was strange that he didn't say a word.

It was all very frightening for two children who had left home that day thinking they were going away to the countryside with their father.

'So, you two settle down now, and try to have a sleep on the way..'

They seemed to have been travelling for a long time, and actually did fall asleep for part of the journey, but eventually Mr Morgan turned the car into a country lane which was very bumpy, and that woke them up. They passed a farm with sheep grazing and a grassy smell of manure that wafted in through the windows.

They stopped at a gate, behind which were three buildings. A white-painted house with a thatched roof, and two large wooden barns. When they pulled in through the gate, a big dog came bounding out to greet the car. He seemed very friendly and, after he had greeted the adults, he came over to the children to be petted. Mrs Morgan said he was a Golden Retriever called Prince.

The house was quite big, and Mrs Morgan showed them to their separate rooms. She told them to unpack their belongings and come down when they were ready. She turned round and just left them to it.

Arnold went into Rose's room and they both sat on the bed and cried. Once again, it was Rose who took control. She gave her brother a hug and dried her own tears, 'Come on, we'd better do as she says. At least we've got each other.'

When they came down, Mrs Morgan had made some tea with fresh bread and jam. The children were starving, and she kept offering them more. She seemed delighted each time they accepted and in the end, between them, they polished off the whole loaf. 'I can see we need to fatten you two up a bit, we'll see what we can do about that,' she said in her sing-song lilt.

She explained that Mr Morgan was an engineer and he worked at a factory near Swansea, which was odd because Mr Morgan was right there and didn't say a word.

She explained that he left home at 7.00am every morning except Sunday, when they went to church. 'I'll be writing to your parents right away, to let them know who to contact if they need. I believe the school have a record of everything, but your Mam and Dad should be able to contact us directly and the school said you are Jewish, so I'll ask if it's alright for you to come with us to church on Sundays.'

They weren't sure if they liked the sound of that.

'Now I think you'd better write a short note to your parents to let them know you arrived safely, and you're ok. When you've done that, look you, maybe you want to explore the place a bit, but don't get dirty outside because supper is at seven.'

They had only seen pictures of houses like this in books, and it seemed quite homely.

'Where's the lavatory please, Miss?' Rose asked, and she was surprised to find that the toilet was outside in a lean-to attached to the house.

It felt very strange to be in someone else's place, and they both wished they could go straight back to their own home again.

It was a nice supper, a stew with meat, potatoes and dumplings, and there was trifle for pudding. During the whole meal, Mr Morgan hardly said a word to anybody, but Mrs Morgan didn't stop. She was chattering away about the farm, the animals, the neighbours and the school. The children found her funny because she spoke with a pronounced Welsh accent, and she kept on saying 'look you.' She also asked questions, but never waited for the answers before going on to the next thing. Maybe that was why Mr Morgan didn't speak much.

They went to bed in separate rooms and Mrs Morgan gave them each a bowl of water for washing, and a chamber pot in case they should need it during the night. She told them that they were responsible for their own rooms, and they were to make the bed each morning, empty their chamber pots, and clean the whole room thoroughly at the weekends.

Rose cried quite a lot at first and didn't sleep much, but Arnold went out like a light.

The next morning Mrs Morgan woke them at 7.00am and said to get ready and come down for breakfast. There was a delicious smell wafting up the stairs and when they were down, they found Mrs Morgan was waiting for them in the kitchen.

'Mr Morgan's just left for work. He likes a full cooked breakfast in the mornings, says it sets him up for the day. I didn't know if you would eat bacon, what with you being Jewish and all, but I can make you some eggs and there's plenty of toast and stuff.'

Arnold said he would love to try the bacon which smelled so good, and he gave a little piece to Rose. After that it was full Welsh breakfasts every day.

Mrs Morgan walked them to school, which was about a mile away and they were pleased to find that many of their friends were there. Their own teachers had returned to London and the Welsh teachers took over. There was a school assembly, led by the Headmaster, a man with an accent so broad, they found him difficult to understand. He was a tall man with jet black hair and moustache, wearing a blue suit that had seen better days. He stood at the front of the stage with twelve staff sitting in a horseshoe shape behind him.

They had to say the Lord's Prayer, and then all the children sat on the floor with their legs crossed. The Head, Mr Davies, told the pupils that these were the evacuated children from London they had been told about, and reminded them why they were there. After that they began to be allocated to classes. Rose and Arnold thought everyone talked funny; funnier still, it turned out that the Welsh children thought the new arrivals sounded funny, too…

After a few days Rose wrote a longer letter to their parents.

Dear Mum and Dad

You probably know, we are here in a place called Gower in Wales with Mr and Mrs Morgan. They seem quite nice, and we have our own rooms. The house is in the countryside, and they have a lovely dog called Prince. We are trying to be very well behaved, but we miss you and the family so much. When can we come home? The toilet is outside, so we don't go much, and Friday night is bath night and hair washing. They have a big tin bath that we have to fill with kettles of hot water, and then I go first and Arnold after me. They put the bath in front of the fire, so it is quite warm. We go to school and a lot of our friends are there too.

Mum and Dad, Mr and Mrs Morgan go to church on Sundays, and they want us to go with them. What shall we do? They say we can't stay in the house on our own, but we don't want to upset God. How is Zeider? How is our little sister? And how are our Uncles and Aunts and cousins? We miss you so much, please don't leave us here too long.

Love from Rose and Arnold xx

It turned out that Mrs Morgan had already written, and their parents had said it was alright for them to go to church, so they went the following Sunday. Although they had not been brought up to be very observant of the Jewish faith, they still felt embarrassed to be in a church. Arnold said he thought that if he didn't actually say the name of Jesus, God would forgive them for being there. They got a letter back from their parents in Rachel's lovely handwriting.

Dear Rose and Arnold

We miss you so much too, and we hope it won't be too long before it is safe for you to come home again. I am going to live in a place called Truro with your little sister, Jeanette. A nice lady down there has agreed to take us both, so only your Dad will remain at home. We are still not sure if your cousins are going away. They would have to go with their Mums, like us. I think they should do it, and Zeider is very angry that they haven't made up their minds. He says it could be dangerous for young children here in London.

I already heard from Mrs Morgan. Don't worry, it's ok to go to the church; while you live in their home, you must have respect for what the Morgans do. Make sure you eat what you are given and behave yourselves. We will all be back together again soon.

All our love,
Mum and Dad xxx

The children did settle down as the days went past. They were able to see their friends and they quite liked the animals, but not the smelly ones. Prince the dog looked on them as friends and they took him for long walks.

Mrs Morgan made nice food and Mr Morgan, when he was home, just sat in the corner smoking his pipe and reading the paper. He smiled sometimes, but not often. Mrs Morgan said her husband had fought in the last war, and had come back quite different, which the children didn't really understand, but they did know she was trying to reassure them. However kind she was, though, as the weeks turned into months, Rose and Arnold grew terribly homesick and kept writing to ask when they could come home.

Life was strange in Acton too, without Ray and the children. Minna decided to stay at home with Lou, so most evenings Leizar and Monty would have dinner with them.

In November that year they were sitting round the wireless after dinner, anxious to know how the war was going.

'This is the BBC Home Service.

It is reported from Berlin that Jewish shops, homes and businesses have been attacked and ransacked. Eyewitnesses say that many Jews have been murdered, synagogues defiled, and graveyards violated. German radio is calling it Kristallnacht, meaning Night of Broken Glass, and it follows reports that Jews have been targeted all over Germany and Poland.

'A broch!' Leizar had his head in his hands. 'This is terrible. Where will it end?'

Monty was shaking his head, causing the ash from the cigarette in his mouth to drip down the front of his waistcoat. Without removing it from his mouth, he added, 'I heard the Nazis were raiding Jewish homes and taking the families away to work camps.'

The Domanskys were full of trepidation and fear. They had no way of knowing who among their family or friends still remained in Germany, and what had happened to them.

Even worse, it seemed that the war was coming to Britain, and that London would be the prime target.

Leizar was worried. He needed to keep his family as safe as possible, and that meant getting them out of the city. 'We have to talk,' he said. 'Lena, help Minna put the little ones to bed and come back.'

When they returned, he said 'Look, bombs are dropping all over Europe and the Germans are advancing on both fronts. Lou and Minna, I know you didn't want the little ones to join the evacuation program, but you must get them out of harm's way. We can pick up property for next to nothing now, go and look for a place outside London. At least you can be away from the worst of the bombing. You can't leave these children here.'

They could see the sense in it, and the family had some cash saved. They started looking.

They found a house in Richmond, a leafy town to the south-west of London. They felt it was far enough not to be a central target, but still near enough that they could stay in touch when the war was over. The truth was they had no idea how far out the bombing would stretch, but Leizar thought it reasonable to expect that the Luftwaffe would target infrastructure in the centre, rather than quiet suburbs, and he also wanted to remain in touch.

He arranged for them to have Anderson bomb shelters dug out in the gardens of all the houses. These were constructed of corrugated iron, partially underground. The roof and walls were covered in soil. They were recommended as protection from flying shrapnel, but of course not from a direct hit. The government supplied them at a subsidised cost of £7 each. Leizar bought three. They could accommodate up to six people, who were encouraged to run into them whenever there was an air raid. Lena swore that she would rather die than go into a smelly, damp hole under the ground. Leizar ignored her.

In May 1940, the Prime Minister Neville Chamberlain resigned, after misleading the country into thinking he had made a deal with Hitler, and Winston Churchill became Prime Minister.

So far, only young men aged 20 to 23 years had been conscripted to join the armed forces, but Leizar warned it wouldn't stop there. He told Monty, Jack and Lou that it was highly likely they would be called up.

He was right again, and shortly afterwards the government announced that all men between the ages of 18 and 41 would now be required to do National Service and join the war effort. This included both of his sons and his son-in-law.

Everyone knew that the lives of the conscripts would be on the line. They were likely to be at the front of the battle lines, because they were the most expendable. All sorts of rumours abounded about how you could get out of it, ranging from physically injuring yourself, to 'joining the Trotters' Regiment', in other words, simply not turning up, running away from your usual haunts and hiding. The latter would lead to a charge of desertion, and imprisonment, but the wives said it might be worth it if the men didn't have to go into battle.

But Leizar knew there was really only one way out of it. Unless you were employed in a key industry such as baking, farming, medicine, or engineering, you would need to be declared medically unfit.

Minna called and said she had heard there was a friendly GP in Richmond, who would write a letter stating why, in his opinion, his patient was unfit.

'I know all about this,' said Leizar. 'Believe me, doctors generally won't deliberately lie to the government, or they could get struck off. I've seen this before. The best you will get from a risky doctor is a letter saying the patient has 'general debility.' These military doctors are not stupid; that won't wash with them for a minute.'

All three of them were required to attend a medical centre in Watford to assess their fitness. They arranged to meet up there on the appointed day. When they arrived, they were shown into a large building with several doors marked 'Examination Room.' They were told to sit in the general waiting area, and wait for their name to be called.

There were a lot of men waiting, a few with bandages around various parts of their bodies, one or two had walking sticks and limps, which, when they stood, they sometimes forgot.

The Domanskys smiled, remembering Leizar's words, as one by one, the bandaged men came out with their bandages removed, and the limpers without their walking sticks.

But Lou told them he had a friend who was a pharmacist. He had given him a liquid to take an hour before the examination. He took it and it brought him out in spots all over. Everybody moved away from him, and he was left sitting on his own.

This was one occasion when Lou's thick accent worked to his advantage. The doctor called him in and was alarmed when he saw the rash.

'When did these spots come up?' said the doctor.

Lou deliberately made his accent worse, 'Ven I vos vaurking.'

'You were walking? Where were you walking?'

'Ney, ney, I vos *vorlking*' Lou said louder, as if the doctor might understand if he shouted. 'I vos *vorlking, vorlking* in my *vorlkshop.*'

'Oh, you mean you were *working*. When was this?'

'Vot you mean ven iss? Diss is now.'

'Oh dear, I mean when was it you were working, and the spots came up?' The doctor was getting frustrated, and he had a queue of men waiting outside.

'I vos vorlking in de vorlkshop mit de shears unt de pepper…'

'Ah! You were working with pepper?'

'Ney, ney,' said Lou condescendingly, 'Not a pepper - pepper! Pattern pepper!'

This went on for a while with the doctor trying to understand Lou, and Lou deliberately misunderstanding, and thickening his accent. In the end, the doctor sent him home, charging him to return in two days.

That was a blow, because Lou didn't have any more of the liquid and of course, all the spots had gone in two days.

The three men were all at the upper age of conscription, and they all received the grade of 'C' – which meant fit for home service only. They were all to report for duty to 10th Buckinghamshire Battalion, Iver Heath. Monty and Jack were deployed as Air Raid Patrollers. Their duty would be to go to bomb sites after an air raid and assist the wounded and homeless.

Recognising that Lou's language skills posed a difficulty, it was decided that he should be deployed in a support role. Due to his skill as a tailor, he was given a role in the supply factory making uniforms, not so very different from his civilian job. Leizar was pleased that his boys were not being sent into the teeth of the battle, and yet still performing important roles in the war effort.

Poland had fallen quickly to the German invasion and by mid-1940 they had swept through Belgium and the Netherlands and they were already threatening France. The war was not going well for the allies. At the same time Hitler invaded Norway and Denmark. Then came the major shock for the Domanskys.

In preparation for Hitler's invasion of Britain, in September 1940 the Blitz started. The Luftwaffe relentlessly bombed London and other major cities day and night. The families were grateful for the Anderson shelters. Every time the sirens sounded, they would run down into the shelter and huddle together. A full night's sleep was unheard of. They began to dread the sound of those sirens, each time they started up warning of a yet another imminent air raid.

Only Leizar and Lena remained in the house in Acton, and Monty was able to come home from time to time. One night when he was there, they had returned to the house after the 'all clear' had sounded at 2.30 am. They had just gone back to bed, and Monty was just dropping off to sleep when the awful sound of the sirens started up again. He jumped out of bed and ran to Lena's room. She was still fast asleep. 'Lena, *geshvint* – quick, get up!' he shook her awake and the first thing she did was slowly to reach for a cigarette.

He ran into Leizar, and nearly tripped over him. He was on the floor writhing in pain.

He could hardly talk. 'Monty… I can't… move. The pain… *Oy a broch*. The pain.'

'What happened, papa?'

'The sirens… I jumped out of bed. My back. *Oy veh*… my back.'

The siren sounds were at their loudest, and Monty could already hear the whine of the Messerschmitts and the Stuka bombers approaching. 'Lena, help me, we've got to get him downstairs.'

But Leizar was having none of it. 'Just get me back on the bed. You go… I'll be alright.' The explosions had started, and they knew this was a serious raid.

Lena turned to go. But Monty became very calm, 'Lena stop, I'm not leaving him here. We must get him out.'

Leizar started shouting 'Go, go… or we will all be in danger.' But the Domansky stubbornness had risen in Monty. He said nothing and just grabbed Leizar under the arms. He told Lena to take his feet. Leizar had lost a lot of weight which worked in their favour.

With Leizar shouting to be left alone, they manhandled him out of the room, and they were halfway down the stairs when there was a blinding flash of light, followed by a massive explosion, and the windows blew out. They stumbled and nearly dropped Leizar who was still shouting for them to go. Their ears were ringing and there was debris everywhere.

Monty was now dragging Leizar, because Lena had been hit by some flying glass. He managed to get him to the bottom of the stairs and out into the garden. Lena followed, bleeding now from cuts to her cheek and arms, and between them they got him into the shelter.

It was dark and damp. Monty lit the candle. He managed to get Leizar onto the camp bed and then took a look at Lena's injuries. She was shaking with shock, but luckily the injuries were superficial. He did his best from the first aid kit they kept down there.

Explosions were going off all round them and they had to shout to hear themselves, but the air-raid was mercifully short and after about half an hour, the All Clear sounded.

Monty ventured up the steps. The smell of cordite hit him straight away. There had been a direct hit on the house next door, and not much of it was standing, dust and smoke was swirling around.

He was astonished to see a large bomb sticking out of the ground no more than a few yards from the bunker. '*Gishvint*, Lena. We've to get out!'

Again, they had to manage Leizar, who seemed a bit more able to help this time. Monty was sweating profusely now. At any moment that bomb could go off and blast them all to kingdom come.

They got back in the house, which mercifully had not been hit except for the bomb that had struck nearby, and blown out the windows. He left Lena with Leizar. 'You'll have to look after him. I have to report for duty. Give him aspirin from the box – but not too much. I'll get back as soon as I can.'

He hurried to the Army barracks; he knew there would be many injuries, and probably deaths to deal with. It had been a terrible night.

They had to wait until morning before it was possible to find a bomb disposal officer, all the while knowing that if it went off, they might not survive the blast, and yet they couldn't move Leizar very far from the danger.

Monty managed to persuade an Army doctor to have a look at his father late the next day. They had been feeding him aspirin to deaden the pain and he had been passing in and out of consciousness. He wouldn't eat anything, and his face was ashen grey. After the doctor had administered an injection, a little colour returned, and Lena then administered the 'Jewish penicillin' – chicken soup!

Monty knew from his rounds as an ARP that the shelters saved many lives, the bombing was relentless, and it seemed the air raid sirens were going off all the time.

No sooner was the 'all clear' sounded after an attack than the air raid warning would sound again. Monty and Lena decided they would not be able to get Leizar down in the shelter again, so they resolved to stay in the house next time and take their chances. They made up makeshift beds downstairs and constructed a 'shelter' under the stairs using the table and pieces of furniture.

The Blitz was a very hard time. Death and destruction were all around, and Monty, Lena and Leizar, like most people in or around the cities, became accustomed to living their daily lives in between the burning buildings and the piles of rubble, with limited food.

Homes that were still standing were ordered to be 'blacked out'- curtains drawn and no lights visible at all times. Monty tried to nail cardboard where the windows had been, to comply. They wondered about Lou and Jack and their families. Had they all survived? The phone lines were down, and there was no way to communicate.

The radio reports said the London bombing was mainly focused on the centre and certain strategic targets, factories, dockyards, airports, and the suburbs were only suffering from misdirected bombs, so they hoped the families that had moved out were not experiencing the same level of fear and disruption.

Monty remained deployed as an ARP in the local area. Other houses in the street were hit and reduced to rubble, forcing survivors to live in shelters or the remains of their homes. Churches and schools helped with accommodation. After each raid he had to assist in gathering up the wounded and dead, and dealing with people who'd been made homeless.

He saw horrors on the streets and on many occasions, they had to lift heavy objects to free someone who was trapped. Although he was short, he was very strong.

The RAF was deployed in 'dog fights' overhead and they would sometimes see planes on fire, or being shot down, both German and British. This went on day after day, week after week, month after month. It was very demoralising. They listened to the voice of Winston Churchill making rousing speeches, but then the bombs would start again.

They endured this from September until May 1941 with the RAF fighting valiantly and inflicting very heavy casualties on the Luftwaffe. They heard that Hitler had successfully occupied Lou's home country, Hungary, together with Romania and

Bulgaria, and earlier that German troops had overrun Yugoslavia and Greece. The German war machine seemed unstoppable.

Churchill was on the radio a lot and he made much of the fact that Hitler had found Britain more resistant than he had thought. There was a rumour that he had turned his attention eastwards, toward his biggest target, Russia.

Churchill's broadcasts were inspirational, and did much to foster the fighting spirit, especially when they heard that France was fully occupied, and the Allied troops had to be evacuated from Dunkirk. The Germans were now only 22 miles away across the Channel.

Leizar heard stories about Jews being rounded up all over Europe and taken to concentration camps. He was worried that this would happen if Britain fell and was occupied.

But in December 1941, they heard on the news that Japan had attacked America at Pearl Harbour, which led to the United States declaring war on Japan, and Germany declaring war on the United States.

Very soon after that news, Monty saw American bases being established around London. Leizar was following the progress of the war very closely, and this news lifted his spirits. He was further encouraged when, in 1942, with Germany preoccupied with the Eastern front and the Americans fighting the war with Japan in the Pacific, the intensity of the bombing in London diminished.

His fear of an occupation of Britain diminished a little, which reduced his dread that Britain could be invaded at any time, and that would be the end of the whole family. He had kept his thoughts to himself, but now at least, he had hope.

Leizar missed his family and the grandchildren. Travel was very difficult, but Lou and Minna's family - who became known collectively as 'Richmond,' - did manage to come and visit.

It wasn't easy to pick their way through the blocked-off streets, but when they turned the corner at the end of the road, the children saw Leizar standing by the front gate. *'Zeider, zeider!'* they shouted and ran all the way to him. Minna and Lou were shocked to see how Leizar had deteriorated. He had lost weight and could hardly walk.

Lena took them to one side. 'I'm worried about him. Since Mama went, he hardly eats.'

Minna was frowning, 'He's so pale, are you sure he's not ill?'

'Doctors don't make routine house calls,' replied Lena. 'They've got their work cut out with the results of the bombing, but Monty got a military doctor to have a look at him. He put his back out during the bombing, and he has painkillers for it, but the doctor says he needs to eat. He's malnourished.

'He got very excited over the Mosley thing, and got himself arrested, and the war has definitely focused his mind. I just wish he would eat! He gets very depressed.'

It was a good visit, and the grandchildren seemed to cheer them all up. They couldn't stay long for fear of a raid and the difficulty of transport. Leizar was very sad to see them go and, although he didn't say anything, it made him miss the family he had left in Poland and Germany.

Bombing raids continued, but with less intensity than during the Blitz. People had been conditioned to the death and destruction all around them, so the odd raid here and there was taken in their stride.

But in June 1944 Leizar, Monty and Lena heard the voice of Winston Churchill telling Britain that the British and American troops had taken part in a massive assault on the French coast at Normandy. The Germans had been pushed off the beaches by the heroes of the Allied army and the RAF. Thousands of vessels had taken part and the Allies now had a stronghold in France. The Domanskys and their neighbours all ran out in the streets to cheer at the tops of their voices. Even Leizar managed to hobble out on his walking stick.

Since the bombing had eased off and the tide of the war seemed to be turning, Leizar felt it was a good time to speak to Monty about something that had been on his mind for some time. 'Jack sent me a letter, the house next door to them in Northolt has become available. Monty, it's a nice quiet suburb on the outskirts of London and not nearly such a dangerous place as Acton.

'Jack says people are buying up these properties during the war for *goornisht*, very little money. We could buy it together, what do you think?'

Monty didn't hesitate long, 'I could apply for an area transfer, but then we could bring Ray and the children back, couldn't we?'

'Yes, the family could be together.'

Lena said she would be happy to get out of the hell hole she perceived as Acton, as long as she could have her own room.

Jack and Lainchen made all the arrangements, and it only took a few weeks. They left the keys to the Acton house with the agent to sell when it became possible, and with the help of Jack and Lainchen, they moved.

———————※———————

Monty couldn't wait to see his family.

He really had difficulty writing in English, but he did his best. He wrote to Rachel right away.

Ray,

Ive got sum good noos! Papa and me, we bought the house next to Jack in Northolt its a luvly qite little subub, away from the bombing. Wit Papa and Lena, we moved in already.

So get Jeanette redy, tank the Penhaligons and get on the next trane home! The fones are still down, so send me a tellygram to let me no wot train yor getting and I will meet you at Padingten.

Do me a fayvor Ray. You no Im not much good at riteing. Will you rite to Mrs Morgan and to Rose and Arnold. Tel them to do the same for them. Tell them also to send a telagram so I can meet them too.

I cant wayt to see you all.

All my luv
Monty xx

As he stood on the platform, he wondered how things would be. He had not seen his family for nearly five years. And they had been horrible frightening and long years. Finally, the train pulled in and he saw his wife schlepping two suitcases with a beautiful little girl by her side. He ran towards her, and they embraced.

He was somewhat disappointed that Jeanette did not remember him, and that, when they arrived home, she could not remember her grandfather, either. She was only two when they went away, and now she was seven - a beautiful little girl.

When Rose and Arnold returned, to the amusement of the family, they had developed quite strong Welsh accents. Arnold was now a fine young man of seventeen and Rose was fifteen. They were very excited to see their new home.

Although it was a terraced house, it had two main bedrooms, a small 'box' room, and a bathroom with toilet. There was a large dining room, lounge and kitchen downstairs, and a very long garden, that the children thought was great.

Monty had got their furniture brought over from Acton and arranged the bedrooms. He and Ray had one main bedroom and the girls had the other, Leizar had the box room and Arnold had to make do with a bed in the dining room.

But they had made an error. Jack had told them it was nice and quiet in Northolt. What he did not tell them was that it was very close to a major RAF base, and therefore a German target. No wonder the place was so cheap!

When he found out, Monty went next door to Jack. 'Why didn't you tell me?'

'Listen Monty, it's not an important base, and the war will be over soon. Don't worry about it. We'll all be safe here.'

Ray was getting to grips with the kitchen. Together with the children they had spent much of the day trailing the shops to buy food and provisions. It was difficult because they needed everything from scratch, and the shops had very little. But she was extremely resourceful at making a little go a long way.

It wasn't long after they got home that delicious aromas of cooking were making everyone feel hungry.

In the dining room they had inherited from the previous owners was a full-size snooker table with a wooden cover which they had converted into a massive dining table. 'Monty, tell Jack and Lainchen to bring the girls and we will all have supper tonight together as a family.'

'What are you making?'

'That *braten* you like.' This was a sort of meat loaf. She mixed a little minced meat with matzo meal and onions, then she roasted it with onion and tomato gravy, and served it with roast potatoes and vegetables. It was a lot of work, but she could feed the whole family with it.

After they had all eaten and everyone said how nice it was to be together again, the little ones went to bed. Ray had found some coal in the bunker in the garden, and she lit a fire in the grate. They sat in the warmth around the radio and tuned in to BBC News.

'The war with Germany is progressing well, and the occupying forces in France are in retreat. The allied army and air forces have now regained most of France and will be pushing into Belgium. On the Eastern front, Soviet tanks have gained superiority over the Germans, and the Red Army is gaining ground through Poland.

In the House of Commons today, in answer to questions, the Prime Minister said he was optimistic that an end to the war may be in sight.

However, the War office issued a warning today, that the Germans have developed a type of rocket bomb which does not need to be dropped from an airplane. Intelligence reports that these are indiscriminate and cannot be controlled. The RAF together with Ground Artillery are alert to this threat, and are confident they can be shot down.

As the family crowded round the radio to hear the announcement, they became aware of a loud whining noise. Looking out, Leizar saw what looked like a group of small fat aeroplanes with no cockpit. One of them, nearest to the streets they lived in suddenly went silent, and dropped like a stone. The deafening explosion demolished houses a little further down the street.

Monty was told these were V1 flying bombs, or what the army called Doodlebugs. They were simply pointed at a target and given sufficient fuel to reach it, but they would drop indiscriminately when the fuel ran out. The RAF base was clearly the local target, but the bombs could drop anywhere.

They were truly terrifying, and the Domanskys became familiar with the ominous whining sound whenever they were approaching. Once or twice when the sound stopped overhead, they thought the bomb was about to drop, but then the engine would start up again and fly on a little further. This was the most dangerous time for Leizar and the family. They had brought the evacuees back and although the news was that the Allies were winning the war, the Germans had found a new way to wreak havoc and terror among the British.

Monty and Jack had been re-deployed as Air Raid Patrolmen locally and every morning when the air raids had been going all night and the 'all clear' was sounded, Rachel and the children would come up out of the Anderson shelter and wait with fingers crossed for Monty to return, praying that he would be alright.

Lainchen and her children were doing the same for Jack. When they did return, they were usually covered in dust and debris from the bomb sites.

One morning when Rachel and Lainchen were both anxiously waiting by their front gates, staring at the end of the road, they had the shock of their lives when Jack and Monty appeared in the distance, covered in blood from head to toe. Thank God, they both seemed to be walking normally and did not seem badly injured, but clearly some terrible tragedy had occurred, and they had been involved in the rescue.

Rachel gasped and Lainchen let out a squeal of anguish, 'Oh my God, what has happened?' They ran up the road towards them.

As they approached, they were expecting to see cuts and bruises and they were already thinking of how they could treat them from the first aid kits they had.

'Rachel was breathless, 'What is it Monty, where are you hurt?' whereupon both men started to laugh. The wives were taken aback at such a strange reaction.

It turned out that they had been called to the Heinz factory, which had been hit by doodlebugs, and while they were helping to extricate a person trapped under a beam, another bomb had hit the tomato stock and covered them all in the fall-out. They thought it was very funny. Rachel and Lainchen were less amused.

Although they were losing ground rapidly on the battlefield, the German war machine still operated, and after a couple of months, they had developed a much more sophisticated version of the doodlebug. The V2 rockets effected even more devastation and they were much more accurately targeted. There was a silver lining for the Domansky though, because the better targeted bombs were falling on the base, and there was not so much danger of a stray bomb falling on the house.

Incredibly, during this time Rachel became pregnant again, perhaps due to the joy of being reunited with her husband. But it was a big surprise to Leizar. It had been eight years since Jeanette was born and Rachel was now 44 years old. It was not uncommon for women to conceive later in life, but Leizar was concerned, and he nagged her to look after herself and not spend so much time on her feet in the kitchen.

There was very little available in the way of medical supervision, but Monty nagged the doctor to come and see her. 'You need to look after her,' he said to Monty. 'Shlepping up and down to the shelter is not good, and she needs good food – she is eating for two.'

'It's not easy. I can't leave her in the house during an air raid, and tell me where all this good food is! But she's had three children already, and she's never had a problem.'

'Yes, but Jeanette was born eight years ago, and now Ray is 44. You have grown up children, they can help. Look after Monty, it's important. I'll try to call again in a month or so'

Having lost so much of his family already, and knowing that childbirth did not always go well in the family, Leizar was worried, and he fussed around Ray, waving his stick and constantly telling her to go to bed. Exhortations to which she did not of course, listen.

The following year, the news was getting better, and the bombing was becoming more sporadic. On the news they heard that British and American troops had entered Germany from the West and the Russians from the East. It seemed that Hitler was defeated.

On the 8th May 1945 Victory in Europe was proclaimed and Churchill marked the occasion by declaring a public holiday. The newspapers shouted it from the headlines, the National Anthem could be heard often, together with Land of Hope and Glory.

The Domansky family joined the neighbours and there was again dancing in the streets, but this time many of the streets were completely devastated and in ruins. Nevertheless, the relief was palpable after six years of war and despite all they had been through, people were hugging and kissing total strangers.

Even Ray tried to join in, but at eight months pregnant, it was not easy for her, and Leizar was worried all the time. He got her inside as soon as he could. The celebrations continued well into the night and Arnold and Rose took their little sister and their cousins and joined in the singing, dancing and firework display parties.

The partying was going on in Richmond as it was everywhere over the country. Lou was not one for partying really, but Minna, Simon and Rita were all in the streets. It was a little more reserved in Richmond, which had not suffered as badly as Northolt. They tried to call the Domanskys, but all the lines were jammed.

At Leizar's behest, Ray and Monty went to bed early, but it was hard to sleep with all the noise going on. In the early hours, the partying had abated somewhat, but Ray was still awake. She couldn't find a comfortable position.

About 2am she woke her husband who was snoring rhythmically. She gave him a dig in the ribs, which he did not appreciate. 'What was that, Monty?' She sounded alarmed. 'I heard a strange noise in the house.'

Monty awoke with a start. 'What, what?' he murmured, as he rubbed his eyes. 'Listen,' she said. And they heard a ticking sound in the house which seemed to be getting louder all the time. Monty was wide awake by now and could clearly hear the noise. He got out of bed and fumbled around to find his glasses, but then they heard the sound of footsteps coming up the stairs.

Monty had an old ceremonial sword he had kept from the first war, nobody knew where he had got it, and it was in a cupboard in his bedroom. He grabbed it, Ray was crying and very frightened.

Monty raised the sword above his head as he went to the bedroom door in his pyjamas. He put his hand on the handle, paused and took a deep breath. He flung the door open shouting at the top of his voice. 'Get out of my house!'

Arnold, who was standing immediately behind the door screamed at the sudden appearance of his father in his pyjamas with a sword raised above his head, shouting at him. At that point the ceiling fell down covering them both with dust and plaster!

It turned out that the vibrations from the nearby explosions over a continued period, had loosened the old 'lath and plaster' ceiling lining, and the ticking had been the sound of it gradually coming away. Arnold and Rose had put Jeanette to bed earlier and returned in the early hours. Arnold was about to get into bed downstairs, when he heard the ticking sound. He had gone upstairs to investigate. Although they were both relieved, they were covered in white powder from head to toe. They looked at each other and couldn't help laughing.

Leizar and the girls came out on to the landing, and they all stood laughing at the sight. Their Monty and Arnold white all over, with white dust swirling round them, and Monty with his ceremonial sword.

The pregnancy was not going well. Ray was exhausted most of the time, but thankfully there was no more bombing, and she was pleased they no longer had to *schlep* up and down into the smelly shelter.

On the 24th June, she started to bleed, and her waters broke. She was in a lot of pain. Leizar was very alarmed; memories of the past coming back to him.

Thankfully, things were slowly beginning to recover in the area, and Monty was able to find an ambulance to take her to Park Royal hospital where she delivered their fourth child, David, designated a peace baby. This time the birth was not easy. Ray suffered greatly and Monty was no help at the hospital, walking up and down and chain smoking. However, he was delighted with another healthy son, and Leizar was relieved when it was all over. Ray had to stay in hospital for five days and needed an operation to correct a prolapse.

CHAPTER 44

THE HORRIBLE PEACE

Times were very hard for everyone after the war, and the Domansky family was no exception. The war had bankrupted the country and almost everything was rationed, most importantly, food. For families with children and elderly or sick people, it was difficult to obtain sufficient nutritious and healthy food. But there was a general optimistic attitude which came with the relief.

News started to come through of unimaginable horrors that had been found when the concentration camps were opened up. Everyone was glued to the wireless and horrific pictures began to appear in the newspapers of scenes of death and mutilation that had taken place. It was scarcely believable.

People had been rounded up and taken from their homes in occupied countries, including a very large proportion of Jews, who had been treated like animals; starved and murdered.

Leizar was desperate to find out what had happened to his family in Poland and Germany. So he started to investigate. The Red Cross were encouraging those seeking loved ones to contact them and they would do their best to provide contact links.

It took some time, but eventually he managed to make contact with Pyotr Borin, the cleric in Poland and he asked Pyotr to see if he could find any information. He was very helpful and made enquiries with contacts in Warsaw. The news was not good.

My dear Leizar

How good to hear from you, and I am pleased that you and your family have finally made your home in England. Thank God you did not stay in Poland or Germany. I am afraid to say that to be Jewish in any of the Eastern European countries during the war was almost certainly a death sentence. Here is some background from my personal experience.

Truly Poland did not put up much resistance to the German invasion. As you know, we are a country that is used to being occupied. The German army only took a few days to control the country. Worse, the Russians moved in from the East and the fighting was terrible, millions died. As a cleric, I managed to survive, but people's homes were destroyed, and I lost many friends.

The German officers were under instructions from Berlin to start a 'cleansing' operation straight away. Bank accounts of Jews were seized, and Jewish establishments had to display a Star of David. All Jews had to wear an armband at all times.

You asked specifically about your sister Marcia and her husband who were living in Warsaw and it is not good news. In 1940 all Jews were rounded up and placed in a ghetto with high walls all round, in the centre of Warsaw.

I found someone who knew your sister. She said the SS had arrested them and bundled them into a van. Marcia was screaming. They were taken to the ghetto. It was mostly Jews, but also some Catholics, Romanies and even some Poles were effectively imprisoned there.

In 1942 the Germans emptied the ghetto, and the prisoners were loaded on to railway trucks and taken away to camps in Treblinka and Auschwitz. No one knew what had become of them, but we are hearing stories of mass murders.

I am very sorry to say, my dear Leizar, I don't think you will see your sister again. I regret that I have to give you this bad news, but at the same time I'm glad that you and your family have survived.

I wish you all health and strength.

Best regards,

Pyotr

Leizar had read about the Warsaw ghetto. The Jewish population of Warsaw was 360,000 and they were rounded up and placed in an area where previously only a few hundred people had lived.

Although he had feared the worst, to read this stark letter hit Leizar very hard. He took to his bed and hardly ate anything for several days. His breathing was already affected by the ash and pollution as a result of the attacks from the doodlebugs and V2 rocket bombings.

Although the devastation in Central London was worse, and Acton had been very badly hit, their close proximity to the RAF base in Northolt meant the area had still suffered. At times the air had been full of dust and ash.

Leizar's breathing started to labour quite badly at times. He was often heard breathing noisily and he had developed a persistent cough. He was heavily dependent on his walking stick and now he didn't talk much either. It was clearly quite an effort for him to do so.

Telephone lines were starting to be re-established and that gave Jack, Monty, Lena and Minna the ability to discuss what might be best for their father. The new baby was keeping him up at night and Richmond was a much quieter place than Northolt. They agreed with Lou and Minna that he should move there.

Leizar was now even more anxious to find out what had become of the family in Berlin, but of course, at this time great security surrounded all postal services and it was extremely difficult to communicate with anyone inside Germany. Hitler was said to have committed suicide, but they had not found the body.

Leizar wrote to Frau Schmitt at the school and amazingly, she answered.

Dear Leizar,

I was so happy to receive the letter from you, and especially that you and the Domansky children managed to escape both wars and Oh! They now have children of their own. I have such fond memories of them.

Things have been dreadful in Berlin. Bombings were relentless, and the apartment block you lived in is now nothing but rubble. Almost the whole street has been destroyed. Your magazine was closed down early on, and the building is destroyed, but I'm afraid I have no idea what happened to any of the people connected with it.

The part of Berlin where we live is now occupied by the Russians, and they make the rules. They are not very kind to Germans.

I know your uncle and your brother got out with their families, I hope they are alright, and I am afraid the owner of the block, I think his name was Ernst, he died when the building was hit.

I am so sorry, I don't have any better news for you, Leizar. Give my love to your beautiful wife, and keep well.

My very best,
Frau Schmitt

PS, A very strange thing happened. I was contacted by a man called Pyotr Borin, a Russian asking after you. He said you were a friend of Trotsky, the Communist. I wonder if you ever heard from him?

This was a seminal moment for Leizar. He got Jack to take him to the library, and there he looked up the biography of Trotsky. At first he could not believe his eyes. There in black and white, it was confirmed that his original name was *Lev Davidovich Bronstein.*

But, when he thought about it, he remembered the intense young Russian, so focused at such an early age, on changing the world. Yes! It made sense.

No wonder the authorities in Glasgow had been so concerned when they heard Trotsky was claiming to be a friend of Leizar! And yet, this man had influenced the path along which Leizar had taken his family. Who knows? - without the time they spent together in Warsaw, the Domanskys' life may have been quite different. They may have remained in Poland and perhaps not even survived. Thanks to the man called Trotsky.

———————✳———————

By 1947 communication throughout the world was beginning to improve as the countries tried to haul themselves back to some semblance of order. Families were desperately trying to contact or discover the fate of misplaced loved ones.

Leizar's breathing grew worse, and the doctor had to come and give him injections to ease it. On his visits, the doctor could be heard shouting at Leizar, 'You must give up smoking cigarettes, they are killing you. It's no good me coming round and injecting you so you can breathe, and then you light up a cigarette and make it worse again.'

Leizar was infuriating. As was his way now, he just stared at the doctor with a very stern face and said nothing. Every now and then he would nod. And when the doctor left, he would light up another cigarette. In fact, after a doctor's visit he would smoke more in defiance.

A year before, Leizar had applied to the American Embassy to see if they could find his brother, Duvid. He knew they had gone to New York with Uncle Shmuel, Aunt Chava and their family. It took a year, but out of the blue came a letter from the Embassy with an address for Duvid and Esther Domansky living in the Queens suburb of New York. Leizar wrote immediately and received a reply a week later.

My dear brother,

How wonderful to hear from you and to know you are all alive and well, and you have escaped the dreadful war. I can't believe the children are all grown up and have children of their own. So many years have passed. I would love to see you all again.

Uncle Shmuel and Aunt Chava passed away some years ago, but Esther and I are well. With Herschel's financial help we fled from Berlin, and travelled directly to New York. There were so many refugees arriving, especially Jews and Irish. This really is the land of opportunity, Leizar. If you work hard, you can earn good money, and everyone respects you. Unfortunately, the opposite is also true, and if you have no money, nobody will care.

We have a nice house in Queens. We have four grown up children, and six grandchildren. We get nachas from most of them (and a little aggravation, sometimes), and we have a Doctor, a Dentist and two engineers in the family. My youngest son is a journalist, Leizar – he writes for the New York Times – following in your footsteps!

The other two boys fought in the war against Japan and returned safely, thank God, but other than that, the war didn't really touch us here in the USA. But we heard about these appalling stories coming out of Germany, horrors beyond belief.

We are so sad to hear about Chaya and Marcia. Do you know what happened to anyone else? I fear the worst!

But listen, we are delighted to hear from you. You must come visit. The ships don't take too long now, and I believe they are quite comfortable. A big hug for everyone there who knows us. Write again, and maybe you could take a photograph, so I can show the family?

With all our love,
Esther and Duvid (and all the family)

The world was shocked as the monstrous atrocities began to be detailed and verified. More reports and pictures came out from the concentration camps it and was gradually realised that the greatest crime against humanity in the history of the world had been perpetrated by the Nazis.

Gruesome pictures of emaciated bodies piled high in front of industrial diggers like so much rubbish. Gas ovens where bodies were burnt on an industrial scale. These camps were being discovered all over the occupied territories and the victims appeared to be mostly, but not limited to, Jews. There were reports of experimentation on humans kept in cruel and starving conditions.

The Germans had kept meticulous records of all the victims. Each had been given a number and their name and circumstances were logged together with their fate, which was usually death by firing squad or extermination by gas.

Names of victims were gradually released and Leizar and the family opened the papers each day with fear and trepidation. Sure enough in the first list of ten thousand names to be published from Auschwitz:

- Marcia Galitzer aged 53 – (Leizar's sister) – Shot in the head
- Joseph Galitzer aged 54 – (Marcia's husband) – Died of pneumonia and burned
- Chaim Galitzer aged 25 – (son) – Experimentation and burned
- Rebecca Galitzer aged 24 – (daughter) – Shot in the head
- Minky Galitzer aged 9 – (granddaughter) – Experimentation and burned
- Yitshok Peretz aged 65 – (Leizar's compatriot writer in Warsaw) - Gassed and burned

There followed lists from Bergen Belsen, Buchenwald, Dachau and Sobibor. The lists kept coming and the scale of this atrocity was shocking the world. These death camps had been established in many countries, but it seemed the biggest had been in Germany and occupied Poland. They even kept records of how many people were exterminated each day as if it was a production line at a factory. Auschwitz, at its peak, recorded a total of around 6,000 per day.

The list from Treblinka included:

- Ernst Schultz aged 65 – (the Berlin landlord) – Gassed and burned
- David Cohn aged 67 – (the magazine owner) – Gassed and burned
- Moishe Domansky aged 50 – (Leizar's brother) – Gassed and burned
- Sheila Domansky aged 48 – (his wife) – Gassed and burned
- Rosie Domansky aged 26 – (their daughter) – pregnant – Experimentation and burned.

The whole families of Leizar's other siblings, Harry, Molly and Sayde were all wiped out, including children and grandchildren.

This news took a further terrible toll on Leizar's health. Occasionally he had delighted in taking the children to school when he felt up to it. His health would no longer allow that, and he could hardly get out of bed. When he moved, he could hardly breathe. The decision for him to move to Richmond with Lena and Minna, meant that his daughters could look after him. He was mostly confined to his room and because he could no longer shout out in his old cantankerous way, when he wanted something he would bang on the floor with his stick. And he wouldn't stop banging until someone came to see what he wanted. This was very irritating and led to many Domansky family rows, but he didn't care. Monty thought the old man derived a little bit of pleasure from winding them up.

Although they cared greatly for their sick father, Lena and Minna objected to being treated as servants, but that didn't stop him, and each row took a further toll on him.

In the end, his mind started to wander, and he would imagine himself back in Kawetchka with his brother Mendel playing with a wheel and a stick, and with Ryfke making chulent. He died in his sleep on 26th June 1948, at the age of seventy-five.

———※———

Following Jewish tradition, Leizar was buried the very next day in the Jewish Cemetery in Streatham. It was a cold day for mid-summer with driving rain, and an awful day for a funeral. Family and friends crowded into the small prayer hall which had no heating, a cold stone floor and a damp and stale smell. Men and women stood on separate sides and the coffin was in the centre on a rickety barrow with a simple black cloth draped over it.

The rabbi conducted the traditional prayers, following which Jack and Monty recited the *kaddish* prayer for their departed father. They stood together with an arm around each other's shoulders and tears in their eyes. Lou stood with Minna and Lena, who were crying and sniffing into damp handkerchiefs. Ray had to stay with David.

They had all collaborated in writing some notes as a eulogy, and Minna had been nominated to read them out. She stood bravely at the lectern in front of the coffin, a diminutive figure dressed in black from head to toe, with a black scarf which she had ripped for *kriah,* the sign of mourning. Jack, Lena, Monty and Lou all stood beside her. She had to hold the paper very close to her face, and even then, struggled due to her very bad eyesight:

> *'Our Papa was our hero, but we didn't know it!' She moved the paper even closer to her face. 'We all had so many rows with him - especially Lena,' everyone smiled.*

> *'But he was usually right and now he has gone and there is a massive hole in our lives.'*

To make it worse, at this point, Minna started crying which meant she couldn't see at all… There was a long pause and Jack (whose eyesight was not much better) took the paper and held it up to his thick glasses, before continuing valiantly:

> *'Although Papa was only five foot one, until he lost our beautiful mama and became ill, he was a fighter through and through. He overcame so much in his life. He spoke English, Yiddish, German and Russian and he could write perfectly in all of them. Writing was his passion, and he was quite well-known for his views.*

Jack paused and blew his nose again:

> *Life was a massive struggle for Leizar Domansky. He was challenged at every turn throughout his life. From the shtetl in Galicia with all the vile pogroms and injustices they had to overcome every day, to the fights against Mosely and his Fascists before the war. Even his own wedding was defiled by the Cossacks. But the worst was when he*

had to watch his innocent brother hanged for something he did not do.

He went to Warsaw to write for the Socialist movement, and it was there he met our Mama. He invented the workers co-operative in our other Grandfather's factory. And then he was badly beaten by jealous workers.

Together with little Lena and Minna, they left Poland intending to go to America, but they got stuck in Glasgow, where Leizar was jailed for nothing, but he overcame that, and the family became British citizens. He then took the family to Berlin, where I was born, and where he opened a business, until he saw the war coming and got us all out again, back to London just before WW1.

Beside him all the time was our beautiful mama. Together they were not only the most wonderful parents, but there was nothing they couldn't overcome. They saved us all from two world wars.

Leizar was a man who made a difference… and he never, ever, ever gave up. And now he has gone to meet our lovely Mama, who was undoubtedly, the love of his life.'

Here Jack broke down and there were a few uncomfortable moments during which someone handed him a handkerchief with which he wiped his eyes and blew his nose noisily. He eventually composed himself.

'Papa used to say that God tests us with challenges, and you must keep your eyes on your goal; don't get distracted. You can achieve anything with guts and determination.

Finally, we ask those of you who knew him. Would you please spare a few moments to do us a great favour in his honour? Our children only remember their zeider from his latter years and mostly when he was ill.

So, we ask you this… Tell them your stories, those you know, and those you have heard. Tell them what a great man their zeider was. He was a wonderful role model for

*us all. And so as we say a final goodbye, here is something he told us over and over...
Never, ever, ever, give up!*

Every time someone bangs on the floor with a stick, we will think of our papa!'

They wheeled the coffin out to the graveyard and Monty and Jack recited the Kaddish again as it was gently lowered into the ground.

Dramatis personae

Marcia: *married Joseph Galitzer*

Moishe Dawid

Harry

Molly

Sayde

Children of Leizar Domansky

Lena: *married Morris Binstock*

Minna: *Married Leopold (Lou) Cohen*

Morris (Monty): *Married Rachel (Ray) Green*

Jacob (Jack): *Married Lainchen (Helen) Phelops*

BENJAMIN FAMILY

Moszek: *married Zelman (2) mother of Leizar*

Esther: *First wife of Dawid*

Moszek: *Second wife of Dawid*

Anna: *sister*

Rebecca: *Sister*

BLASS FAMILY

Ryfke: *Married Zelman*

Lena: *Mother of Ryfke*

Reuben: *Father of Ryfke*

OTHERS

Avram Groisse: *Friend on the ship*

Bryan Bell: *Pub Landlord - wife Rosie*

Chaim Farshinsky: *Farmer, Father of Gitte, Brother of Izabella*

Chana Bubitke: *Shiddach macher*

David Cohn: *German magazine owner*

Dmitri Belakov: *Russian Captain – sons Alexei and Igor*

Edvard Abramovski: *Founder of the Polish co-operative movement.-wife Zelda*

Ernst Cohn: *German landlord*

Frau Schmitt: *Teacher*

Gyorgy Berkov: *Solicitor*

Herschel Eisenbaum: *Father of Chaya*

Joseph Galitzer: *Pseudo Doctor*

Lev Davidovich Bronstein: *Russian Communist party member*

Manny Gold: *Factory Owner*

Mary Dunbar: *Midwife*

Maynard Campbell QC: *Barrister*

Menachim Cohain: *Family friend*

Menachim Ochter: *Father of Ada Ochter who marries Mendel*

Morris Binstock: *Married Lena*

Moshe Vasilinsky: *friend of Edvard Abramovski – wife Gitte*

Pyotr Borin: *Cleric and agent for travel*

Rabbi Cornbloom: *Glasgow*

Reb Bendle: *carpenter*

Rudi Vostok: *Translator*

Sian Rafferty: *Market Controller*

Sokrates Starynklewitz: *Mayor of Warsaw*

Yitshok L Peretz: *Famous writer and agitator*

GLOSSARY OF TERMS

Although I have tried to make the Yiddish terms obvious, or explained in the text, here is a glossary with, in many cases a fuller explanation of how the expression is used in the book. Yiddish is a hybrid language handed down verbally from generation to generation, so spellings and translations may vary slightly. It was rarely written.

Where the words used are German or Russian, it is noted.

A chazer bleibt a chazer: A pig is always a pig, ie, the leopard never changes his spots

A mama hot glezerne oygn: A mother has glass eyes, ie is blinkered about her children

A meesa meshineh oyf zey: A horrible death on them

A meesa meshineh oyf im: A horrible death on him

A viste pgire oyf dein!: He should die a dismal death like an animal

Ale tsorris vos ikh hob oyf mayn hartsn, zoln oysgeyn tsu zayn kop: All the troubles I have in my heart should go to his head

aleichem shalom: reply to sholem aleichem: Peace be with you, And with you, peace.

aliyah: Rise up. In this context, called to the reading of the Torah

alter dumkopf: Old fool

apfel strudel: Apple strudel

ark: The sacred cupboard where the Torah scrolls are stored

Az men shloft mit hint, shteyt men oyf mit fley: If you lay down with dogs, you get up with fleas

baal korei: Expert Torah reader - in the synagogue

bedeken: The ritual raising of the bride's veil, ostensibly to be sure it is the groom's intended.

balabusta: Home maker

balbattishe: One who makes a good home

bar: Son, as in Bar Mitzvah,

beshert: Fated, meant to be

bimah: Raised dais in a synagogue from where the Torah is read

boychik: Endearing term for young boy

braten: A way of serving meat, usually stewed with a thick gravy

bris milah: Ritual circumcision

brocha: Blessing

bubba: Grandmother

bubba meister: Story, often untrue, literally grandmother story

bubele: An endearing term for a person or child. But also a potato pancake

chai kak: Big Shit. Used to describe the receipt of nothing at all.

challah: Plaited bread

chanuka: Festival of lights, usually falls in December with the eight pronged candelabra

chazan: Cantor or singer at a synagogue service

cheder: Hebrew school

chulent: Stew, often cooked a day or two before it is needed

chuppah: Canopy at a wedding.

cuppel, kippah or yarmalka: Skullcap

daven: To pray in Hebrew

Din: The law according to Moses and Israel

Du farkirtst mir di yorn: You'll be the death of me

ein funt: One pound

El Maleh Rachamim: God who is full of compassion, prayer for the departed

es iz a umglik: It's a disaster

farkukte: Shitty

farmisht: Mixed up

farmisht dein kopf: Messes up your head, stops you thinking straight

farshtinkeneh: Stinking

farshtinkener chazer: Stinking pig

frum dein moil tsu Gott's erin: From your mouth to God's ears

geh shlogn zich kop in vant: Go and bang your head on the wall

gefulte fish: Chopped fish, usually carp or pike, rolled into balls with matzo meal, can be served boiled or fried

gefulte fish balls: As above

gepipchged: Having the umbilical cord attached, ie. wet behind the ears, a novice

geshvint: Quick

geh gazunte heit: Go in good health

gezunt: Good

gib mir avek: Fob me off, sell me something I didn't want

goornisht: Nothing

Gott zei danken: Thank God

goyim: Gentile

groisse knucker: Big shot

grunderzeit: Good times

gutte neshuma: Good soul

haftorah: Chanting from the 'Prophets' section of the Torah

hak mir nisht kayn tshaynik: Don't hit me with a teapot, don't drive me mad

Hashem: 'The name'. Jews are not supposed to utter the name of God, so saying Hashem is one of the ways they show their reverence

hassids: Extremely religious Jews, focussed on the imminent return of the Messiah

hartzshklupinsht: Heartache

Ich glaube, er hat dein geld genommen: German: I think he took your money

Judenscheiss: German - Jew shit

Judenschwein: German - Jew pig

kaddish: Mourners' prayer

kapotes: Long Hasidic coats

khala: Bride

khochick: No real translation. It's a question at the end of a sentence, nearest is 'really'

kichels: Little cakes

kiddush: Usually after a religious service, snacks and drinks

kim gishvint: Come quick

kim shoyn: Come already, stop messing

kindele: Little children

kippah: Skullcap

Kleine kinder lozn nit shloffen, grosse kinder lozn nit leben: Little children don't let you sleep, big children don't let you live

kreplach: Matzo balls, usually in soup

kriah: Mourners' ritual rending of a garment at a funeral

kvater: Plays a ceremonial role in the bris, by bringing the baby to the Mohel

kvelled: Filled with pride

lechaim: Traditional Jewish drinking toast "To life"

latkes: Potato pancakes

levaya: Funeral

liebchen: Darling, loved one

leining: Ritual reading and chanting from the Torah, must be 100% accurate

liebe fun meyn lebn: Love of my life

lokshen: Thin pasta for soup

mach gishvint: Hurry quickly

maftir: Final verses of the Torah portion

magela: Stuffed chicken neck

magen dovid: Star of David

mak kliner: Muck cleaner

matzeers: Bargains

matzo pudding: Pudding from matzos, with dried fruit

mazel und brocha: Luck and Blessing

mazeltov: Good Luck

mechitten: The father of your child's spouse - Male in-law is the nearest in English

meiskeits: Cursed face, very ugly

Men zol zikh kenen oyskoyfn fun toyt, voltn di oremelayt sheyn parnose gehat:
If the rich could hire someone to die for them, the poor would make a good living

meshuggener: Madman, idiot

mezuzah: Small decorative case containing the sacred prayer "Hear O Israel."
Placed on the door frame

Mi adir al hakol: 'He who is mighty above all beings', a beautiful hymn sung at
the start of the wedding ceremony

mikvah: Ritual bath for women

minyan: Ten men over the age of 13, the necessary quorum for a full religious
service

mishigarse: Something that is meshugge, mad, crazy

mishpocha: Family

mitzvah: An act that is a blessing to perform

mohel: One who is qualified to carry out ritual circumcision

Moishe Groisse: Big shot, thinks he is a big man, literally Morris Large

momzer: Bastard

nahora: Evil eye

nemen keir: Take care

noch: An idiom with various meanings such as still, yet, also, even, again. Eg
Noch a mol – another time, again; Er iz noch mayn zun – he is still my son, or
even 'he's my son - isn't he?'

nu: Now/so. An idiom usually said as a question. Nu? What is happening?

noshes: Little treats to eat, sweet or savoury

olav ha sholom: Rest in peace

oleh: One who makes Aliyah. Goes up. In this sense to the bimah to read from the
Torah

Omayn: Amen

Oy a broch: Broch is a curse, Oy is used a lot in Yiddish to express surprise or pain

Oy gevalt: Used to express surprise at something bad. Literally Oh! Violence

Oy veh: Another expression, nearest is Oh dear! Oh woe! Eg Oy veh iz mir – Oh woe is me

payot: Ringlets of hair worn at the side of the head by male orthodox Jews

pidyon haben: Ceremony held 30 days after the birth of the first son. He is ritually 'offered' to the Cohainim – the priestly elite who ran the temple in ancient times – then bought back.

pippick: Belly button

rugelach: Sweet cakes with dried fruit inside

sandak: Man who holds the baby at circumcision

shapsele: Little darling

shemozel: Confusion, mess, calamity - of people (see also shlemazel)

shlemiel: A clumsy fool. Someone for whom everything seems to go wrong.

shlepped: Carried, dragged, or a long journey you don't want to make

shmegegge: Nonsense, of no consequence

shmoozing: Buttering up, flattery with a purpose

shmuck: Literally, a penis; a derogatory term for a man. According to the saying, the shlemiel spills his soup, the shlemazel is the person it lands on, the shmuck charges them for a napkin.

sedra: A portion of the Torah

Sefer Torah: The Book of the Torah, in this case the scroll

shabbas: The Sabbath, starts at dusk on Friday, ends at dusk on Saturday

shalom aleichem: Peace be with you

shamas: An official in the synagogue who manages it day to day

shashkra: Russian sword

sheitel: Wig worn by observant, married women to hide their hair

shiddach macher: Matchmaker, one who puts people together for the purpose of marriage

shiva: Seven days of mourning. The mourners sit on low chairs, and people pay respects

shkoyach: Respect. Often said after to someone who has been called to the reading

shmerel: Another type of fool. Someone with no common sense

shofar: Ram's horn. Blown many times on New Year, very difficult to do

shomer: One who watches. In this case to watch over the body

shtetls: Villages, or small towns in Eastern Europe with primitive housing and facilities

shteyn in zeyn shukh: Stone in your shoe, ie something that is bothering you, and won't go away

shtiblakh: Small room

shul: Synagogue

simcha: Happy occasion, celebration.

simentov: A happy song of congratulations

Sipurim be-shir ve-shirim shonim: Stories in verse and selected poems

s'iz shver tsu zayn a Yid: It hurts to be a Jew

shtrimmel: Large, round furry hat worn by Hasids

tachlis: To talk tachlis, to get to the real point

tallis: Prayer shawl

tallisim: Plural of Tallis

tatele: Translation is Little Father, but used as endearing term for a boy

tefillin: Small black leather boxes containing verses from the Torah.

The Din: Jewish Law, according to the Torah

traif: Non-kosher food

tsorris: Troubles

tzadiks: Religious Leaders

tzitzis: Fringed undershirt worn by orthodox Jews

untermensch: German - sub-human

vershtay: Understand

vi fil?: How much?

völkisch movement: German Nationalist and pseudo-scientific movement based on a hierarchy of races, with blonde haired Nordic 'Aryans' at the top, and Jews and Roma at the bottom.

yachner: One who talks too much

yarmulka: Another word for skullcap

yeshiva bocher: One who attends the Yeshiva or Jewish school to study Torah

zeider: Grandfather

Printed in Great Britain
by Amazon

31878436R00249